a sweet celebrity romance

Moonstruck

DANA LeCHEMINANT

This book is a work of fiction. The characters, names, incidents, places, and dialogue are either products of the author's imagination or are used fictitiously. Any resemblance to actual persons, living or dead, events, or locales, is entirely coincidental.

Copyright © 2024 by Dana LeCheminant
Cover Design Copyright © 2024 by Dana LeCheminant

ISBN: 978-1-951753-24-5
First Print Edition: March 2024
Bow and Arrow Press, LLC

All rights reserved.

No portion of this book may be reproduced in any form without written permission from the publisher or author, except as permitted by U.S. copyright law.

To the creators of the world—
never give up on your dreams

Moonstruck:
acting foolishly or out of character, especially because of love

Hollywood Hot Scoop

Too much Trouble for the Tune Titan?

AFTER WHAT SOME MIGHT call his best show yet, Liam Connolly was spotted fighting a fan in what many think is a sign of the majorly popular musician's inevitable breaking point. While some, like me, might find Liam's macho display something akin to mouthwatering, we can't help but wonder if the fame has finally gotten to our guitar-wielding hero. Up until now, Liam has been nothing but smiles and good vibes, but we all know everyone has to crack at some point. I mean, look at that punch in the videos below! The man clearly had some aggression to let out.

With the smooth-voiced artist currently MIA, the world of music is full of one important question: Where is Liam now? We've got our theories, and whether he's in rehab or a luxury prison upstate, we are eagerly awaiting more news on our favorite male singer. Maybe this is the end of Liam's chart-topping reign.

Only time will tell.

Stay up to date on all things Hollywood by hitting that subscribe button, and we'll make sure you get all the info on Liam Connolly. Until next time! XO

CHAPTER ONE

LIAM

Look, I'm as pro-peace as the next guy, but some people deserve to be punched. It's a known fact. And yet, no matter how many people agree with me, my publicist, Ethan, seems to think otherwise.

"Could you show at least *some* remorse?" he asks for the fiftieth time this afternoon. (It's only the third time, but I stand by my hyperbole.) "You're acting like this isn't a big deal."

I twist my kitchen stool back and forth a few times, trying to make it squeak as loudly as I can because it will drive Ethan crazy. "I miss when Jordan was my publicist," I say wistfully. "He would have fixed this by now."

"You are probably the reason Jordan quit," Ethan shoots right back.

I really hope not, though Jordan *did* leave his PR firm without any heads up, which is strange. He had a lot of high profile clients, myself included, and he left us high and dry a couple of years ago. He's the only publicist I know who managed to keep every single one of his clients in the clear. Ethan's fine, but he's not the kind of genius who could turn an arrestable offense inside a Costco into an endorsement goldmine.

I knew it was a bad idea to climb the racking inside the warehouse, but a kid had just thrown his toy up there and was seconds away from a world-class meltdown, with no employees in sight. I was trying to help.

Just like this time.

I squeak the stool a few more times until Ethan looks like the vein in his forehead is going to burst. It's a good thing we're having this chat over video conference, or he would have lost it by now. He has the benefit of muting me if he needs to. "I know I shouldn't have punched the guy," I say, trying for some sobriety. It's not easy. "But he wouldn't stop harassing the girl. What was I supposed to do?"

"Alert security and let them deal with it?" Ethan groans when he sees my answering glare. He knows as well as I do that my security team had been busy with some overeager fans trying to sneak onto the stage to get to me. "I know, I know. 'There was no one there.' But that doesn't change the fact that you decked a paying ticket holder at your own show, Liam."

"It's not my fault there's never anyone around when the bad stuff goes down!" I complain.

It's my literal curse and has been my entire life. That whole "luck of the Irish" thing doesn't apply to me in the slightest, despite my mother being from Dublin.

I encounter more nasty events than most just by nature of being a famous musician, but even then, most people usually aren't alone when the bad things happen. Then there's me. Like the time our tree in the backyard got struck by lightning and caught on fire, and my six-year-old self was temporarily home alone while my mom brought dinner over to the neighbor? Did I know how to call 9-1-1? Of course not, so half the yard burned before someone noticed me covered in ash and trying to put it out with the garden hose. I still have a burn scar on my wrist because my smart little self thought getting closer to the fire would put it out faster. Or that day after school in sixth grade when I came across the biggest bully in our grade trying to shake down another kid for his lunch money even though he'd already spent it at lunch that day? I couldn't stand by and watch, and I got suspended for fighting even though I never threw a punch.

I *did* throw a punch at my concert three days ago, though. And I won't apologize for it. The guy had it coming.

Ethan must see my defiance because he groans again. "You really won't post an apology video? Your image is looking really bad right now, Liam, and I don't say that lightly. Especially with you on house arrest for the next six weeks, we have to find a way to fix this."

I look down at the ankle monitor gracing my right leg. While I'm almost certain the charges are going to be dropped once we go to trial in a month and a half, thanks to a witness willing to testify that I was not the first one to throw a punch despite what all the videos show, I'm not fond of this little precaution. The LA police thought it best if I keep out of the public eye until things calm down, given my high profile.

Honestly, if they had asked me to lie low, I would have done it. I think. But this little black box is practically taunting me, begging me to see how far from my front door I can get before it goes off and I'm noncompliant. It's a bad idea to give me strict boundaries; all I want to do is cross them.

My left foot is the one that makes me even more frustrated though, encased in its thick and unwieldy boot. Turns out when you get into a fight on a stage, chances are high that you're going to misjudge where the edge is and accidentally take a little tumble. And you're likely to end up with a hairline fracture.

At least it's not completely broken? And I don't know where I would be if I'd broken my wrist or something. These hands are valuable.

"Honestly, I should be pressing my own charges, after what happened to me," I say, immediately regretting my joke when Ethan lets out a bone-weary sigh. I like messing with him, but not to the point where he quits like Jordan did.

"Liam, your career is in danger. Can you be serious for ten minutes? I'll even take five."

I sit up straight, recognizing his request for what it is—a straight up plea. "Yes. Sorry. I know we need to do something, but I can't apologize. I just can't."

I've spent my life apologizing, so it's not like I don't know how. Neither am I too proud. But in this instance, I would do what I did a thousand times over with no regrets. I wish other people had done it with me.

Ethan runs a hand down his face, probably contemplating how difficult it would be to find another job that pays as well as his does now. "Fine. Will you just...stay off of social media until I figure out what to do about all this?"

"Duh." I don't like socials anyway. The only reason I even got an account is because my record label required it, and I pay someone else to post for me and answer DMs. No one can convince me there's anything good on social media when it's full of trolls and people invading my privacy, so I steer clear. I should probably remind my gal who has my account to take a break for a couple of weeks, in case she missed that memo when I got arrested.

"And don't leave your house for any reason," Ethan adds.

I don't even bother gracing that one with a response. "Let me know when you've got something," I tell him, and then I shut my laptop and let the kitchen fill with silence.

That's a lie. I don't do silence. I've got a fountain in the backyard, its soothing sounds coming in through the open door behind me, and Nelson the budgie is singing something in the front room. It sounds a bit like a remix of one of my older songs with lyrics from a Taylor Swift classic instead of mine.

"Interesting choice," I murmur. It never ceases to bother me that my parakeet likes Taylor more than he likes me. I've thought about telling her, but I don't need to give her more reasons to be awesome.

Someday I want to be Taylor. Just, like, the guy version of her.

Grabbing my phone, I struggle up to my foot and snag a crutch so I can hobble out to the back patio. The doctor said I shouldn't try to put weight on the fracture for another week or so, and I'm actually going to listen to his advice because it hurts like the dickens. But it sure makes it hard to get around.

I don't even know why I'm coming out here. With the monitor on one foot and the boot on the other, it's not like I can go for a swim in the pool, and the officer who attached the monitor said it will only take me as far as the edge of the yard, so I won't be able to take the stairs down to the private beach below. Living in Southern California is great until suddenly you can't enjoy any of it.

Plopping onto a pool chair, I get myself situated and then tug my shirt free. At least I can work on my tan, though it's not like anyone will see it. Then I grab my phone and hope Jordan never changed his number.

He answers surprisingly quickly, and I can't help but grin at his response.

I sigh, suddenly both bored and lonely because my friends are all too busy to keep me company while I'm stuck at home. Derek's off filming a movie in South America, and Cole has a bad habit of disappearing when it isn't rugby season, though I have yet to figure out where he goes if he's not with his longtime girlfriend in Oregon.

I type out another text to Jordan, wishing I had more friends so I could have someone to talk to. Maybe Bonnie is around, though I don't think Derek would love me hanging out with his girlfriend without him. He's extra protective of her lately, even though she was part of our friend group before they started dating. And it's not like I'd ever make a move on her. She's practically a sister to me.

I try to remember back in the day when Jordan first took me on as a client, but I don't think I ever met his wife despite knowing he was hitched. Clearly it didn't work out.

Liam:

It's not that I'm anti-love. I just don't think it exists.

Jordan:

Says the guy who became famous because he wrote a love song.

Liam:

It was multiple love songs thank you very much.

Jordan:

Been waiting for your new album.

"You and me both," I murmur, peeking inside the house to where my favorite guitar sits innocently in its stand in the middle of the dining room. Freya, the fifth member of our group, left it there when she was here last as a not-so-subtle hint that my next album is overdue, and I've been sorely tempted to tuck it away in a closet in one of the guest rooms so it will stop staring at me so judgingly. I keep hoping the album will write itself, but so far no luck.

Liam:

It's coming along.

Ah, how I love lying to people. *Not.* But I've gotten a little too used to saying that to my agent as well as my group of friends, so it rolls right off the tongue. Er, thumbs.

Liam:

Are you still in Cali? We should meet up.

Jordan:

Nope. In Sun City now.

Liam:

> No beaches? *skull emoji*

Jordan:

> I'm way happier here than I ever was there. You should try life somewhere else.

I would if I could. Except, even without the ankle monitor, I would still be here. I grew up in rural Oklahoma and a million other places, and California was the first place that ever felt like home. I don't see a reason to mess that up.

Liam:

> So no chance you'll come work for me again? Ethan is *vomiting emoji* *poop emoji* *snowflake emoji*

Jordan:

> Ethan is one of the best.

Liam:

> Not as good as you. Move back here with your wife and get me out of this mess.

Jordan:

> Not taking Brooklyn away from her family. Sorry. Besides, I've got my own business now.

Liam:

> PR?

Jordan:

> Landscaping.

Liam:

> Okay weirdo. I can't imagine that pays as well as I did.

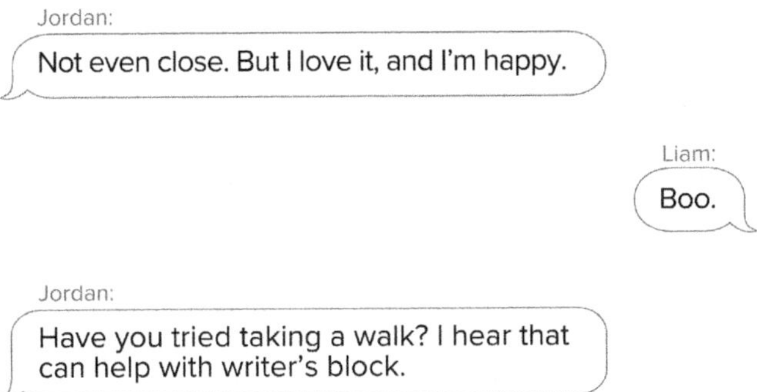

That catches me off guard, and I glance around my backyard as if I might find Jordan lurking in the bushes. He's a pretty intuitive guy, but this seems a little extra. Just in case, I send off a text to the head of security for our gated neighborhood, asking him to send someone to do a sweep of my yard to make sure the paps haven't gotten in somehow.

Then I take a picture of both my feet and send it to Jordan.

And I probably shouldn't be texting this to anyone outside my team. I trust Jordan, but I also don't know for sure that it's him on the other side of the phone. He's got the right vibe, but it's been long enough that he could be anyone.

> Ethan's got your back, so trust him and do what he says.

Liam:
> I'd rather do what you say.

Jordan:
> Sorry, man. I'm out of the game.

> By the way, my wife is a huge fan. She's screaming right now because she just realized who I'm texting.

> Apparently I wasn't supposed to tell you that.

I chuckle, imagining some gorgeous woman sitting next to him because Jordan has the charm of a Hollywood heartthrob and would absolutely land himself a bombshell. I'm glad he found someone, and I hope it works out this time.

Liam:
> Send me your address and I'll have my team send her a signed vinyl or something.

Jordan:
> I think she just burst my eardrum, dude. But thanks! She's clearly excited.

And I don't know what to say after that. It's nice to know I still have at least one fan after all the videos went viral from the fight at my last concert, though Jordan's wife might be the only one left. The best part about not being on socials is not knowing what people are saying about me, though I have a pretty good guess. Especially after the article *Hollywood Hot Scoop* posted only minutes after the fight went down.

I hate that site. It brings nothing but trouble, and I blame it entirely for the stupid thing I type next.

I mean that. In my twenty-six years, I've never met anyone I wanted to keep around that close. Certainly not anyone who wanted *me* that close. I've got my friends, few though they are, and that's enough for me. I'm glad Jordan is happy, but you won't see me falling head over heels for anyone. In my experience, love is a waste of time. My music is all I need.

My doorbell rings, and I frown as I pull up the front camera to find a woman on the front steps with a bright purple bag in her hands.

"Lunch!" I realize out loud. I ordered it when Ethan started droning on and on about my image and then totally forgot. I don't even know what I ordered. Something delicious...

I look at my fractured foot and sigh before unlocking my front door with my phone and turning on the intercom. "Hi, can you bring that inside?"

The woman jumps at the sound of my voice and starts looking around, though she can't seem to find the camera. Good. It's fairly well hidden. "I'll just leave it on the porch," she says to the doorbell and starts pulling my food from the bag.

"Ah, but I can't come get it from the porch, so I would really appreciate it if you brought it inside."

"I'd really rather not," she replies.

Most people would kill to get a look inside my house. Pulling my phone closer to my face, I try to get a good look at her, but she's keeping her head down enough that I don't have a clear view of her face. Her voice is lower than I would have expected from a delivery driver, a bit on the husky side.

"Tell you what," I say right as she's about to set my food on the step. Sushi! That's what I ordered. Definitely don't want to leave that on the porch. "I'll tip you an extra hundred if you bring it into the backyard so I don't have to use my crutches and probably drop it on my way to the kitchen table."

Her shoulders tense, and she searches for the camera again. "Really?"

"Really. Crutches and sushi don't mix."

"I mean will you really give me a hundred?"

My stomach growls as if it knows how close I am to food. I slept through breakfast, so I technically haven't eaten anything yet today. I'm only a few days into this house arrest thing, and already my schedule is all over the place. "I'll give you two hundred if you stop talking and start walking."

She scoffs, but then her hand reaches out for the doorknob. She mutters something that sounds a lot like, "Please don't murder me," and then she pushes her way inside.

Nelson is quick to greet her with a cheerful, "Chicken noodle soup!"

"I don't think this is soup," the woman replies, her voice carrying through the open door. It has risen in pitch from where it was on the porch.

"Why chicken cross road?" Nelson says.

I sit up a little, figuring I shouldn't look like I'm totally lounging out here and too lazy to get up. "I'm back here!" I call, eyes on my phone as I figure out how to add an extra tip to my order. I've got cash somewhere inside, but I'm not about to get up to find it.

"Other side!" Nelson shouts right as the woman walks directly into the half of the glass door that *isn't* open. She collapses on the tile right as my budgie starts whistling the melody of "Shake it Off," and I'm suddenly regretting this whole *bring the food to me* idea.

"Hey, are you okay?" I ask, jumping up and hopping in her direction. Only, I lose my balance halfway there and tumble sideways into the pool with a splash.

CHAPTER TWO

KASEY

Whoever Brent Fallsteen is, he is too lazy to get up and get his own food. Strike one.

He owns a terrifying bird that he keeps in his front room, likely to give his visitors a heart attack as they enter. Strike two.

His windows are too clean. I can't decide if that's a strike or not, but I'm going to have a bruise on my forehead because said terrifying bird failed to warn me in time that I was walking in the wrong direction and straight into a glass door.

And the man is clearly an egotistical, vainglorious jackhole who feels the need to show off by swan diving into the pool instead of coming to help me, which is unequivocally strike three.

Not that he is even aware I'm taking a tally.

As I scramble to get all his food back into its containers before he notices how much of it went tumbling when I walked face first into the door, I force my expression to stay neutral. I'm no actor—thank goodness for that—but it's a bad idea to show weakness to anyone in this celebrity-filled corner of the world.

I get out to the back patio just as Brent climbs out of the pool in that sexy, James Bond sort of way where he uses his arms to lift himself up and put his rippling torso on display. And yeah, while thus far I've hated everything else about the man, I can appreciate well-formed pectorals and abdominals while I've got them displayed right in front of me. Time seems to stall and grace me with the view of water sluicing off his tan skin and glittering in the sun, like the best kind of slow-mo shot.

But then I realize he's just frozen in place, hands on the cement and vivid blue eyes fixed on me.

I don't know what I hate more, the fact that he caught me staring or the way he looks like Zac Efron and Chris Hemsworth had a baby.

He coughs and lifts himself up the rest of the way, sitting on the edge of the pool before tugging his well-toned legs out of the water. "Sorry about the, uh, door. Are you okay?" Then he curses under his breath and starts undoing a big black medical boot on his foot.

I glance over at the chair he'd been sitting in before I arrived, and seeing a crutch there makes me feel a little bit better. I guess he's only on strike two.

"Where should I leave this?" I ask, glancing down at the food in my hands and then wincing when I see the smear of wasabi on my shirt. Hopefully he won't notice? I shake my hair over my shoulders to hide it, just in case. The sushi rolls are a little worse for wear, but there's not much I can do about that now.

With his foot now free of the boot, he pushes his blond hair from his forehead and then runs a hand down his face to clear it of water. "Would you mind handing me a towel?" he asks, pointing to a cabinet to my left.

"Do you want the food or the towel?" I cringe. The only reason I came into this house was to get that extra tip, and I probably shouldn't let my mouth ruin that for me. "I mean, I should probably set this down first so I don't drop it. Again," I add under my breath.

Brent flashes a wide smile that is full of more mischief than I would like. "Table over there?" he suggests, pointing to my right.

My eyes nearly bug out of my head when I see the dining setup he's got out here, complete with luxury chairs around a firepit and a stone table that seats six but could easily fit twice that. I knew I was coming into a fancy neighborhood, but my goodness. Brent must be good at what he does.

Unless he's a trust fund baby. In which case I guess he's good at being a trust fund baby because this house is impossibly fancy.

Unloading the food onto the table, I take a few deep breaths and remind myself of the two hundred bucks he promised me. It had better be worth it. And he'd also better give me a good rating because it wasn't easy to get enough five-star ratings to get gigs in swanky Malibu neighborhoods like this. I refuse to lose my well-earned high-level status to a nineteen-year-old driving a beat-up minivan.

Seriously, Milo needs to get himself a better car if he's going to keep doing food deliveries and work his way up to the bigger payouts. Every time I happen to run into my fellow delivery driver picking up food for a customer, I'm worried his car isn't going to start when he heads out for his delivery, but he keeps telling me it'll run forever. Oh, to be carefree and optimistic. "I don't want to have to rescue him," I mumble.

"How about that towel?" Brent asks, giving me another leering smile. It's way too big, and his teeth are too white. "Unless you want me to stay on full display," he adds with a wink.

Body like that, he has a right to be a bit cocky. But this is over the top.

Stalking across the patio, I tug open the cabinet and hold back a groan when I see that it's full of the fluffiest white towels I've ever seen. Because of course it is. These are the towels of dreams. I grab one and throw it, accidentally tossing it too hard. It flutters right over his head and lands in the pool with a splat.

Brent chuckles. "Nice arm."

I take the safe route and hand him the next towel instead of throwing it, which means I get an up close view of those abs as he dries his face. My goodness. Muscles like that should be illegal. Is he an MMA fighter or something? Why is that the only explanation I can come up with for muscles? That would be terrifying.

"Well," I say, as much to move things along as to remind myself that I shouldn't be staring. "Enjoy your lunch."

Gathering the towel up in a ball, he turns his gaze to his now-free foot. Up to me. Back to the foot. It looks wrinkly and purple and honestly a bit gross. For the first time since I got here, his smile falls, making room for what I can only describe as a pout.

"I hate to ask," he starts.

"Nope." I take several steps backward, hoping I remember how I got to the back door through that far too large house. The last thing I need to do is start wandering. "I only do deliveries."

Infuriatingly, his smile comes right on back. "What do you think I'm going to ask?"

"Doesn't matter. If it doesn't have anything to do with your food, I can't help you." I'm not keen to encounter that bird again—it seems to be making up its own song right now—but it's better than anything this guy might ask of me. "It's not worth two hundred bucks," I mutter under my breath.

"I already tipped you the two hundred."

"Oh." Apparently I need to work on my "under the breath" volume, since I already know I'm terrible at keeping those comments to myself in the first place. As my face lights on fire, I watch as the guy shifts his weight, lifting himself up on his hands and flexing all his muscles again.

Pain lances across his face, along with a good deal of frustration as his eyebrows pull low. His hair might be blond, but his eyebrows are a darker brown. He must bleach his hair, though it looks surprisingly natural.

With a groan, he gives up on whatever he was trying to do and looks over at me again. "So, I could really use some help getting up. I fractured my foot earlier this week, and it hurts so much more without the boot."

Curse him for appealing to my bleeding heart! But I stand my ground. I've already made the extra cash, so I could leave and never look back. But if I do that, he could give me a low rating, and then I'll be back to dropping off pizzas in Lynwood where they can't afford to tip more than the bare minimum.

Milo loves delivering in the heart of Los Angeles, but I think it's because he's not worried about his piece-of-junk car getting stolen. And he's not paying off student loans.

"I'll give you another hundred if you help me to the table," Brent says, pressing his palms together in a prayer pose.

"Why'd you take the boot off?" I ask instead of walking away.

His eyes, which are so blue it should be a crime, jump to the sopping mass of plastic and Velcro lying discarded on the stone near where he's sitting. "Because I wasn't supposed to get it wet."

"Then why jump in the pool?"

"I, uh, fell in."

And I'm not sure I believe him. With this being Malibu, one can never be too careful when it comes to trusting beautiful humans. There are all sorts of creeps and crazies out here. "You fell in?" I repeat.

He nods, his expression a picture of innocence. "When I got up to help you."

Sure he did. I turn to go. "Sorry, Brent, but I've got another—"

"Three hundred bucks to not leave me stranded here."

I hate how quickly that pulls me to a stop. That would put me at an extra five hundred for the day, enough to convince Val not to kick me out of her house just yet. Not enough to pay rent, but I've got another six hours of deliveries in me before I'm completely brain dead. Maybe I can hit a couple more houses like this one and make enough to pay for all of July.

Yeah, I know it's September. I'm working on it.

Brent holds out his hand and then sticks out his bottom lip, looking ridiculous. "Please?"

"Three hundred to get you to the table?"

He cocks his head to the side. "Yeah."

"Fine."

Turns out, when a guy can't use one of his legs, he requires quite a lot of assistance, and muscles don't come lightly. The dude is *heavy*. And getting him up to his feet involves a lot of hands. Hands against bare skin because he's still not wearing a shirt. He does his best to help, but he's so slippery that I accidentally get way too familiar with the guy's abs.

It feels like an eternity before he's on his feet. Foot. But that's only half the battle. Regretting my decision to stay and help, I tuck his well-toned arm around my shoulders to help him hop, forcing myself to ignore the fact that he's half a foot taller than me. And my goodness, he smells so good. It's a mixture of chlorine and something tantalizingly fresh and clean.

I should have just handed him his crutch and called it good.

"Wait," Brent says, somehow managing to hold me back despite his questionable balance. "Do you see my phone anywhere?"

I almost don't hold back my groan, but he'll be helpless without his phone as soon as I leave. So even though it means an extra few seconds with his arm around me, I search the patio to no avail.

"It might be..." He points to the pool.

I sigh and force him to hop a few times so we can look down into the glittering water and get a good look at the little black rectangle at the bottom. Right in the middle.

He swears under his breath and then turns to me.

"Nope," I say before he can open his mouth. "I agreed to help you to the table. That's it."

"Thousand bucks."

"I knew you were trouble," the bird says inside.

I agree with the terrifying bird, but my refusal is stuck on my tongue. Is this guy serious? "You could almost buy a new phone for that much."

"I could," he agrees, lifting his eyebrows high. "But then you'd be out a grand. It'll cost me the same either way."

He is too handsome for his own good, and I'm pretty sure he knows it. There's mischief in his tropical blue eyes and laughter in his smile, and I'm only just now realizing I still have a hand pressed against his stomach even though he doesn't need that added support.

I clench my jaw, but that kind of money is too hard to ignore. What kind of person does it make me if I'm actually considering jumping into that pool to the amusement of a creep who should not be this entertained by my indecision? I'll have to put my head under the water to reach it, and I'm already panicking about it.

"You must be really attached to that phone," I say, hating that I sound breathless. It's just because he's maintaining more eye contact than I'm used to. Not because I'm actually affected by this guy. Or terrified of that pool. Gah, there are too many things happening right now for me to think straight!

His smile stretches wider. "Something like that. What do you say, unnamed delivery girl?"

"It's Kasey."

How can his grin possibly get any wider? "Kasey," he repeats, and a shiver runs through me. He has the kind of voice that would make a good audiobook, like one of those romances I will never admit to listening to while I drive around. It's deep and smooth and far too alluring, given the circumstances.

Why in the world did I tell him my name? The delivery service I work for doesn't even show customers our real names. It assigns one at random each time to keep us safe, for which I am grateful. I could have told him my name was Flora, and he would have believed me because that's what the app says.

Ethereal music starts coming from the pool, muffled and only audible because we're both silent at the moment.

Brent shifts, moving his arm to free me. "Help out a cripple? What if it's my mom calling? She might think something happened to me."

"Phones can't receive a signal underwater," I say, which sounds stupid considering his phone is ringing. But it's true! His phone shouldn't be receiving anything down there, given it's sitting in several feet of water.

In response to my fun bit of trivia, Brent drops onto his belly—far nimbler than I expected given how difficult it was to help him stand—and sticks his whole arm into the pool. He may be tall, but he's at least six feet away from reaching that phone. Doesn't look like that will stop him from trying. His whole body flexes taut as he reaches and strains.

By some miracle, I keep my eyes to myself even though his linen pants are hugging his thighs. Not staring is a feat that would be difficult for pretty much anyone in my situation, let me tell you. The sight of him is...nice. Really nice.

Focus, Kasey.

It's my fault he lost his phone. I walked into the door. He got up to help me. Assuming he was telling the truth, I should probably help him out, even if pools and I really don't mix.

"I can't believe I'm doing this," I mutter and then unload my pockets, lining up my phone, wallet, and keys in an orderly row. I slip off my shoes, tuck my socks neatly inside them, and silently wish I had a hair tie with me. It's one of those things that I should really keep on my wrist, but I can never remember to grab one to begin with.

"A thousand dollars," I remind myself, repeating that over and over as I creep to the edge of the pool and then sit on the edge, gingerly sticking my feet into the water only to realize it is a rather pleasant temperature. That'll help, but it doesn't make it any easier to jump in.

How deep can it be? Five feet? I'm taller than five feet. I'll be fine.

I'm not fine. With a mental countdown, I plug my nose and force myself into the water, only to let out a scream when it completely engulfs me. Water fills my mouth. I try to cough. Flail my arms. My toes hit the bottom, and I kick frantically, trying to push myself up. It's no use.

I'm drowning.

CHAPTER THREE

LIAM

WHY DO THINGS ALWAYS happen to *me*? I should have known Kasey wasn't keen on getting in the pool when it took her so long to jump in, but it wasn't until she started flailing that I realized she *really can't swim*.

I glance at the discarded boot, wondering if I have time to put it back on, and then I curse myself for being stupid and slide into the pool like a penguin. My arms wrap around Kasey's midsection at the same time pain lances through my foot as the water moves it around. The pain quickly becomes second to the way Kasey thrashes around, like she's trying to free herself from my hold.

I tug her toward the other side of the pool, a stream of curse words on repeat in my head, until I can touch the bottom again, and then I shove her upward. She fights, her hands finding my face and pushing me down into the water again.

If she doesn't drown first, she'll certainly make it happen to me.

Grabbing her hands this time, I pull her another foot shallower and shout her name. This time, her legs wrap around me, which is a far better way to keep herself from slipping back into the water. She coughs, and I help push her dark hair out of her eyes even though she's coughing right into my face.

"Hey," I say, feeling as breathless as she is while my racing heart tells me installing a six-foot pool was apparently a bad idea. "Hey, you're okay. Just breathe."

She keeps coughing, but she's relaxing into my arms as the water settles around us. Her wide eyes find mine, big and golden-brown and vulnerable.

I try to straighten her hair for her as I slowly start moving us to the shallowest part. She's still clinging to me, and I'll let her stay here until she feels safe again. "I'm sorry," I tell her.

"For saving me?" she croaks back.

I can't stop my smile even though it's not an appropriate gesture right now. "For asking you to get in the pool in the first place. You could have said you can't swim."

Her arms snake around my neck as she looks around us, like she isn't sure what just happened. "I...I didn't think it was going to be that deep."

"I make that mistake all the time."

As her fingers curl into my hair, a shiver runs through me. I don't think she's doing it on purpose—she looks around again and furrows her brow—but dang, she's doing something to me. It's not just her hands in my hair that are affecting me either. I don't remember the last time I was in a pool with a woman, and Kasey is checking a lot of boxes. Dark hair, warm honey eyes, next to no makeup but still absolutely stunning. Not to mention her wariness around me and complete obliviousness to who I really am. She called me Brent, which is the name I use on any deliveries to try to keep a small sense of anonymity.

Call me crazy for finding a woman's disdain attractive, but I've spent too long being women's fantasies. I have literally had to pay Kasey to keep her around this long, and I must be a glutton for punishment because I want to keep her here as long as I possibly can, no matter what it costs me.

I'm fully aware that this is bordering exploitation, but it's not like I'm going to do anything with her. I simply want to get to know her better.

Kasey's eyes return to me, and something snaps into place in her expression as she seems to realize how she's holding on to me. "Oh. Uh. Sorry." She drops her legs, though she seems unsteady on her feet. We're still between four and five feet, so her chin is touching the water, and that seems to make her nervous.

"I've got all day," I tell her, hoping she takes her time calming down and climbing out of the pool. Yes, I want to keep holding her, but she also almost drowned just now. I can't imagine how terrifying that was for her, and I keep waiting for her to go into shock or something.

Instead, irritation flashes in her eyes, and she glances down at my hands around her waist. "Will you let go of me?" she demands.

I comply.

She squeals and jumps right back into my arms. "Will you help me get out of here?" she asks instead.

I know I should do as she asks and take her right to the edge. I could lift her out, no problem, and she deserves anything she wants because the reason she almost drowned right now was because she was trying to rescue my phone, which is still chilling at the bottom of the deep end. Derek would have had her out of the pool already. Actually, he wouldn't have asked her to jump in the first place.

But here I stand, unmoving, trying to tell myself to stop staring at her. Even if she is possibly the prettiest woman I've ever met, that doesn't mean I have any right to gawk at her.

"Here's the thing," I mutter, and it almost feels like someone else is talking for me. "I can't really move right now. My foot..." Granted, my foot *does* hurt. Like, a lot. Anytime I move it, it seems to be telling me that the fracture could turn into a break if I'm not careful. But that's the stupidest reason for not helping her out that I've ever heard.

Kasey clearly agrees with me, her fearful gaze turning into a searing glare. "Okay, seriously, let go of me. I can get myself out."

She makes it two steps before her foot slips out from under her, sending her face first into the water.

Coming to my senses, I grab her again and push her toward the edge, gritting my teeth against the pain as I hop along with her. When we reach the edge, I twist her around and then lift her by the hips until she's sitting on the stone, and it takes all of my willpower to pull my hands away.

"Thanks," she says, obviously reluctant to be nice to me.

Instead of replying, I slowly make my way back to the deep end, growling through the sharp pain stabbing my foot, and then sink down when I reach my phone so I can grab it. When I surface, Kasey is wrapping herself in my towel and looking like she's on the verge of tears.

"Please don't," I say.

She looks over at me. "Don't what?"

"Don't cry. I never know what to do when people cry."

Setting my phone on the stone, I pull myself out of the pool and basically collapse onto the patio like a harbor seal. I feel a bit like crying myself when my foot throbs, and I'm exhausted. Now that Kasey is safely on land, my adrenaline levels are dropping and leaving me somewhat shaky. That could also be due to the fact that I haven't eaten anything yet today, but I'm blaming the excitement and terror of someone nearly drowning in my backyard.

With my track record, I would probably be charged with murder for that one.

Turning on my back, I close my eyes and soak in the sun for a moment before looking back up at Kasey, though it takes me a second to find her again. She's over by the doors now, still barefooted and holding her shoes in her hands.

Something like alarm shoots through me, and I sit up. "Don't go either."

She frowns. "I have to work."

"I'll pay you." I wince as soon as the words are out of my mouth. Three days without any in-person interactions, and I'm clearly losing my mind. "I don't mean... Will you at least share my lunch with me? I feel terrible for what just happened, and I want to make it up to you." And I really don't want to spend the rest of the afternoon on my own.

She still seems skeptical, and she winces when Nelson starts singing "All By Myself" like he's reading my thoughts. When I bought the bird through a Craigslist ad, I thought his last owner was making excuses when she said the budgie creeped her out, but I am fully convinced he reads minds. Kasey doesn't seem too fond of him either, but I like him.

He keeps my house from being too quiet.

"It's just lunch," I add.

Half a dozen different expressions cross her face as she stands there, dripping on the patio, and she mutters something that's too quiet for me to hear this time. I'm pretty sure she's going to say no and leave with my towel as a souvenir, but then she sighs and drops her shoes onto the patio so she can slip them on. "Fine. But if you make any sort of moves, Brent Fallsteen, I'll—"

"Liam."

"What?" She narrows her eyes and looks like she may still try to finish her threat despite her confusion.

I smile, wishing I weren't sitting like a dead fish on the cement so I could give her a proper handshaked hello. "My name is Liam. Not Brent."

She thinks about that for a second, eyebrows low and lips pursed. Then she gapes at me. "Wait, did I deliver to the wrong—"

"I use a fake name so no one figures out where I live."

"And you picked the name Brent Fallsteen?"

I can't decide if she's annoyed that I gave her a fake name or disgusted by my choice. "I thought it was funny," I say with a shrug. "You know, like Bruce Springsteen, but with fall instead of...you know what, it doesn't matter. My name is really Liam Connolly, and I have no plans to make any moves. Just offer some delicious sushi so I don't end up eating it all myself. No one needs that much seaweed."

I wait for recognition to set in, as it always does. I mean, usually people recognize me immediately, but on the rare days they don't, the name always does it. Not to toot my own horn, but I've topped enough charts to say I'm on the famous end of the musician spectrum. Not like Taylor, who will be my best friend someday if I have anything to say about it, but certainly more famous than the guy who only plays at open mic nights at the local pizza parlor. I'm not knocking that guy—I *was* that guy once upon a time—but I've come a long way since then and refuse to think less of myself.

But as I watch Kasey, that recognition never comes. In fact, she lifts an eyebrow as if waiting for me to give her the go-ahead to start eating because she couldn't care less about who I am, just that I'm going to share my fishy bounty.

I guess I'll take that hit to my ego and hope it doesn't make this lunch all awkward. At this point, I barely know how to interact with anyone who doesn't know I'm famous.

My phone starts ringing again, the sound muffled because the speaker is probably full of water, and I'm exceptionally glad I happened to pick a water resistant variety this time after my last phone-breaking incident, which happens way more often than it should. I should really stop trying to take videos at my concerts; I'm a little too good at dropping my phone from the stage and shattering the screen. My phone budget is honestly ridiculous.

Freya's face lights up the screen as it rings, and it's like she knew I was feeling a bit too self-important.

"You should start eating," I tell Kasey and then answer the phone. "Isn't it your bedtime, Peach?"

Freya scoffs. "Is that really your best greeting? Have you forgotten how to speak to royalty?" Her accent, somewhere between British and Scandinavian, fills the phone with the sounds of her importance. I mean, she really is important, but she doesn't have to *sound* important.

"Don't have royalty here in the States," I argue. "Not really a habit of mine." Kasey starts tip-toeing toward the table where she left the sushi, and I can't help but watch her. Her jeans are drenched—naturally—and I can't imagine she's very comfortable. I wonder if Bonnie or Freya have left any clothes in one of the guest rooms. Freya usually stays at Derek's place when she's in town, but when he's off shooting a movie, everyone comes here to hang out.

I bet if I offered Kasey some clothes, assuming I found anything, she would think I was trying to "make a move," as she put it.

"Did you hear me, Connolly?"

"Nope." I pull my focus back to the phone. "Why are you calling, Your Majesty?"

"Highness," she corrects, making me roll my eyes. "And I am calling because you promised I could hear your new song this week, and I have yet to receive an email."

I curse. "You sure I promised that?"

"Am I sure?" She clears her throat, and I already regret not believing her. "You said, and I quote, 'Freya, darling, I am never going to write this song if I don't have someone breathing down my neck, and you're the best neck-breather I know.'"

I wince, glad that I didn't put the phone on speaker so Kasey could hear all of this. "I said that?" I ask, voice squeaking.

"When was the last time you worked on a song, Liam?"

"What's that? You're breaking up. The connection—"

"Do not hang up on me, Liam Connolly."

"Dropped my phone in the pool. It must be dying." I hang up, knowing she's going to tell the others to start hounding me about my album. Bonnie will be nice about it but pushy. If Derek wasn't on location, he would probably come over here and force me to sit in front of my piano until I plunk something out. Cole...who knows what he would do? I don't really want to find out. I'm decently strong, but I'm not rugby player strong.

I love my friends, but they don't take any crap.

With Freya dealt with for now, I struggle up to one foot and hop over to join Kasey. Right as I reach her, she tosses my t-shirt at me.

"Don't like what you see?" I ask as I slip it over my head and then collapse into a chair.

Scoffing, Kasey stuffs a spicy tuna roll into her mouth instead of answering. She's still standing wrapped in the towel, and she has even started shivering. At least she seems to be enjoying the food.

And...cue the awkwardness. What are we supposed to talk about?

"So..." I grab a pair of chopsticks and try not to smile when Kasey uses her fingers to pop a cucumber roll into her mouth. "How long have you been delivering food?"

Girl's got an impressive side eye, I'll give her that. Now that I'm getting a good look at her, she's younger than I originally guessed, probably in her early twenties. She's literally my target demographic, which makes it even stranger that she doesn't know who I am.

She swallows and adjusts the towel around her shoulders. "We don't have to do small talk. I'm here for the food and that tip you promised me."

"Technically, you didn't get my phone, so..." I hold my hands up as soon as the panicked look enters her eyes. "I'm kidding! You jumped in the pool, so you'll get paid. Probably not through your delivery app, though. Can't imagine how much they tax you on that stuff."

She blinks at me. "Oh. Uh. Thanks."

And we're back to silence again. I pick up a California roll with my chopsticks, searching for something to say.

"Clearly you didn't actually need my help getting up," Kasey says, nodding toward the pool.

I grimace. *Busted.* "Need? No. But it was a lot easier when you did help."

She grunts in reply.

Nelson decides to fill the space between us with a thrilling rendition of "Look What You Made Me Do."

Kasey frowns, looking back toward the open back door. "Is your parrot singing Taylor Swift?"

"He's a parakeet. But yes. Nelson loves her almost as much as I do."

"I can't say that I'm a fan."

I gasp, pressing a hand to my heart. "Well, now we can't be friends."

"I didn't want to be friends with you anyway." She says it so quietly that I'm pretty sure she didn't intend for me to hear, like a few other things she's muttered since arriving.

I should really take the hint, but I'm not the smartest guy in the world. What's that they say about cats and curiosity? Plus, I'm a bear-poker, and Kasey is begging to be bothered. "Why wouldn't you want to be friends with me? I'm awesome."

"I'm sure you are," she grumbles back. "Luckily for you, I'm not a Swiftie, so we can part ways as strangers and be perfectly fine."

"I wouldn't call us strangers. You did feel me up earlier, so..."

A fire bursts to life in those honey-colored eyes of hers, and I'm enchanted. So she's not just a stoic beauty... "I did not feel—you said you needed—clearly you can move around on your own just fine!" Then her eyes drop to my torso, and a delightful blush fills her cheeks with color.

I grin. "I'm glad someone got to appreciate the hard work I put in. My manager doesn't let me take my shirt off on stage anymore since *the incident.*"

That gets her. She even sinks into a chair as she stares at me. She's curious, and I can tell she doesn't want to ask but she's going to anyway. "The incident?"

Nodding as seriously as I can, I finally put a piece of sushi in my mouth and take my time chewing to make her anticipation grow. "See, I used to do it all the time, but last year I was playing a show in Miami over spring break season, and things got a little crazy."

"You're a musician?" Her leg is bouncing beneath her, though I can't decide if it's because she's anxious, cold, or trying not to ask for more details to my little story.

"Yup. Maybe you've heard one of my songs."

"I'm not really a music person."

My hand goes right back to my heart. "Kasey, you wound me. That's my bread and butter right there."

Her eyes jump around my backyard and the house behind her, taking it all in once more. "Ever think you should cut back on the carbs?"

I burst out laughing. Beautiful, disinterested, and funny? Kasey is quickly turning into the most interesting person I've ever met. "Yeah, well, when you have hundreds of thousands of fans clamoring for new music, it's hard to ignore them."

And yet I'm doing exactly that, pretending I don't have a looming deadline for my next album. It's not like I haven't tried to write it, but writing songs without inspiration is like having a conversation with Freya without making fun of her high-and-mightiness. It can be done, but there's no satisfaction.

Nelson starts whistling one of my oldest songs, as if subtly telling me I'll be a has-been if I don't pump out something new, and soon.

"Oh, I like this song," Kasey says, perking up. "I think I've heard it on the radio. Is this one of Taylor Swift's?"

Oh, I could die happy right now. And I'm definitely getting Nelson a bigger cage for choosing to sing this one when he's got a whole arsenal of melodies from Taylor's catalog.

"*Don't go forgetting my face,*" I sing along, pulling Kasey's attention back to me. "'*Cause I've got the color of your eyes burned into my mind. If we ever get out of this place, there's no limit to the joys we might find. Stick with me on this journey called life, and someday I might call you wife.* Man, I wrote that ages ago."

As red splotches her cheeks again, Kasey drops her gaze to her lap. "That's one of your songs?"

"Not my best work, but yeah." Honestly, I don't love that song. It was one of my first ones after my record label discovered me, which is pretty obvious when it comes to the lyrics, but the melody is good. I think that's why Nelson likes it.

Kasey shivers, though she tries to hide it by adjusting her towel and eating another spicy tuna roll. At this point, she's eaten at least half of my lunch, and I'm tempted to see if she keeps eating, even if it means my lunch will be dismal. If she's hungry, I'd rather she eat it.

If the woman is willing to risk drowning for a measly thousand bucks, she needs all the free food she can get.

"I probably have some dry clothes you could change into," I tell her instead of nudging the rest of the sushi closer to her.

She winces. "Oh no, that's okay. I need to get going anyway so I can make some more deliveries before it gets dark."

"You're freezing."

"I've got a heater in my car."

"Do you really think it will be comfortable to drive around soaking wet?"

"I'm almost dry."

Why in the world is this woman so stubborn? Hopping up, I slowly make my way back to where I left my crutch. It may be unwieldy, but it's a million times easier to move around with this thing than by hopping. "Kasey, take the clothes."

Of course, she keeps arguing as she follows me. "I'm pretty sure I'll drown in your clothes."

"Better than in my pool." Yeesh, that was a terrible joke, and I start making my way inside so I don't have to see her reaction. I can't imagine it was in my favor. "I'm sure Freya has some clothes around here somewhere."

"Your girlfriend?"

I stop at the base of the stairs. I can't help myself. Either that was disappointment in her voice or it was relief, and it's going to drive me crazy if I don't know which. I turn, pleased to see her right behind me with her shoes in hand. "Not my girlfriend. Just a friend."

"Oh." She frowns, though I think it's more in confusion than as something to help me clarify. "Why are you looking at me like that?"

I grin. "Because I'm trying to figure you out, Kasey."

"Good luck with that," she mumbles back. Probably not for me to hear, but she seems to say a lot of things to herself.

I don't have anything to say for the next couple of minutes because it takes all my concentration to get up the stairs. This large, curving staircase appealed to me when I bought this house—granted, pretty much anything appealed back then—but I'm regretting it wholeheartedly right now. Stairs and crutches don't mix, and without the boot there is no way I'm putting weight on my foot.

"I really don't need dry clothes," Kasey says when I'm halfway up.

Desperate for a break, I plop myself down on a step and raise an eyebrow at her. "I'm already this far. Might as well follow through with my promise. Though, if Freya didn't leave anything here before she left for Candora the last time, then I'll probably just have my own stuff to offer. Bonnie keeps most of her spare clothes at Derek's."

At first, Kasey looks ready to keep arguing, but as soon as I say Derek's name she seems to freeze, her eyes the only part of her that still looks alive.

Apparently Derek is more famous than me. Which I already knew, but it still stings. This is what I get for befriending one of the biggest names in Hollywood.

Breaking from her trance with a blink, Kasey clears her throat. "When you say Bonnie and Derek, do you mean—"

"Hollywood's darlings? The two halves of Dennie? Captain Jupiter and the shy but gorgeous Dr. Adeline Price?" I snort a laugh at the look on her face. Kasey may not be a music lover, but I'm going to hazard a guess that she's a movie buff. At the very least, she knows the two movies I referenced with Derek's and Bonnie's most iconic roles so far.

Derek has a lot of those. Bonnie's still working up to his range, but she's hustling to try to get some different parts in the works. She's a phenomenal actor, but casting directors have been locking her into a type since the beginning of her career.

"You know them?" Kasey asks. Her eyes seem to sparkle, though they're more brown than golden like they were in the sunlight.

I let out a little sigh. So much for disinterest. It's just me she doesn't care about. "Derek is one of my best friends," I admit, though reluctantly. "And Bonnie too." I'm not sure where this is going to go now that Kasey has taken an interest in my friends. If she tries asking for their autographs, I'll probably have to send her packing.

Living a life of fame isn't easy, and we take care of each other. Too many people try to get to their idols any way they can, and it wouldn't be the first time someone tried to get to Derek through me.

"How about those clothes?" I ask, curious to see how she responds now that she knows I've got connections.

To my relief, her wariness comes right back. "I really should be getting back to work." But there's hesitation there.

I nod up the staircase. "First door on your right is the best guest room. If you find anything that works, it's yours."

"Won't Freya miss it?" Though she asks that question, she's already on her way up.

I chuckle. "She's literally a princess, so she'll be fine."

Kasey trips, looking back at me. "Do you mean metaphorically?"

"No, I mean literally. She's the heir to the Candoran throne and a royal pain in my neck most of the time."

"Who in the world are you?" she mutters as she continues onward.

When the door to the guest room closes, I push myself up so I'm sitting on the next highest step, and then the next, feeling pathetic but knowing it's my best chance at getting my own change of clothes so these wet pants stop riding up. As long as I can get changed quickly enough that Kasey doesn't sneak out while I'm in my room.

Better to leave the door open, just in case.

As soon as I hit the top of the stairs, I hop as quickly as I can, using the wall for support and cursing my stupid foot for causing so many problems..

I stumble when I reach my closet, smashing into the door with a grunt and a curse. I never skip leg day, but it's obvious I need to build up more muscle because my right leg is screaming at me almost as loudly as my fractured foot. I grab a pair of sweatpants, curse again when I realize my underwear is clear on the other side and requires more hopping to get to it, and then I plop onto the ottoman that sits in the center of the closet and imagine what it might be like to go back to a normal-sized house again.

"Ha! Normal," I mutter to myself, shimmying out of my wet clothes, which isn't especially easy while sitting down. "My houses were never normal."

They were derelict trailers and tiny apartments and some creepy guy's basement because he offered cheap rent. My walk-in closet now may be bigger than my bedroom when I was twelve, but it still feels more like home than anything I had growing up. I'll take this massive house and all its silence any day if it means I'm not living in squalor.

"Hey Liam, could I—"

I shout at the same time Kasey shrieks and claps a hand over her eyes.

"Why are you naked?" she hisses, spinning around so her back is to me.

I scramble to pull on my dry pants, another stream of expletives spewing from my mouth every time I bump my foot. "Why are you in my bedroom?" I shoot back.

"I didn't realize you'd be..."

I can see her blush climbing her neck even though she's facing away from me, and though my heart's pounding from her sudden appearance, I can't hold back my grin. "You know," I mutter, standing again so I can find myself a dry t-shirt, "I have to say this is a first for me."

"Says the guy who apparently takes his shirt off at all of his concerts."

"Not anymore. Not since—"

"The incident," she finishes for me. "Can I look yet?"

I pause instead of grabbing a shirt from the drawer. "Depends on what you want to see."

"Liam."

"Yeah, I'm decent."

With her hand still covering her eyes, she turns toward me and peeks through her fingers, sighing with relief as soon as she realizes I'm clothed. Well, *mostly* clothed. I have yet to grab a shirt, too curious to see what she'll do. "Decent," she mumbles with a scoff. "I'm sorry for, uh, walking in on you. I wasn't thinking."

My eyes travel over her drenched outfit, and I purse my lips. "Didn't find anything?"

She shakes her head. "Just some fancy ball gown, and I'm not wearing that."

Since I'm still standing by my drawer full of t-shirts, I grab one and toss it at her. "And there are some sweatpants there," I say, pointing to her left. "Forgive me for not grabbing something myself, but…" I gesture to my legs, realizing with a grimace that in my haste I pulled the bottoms of the sweatpants all the way up to my calves.

Though she grabs herself a pair of black sweatpants, Kasey's eyes fixate on the ankle monitor sitting so suspiciously above my foot. Some of the color drains from her face, and she looks back up at me. She must not have seen it earlier, though I'm not sure how she could miss something like that.

"It's not what it looks like," I say quickly, bending to hide the stupid thing beneath my pants.

"It looks like you're a criminal."

"Technically? Yes. But also no."

She folds her arms. I expected her to run, so I'm not really sure what to do with the judging look in her eyes. "What did you do?"

"Uh. Punched someone."

"That was enough to get you arrested?"

I drop back onto the ottoman, clenching my jaw and wishing I had something other than the truth to give her. "When it's one of my concertgoers and I deck him on stage for everyone to see, yeah." It sounds so bad out of context. "But he was—"

"I should go." Kasey shakes her head, and I can almost feel her disappointment. I just don't know what she's disappointed *about.* "Thanks for the clothes, Liam."

"He was harassing a girl after the show." My words come out somewhat desperate, probably because I *am* desperate. I don't know what it is about Kasey, but she has me all out of sorts. Or maybe it's because I've been cooped up here for three days with no one but a budgie to keep me company, and Nelson doesn't exactly have great conversational skills.

Thankfully, Kasey looks back. She's obviously wary, but her curiosity has kept her here. At least for a little longer.

I keep talking. Maybe if I give her all the details, she'll stay. "They were both part of a VIP group who got to come up on stage and meet me after I finished my set. Everyone was on their way out when he went after her, and she clearly wasn't into him. So I broke them apart. He was totally wasted and fought me off. Said some things about the girl I'm not about to repeat." I grimace, dropping my gaze. I've been around guys like that too many times in my life, and I hate that they can't get into their thick skulls the concept of consent.

"So you punched him?" Kasey says, bringing my eyes back up to hers. She has a small smile now, enough to give me hope that I haven't fully scared her off yet.

I nod. "So I politely asked him to apologize, and *he* punched *me. Then* I punched him, but at that point people had noticed our little, uh, conversation, and started filming, so a lot of people think I started the fight."

She leans against the door frame, her smile growing. She's suddenly way more relaxed than she was a second ago. "You know I have no reason to believe anything you say, right?"

I jump up, hopping closer to her and praying she doesn't run. She stays put, allowing me close enough to tilt my head and show her the fading bruise on my left cheekbone. "You can watch the videos and see that he never touched me before security arrived. It's because he's the one who hit first, before anyone looked our way and started recording it all."

"A bruise doesn't mean you got punched at the concert. With your charming personality, I can see a lot of people wanting to punch you."

I chuckle. Up this close, I've got a great view of the light dusting of freckles across her nose and the way her eyes crinkle at the corners when she smiles. It's more of a smirk than a smile, but I'll take what I can get.

"You do believe me, don't you?" I ask, leaning ever so slightly closer. I can't help it. Nothing feels close enough, and I'm not detecting any discomfort in her expression. "Because I really want you to believe me."

She tilts her head up, honey eyes glittering. "I guess we'll see."

"Do you really think I'm charming?" I must be, with the way her eyes flick down to my mouth for half a second, sending a thrill through me. She may not like me, but I might have a chance to change her mind. Everyone likes me eventually.

Her smile twists as she shifts her weight, fractionally closing the space between us. And then the last thing I expected to happen happens. Her fingers lift and press against my sternum, almost like she's going to push me away. But then they slowly glide down my abdomen. I'm not even sure she knows she's doing it, but my brain is short-circuiting as goosebumps pepper my whole body. "I think you're far too aware of how attractive you are," she says carefully, "and that makes you dangerous."

I grab hold of the door frame for some stability and smile down at her. I'm not even going to touch on the fact that she thinks I'm attractive, as much as I want to. I can barely focus on anything but the way her fingers are still pressed against my skin. "Dangerous?"

"Yeah." Color fills her cheeks at the same time her tongue darts out across her lips. "I've known too many guys like you, Liam Connolly."

"There are no guys like me." I move slowly, almost painfully slow, bringing my face down to hers and watching every micro expression that crosses her face. Begging for a clear sign of permission because I'm not sure I can get the words out to ask. When my nose brushes hers and she doesn't move, I take that as a go-ahead.

Before I can press my lips against hers, a high-pitched whistling fills the air, like the sound of a bomb falling from the sky, and then Kasey screams.

CHAPTER FOUR

KASEY

"It's in my hair!" I shriek, throwing both t-shirt and sweatpants as I swat at the air around my head, knocking the bird loose. Excited twittering fills the room, and the only reason I'm not running for my life is the crippling fear and the horror of little bird feet clinging to my scalp.

"Nelson!" Liam stumbles out of the closet at the same time I dart inside, and he collapses on the wood floor with a thump. A string of words comes out of his mouth in a language I don't understand as he flips around and tries to keep his eyes on the green and yellow bird circling the room like a vulture looking for its next meal. "Nelson, you stupid bird, how did you get out of your cage again?"

I grab the closet door and slide it shut, except the bird flits inside at the last minute, trapping himself in here with me. I scream again and scramble into the wide array of clothes hanging along the left wall. This is what I get for falling for the charms of the gorgeous musician—death by parakeet.

"Please don't eat me," I beg of the bird, though I can't see it through the suit coats and silk shirts that are the only thing protecting me from the Taylor-tweeting terror. I think I might have nightmares if I hear "Shake it Off" again.

The closet door slams open, and it sounds like Liam is shouting some sort of battle cry to compete with the parakeet's whistling song, again in that language that is completely indecipherable. There's a crash and a curse, a shrill shout of "Stupid bird!" from the bird itself, and then a sharp squeak and a "Gotcha!". Not sure who squeaked, though the shout came from Liam.

Though the bird starts up a chant of "Chicken soup, chicken soup!" like some little demon, I poke my head out, holding my breath.

Liam is sprawled on the carpet with the bird clenched in his fist and a wild expression in his eyes as he glares at the little beast. "Don't make me send you back where you came from," he warns breathlessly. Then his eyes jump over to me. "Kasey."

"I need to go." With my eyes locked on the bird, I crawl out from my hiding place and inch my way back into the bedroom, trying to calm my breathing. "Thanks for lunch. And the clothes. Don't worry about the extra tip." I don't mean that last part, but I'm not sticking around long enough to get attacked again.

Snatching up the t-shirt and sweatpants—I really am freezing in these wet clothes—I ignore Liam's calls after me and hustle back down the stairs and to the front door, which is thankfully easy to find. I glance at the open door of the big birdcage in the front room, but that's the only glance I allow myself until I reach my car.

Thankfully, it starts up despite my paranoid fears that my generally functional car will crap out at the most inopportune moment, which means I have a free and clear escape.

Before pulling away, I look back at Liam's house just as he reaches the front door and gives me the most mournful look I've ever seen. It's almost enough to make me want to stay. *Almost.*

I don't breathe easily until I'm on the PCH heading back to LA. I stop at the first gas station I come across and change my clothes, but I don't think I have the stamina to keep doing deliveries today as I look at myself in the warped and dirty bathroom mirror. It's not just the bird, though my irrational fear of the flapping creatures has certainly taken it out of me. It's nearly drowning in a pool because I was desperate for money.

It's the fact that I almost *kissed* a practical stranger, which for some reason feels crazier than the drowning thing. I don't kiss strangers. I don't know if it was his easy and lighthearted nature or his pretty face or the way he gave me the best sushi I've ever had and then offered me dry clothes. Maybe it's that whole savior complex thing, but reversed. What's it called? White knight syndrome, or something like that.

I mean, the guy *did* save me from drowning. It's almost a pity he didn't have to give me mouth-to-mouth.

"Oh, get a hold of yourself, Kasey."

"Pardon?"

I jump, glancing behind me to the one occupied bathroom stall behind me. Should I reply? No, probably not. Washing my hands quickly, I gather up my wet clothes and dart back out to my car before the lady finishes her business and gets a look at the kind of person who talks to herself in a gas station bathroom. I have to hold the sweatpants up, and this t-shirt is far too big, but it smells like Liam and that's...

"A problem," I growl, slipping back into my car. "Dang it all, why does it smell so good? Does he douse his laundry in cologne or something?"

He probably uses his tantalizing scent to lure women in, and then he kisses every one of them because that's how all celebrities seem to be. I just happened to be his next conquest. I have to keep telling myself that, no matter how untrue it feels, so I don't keep feeling so disappointed that we were interrupted. Kissing Liam Connolly would have been bad. So bad.

"Oh my gosh, did I *stroke his abs*?"

I refuse to think about what went down in that closet. Any of it. Except now I'm thinking about it, and my mind is fixed on the way he looked at me and how his muscles felt and *I desperately need a distraction.*

As I turn my car on, far more comfortable now that I'm not sitting in wet jeans, my phone buzzes with a notification from Diner Delivery, the app that I work for.

I squeak when I see the five-hundred-dollar tip Liam just sent me on top of the three hundred he's already given me with his original tip and the two hundred to bring the food inside. He also left a five-star review, which I open with hesitation.

"Flora was everything I could have hoped for in a delivery driver. Incredibly helpful in every way and completely discreet when it came to my somewhat sensitive package."

It's a warning, and I know it. Granted, I didn't actually see anything when I accidentally walked in on him in the closet—praise the heavens he was sitting down—but if he's as famous as he seems, I can imagine he doesn't want me shouting to the rooftops anything about his, uh, *sensitive areas.* I bite my lip as I keep reading.

"She showed professionalism to the highest degree, and I hope she delivers my food again. Best delivery driver I've ever had, and I owe her big."

Does that mean he still wants to pay me the full thousand he promised? This five hundred is way more than I deserve as it is because I was neither nice nor grabbed his phone. Don't get me wrong, I'm incredibly grateful for the money, and I could really use it. I never did give him a way to send me money outside of this delivery app, so this review makes sense. He was right when he guessed that the taxes are pretty awful, and Diner Delivery takes their cut of tips, even though I'm not sure that's entirely legal. It doesn't matter because they're the only delivery company that's used in the richer parts of Los Angeles and they keep a small employee base, so I'm not about to work for someone else.

Especially if I can encounter more people like this strange musician who isn't anything like how I would expect someone like him to be.

If not for his murderous bird, I might even go back.

"Ha!" I pull out of my parking spot and start heading for home, too tired to do any more deliveries today. I can't go back. I nearly drowned, ate most of his lunch, and made a fool of myself when a parakeet landed on my head. No matter how nice he might be, I'm not sure I could ever be brave enough to show my face there again.

I would have no argument if he accused me of feeling him up again because I definitely did that. I thought his whole "shirtless incident" thing was a joke, but after the way I reacted to his bare torso, it's not so unbelievable that something bad could go down when he's out in the open like that.

Val is home when I enter the little East Hollywood house that has been my home for the last year. She's in the middle of filming a yoga video in the sun room, so I tiptoe toward my bedroom to avoid interrupting—

"Whoa, where do you think you're going, looking like that?" Though still in the middle of one of her poses, she fixes me with a pointed stare. She figured out in the sixth grade that this stare is super effective whenever I'm trying to keep something to myself because it makes me feel like she can see into my soul. I'm not much of a liar.

I tuck my wet clothes behind my back. Stupid, considering she's probably already seen them. "Looking like what?"

"Looking like you're doing a walk of shame, though I know you weren't out having fun." She whispers some sort of prayer and waves her hand over me. "Heaven forbid you actually meet a guy and get some action."

"I don't want any *action*, thank you very much." Though, my hand against Liam's abs might disagree.

"Yes, yes, I know you're old school and adorable." Unfolding herself, Val comes over to me and pinches the sleeve of Liam's t-shirt between her thumb and pointer finger. Then she takes a big sniff and tilts her head to examine the sweatpants that are barely holding on to my nonexistent hips. "Honey, you had better start explaining why you're wearing a man's clothes before I start thinking you've crossed over to the dark side."

I don't want to explain anything, but Val has been my best friend since we were ten. It's not like I'll really be able to keep anything from her. "I, uh, met someone while I was out delivering."

Val *tsks* and tugs on the rolled waistband of the pants. "*Met* someone?"

I slap her hand away. "Not like that! No, I ended up in his pool, so he lent me some clothes." Clothes I have no intention of returning. I'm pretty sure he can afford more, and it's not like he wears them anyway. "I have some rent money, by the way. Or I will, as soon as I cash out my tips."

I try to step toward my little bedroom, but Val moves into my path. "Kasey Elizabeth Graham, please do not tell me you have gone the way of selling your cute little body for money."

"No!" Good heavens, she's jumping to all the wrong conclusions. I might as well give her all the details. The important ones, anyway. "I brought food to Liam Connolly's backyard in Malibu and helped him get his phone out of the pool, and then he gave me some clothes to change into so I wasn't freezing and wet the rest of the day."

That shuts her right up. She takes a step back, brown eyes narrowed and suspicious as she studies me. "Liam Connolly," she says after a moment.

I nod once. "Yep."

"Like, the world's most sexy guitar player and vocalist, Liam Connolly?"

"Is he?" Even as I ask that, heat floods my face. Yeah, Liam is wildly attractive, though I've seen way too much of him at this point. And also his voice was... I may have been too hasty when I told him I wasn't big into music. I can see myself getting big into *his* music, with the way he sang to me on his patio. Even with a parakeet as his background music, he was incredible.

Val gasps as if she's reading all of my thoughts. She probably is. "*You actually met Liam Connolly?* How? And why are you here instead of making out with the man? He gave you his *clothes*, for goodness' sake!" As if she needs to emphasize how monumental that is, she buries her face in my shoulder and inhales deeply. "Oh, he smells *so good*!"

"Trust me, I know." I was smelling him the whole drive home, though it was all a reminder of how delicious he smelled when he crowded my space in the closet doorway.

It might have been me doing the crowding. At this point, I don't even know.

"And you didn't kiss him?" Val asks, narrowing her eyes.

"I would have told you if I had." I could tell her I *almost* kissed him, but I keep that to myself. An almost kiss is nothing to write home about, no matter how much I was enjoying the moment. "Val, this isn't a big deal."

"Not a big deal." She scoffs, grabbing hold of my wrist and tugging me to the couch. "Do you have any idea how wrong you are? This is *Liam Connolly* we're talking about. Wait!" She jumps back up, rushing to grab her phone and end the recording she was doing. Then she furiously starts typing until she shoves it in my face.

A picture of a shirtless and sweaty Liam singing his heart out on a backlit stage is front and center. My goodness, pictures like that should be illegal. It's as much the reminder of his muscled torso as it is the pure, raw emotion in his face that fills my own face with heat again.

"This is the guy you met?" Val demands.

I groan. "Is there more than one musician named Liam Connolly in Malibu? Yes, that's him."

Squealing, she curls her legs up underneath her and takes hold of my hands. "Allow me to educate you. Liam Connolly is not just a *musician*. He's like a unicorn among men. He writes all his own songs, never lip syncs, doesn't sleep around, and is always *so nice* to all his fans. Not to mention his scrumptious face and gorgeous bod. This man is the *whole package*. And you know where he lives!"

I roll my eyes. "You know I can't tell you where he lives, right?"

"You don't have to tell me. I will graciously let you have him."

"Have him?"

Val nods like it's a done deal. "Yes. Because you, my beautiful starfish, need an equally beautiful man in your life, and you literally can't find a more attractive man than Liam Connolly."

I'm glad she thinks so highly of the man, but I have no intentions of ever seeing him again. The mortification alone is one thing, but it's not like I can get access to his neighborhood anytime I want. The place is more secure than a prison.

"I highly doubt I'm going to get assigned a delivery to his place again," I mutter, though I'm surprised by the disappointment in my voice. "I don't want to go back, anyway."

"Why not?" She gasps again. "Did he come on to you? You know, you could totally sue him if he—"

"I thought he was a unicorn among men," I grumble, cutting her off. And okay, yeah, he almost kissed me, but I was clearly giving him all the signs that he should take his chance. "He gave me a great tip, which is nice, but I don't need a guy like him in my life. You know that."

She doesn't argue, for which I'm glad. At least, I'm glad until she says, "You know who Liam's best friend is, right?"

I sigh. "Derek Riley?" Honestly, I've been trying not to think about it because that connection is going to be far too tempting to exploit. Liam seems like a nice guy for the most part, if a little full of himself, and he doesn't need me trying to get to his famous actor friends through him. He closed off as soon as I asked about Derek and Bonnie. It was the only time he seemed reluctant to say anything.

Besides, that's not exactly a path I want to take again.

Val whacks my arm. "Don't get that look. You've said a million times that the only way to get into the movie business is to have connections. A gorgeous guy who is best friends with the biggest name in Hollywood? That's a *connection*."

"Yeah, well, the last time I tried using a connection, I ended up getting my screenplay stolen from me and it turned out to be a huge hit." Pulling my knees up to my chest, I take a deep breath full of Liam's fresh scent and let it out slowly. The smell of him is weirdly calming. "Maybe I'm not meant to be a screenwriter. If I was any good at it, someone would have been interested by now."

"Kasey, honey, you haven't sent anyone anything new. That screenplay was not a fluke." Her argument stings because she's entirely right. I really have no right to complain. "Besides," she continues, "sometimes things take time."

"Your thing didn't." Val moved to LA two years ago after quitting her nursing job in Wichita because she wanted to start an ocean-based yoga studio. While she picked up a waitress job to pay the bills until she could find a location, she started filming her morning yoga sessions on the beach and built up millions of followers in mere months. She's well on her way to being famous herself.

Clucking her tongue, Val curls up next to me, though I'm pretty sure it's so she can breathe in Liam's scent again. "I got lucky," she argues. "And Vince is good at the algorithm stuff."

"I still don't know how you managed to find the one normal man in Los Angeles and convince him to propose to you," I mumble. "Seriously, you are one lucky break away from winning the lottery and becoming a millionaire."

Humming thoughtfully, Val cuddles up closer. She's way more touchy-feely than I've ever been, but I've gotten used to it. When her adorable fiancé is on one of his many business trips, like he is now, she gets even clingier than normal. "Kasey, I know He-Who-Will-Not-Be-Named did a number on you when he took credit for your story, but that was almost a year ago. Someday you have to pick yourself up, put on your big girl panties, and tell yourself that you're better than what he put you through. You're a better writer, a better woman, and a better human because you're not the kind of person who would take advantage of someone else's desperation."

'Help out a cripple?' I can easily picture the look on Liam's face when he said that after asking me to grab his phone from the pool. And while I know full well he would have been fine without me, I still refused to help him until he promised me money. Guilt settles deep in my belly as his offers replay in my mind.

Two hundred bucks to bring his food to him so he didn't have to hobble around.

Another three to help him over to the table so he could eat his lunch, which he didn't actually do because I ate most of it.

A thousand for him to save my life and offer me his own clothes to keep me warm, and I didn't even grab his phone.

What kind of person does that make me? I really shouldn't go back there, especially after the way I left, but something in me is desperate to see him again and find out if he really is that wonderful of a person. He feels too good to be true, which, in my experience, is a bad omen. I know better than to risk it, and yet…

I'm not sure I'll have the fortitude to stay away if I get another chance.

CHAPTER FIVE

LIAM

"Wow, you've got a nice house, man." George, though I'm starting to guess that isn't his real name, pokes his head in through the door as he hands me a brown paper bag. "What kind of mortgage do you have?" He even takes a step inside, as if he's planning to take the grand tour.

I shift my stance to block him off, almost wishing I had a crutch with me to use as a barricade. Though I've kept the boot on, I stopped using the crutch two days ago, and it would have come in handy today. "Thanks for the food. Tip is in the app."

Disappointment washes over George's face, but he's got nothing on my own disappointment. It's been a full week of ordering food from Diner Delivery, and so far I've only gotten men dropping things off and one lady who looked like she was nearing eighty years old. At this point, I'm not even hungry, and my fridge is full of enough leftovers to feed a small army. I might have offered tonight's dinner to George if he didn't decide to overstep. Literally.

"Oh, sweet tip!" he says as he bounces down my walkway to the street and waves his phone in the air. "Thanks!"

I give him four stars for tactlessness.

Once I'm sure he drives off, I send a heads up text to the security guard at the gate to make sure "George" actually leaves the neighborhood instead of trying to sneak into someone's backyard, and then I limp into the front room where Nelson has been trying to break out of his cage, without success.

At some point, he learned how to undo the latch on the door and let himself out, which is why I've wrapped an unfolded paper clip around it as many times as I can. In the increasingly unlikely event I can get Kasey back here again, I don't want my idiotic parakeet scaring her off before I can at least get her number.

Plopping myself onto the rug in front of the cage, I pull out tonight's attempt and wrinkle my nose. I've been trying different restaurants to see if any of them might bring Kasey, but so far I haven't had any luck. At least now I know I don't need to order from Auntie Elsa's Potato Sandwich Emporium again. I didn't look too hard at the menu before ordering the highest rated entree, but I'm not sure how I feel about mashed potatoes sandwiched between two baked potato "buns."

"Well, Nelson," I mutter, picking out a fingerful of potato and sticking it in my mouth. At least the mashed potatoes are decent. "It looks like it's you and me tonight, as always."

Nelson starts whistling "We Are Never Ever Getting Back Together," and I flick a bit of potato at him.

"Don't be rude," I grumble. "It's your fault she left in the first place, you know."

He switches his song to one of mine, as if he thinks that will make me feel better.

I groan, flopping spread-eagle onto my back and staring up at the vaulted ceilings. "I don't know what else to do, Nels. I don't even know if her name is really Kasey, and I can't stop worrying she's ignoring my orders on purpose."

"Other side," Nelson says.

I have no idea what that's supposed to mean, but I do know I should probably start talking to other people instead of a bird.

As if my thoughts are manifested by the universe, my front door opens, though I have no idea who is walking inside. Heck, I'll even take George at this point, though I'll be sure to educate him on proper guest etiquette. But the voice that speaks over Nelson's excited whistling is a familiar one.

"House arrest is not a good look on you, Connolly."

My head snaps up, my body quickly following. "Derek!"

He tenses just in time for me to leap onto him, grunting a bit on impact but holding steady like the beast he is. When the guy is used to playing superheroes and spies, he's pretty constantly jacked in a way I aspire to be. If not for him and Cole, who is a beast of a man, I wouldn't work out nearly as hard as I do.

"I didn't know you were back in town!" I shout at him.

He laughs, fighting me off until I let go. "Maybe if you would stop ignoring our group chats now and then, you'd be better informed."

I usually drop everything for our video calls, so he has a point. With the five of us constantly on the road—and Freya most often on the other side of the world in her own country—those video chats are the only way we stay in touch beyond texts. But after my phone call with Freya last week, I've been wary of interacting with my friends in case they try holding me accountable for my album.

In my defense, I *have* tried working on a couple different songs, but nothing has worked. Writer's block is the bane of my existence.

"Hungry?" I ask, working my way to the kitchen.

"How's that foot of yours?" Derek replies as he follows.

I shrug. "Depends on the day, but it's better than it was a week ago." I pretty much didn't move from my bed the day after I met Kascy, too much of a baby to deal with the aftermath of walking around as much as

I did. The pool and my chase after Nelson weren't kind to my poor foot. "How was filming?"

I pull open both doors to the fridge, wincing when I see the full scope of my delivery binge.

Derek comes up beside me, his eyebrows low. "I think you can ease up on the food orders, Liam."

"It's not my fault."

"Lies."

I roll my eyes, though I should have expected that response. It's something our little group—me, Derek, Bonnie, Freya, and Cole—started a couple years ago when we realized we were all pretty good at keeping things from each other. It's an occupational hazard, a side effect of fame that we've all developed, not necessarily by choice. We're also good at spotting BS, so we started calling it out.

Normally, I'm pretty open, especially with Derek, but I feel like this week has been the start of my slow descent into madness. I don't need that out in the world for others to know.

Sighing, I sit on the edge of the counter as Derek starts sorting through the contents of my fridge. "I met a girl," I admit.

"You meet girls all the time. It's maddening."

Not like this.

"Says the guy who's been dating Bonnie for over a year now," I argue. "I expected you two to split six months ago, based on her track record." Bonnie is one of my best friends, but she's not a long-term kind of gal. It was strange enough when she and Derek moved from friendship to a romantic relationship, and even stranger still when that relationship continued beyond a few months.

Emerging with a carton of tikka masala, Derek scowls at me. He's sporting a dark beard right now, probably for whatever movie he's currently working on, and it makes him look more intimidating than usual. "You like Bonnie."

"Oh, I know. I don't understand why she's content to date a bone-head like you." That, and Bonnie has a past full of short-term relationships that always seemed somewhat sketchy. She's too flighty for a guy like Derek, who isn't shy about his end goals of settling down and starting a family. Bonnie's great, but I don't see her as family material.

She and I have that in common.

Grabbing a fork, Derek starts eating the chicken cold. "I know she's too good for me," he says calmly. Everything Derek does is calm unless he's in front of a camera. "But we're not talking about my relationship with Bonnie. Tell me about this girl and what she has to do with you single-handedly keeping Diner Delivery in business. You don't even like Indian food."

"It's food. Don't care where it's from."

Snickering, he lifts his eyebrows and leans against the granite countertop. "I can't wait for you to hit thirty and experience the nightmare of your metabolism slowing down."

Ugh, I'm trying not to think about it. I've still got a few years before I start to feel old like him. "Anyway, this girl delivered my lunch last week."

Derek immediately stops eating and looks up at me. "What did you do?"

I flinch. "Why do you always assume I did something?"

"Because you're you. Spill it, Connolly."

I do, regaling the whole encounter with the intriguing and mysterious Kasey. Minus a detail here and there, like her walking in on me while exposed. I haven't gotten any angry phone calls from Ethan about unseemly mentions of my unmentionables, so I have to assume Kasey got my message in the review I left her.

"There's something about this girl," I tell Derek. "I can't get her out of my head."

"Have you tried contacting Diner Delivery to get her info?"

I laugh. "Surprisingly, they're pretty tight-lipped about their employees and wouldn't tell me anything. The drivers don't even use their real names. Kasey was Flora in the app."

"Hmm." Derek pulls out his phone and types out a quick text.

I narrow my eyes. "Who did you just text?"

"Doesn't matter." He's a bit *too* calm now, and that's worrisome.

Sliding from the counter, I step forward so I'm in his face, though he's got two inches and twenty pounds of muscle on me and isn't the least bit intimidated by me. He's also five years older, though I've never let that get in my way. "Derek Riley, I know you have this freakishly wide circle of connections around the world, but I don't need you hunting this girl down for me. If we're going to meet again, it has to happen naturally."

He lifts one dark eyebrow, glancing at the fridge behind him. "There is nothing natural about the state of your fridge right now."

He doesn't need to tell me as much. I know I've crossed into full-blown crazy. "I've got some boxes in the garage if you're up for taking some of this to a shelter or something. I'm never going to eat it all, and it's not like I can take it out myself."

As if on cue, my ankle starts itching underneath the band of the monitor, and I resist the urge to scratch it. The moment I start, I'm doomed. I spent a whole hour the other night trying to ease the itch and nearly went mad before I tore off the boot and dove into the pool. Thankfully, the monitor is more waterproof than I expected, and I managed to get in a decent swim before my foot started hurting too much.

Derek agrees to take the food when he leaves, and then we move to the back patio to watch the sunset over the Pacific. Outside of my quick dip last night, I haven't spent much time back here since the Kasey incident, so it's nice to get outside. Fall is my favorite time of year, when the nights drop into the sixties and the days are the absolutely perfect temperature for kicking it on the beach without boiling in the sun.

Granted, I can't actually go to the beach right now, but it's still pleasant out.

As he settles himself on a pool chair, Derek points to the monitor on my ankle. "Think you'll get that off when this is all said and done?"

I've been trying not to think about it, though Ethan has been calling every other day with pointless updates. I'm tempted to start ignoring his calls. "The girl who got harassed is still willing to testify in my favor, and Ethan doesn't seem too worried," I say with a shrug. "The hardest part is the waiting."

"If only you had some sort of project to work on."

I growl at his sarcastic tone. "I don't want to know what you four have been talking about behind my back."

"Three. Cole has been pretty radio silent too."

That's strange. Cole is a quiet guy in general, but unless he's got a match that day, he's always on the video calls. "I've got a bad feeling about that," I mutter. "Rugby season is over now, so he has no excuses."

"I know," Derek agrees, frowning. "Last I heard from Bonnie, he was planning to head to Oregon to visit Sage, but he hasn't told me anything."

I send Cole a text, curious to see if he'll respond. It's unlikely, if he's with his longtime girlfriend. "Maybe he finally decided he's too cool for us."

Of the five of us, Cole possesses the least amount of celebrity status, though he's far from unknown. At one point, he was one of the most widely discussed quarterbacks in the NFL, on his way to becoming one of the greats until he gave up his career out of the blue to play a sport that hasn't taken hold in the States like it has in the rest of the world. To this day, I still don't know why he left football, though he's killing it in rugby and is probably one of the best players in the league.

Cole generally keeps to himself, but he and Derek have been friends long enough that it's weird for him to ignore his oldest friend.

Time to change the subject before Derek gets stressed out by Cole's silence.

"Are you ever going to collect another famous friend?" I ask.

Derek looks over with a spark of amusement in his eyes. "Why?"

"We're all *too* famous. Who am I supposed to hang out with for the next four and a half weeks when all y'all are off living your celebrity lives? I need a wider pool of options."

He laughs. "Going stir crazy already? That's a bad sign. You know you can make your own friends, right?"

My scoff comes with a smile because we've had this conversation before. "I'm sorry, but I'm pretty sure you tell me at least once a month that I'm too trusting."

"You are."

"There's your answer then." With my track record, I would only befriend someone who's in it for what they can get from me, not for genuine friendship.

My phone buzzes, and I roll my eyes as soon as I read Cole's response.

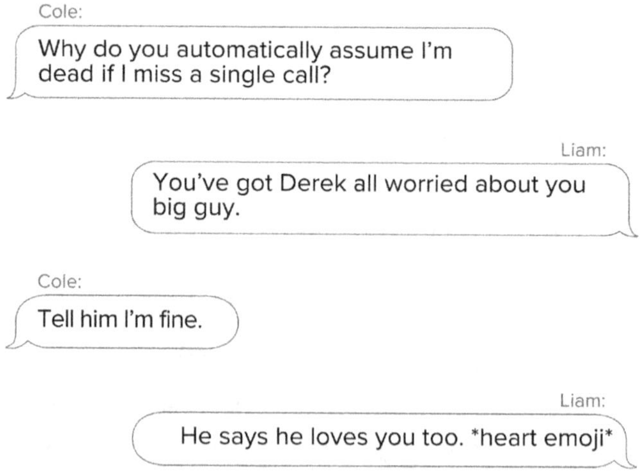

Derek groans as he looks over at my phone to see what Cole said. "Why do you always make it weird?"

"Because life is more fun that way."

Standing up, he gives me a stern look and then heads for the door. "Bonnie's home from her shoot, so I'm going to leave now so you can write those non-existent songs that you keep telling me are 'almost done.' Try focusing on your job instead of the girl you probably won't see again, okay? Stop overthinking and start doing."

"Take the food!" I shout back. Then I slump back in my chair as silence settles around me. Even with the fountain splashing away in the corner, it's way too quiet. Nelson must be asleep now that it's getting dark, and this neighborhood is tucked away from any roads that would add much to the ambience.

Seriously, why doesn't Derek make more friends? He's the reason our little celebrity group formed in the first place, and he's the type of guy everyone likes because he's calm and friendly and mature. He really does have an enormous array of connections both in and out of the movie industry, so it would be so easy for him to grab a couple more fellow fame-finders and give me someone else to bother.

I send another text to Cole because it's like three in the morning for Freya and Bonnie is going to be fully focused on Derek as he makes the short drive to his house. They have a habit of talking on the phone whenever they're not together, which is both endearing and annoying.

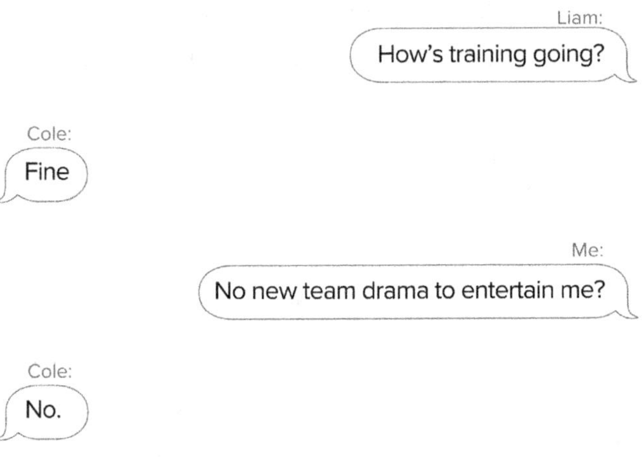

Ugh, he's really not giving me much to work with, and I'm already bored. I'm not used to sitting still like this, but what am I supposed to do to keep myself occupied when I can't venture outside my house? My home gym can only do so much.

Pulling up the Diner Delivery app, I start humming to myself as I peruse my many ice cream options. Ice cream is a minor distraction but a delicious one, and there's the slim chance Kasey will come with it.

What would I do if she did come? I have no reason to expect her to come inside again, especially now that I can walk almost normally, but maybe she'd be open to a conversation on the front step. Or in the backyard after I show her that Nelson can't escape like he did the last time. I'm desperate to know more about her because I've gotten next to nothing so far.

"Who are you under all that fear?" I mutter as I hit the order button. I'm not even sure what I picked, but it's ice cream, so it doesn't really matter.

I'm still humming as I settle back in my chair and look out over the darkening ocean. It's a good melody, though I can't place what song it's from. A bit melancholy and hopeful at the same time, and I'm pretty sure it's got some sort of string layer over top of the harmonies running through my head.

This is going to drive me crazy if I don't figure it out, so I wander back inside and settle down at the piano in my music room to see if I can solidify the melody.

CHAPTER SIX

KASEY

FINALLY. I'D ABOUT GIVEN up hope on getting another route to Liam's house, and then bam! Brent Fallsteen pops up right after I drop off a delivery. I have never accepted a job so quickly, and I can't decide if that makes me opportunistic or desperate. Probably desperate.

But here I am, clutching six pints of artisan ice cream and seriously debating leaving it on the step and running away.

But it's ice cream! I have to make sure it gets to a freezer before it melts or it'll be a tragedy, so I awkwardly shift my bounty and ring the doorbell again. I'm still not sure where the camera is, and looking around doesn't give me any clues. Probably a good thing; people act differently when they know they're being watched. Like me, for instance. If I didn't know Liam had a way to see me, I'd consider trying to look into the windows and see if he's even home.

"Don't be stupid," I tell myself. "Of course he's home." He's got that fancy little ankle tracker keeping him here and, based on my deep dive into all things Liam Connolly on the internet, he's either trapped in his house for the rest of his life or for the next month or so, depending on who you believe.

By the way, I don't recommend Googling someone as famous as Liam. There's a whole lot of info on the internet, and it's really hard to decipher what's real. I know his concert in Miami resulted in several broken bones when the crowd of drunk and crazed females swarmed his stage after he took his shirt off and several of them got pushed off in the madness. He told me about that one, the "incident" in Miami, and I had multiple up close encounters with shirtless Liam so it's easy to believe the pictures are real.

It's not as easy to believe he once rescued an injured surfer by punching a shark, though the internet seems to think that one is definitely true.

"Where are you, Liam?" I ask, loud enough that maybe he'll hear me through the microphone, wherever it is. I can't stand here all night, especially because the security guard at the gate told me that I only had ten minutes to drop off my delivery and head out of the neighborhood before he comes looking for me. He didn't tell me that last week, so I wonder what's changed.

I glance at my watch, grimacing when I realize I've already been standing here for six minutes. "Come on, Liam!" I ring the bell again.

This time, a cheerful, "Knock knock!" replies through the door, and I instantly go on high alert. If that bird is loose again, I swear I'll drop the ice cream and make a run for it, no matter how much I want to talk to Liam again.

Val told me in no uncertain terms that I am required to ask for an introduction to Derek Riley if I ever get the chance to see Liam again. I have my doubts that I won't chicken out—assuming I get the chance in the first place—but Val was pretty clear when she said she'll demand my back rent if I don't (which I can't pay). And while she's my best friend, she doesn't make threats lightly. She *will* kick me out if I blow an opportunity.

Honestly, she should have kicked me out months ago when I stopped making regular rent payments when my savings ran out. She's too good to me.

"This is getting ridiculous," I say, my frustration mounting. But if Liam doesn't answer his door, I have an excuse for not asking about Derek, and Val can't demand all my money.

I wait one more minute, during which I ring the doorbell and knock three more times—each time with an excited response from the parakeet inside—and then I give up. Might as well pick up some more deliveries before it gets too late.

When I crouch to set the ice cream on the porch, however, my eyes catch on a little piece of paper tucked under the welcome mat. Welcome mat? I didn't think rich people used regular welcome mats like this. Certainly not ones that say "welcome, y'all" in cursive. But whatever. Too curious to leave it alone, I tug the paper free and squint at the scrawled words, though they're almost illegible.

If you're here to deliver food leave it on the step. If you're Kasey you know where to find me.

Oh. Heat fills my face at the thought of Liam expecting me to show up again. It's not like I made a good first impression. "Are you expecting me to just walk inside?" I wonder out loud, staring at the huge wooden door in front of me. Given his celebrity status and the sheer value of everything inside his house, it seems unlikely that he would leave his door unlocked, especially if he has fairly constant food deliveries thanks to his house arrest situation.

Besides, what am I going to gain from letting myself in if it *is* unlocked? A part of me wants another massive tip like the last time, while another part wants to steer clear of this man and his connections. I don't like the idea of using Liam to get to Derek, nor am I confident that doing so would work out well in my favor. The last time I met someone from the movie industry, he screwed me over right alongside He-Who-Will-Not-Be-Named.

What if Derek likes one of my screenplays and tries to pass it off as his own?

I let out a humorless laugh. "As if I could write anything Derek Riley would like," I grumble. Val thinks my first movie script was the first of many, but I'm leaning more toward it being a fluke. I highly doubt I could write something like that again. Something people would actually want to watch.

I groan. "This is getting ridiculous!" I tell myself and then grab the door handle before I fully chicken out and run away. Liam wants me to find him in the backyard, according to his note, so that's what I'll do.

To my shock, pleasure, and slight horror, it opens easily, swinging inward on silent hinges.

"This is how you get robbed," I tell the empty foyer. "Or murdered." I scope out the birdcage to my right, glad to see the overeager, lemon-lime parakeet failing to open the cage door, though he's giving it his best effort. Aside from his chirping and strings of random words, the house is otherwise silent.

And darker than I'd like it to be. There are some lights farther in, but I already feel weird about letting myself in. It's not like his note said, "Come on in!" There's a good chance I could lose my job if I'm overstepping. I'm taking a huge risk right now, and yet my feet are glued to the floor, refusing to carry me back out to where I know what to expect. I certainly don't have any clue what I might find if I keep going.

The last time I let myself into this house, it didn't exactly go well for me.

"Maybe I'm the one about to be murdered." Saying it out loud isn't exactly comforting, but it gives me a weird boost of courage as I start creeping deeper into the house. I'm hoping Liam is still slightly crippled, either so I have better chances if I have to fight him off or so I can run away without him catching me.

I make my way to the kitchen, and the silence is still so disconcerting as I set the ice cream on the counter. I have a small view of the backyard from here, but it's all completely dark except for the glowing pool. I have a hard time envisioning Liam sitting back there in the dark, but what do I know? I have about thirty seconds before that security guard starts hunting me down anyway, so I might as well leave the food and be on my way.

But since I can't leave it on the counter to melt, I tug open his industrial sized freezer and then stop dead when I see the sheer amount of ice cream already in here. There's even a few pints from the shop I just picked up from, which makes absolutely no sense. I suppose he could want different flavors, but as I start stuffing the new pints anywhere I can fit them, I notice several repeated flavors.

I'm probably overthinking it, but it almost feels like he ordered this ice cream in the hopes of bringing me back here.

I don't like the small flame of hope that bursts to life in my chest.

"Don't go there, Kasey," I mutter, shaking my head as I stuff the last pint into the freezer and close the door. "You know better than to get involved with someone like him."

Piano music suddenly fills the house, making me jump, but it's far enough away that I quickly realize I'm still alone in the kitchen. But not alone in the house. Liam is most definitely somewhere else in the house and not where he said I would find him. That alone is reason to head back to my car and pretend this delivery never happened, but I can't bring myself to get to the door.

The song that starts playing is gorgeous and unfamiliar and pulls me immediately to the far end of the house.

I've entirely forgotten my plan to stow the ice cream and leave. I don't know what it is about Liam Connolly, but so far he has an uncanny ability to make me forget how to think like a proper adult and do things I shouldn't do.

The music gets louder as I make my way down a long hallway that I assume runs along the big garage, and though I pass a couple of closed doors on my way, it's the open doorway at the end that I'm aiming for. But right as I reach it, the music stops, bringing my feet to a stop right along with it. It felt easier to sneak with the speakers doing their thing.

A moment later, the sounds of an acoustic guitar replace the piano, and with a flutter in my heart I realize that it might have been an actual piano I heard, not a recorded song. I knew Liam played the guitar—thank you, videos on the internet—but he is clearly as talented on the piano as he is with his main instrument of choice.

I poke my head into the doorway with eager anticipation as the guitar music washes over me, and it takes me a good ten seconds to fully take in the sight in front of me.

As I suspected, Liam has a guitar in his arms as he stands in the center of the room, his booted foot propped up on a wooden box so he can rest the guitar on his knee. His head is bowed over the instrument as he fluidly plucks the strings, blond hair flopping on his forehead. There's a laptop open on the gorgeous grand piano, and about a hundred different instruments are strewn across the room, including a dozen various guitars hanging on the wall. It's a musician's paradise in here.

I notice far later than I should have that Liam is once again shirtless.

"What does this guy have against wearing shirts?"

His head snaps up in surprise at the sound of my accidentally outspoken question, and he nearly drops his guitar as his vividly blue eyes lock on to me. Though there's a pencil clenched in his teeth, his smile still comes quickly and heats the room by a thousand degrees.

To my surprise, he picks right back up where he was playing, only now his eyes are on me instead of his guitar. The moment is weirdly intimate despite the expanse of room separating us, probably because he doesn't break eye contact. Am I complaining?

Not even a little bit.

The song he's playing seems to come to a natural conclusion, and he waits a moment before setting the guitar in a stand and moving to the laptop, pencil still lodged between his teeth as he starts clicking away. I'm not even sure why he has the pencil in the first place, given the lack of paper in the room. A moment later, the pencil is on the piano and a look of concentration replaces his smile.

I feel like I should say something, but nothing comes to mind. Though, it's hard to concentrate when there's no longer a guitar blocking the bulk of his torso. Living on the coast provides an ample supply of men who use every opportunity to show off their time in the gym, but there's something different about Liam's partial lack of clothing.

He seems so completely comfortable in his own skin and isn't trying to prove anything. He's just existing.

And I'm just standing here in the doorway, waiting for him to say something. Do something. I would almost wonder if he even realized I was here if not for that heart-melting smile when he saw me.

Right as I'm about to tell him the ice cream is in the freezer, he hits a key on the computer and then hops over to me, grabbing my hand and pulling me deeper into the room, toward the piano. He takes hold of my shoulders and sits me down on the bench, and in the next second he's shoving a pair of headphones over my ears.

I have no idea what's going on. "This is the strangest—oh!"

Music fills my ears, starting with the guitar riff he just played until the piano joins in. It's beautiful, and emotional, and so moving that suddenly I feel like I'm about to cry. "Liam, this is—"

He cuts me off when he hops over to a digital keyboard and starts playing, and the artificial strings layer on top of the piano and guitar in the headphones.

Then he starts humming.

Before I can think better of it, I shift the headphones off of one ear and stand up, moving closer to better hear the melody he's singing. There aren't any words, but he doesn't need them to convey everything he's trying to say in this song. I'm almost mad there's a keyboard between us because I want to get as close to him as I can, but a little voice in the back of my head—the voice of reason—keeps me in place.

This guy is still a stranger to me, no matter how much this song is making me feel like I have a clear view into his soul. I've never understood the way people obsess over music—the closest I've come has been movie scores—but something just clicked, like I had a loose wire that got woven into place and suddenly I get why someone can be sitting at a stoplight, tears pouring down their face as they sing along to their favorite song on the radio.

Something about this song is speaking right to me, creating a bond between me and the man singing it.

"Maybe fate was right all along," he finishes, almost speaking those words rather than singing them. The music fades around us, and then the biggest smile lights up his face as he looks at me. *Studies me.* Like I'm the most fascinating thing he's ever seen.

I'm speechless. Breathless. Thoughtless.

"Hi," he whispers, sending a shiver through me.

I'm in trouble.

"Sorry about all that." Liam hands me a bowl of double mint fudge ice cream and then settles on the other end of the couch from me, kicking off his boot as he gets comfortable. "I don't always get into manic composing mode, but when I do, it's better if I don't stop the momentum."

Honestly, I'm not even sure how I've ended up in his...lounge? I don't know what I would call this room, but the couch is insanely comfortable and the whole west wall is made of windows looking out over the coast. It's too dark to see much more than the moon reflecting in the ocean, but I doubt the view, even in daylight, would compare to what I just witnessed in that music room.

"Liam, that song was amazing."

Though nothing compares to the smile when I first walked in, his grin now is still incredibly potent, bringing a burning blush to my cheeks. "It needs a lot of work, and I still have to hash out the lyrics."

"That song was loads better than anything on the radio right now," I argue.

Biting his lip, he grabs a throw pillow and hugs it to his chest. I'm immensely glad he put on a shirt before suggesting we dig into the ice cream I brought, or being this close to him would be messing with my head. I thought he was attractive before, but after that display of pure, unfiltered creation, I totally understand why the Miami girls went completely crazy. I can't imagine what his live shows are like, when he's giving it his all.

"I thought you weren't a music fan," he says. I swear his eyes twinkle as he waits for my response.

I try to play it cool by shrugging. "I'm not." But I am a Liam Connolly fan now. I take a bite of ice cream, hoping to cool myself down.

Somehow, Liam's smile grows. "I was worried I was never going to see you again."

"You still owe me five hundred bucks." I don't know why I say that. It wasn't even on my mind, and I regret the instant effect it has on Liam's bearing.

His smile drops, shoulders drooping, and it's like a chill enters the room. He's the definition of wearing his heart on his sleeve. "Right. I've got some cash upstairs."

"Wait." I grab his wrist before he can get up. "I didn't mean...sorry. Sometimes I say stupid things. I wanted to come back. Really. And not for the money."

Now would be a great time to tell him why I'm really here, since a relationship is out of the question, but I already know he's not going to respond well if I tell him I need an introduction to his friends. I take a big bite of ice cream instead, taking the coward's way out.

He nods to the bowl in my hands, still without that gorgeous smile of his. "How is it?"

"Amazing," I answer honestly. I've always wanted to try this place, but I can't justify spending fifteen bucks on a pint. "Don't you want any?"

He shakes his head as he stretches an arm along the back of the couch, slightly bridging the gap between us. "I'm not really an ice cream person."

"Your freezer would say otherwise."

There. A small smile, as if he can't help himself. "Okay, I love ice cream, but it doesn't especially love me. I've maybe been trying to bring you back the only way I know how." He reaches into the pocket of his sweats, pulling out his phone and then holding it out to me. "Maybe you can make it easier for me?"

I shouldn't. I really shouldn't. But this man is like the sun, gravity pulling me toward him until I come dangerously close to getting stuck in his orbit. The last time I let myself get attached to someone, I lost what little footing I had and ended up at rock bottom. I can't picture Liam being that kind of guy, but what do I really know about him? Nothing. Nothing except the fact that he's known around the world and constantly in the public eye, which sounds awful.

Liam gives his phone a little wave. "It's just a phone number."

"Last week was *just lunch*," I mumble, "and I ended up seeing you naked."

Liam poorly covers a laugh with a cough. "That wasn't my fault."

He's right, but I still argue even as I take hold of his phone. "Your door was wide open."

He waits until I've typed in my phone number and handed his phone back to him. "I guess I've gotten too used to being alone." Does that mean he hasn't had a girlfriend for a while? I can't say I'm mad about the idea.

My phone buzzes with a call in my lap, making me jump, and it's a number I don't recognize.

"Just wanted to check," Liam says before ending the call and returning his phone to his pocket. "So, Kasey." He inches closer in his seat, eyes wary as if he expects me to run away if he moves too quickly. Honestly, I might. I am way out of my depth here. "I know three things about you. You have no taste in music, you should not be allowed near bodies of water, and you have an irrational fear of tiny little parakeets who want to be your friend."

On cue, the "tiny little parakeet" in the front room does several wolf whistles in a row, followed by the theme song from *Jaws*.

I pull my legs onto the couch as a shudder runs through me. "You can't tell me that's not terrifying."

He chuckles. "Nelson is harmless. He watched too much TV with his last owner and doesn't fully understand social etiquette. He's the only thing keeping me sane right now, so give him a break."

I roll my eyes. "I would be way better company than that nightmare."

"I agree. What are you doing tomorrow?"

I laugh until I realize he's not kidding. "Oh. Uh, deliveries. I have to pay the bills somehow." Though, if I don't bring up Derek Riley at some point, I may end up homeless before the night is over. I'm not good at lying to Val, so she's going to hear all about today's visit.

"Have you always wanted to deliver food?" Liam asks.

I snort, shaking my head. "I want to be a writer." And the fact that I just said that out loud without any hesitation catches me off guard. I'm not ashamed of my dreams, but they're a lot harder to fess up to after everything He-Who-Will-Not-Be-Named did to me last year.

I *was* a writer, but I haven't written anything since he stole my screenplay.

Curling one leg onto the couch, Liam scoots closer again. "What kind of writer?"

I know there's more to this guy than his body, but I can't stop cataloging everything about him when he's right in front of me like this. From the wave in his blond hair to the sharp angles of his jawline, from the hard-earned lines of his arm muscles to the way he sits so completely at ease. I wish I could be as confident as he clearly is, but I don't have many reasons to be. Liam is talented—*so* talented—and wealthy, personable and attractive. He has friends in high places and a happy-go-lucky personality that would be impossible to dislike.

I...

I'm realizing I have no idea why I'm here. I can't imagine why a guy like him would want to know a girl like me. "Um." I tuck my hair behind my ear. "Your security guard is probably going to come looking for me. He said I only had ten minutes." Never mind it's been at least twenty by this point.

Liam shakes his head. "I texted him. You're allowed in whenever you want now. You just have to tell him you're here for me, but he should recognize you, no problem."

"Oh." That feels like a privilege I shouldn't have.

"Do you not want to tell me what you write? That's okay." Based on the disappointment in his eyes, it's not okay. He looks like a pouty golden retriever who was just told he isn't allowed to go on a walk.

He literally isn't allowed to go on a walk, I realize, and I remember what he said about the parakeet being the only thing to keep him sane. From the little I know about Liam Connolly, I doubt he's thriving with this house arrest thing, and if his friends are actors who are out filming movies and a princess who lives in a completely different country, I can't imagine how bored he is.

I smile a little. "I only tell my friends about my writing."

"Aren't we friends?" He shifts again, now sitting on the middle cushion and only a few inches away from me. I don't know how he managed to get so close to me so easily.

I shrug, though my smile is growing. I can handle friends, as long as he doesn't come close to kissing me again. If he tries, I'm not sure I'll be able to stop him. I'm not sure I'll *want* to stop him. "I dunno," I say, trying to sound thoughtful and get my mind off of kissing him. "I don't usually see my friends naked."

Why do I keep bringing that up?

As his smile shifts into a smirk, I realize my mistake. "We could be more than friends," he says, lifting his eyebrows.

He has no idea how tempting that is. Who wouldn't want the chance to call an international music star their boyfriend? But I need to stand firm, for the sake of my sanity and my emotional stability. "I'm not looking for a relationship, Connolly."

His smile doesn't change. "Neither am I."

"So you're suggesting friends with benefits?"

"Only if you are." Somehow, he doesn't sound smarmy, which seems to be a skill most men lack.

Still, we're getting into dangerous territory, so I put my hand on his shoulder to keep him from leaning closer. If I'm going to open up a small corner of my life for this man, he needs to know the boundaries. "I'm not that kind of girl, Liam."

His hand wraps around mine, holding it in place. "And I'm not that kind of guy. Friendships are hard enough without making them messy and complicated." He bites his lip, amusement dancing in his eyes. "You seem surprised."

"I am," I admit. "You're not exactly the typical celebrity."

"That's not a real thing. All my friends are celebrities, and they're too different from each other for 'typical' to exist."

It's another perfect opening to bring up Derek and how much my future career needs me to meet him. I ignore it. "Do you always hold your friends' hands like this?" I squeeze his fingers where he's holding them against his shoulder.

He laughs. "Actually, yes. At least, I hold Freya's hand, when she lets me. Derek gets jealous if I get too close to Bonnie."

He's giving me all sorts of softball pitches tonight, and I must be stupid because I gloss over this one too and ask, "How did you become friends with a literal princess?"

"I'll answer that if you tell me what you write."

Heat fills my face, though I'm not sure if it's because he's doing a great job at showing me he's really interested or because he is an eye contact master. I would never call myself intimidating, but Val says I have developed a resting grump face which tends to dissuade guys from giving me too much attention. I don't think many girls consider that an accomplishment, but it's pretty much my only claim right now, so I'll take it. It comes in handy when my slimier customers are as eager to see me as they are to get their food.

While I'm fully aware Liam technically fits into that category, nothing he does is slimy. He's like a mythical creature that exists only in women's dreams. No wonder Val called him a unicorn.

His charm is so, so dangerous.

I clear my throat, trying not to sound terrified when I say, "I'm trying to be a screenwriter."

"Trying to be, or you are?"

I shrug, all too aware that he's *still* holding my hand, though he's moved it to his thigh instead of his shoulder. "Well, it's not like I'm credited for any movies, so—"

"But you've written a screenplay?" Liam's gaze is so intense that I almost can't look at him.

I nod, hoping he doesn't read into what I just said.

"Then you're a screenwriter. You wouldn't say a guy playing a violin on a street corner isn't a musician because he's not in a concert hall, would you?"

Well, how am I supposed to argue against that? I'm not, which is exactly why he said it. Frustration builds inside me, hot and heavy as I set my ice cream on the floor by my feet. "The guy playing on the street is probably also broke, just like I am," I grumble. "Yeah, okay, I'm a screenwriter, but writing is not the same as someone turning it into a movie. Would you still call yourself a success if you hadn't signed with your record label three years ago?"

A slow smile stretches across his face, and he drops his head against the back of the couch at the same time he laces our fingers together. He looks so...cute. Like, to the point where I'm convinced a picture of him right now should be in the dictionary next to the word 'adorable.' I have no idea how he's pulling this look off in a way that is sexier than anything I've ever seen because 'cute' and 'hot' are generally mutually exclusive.

"You didn't even know who I was last time you were here, Kasey," he says. "Did you look me up?"

Crap. Knowing I'm probably bright red, I shake my head as if I have any sort of defense here. "I wanted to make sure you weren't some creep if I ever got assigned your delivery again."

"You keep telling yourself that."

If I keep looking at that smile of his, I'm going to fall for this man so hard, so I drop my gaze to our hands. As if that might help. He's got some crazy calluses from his guitar—I want to touch them, just to see what they feel like—and his fingers are long and rough. There's also a small whale tattooed on the inside of his right wrist that I haven't noticed before now.

Unable to resist the urge, I brush a finger along the whale's long, arched body. "Is this a blue whale?"

"Yeah." His voice has dropped to a whisper that sends a shiver through me. "For my mom."

I look up. "Is she...?"

He smiles softly. "She lives in Santa Barbara and is happy as a clam working at a salon up there."

"Why a blue whale?"

"It's the biggest animal in the world, and she's made the biggest impact in my life. I owe everything I am to her and the sacrifices she's made to get me here."

"I love that." I really do. But this man is making it entirely too difficult to remember my own boundaries. No matter how good he seems, there's too much risk right now. He's barely more than a stranger and even said himself that he prefers to be friends, so I need to stop looking at his full lips and wondering how they would feel against mine.

Pulling my hand free, I pick up my ice cream again and rise to my feet. "I should go. It's getting late, and I have to drive back to East Hollywood."

He wrinkles his nose as he gets up to follow me to the kitchen, limping as he goes. "That's where you live? Yikes."

"It's not that bad, and it's what I can afford." Not actually, but Liam doesn't need to know I'm two months behind on rent. I'm so lucky Val makes decent money from her yoga sessions on YouTube so she can afford to pay for the house herself.

When she gets married in the spring and moves in with Vince? That's a different story, one I refuse to think about until at least March.

What I wouldn't give to be so financially secure that I can afford a Malibu mansion. Not that I want a mansion, but I doubt Liam knows how it feels to live paycheck to paycheck or worse. He's got the rich life nailed down.

"Thanks for the ice cream," I tell him, setting the bowl in the sink. I turn to wish him luck on the song, but he's standing right behind me. Like, *right behind me.* So I end up stepping right into him, face planting in his chest.

He laughs and wraps his arms around me long enough for me to know a deliberate hug from this man would be lethal. So, naturally, I lock my hands behind his back and keep him in place.

"I didn't realize we were at this level of friendship," he says, his voice rumbling in my ear. "But I'm not complaining. And I'm not sure you can really thank me for the ice cream when you only ate two bites."

"It's a bit fancy for my taste."

I reluctantly pull away from his embrace and mourn the sudden drop in temperature. It's not like Southern California gets that cold in the fall, but I'm perpetually cold no matter what degree the thermometer says. Anything under eighty-five is too cold, and Liam is surprisingly warm for someone who rarely wears a shirt. Maybe that's *why* he rarely wears a shirt?

"Well, this was fun," I say. He's blocking the way out of the kitchen, or I would be making a mad dash for the door before things get *too* awkward.

He smiles. "You're going to come tomorrow, right?"

He has no idea how much I want to say yes, but I need to make sure I get this man in moderation. If I'm not careful, he'll have me convinced that not all people with connections are thieves and cheats. I don't see him doing anything against me, but I can't say the same for his friends. Not yet.

Nor do I want to burn this ramshackle bridge by demanding anything from him without having a solid basis of trust. Val can't blame me for not wanting to take advantage of his trusting nature, can she?

"Please," he says, reminding me that I haven't answered his question. "It's just hanging out."

I can't hold back my smile, nervous though I am about balancing the line between genuine friendship and networking to boost my career. "Fine."

He walks me to the door, shushing Nelson the parakeet as we pass the cage, and then follows me onto the front step. Well, almost follows. When I turn to bid him goodnight, I realize he still has one foot in the house and is leaning as far as he can. I'm guessing his ankle monitor doesn't allow him to go past his front door.

I fight my laugh. "Goodnight, Liam. Maybe ease up on the ice cream orders, and I'll come as soon as I can tomorrow."

The eagerness in his eyes is both endearing and concerning. I don't want him getting attached any more than I want to get attached to him. "Promise?"

I nod, as much as I worry it will be a difficult promise to keep. "You clearly need a friend, and so do I."

He leans in, hand clasped around the door frame, and presses a kiss to my cheek. "I'm good at keeping people to their promises."

I'm sure he is. I don't think anyone would ever be able to say no to this man when he's got a perpetual puppy-dog look.

With one last smile, I take a step back. Then another. Telling myself that I can't get used to this sight of him stretching as far as he can to follow me.

CHAPTER SEVEN

LIAM

THERE WAS SOMETHING DEREK said to me soon after we met that stuck with me more than he probably thought it would. "Being known is great until someone decides they know enough." I thought I knew what he meant, but as I finish recording the instrument tracks for the song idea that hit me tonight, my brain won't stop thinking about it even though I should really go to bed.

Few people in the world truly know me. My mom obviously knows more than anyone, but I still surprise her sometimes with little quirks and traits she claims she's never seen before. Plus, she refuses to move closer no matter how many times I offer to buy her a house here in Malibu, so it feels like the last few years we've drifted apart. Not in a bad way, just in a way that means she doesn't know everything about my life the way she used to.

And my friends know me...to a point. They like to dig deeper when they sense something I've hidden, and I both love and hate them for it.

When it comes to romantic relationships, however, I've experienced plenty of "enough" to know that some people want an ideal. They aren't willing to see all the nuances that make up a human being. The things that defy expectation and bias.

In the three years since my music caught my record label's attention, launching me into the mainstream world, I haven't had any relationships worth pursuing beyond casual. Any time I tried, the women I dated couldn't understand why I was suddenly acting weird or "out of the norm" despite me finally getting comfortable enough to let my guard down. Derek's lucky to have someone like Bonnie, who knows exactly how it feels to be famous and constantly in the public eye. He doesn't have to worry that she's with him for his fame and fortune because she has her own.

I've gotten used to the signs of someone looking for a step up, and Kasey has them all. And it sucks. Her hungry look every time I mentioned Derek felt like a knife in the gut.

After emailing the finished song to Freya so she'll stop sending me pushy texts, I make my way to the front room and untwist the paper clip holding Nelson's door in place. He starts whistling one of my old songs in his excitement, which makes me smile, but my smile is short-lived.

"I like this girl way more than I should, buddy," I tell him as I flip the door open and duck before he careens right into my face.

He does a few circles around the room before coming to land on my shoulder. "Hi buddy," he says cheerfully. "Good bird buddy."

"I have never called you a good bird in my life," I reply. "Especially after the way you scared Kasey. You're lucky she came back."

And hopefully she'll come again tomorrow. There's something wrong with me, given the fact that she clearly just wants to use me to get to Derek, but I can't help it. Something about her keeps pulling me in, like there's a melody surrounding her that is too intriguing to ignore.

She'll be back—she promised—and I really shouldn't get my hopes up for more than one more day. Befriending me would be a great way to get someone in the business to look at one of her screenplays, and I'm surprised she hasn't brought it up yet.

I haven't either, but that's because I'm terrified she'll stop talking to me as soon as I do. How masochistic is it of me that I don't really care that that will be the conclusion of this friendship? I still want to see her again.

Desperately.

There's something wrong with me.

"I'm going outside," I tell Nelson, moving him from my shoulder to the top of his cage.

"Other side!" he replies, bouncing his head several times. "Why chicken cross road?"

"That joke's getting old, bud. Behave, okay?"

"Good buddy bird."

"Sure." I slip out the back door, making sure Nelson isn't trying to sneak out after me, and then take a lap of the whole patio, walking alongside the wall that keeps me from tumbling down the hill to the coast. Maybe one of these days I'll "fall" down the hill to get a feel of the sand in my toes and hope the officer over my case accepts the whole thing as an accident.

This hill would be brutal though, and I would have to make it authentic. Probably a bad idea. Still, I peek over the edge even though it's too dark to see anything now that the waxing moon has sunk below the horizon. How bad could it really be? The trees and shrubs would slow my fall.

And probably break both my arms while they're at it. It might be worth it for a taste of freedom.

"You're losing your mind, Connolly," I mutter and turn to head back inside right as my neighbor turns his patio light on.

Huh. I've never seen him out this late before. I rarely see him at all.

The houses in this neighborhood aren't especially close—we pay for the luxury of privacy—but the corners of our yards aren't all that far from each other, now that I'm really looking.

My neighbor, Ted, grumbles something, way closer than I expected him to be. I don't understand what he says, but then he keeps talking. "Always complaining, she is. Whining and nagging like I haven't given her the dream life."

This probably isn't something I should be listening to. I haven't met Ted's wife, Martha, but he has mentioned how long they've been together and how much he loves her. This sounds like trouble in paradise.

"Take me out," Ted grumbles. "Buy me new toys. Feed me expensive dinners. It never stops, and she's never satisfied. I'm tired of it." He lets out a huge sigh, and his footsteps seem to take him back to his house, leaving the night quiet again.

What in the world? I feel like I should do something, but I have no idea what a person is supposed to do in a situation like this.

My phone is in my hand almost immediately as I make my way back inside. I type out the text quickly.

Liam:

> I think my neighbor is fighting with his wife.

The responses come almost as quickly.

Cole:

> Why do we care about your neighbor?

Derek:

> Exactly what Cole said.

Bonnie:

> Oo, which neighbor?

Freya is probably still asleep, but that's a good thing. She would most likely judge me like the guys are doing. But they didn't hear what I did. Ted was angry in a way I've never seen before.

Liam:
Ted to the northeast. He's always been madly in love with Martha but he sounds like he's about to snap.

Bonnie:
You heard them fighting?

Liam:
No. I heard Ted complaining about her though.

Derek:
You're an idiot.

Cole:
I complain about you all the time, Connolly. Doesn't mean we're fighting.

Bonnie:
Has Derek ever complained about me?

Liam:
Are you guys fighting?

Derek:
Of course not.

Bonnie:
Was that answer for me or Liam?

Derek:
Both.

I know better than to mess with the princess's beauty sleep, so I let the group chat die. Though, I'm bummed Bonnie was the only one who seemed interested. Cole, I understand, but I thought Derek would appreciate a good story.

Hmm. Story. Though I have no idea how she'll respond, I take a chance and send a text to the number Kasey gave me. I don't know why, but I still have a decent amount of fear that she gave me a fake number even though I verified when she was here.

I grab a pint of ice cream and settle on my kitchen counter to wait for her reply, if she even sends one. She might have gone to do a couple more deliveries before bed, but if not, it's been long enough for her to have made it home.

I shudder as I think about the neighborhood she lives in. It's not the worst place, but it's not great either. I've lived in similar situations, and I wonder if she feels safe when she's home. Maybe that's why she's so determined to get into the movies. A good screenplay could get her into a better apartment.

Oh, this ice cream is good. I haven't actually eaten dinner—I gave up on the potato sandwich and then got distracted by that song—and I'm going to regret this much dairy, but I can't stop eating it while I stare at my phone.

"She's not going to respond," I tell myself.

Nelson flutters into the kitchen and lands next to my phone. He taps it with his beak and whistles my ringtone, which at the moment is a snippet from Taylor Swift's "Anti-Hero," though it changes regularly.

"I don't know what you're expecting," I tell him right before my phone lights up with a text.

I snatch it so fast that Nelson screams and hops out of the way.

> Kasey:
> I would say that character is looking sketchy and should probably be watched in case he's heading to a breaking point.

I throw my fist in the air in triumph. "See?" I say to Nelson. "It's not just me who's concerned!" I hit the voice-to-text button because I don't have the patience to keep typing.

> Liam:
> This character has spoken fondly of his wife we'll call her Martha for as long as I excuse me the protagonist has lived in his neighborhood. But tonight he I'll call him Ted was just complaining out loud to himself about how he's tired of her complaining that her life isn't perfect.

> Kasey:
> Is this still a hypothetical, or are we talking about your actual neighbors named Ted and Martha?

> Liam:
> They might be real.

I laugh and roll my eyes. I knew she was a writer, but I didn't realize she was one of *those* writers. To save her more grief—who has time for properly punctuating texts?—I hit the call button.

She answers with a healthy dose of hesitation. "Hello?"

"I don't know how friendships work where you're from, but where I come from, friends don't judge each other's texting abilities unless it's completely incomprehensible. Where are you from, by the way?"

She hesitates again, pausing long enough for me to take a bite of ice cream as I wait. "Kansas," she finally says.

"No way, me too!"

"Really?"

"Nah. Oklahoma. Though, I did live in Kansas for a week when I was ten, if that counts."

She doesn't seem to know what to say to that, which makes me smile. Maybe if I keep catching her off guard, I'll be better able to tell what her motivations are. And maybe I'll learn a few more things about this woman and start to understand why I like her so much. I don't know enough about her to justify how happy this conversation has already made me. She's only been gone for three hours.

"Why did you live in Kansas for a week?" she asks eventually.

"Other side," Nelson says.

I shush him, but it's too late.

"Why is your awful bird on the phone, Liam?"

"Good bird buddy!" Nelson hops a few times and taps the phone screen. "Buddy bird!"

"Aww," I say, "I'm so glad the two of you are becoming friends."

She scoffs. "If that bird is roaming free tomorrow, I'm not coming over. I don't care if he's a good bird buddy."

"Good buddy!" Nelson hops again.

I laugh. "I'll make sure he's stowed away, though he'll be very sad not to hang out with you and be your friend."

"I'd rather just be your friend," Kasey replies. "You don't scare me."

"You have no idea how glad I am to..." But I stop as words start interlocking in my head, following a line of melody I've never heard before. I swear loudly, tell Kasey I'll text her tomorrow, and then rush to my music room with Nelson right behind me.

It's going to be a long night.

Who needs sleep when I've got another song to record?

CHAPTER EIGHT

KASEY

THIS TIME WHEN I get to Liam's house, I pull into his driveway as he instructed instead of parking on the street. I've got two steaming bags of food from my favorite diner along Sunset Boulevard, though I doubt Liam knew it was my favorite when he placed the order and begged me to pick it up on my way. It wasn't through Diner Delivery, which kind of stinks because I won't get paid for it, but I almost don't care.

Liam has been texting me all morning, mostly in voice memos that are either incredibly random bits of music trivia or pieces of what I would guess is another new song he's working on. It's both strange and sweet that he's treating me like we're best friends.

With the food in my arms, I make my way up to the garage door and punch in the code Liam sent me, more surprised than I should be that the door starts to slide open with hardly a noise. I was neither expecting the code to work nor the door to be that quiet. My parents' garage back home is like an earthquake every time it opens, so much so that half the time they don't even bother closing it.

"Of course the code works," I mutter as I step inside. Just like with the security guard giving me a nod and waving me forward, Liam has yet to do anything against his word.

The house is almost silent again. Only the soft sounds of a guitar tell me to turn left toward the music room rather than looking elsewhere, though I have a feeling he spends a lot of time in that room, given his profession. Following the music, I can't help but smile when I step through the doorway and find him sprawled out on a couch at the back of the room, a guitar on his bare chest as he plucks the strings.

"Is this going to become a regular thing with you?" I ask, nodding toward his shirtless torso.

He grins without skipping a beat in his song. His fingers fly so effortlessly over the strings that any claims on the internet that he doesn't really play in his shows are the stupidest thing I've ever heard. He has some serious skills, and I wonder how much is pure talent versus hard work and practice.

"How much do I owe you for the food?" Liam asks as I approach. He finally stops playing, setting the guitar aside and sitting up.

I frown. "You already paid for the food, didn't you?"

"I mean how much would you have gotten paid if this had been a Diner Delivery order?"

"Oh." I look down at the food in my hands, which smells so good that my stomach is starting to rumble. I'm all for people ordering fancy food because it usually brings me a good tip, but give me a burger and fries any day and I'll be happy. "Um, I don't know, like twenty bucks?"

Liam stuffs some bills into my hand and takes one of the bags, diving right in and shoving a few fries into his mouth. He moans before pulling out the burger and taking a massive bite. "I haven't eaten since yesterday's lunch," he says. At least, that's what I think he says.

I pull my eyebrows together, half because that's a long time to go without food and half because I've just realized there are two hundred-dollar bills in my hand. I can't decide if I like that he paid me for picking up the food or if I hate the idea that he doesn't really consider us friends, no matter what he says.

"Liam…"

"Are you going to eat?" He raises his eyebrows as he finishes off his burger. "You're making me look like a pig."

This other bag is for me? I must look confused because Liam laughs and reaches into the bag on my lap, pulling out the burger and handing it to me. "I know it's not the fanciest meal, but this is one of my favorite places to eat. It's better than it looks."

"I know," I reply automatically. "I'm just…"

"Just what?"

I feel so out of sorts with this guy, and I don't know how to navigate any of this. I eat a fry, hoping that gets my mind working again. From the first moment I rang Liam's doorbell last week, I've been off balance, and that's not really something you can tell someone. Especially not someone like Liam Connolly, who is from a whole different world from me.

I sigh, slowly unwrapping the burger because I might as well eat it while I make things weird. "I don't understand why I'm here," I admit. "I'm just a food delivery girl, and you are an international music icon. Your friends are famous actors and princesses. You literally had to save my life when we met, and now you're…" I hold up the hundred-dollar bills. "I feel like you're trying to buy my friendship, but I don't know why."

As much as I want to take a bite, I wait in silence, my eyes on the burger instead of him.

After a long, quiet moment, he reaches over and curls my fingers over the money, leaving his hand over the top of mine. "Kasey," he says, his smooth voice gliding over my name and sending a shiver through me. "I'm sorry for making you feel that way. I'm not trying to buy anything from you. I'm desperate to know you better, and I'm using the few tools I have to make that happen."

I meet his gaze, finding nothing but sincerity in those vividly blue eyes of his. "Why me?"

He grins. "Because you don't like me." His grin shifts to a laugh, and he wipes his hands on a napkin before picking up his guitar again. "And I mean that as a compliment."

"How is that a compliment?" Now that he's occupied, I finally take a bite of my burger and hold back a groan because it's so good. Apparently I was hungrier than I thought, and I dig in.

Though he starts playing the same melody he was running through before, Liam keeps his eyes on me. Impressive. Then he starts talking without missing a beat, which is even more impressive. "It means I can trust your opinion of me, which is a rare commodity nowadays. When you first came over, you couldn't stand me, and I don't remember the last time a woman didn't swoon over me."

I choke out a laugh. "I still don't see how this is a good thing. And I didn't *trust* you. It wasn't that I didn't like you."

"Either way," he says, his eyes glittering with happiness now, "you weren't impressed by all of this"—he glances down at his body and then looks around the instrument-packed room—"and it was nice to feel sort of normal for the first time in a long time. It was like old times."

He's being awfully honest right now, and I feel like I should be the same, though I worry how he might respond. Still, Liam seems like the kind of guy who values honesty, so I might as well chance it. "I actually was impressed," I admit. "But I didn't like the ego that came with all of this."

He laughs again. "See? Outside of my friends—only one of them is a princess, by the way—no one is brave enough to knock me down like that. You're a breath of fresh air, Kasey."

Heat fills my face, telling me it's time to change the subject. "Is this a new song?"

He nods, his smile shifting into something closer to contentment than amusement. "It hit me last night after we talked."

"It sounds really fun." Whereas the song yesterday evoked every deep emotion I can think of, this one feels light. Breezy. "Do you have any words yet?"

He starts to nod but stops himself halfway, a little crease forming between his eyebrows. "I'm still working out the kinks."

I try not to let my disappointment show. "Do you always come up with the music first?"

He shakes his head. "Sometimes it's the lyrics that speak to me."

"Where do you get most of your inspiration?"

To my utmost disappointment, he stops playing and returns the guitar to its stand, stretching his fingers and then his arms.

I try not to stare as he puts his whole, muscly body on display.

"It comes from all over," he says lightly, and I'm pretty sure he's uncomfortable with my question because his answer doesn't feel like him. I didn't think this guy could *get* uncomfortable. "What about you? Where do you get ideas for your screenplays?"

Okay, now I get why he didn't like my question. I instantly hate this. It feels invasive and far too personal despite being an innocent question. "Oh. Uh, all over, I guess. Like you." I stuff a few fries into my mouth, but Liam stays quiet. Watching me. Swallowing, I search for a better answer to fill the silence. "I guess I watch people around me. Find compelling characters whose stories would be interesting to watch."

"What kind of stories do you like to tell?"

I probably shouldn't tell him I love writing the gritty stories. The ones where people go through hell before coming out the other side as the strongest versions of themselves. The truth would make me sound slightly sadistic, so I shrug and mutter, "I like mysteries."

"Like a usually calm and content man complaining about the wife I've never met?"

I perk up, remembering our conversation from last night. I nearly had a heart attack when Liam texted me, followed by a freakout a million times worse when he called. *Liam Connolly called me.* I was so glad Val was hanging out with her fiancé, or she would have compounded my freakout a thousand times. And she probably would have asked about Derek for me, which would have been a disaster.

"Okay, yes, that," I say. "Any updates on that hypothetical situation?"

Chuckling, Liam shakes his head as he sits up straighter. I try to hide my disappointment, but then he says, "I've also only left this room long enough to pee and get Nelson back in his cage, so I haven't done any investigating. Do you want to?"

"Do I want to spy on your neighbors' private lives?"

He droops. "Ah, yeah, I guess we shouldn't—"

"Of course I want to do that, Liam!" I shove the last few fries into my mouth and stand up to show him I'm serious. Murder mysteries—even suspicions of them—are my kryptonite.

He doesn't seem to believe me, raising an eyebrow at me without moving.

So I grab his hand and tug him off the couch. "Don't underestimate my curiosity. What if this turns into a murder and makes for an epic movie?"

"Should I be concerned about the way your eyes just lit up when you said 'murder'?" But he's grinning, clearly appreciative of my enthusiasm. "Come on, we might be able to see something from upstairs."

As I follow him down the hall and to the big, curved staircase, I notice him limping a bit and not wearing the boot.

"How's your foot?" I ask. "Shouldn't you be wearing the boot?"

He shrugs and continues forward. "It's on-and-off painful, but the boot was driving me crazy. I'd rather let my foot do its thing. By the time my house arrest is over, it should be mostly healed, so I'm trying to see that as a positive."

"How long are you stuck in here, anyway?"

"Until the first week of November, when my case goes to trial."

I do the mental math as we climb the stairs. "You still have four weeks stuck inside?" I shudder. "I don't know how you're doing it."

"I'm not. I'm going crazy." We reach his bedroom, which gives me pause—I remember too well what happened the last time I was in here—but he walks to the large glass doors on the north end and steps onto a balcony.

Telling myself I'm being ridiculous by being so paranoid, I follow, and then I gasp when I realize the balcony runs around the whole upper level of the house. I can see the glittering ocean to my left, but Liam is focused to the northeast, looking at the house that is just visible through the trees.

"This is amazing up here," I tell him, tempted to take in the whole view. But I don't especially want to leave Liam's side, which could easily turn into a problem. I really can't get attached, but he's making it difficult.

"When I was looking for a house to buy," he says as he leans on the railing overlooking his pool, "I wanted it to be the tallest in the neighborhood."

"Why?"

He chuckles. "Because I've lived in too many basements over the years."

"Really?"

"I wasn't always famous, Kasey. This life is still pretty new for me."

I find that hard to believe, given how easily he throws money around. The man literally sent me more than seven hundred dollars the first day he met me. If I were in his position, I would be clinging to my money for dear life.

Or maybe he's even wealthier than I'm assuming?

He's watching me—I can feel his gaze heating me from the inside out—but I keep my gaze straight ahead. "Do you like being famous?"

When he shrugs, he brings his shoulder close to me so it touches mine. It doesn't help the overheating situation, but I do my best to pretend I'm perfectly fine.

"It has its perks," he says. "But it also has its problems."

"Like what? Struggling to find a tall enough house?"

He snickers. "Well, now I don't want to tell you. I feel like you're going to have an argument against anything I say."

Despite the mild criticism, something in his words settles warm and comfortable in my chest. My smile feels more like a smirk, but it keeps growing the longer I look at him. "I'll do my best not to argue," I say, though I'm sure I'm not at all believable.

Nudging my shoulder, he points to his neighbor's house. "That's where Ted and Martha live. He used to manage actors, and he has all sorts of stories he could tell you about dealing with fame. He wasn't even the famous one, but he was more than happy to retire and get out of that world. For me..." He sighs, shaking his head. "I'll admit I was glad to get recognition and attention after spending so many years playing in bars where no one is actually listening. And getting that record deal meant I could play for more people. But I..."

I wait for him to keep talking, and when he doesn't, I return his nudge with my own. "But?"

He smiles at me, the gesture tinged with sadness. "But it's hard to know when people get close to me because of me instead of my fame. This life is full of insincerity, which means I can't trust easily. It's not in my nature to think the worst of people, but now I have to if I want to protect myself and the people I care about."

In other words, if I bring up wanting to meet Derek Riley, Liam will take that as a sign that I don't care about him and want to use him to further my own ambitions. He wouldn't be wrong, but only because I have my own trust issues. I already like Liam more than I should, but what happens if I trust him too much and lose another story? I hope he wouldn't keep company with terrible people, but I can't trust that Derek is as selfless as Liam seems to be.

I couldn't even trust my boyfriend. Derek is a complete stranger.

I shouldn't have come here. I know that, and I know moving forward with this friendship is dangerous for us both. But I can't bring myself to leave. I want to know Liam better and learn everything there is to know about him because what I've seen so far has been nigh on perfect, even with his terrible first impression.

I take a deep breath. "If it makes you feel better," I say slowly, "I don't like your fame or your wealth. If I didn't owe my roommate rent money, I would be mad that you tipped me for picking up my own lunch."

There's that smile, the one that seems to reflect the sun. "It shouldn't make me feel better, but it does. It's why I liked you in the first place."

"Mm, yes, I do tend to make a great first impression. I accused you of asking me to do some morally questionable things, nearly drowned in your pool, walked in on you when you were naked..." Seriously, why do I keep bringing that up?

Laughing, Liam grabs a chair from farther down the porch, setting it within view of Ted's house. Then he grabs another, and I realize too late that I should help him when he limps over with the second chair and places it next to the first.

"I don't remember the morally questionable part," he says as he gestures for me to sit. Gentleman that he is, he waits until I'm settled before he takes his own seat.

I've replayed our first encounter far too many times, so I remember the moment vividly. "Okay, well, I didn't accuse you outright, but I thought it."

"And look at you now." He gestures to our view.

We can see a decent amount of Ted's backyard and just a glimpse inside his house through the back door. All looks quiet for Ted and Martha. "What do we know about your neighbor?" I ask, all too aware that a normal person wouldn't be this interested.

Liam rests his bad foot on his knee and shrugs. "I know I moved in about two years ago, and Ted had already lived here for a while. He's a quiet guy, keeps to himself, but I talk to him now and then if I'm going for a walk around the neighborhood to clear my head. He likes to grow tulips, so he's usually out in his garden."

"Oh, I've seen his flowers. They're great." I frown. "He doesn't sound like the kind of guy who might murder his wife."

"You're going straight to murder?" Liam chuckles. "I've never met his wife, but he usually only has good things to say about her."

I curl my legs up to my chest, resting my chin on my knees. "Do you know how long they've been together?"

"He told me he met Martha at a farmers' market a decade ago. Or thereabouts. From what I've gathered, she's very affectionate but not super social."

"Hmm." There seem to be a lot of missing pieces to Liam's little mystery, but I can't help but be intrigued. Liam seemed to think Ted's complaining was enough to be concerned. Still, unless something happens within our vantage point, we're probably not going to learn much more.

I shift, settling more comfortably in my chair, and Liam watches my movement with keen eyes and an excited smile. He seems to like the idea that I'm settling in for the long haul, and I know he's bored and lonely. He would probably ask me to stay all day if I gave him a reason to think I would agree.

I'm losing a lot of money by hanging out here instead of out making deliveries, but I would hate to disappoint him. It's amazing what this guy can make me do without saying a word.

"How well do you know your other neighbors?" I ask, trying to sound casual and not like I'm searching for a reason to stay. "I'd bet they have some character traits that could make for a good story."

Liam grins, relaxes against the back of the chair, and starts spilling all the secrets.

CHAPTER NINE

LIAM

"I promise he's not going to eat you."

Kasey shakes her head, excessively pale as she stares at the cage door I've got pinched between my fingers. She hasn't moved since the moment I told her my plan to let my budgie out of his cage, even though I know she wants to run from this house the moment I do. She's standing in the middle of the foyer, not even in the room with us. "You can't promise that," she argues.

It's been three days since our first attempt at spying on Ted (to no avail). The first day, Kasey spent the day making deliveries and showed up with dinner. The second day, she brought lunch and didn't leave until after ten o'clock. This morning, she arrived with breakfast, and now it's after seven in the evening and Nelson hasn't been out of his cage in days.

He has been singing "I Want to Break Free" on repeat. The poor bird needs to stretch his wings, and I know better than anyone how that feels.

"He eats fruit, Kasey. Seeds. Sometimes the occasional cabbage. I don't think a big chomp of human flesh is going to appeal to him."

Shuddering, she wraps her arms around her middle and keeps her eyes on Nelson, unblinking. Over the last few days, I've started to become well-versed in all things Kasey Graham, and I know she's trying her best to pretend she is totally comfortable. She always hugs herself like this when she's trying to be more confident than she is, like when she agreed to sing some harmonies on the demo track of a song that came to me yesterday.

I needed to hear how a different voice layered on top of mine, and while Kasey won't be winning any Grammys anytime soon, she has a decent voice. I almost want to try to get her to sing on more of my tracks as I get them all recorded. I may only be three songs deep into this album, but I have a good feeling about this one. My block seems to be gone whenever Kasey is around.

That, or my music is what is *keeping* her around. Either way, I'll keep playing and hope she keeps hanging out with me.

I want her to stop feeling the need to hide or retreat when she's around me. Whatever she's afraid of (outside of Nelson, I mean), I want to show her she doesn't have to be so scared.

I'll take care of her.

"Liam," she says weakly, "maybe don't say the words 'human flesh' when you're trying to convince me to face one of my demons."

"Chicken soup," Nelson says, nipping at my finger impatiently. "Good buddy bird buddy."

"You are a good buddy," I agree, then turn back to Kasey. "Why are you so afraid of birds anyway?"

She shrugs. "It's irrational. I don't know. But I do know they can all sense it, and they always exploit it. Like that seagull on the balcony! It smelled blood and went for the kill."

I burst into laughter at the memory of yesterday's lunch, which we ate on the back balcony in the hopes of catching sight of Ted or Martha, neither of whom have made an appearance. "That seagull came after you because you were holding pizza," I tell her. "They go nuts for that around here." I won't tell her that it's because I have a bad habit of tossing them my crusts whenever I get pizza. Yesterday, I had to fight the thing off and then beg Kasey to unlock the balcony door, which she locked behind her when she ran, as if the seagull might try to get inside.

Groaning, Kasey studies Nelson while he starts doing a dance and whistling one of my songs—the one Kasey first said she likes. I bite back my smile, though it seems Nelson is trying to convince Kasey as much as I am.

"Okay," she says, tensing up. "If you promise he won't hurt me."

Can I promise that? Nelson nips at me every now and then, but usually it's because I have food in my hand and am taking too long to give it to him. He can get hyperactive, but I don't think he has a malevolent nature. "You'll be fine," I say, which will be true regardless of what happens. "You just have to trust me."

"I trust you."

There's no hesitation in her words, which makes me smile. After our rocky start, I feel incredibly lucky that she keeps coming around.

"It's the bird I don't trust," she adds.

I turn to Nelson and narrow my eyes at him. He keeps dancing and singing, but he seems to be watching me. "I am counting on you to not mess this up," I tell him, keeping my voice low. "I like this girl, and if you scare her off again, I'm putting you up on Craigslist. Do you understand?"

"Good bird," he says. He's either mocking me or agreeing with me, and there's really no way for me to tell which it is outside of opening the cage door and seeing what happens.

This might be a bad idea, but I want Kasey to be a part of my whole life, not just the parts she's comfortable with. There's so much more to me than this quiet life inside my house, and my fame can get messy. If she can't handle a parakeet, what is she going to do when I'm out singing to my fans and dodging photographers?

I know it's only been a few days, but I'm not all that patient. Might as well rip off the Band-aid and see if she'll stay through the sting.

I take a deep breath. "Here goes nothing." I pop the cage door open and hope for the best.

At first, Nelson doesn't move outside of bobbing his head in his little dance as he sings. Then, when I start to wonder if I kept him in there too long and he has somehow forgotten how to fly, he hops out and lands on my shoulder like he usually does.

Kasey relaxes, a smile forming on her lips. "I guess he's not so—"

Nelson leaps, zooming right for her like he's hell-bent on destroying everything I hold dear. Kasey screams and ducks into a crouch, and Nelson starts circling around her and chirping like mad.

Swearing, I lunge toward Kasey and nearly tackle her as I wrap my arms around her, trying to protect her head. Nelson doesn't seem to care that I'm covering as much of Kasey as I can, continuing his shrieking and fluttering all around us, trying to get to her.

I glare at him. "*Go n-ithe an cat thú is go n-ithe an diabhal an cat.*" I spit out the Irish curse even though I know he doesn't understand it. The Irish words feel more appropriate for this moment than telling him in English that I hope he gets eaten by a cat. "You idiotic bird," I add on, just so he has something he *does* understand, and then I throw in a few more curses for good measure.

It takes longer than I'd like for Nelson to start calming down and eventually take up his perch on the light fixture above us, still chirping away like he didn't scare Kasey so bad that she's trembling in my arms. I've got a stream of curses still running through my head, but some of them are for myself. What was I thinking, forcing her to face her fear of birds? I had good intentions, but that's always my problem.

I should have known my bad luck would get in the way.

I pull her closer, settling on my knees beside her. "Kasey?"

She snuggles into my chest, and it feels like she's gasping for air as she grips my t-shirt. I've never seen anyone this scared, and I hate that it's my fault. I take full blame on this one when I should have known better than to think everything would go how I wanted it to.

"Kasey, I'm sorry. I swear he isn't usually like that."

Sniffling, she shakes her head. "I'm sorry," she whispers into my neck. What in the world is *she* apologizing for?

As a shiver runs through me from the feel of her warm breath on my skin, I look up at Nelson and narrow my eyes at the way he seems to be smirking at me. Either he really is a devil incarnate, or he thought he was doing me a favor by scaring Kasey into my arms. Granted, this is closer than I've been to her since the day I rescued her from the pool, but I've been telling myself this is never going to be more than a friendship and therefore I shouldn't get used to being physically close to her.

Even if I want to be.

Why can't I get something right for once?

"He's not moving right now," I say gently and throw a silent threat up to the budgie. He had better stay put, or so help me... "We can head outside if you'd rather get away from him."

"I'm not sure I can move," she whispers back.

Geez, this girl really is terrified. There's not a lot in the world that scares me—space is terrifying, but it's not in this world—so I don't fully understand this level of terror. Plus, Nelson never even touched her, though he sure tried.

"We can sit here as long as you'd like," I tell her. I guess I can't be too mad that I get to hold her for a bit, since I won't get many other reasons after this disaster. I'll take what I can get.

"What language was that?"

I tilt my head to try to see her face. Her eyes are shut tight, face still pressed into my chest. She seems to like it there, which is fine by me. "Uh, that was Irish."

"You speak Irish?"

I chuckle and hope this change of subject will loosen the tension in her body. "Mostly bad words. My mom moved from Ireland when she was nineteen to follow an American musician she fell for when he visited Dublin. He ditched her as soon as she got pregnant with me, but she didn't want to take me away from the States, thinking I might have a better chance here."

I've told her a lot about my life over the last few days, but mostly things from after I got famous. It feels weird to tell someone about my origin when I've done a pretty good job of keeping it all hidden from the world. I have to hope my instincts aren't wrong about Kasey. If I get a call from Ethan tomorrow, telling me my history is all over the internet, I'll know who to blame.

"My granddad, according to Mom," I continue when Kasey remains silent, "had a mouth on him, and curse words are pretty much the only thing she remembers from growing up. Passed them right along to me because she thought swearing in Irish was better than swearing in English because I wouldn't be scandalizing my teachers if I said anything I shouldn't at school."

Kasey relaxes enough to look up at me, though I immediately miss the feel of her warm breath against my body. I'm usually running warm, but I don't mind sharing heat with Kasey. A part of me hopes she never leaves my arms, which is a very bad hope to have when I know I won't get to keep her. "That sucks about your dad. Do you know where he is?"

I shake my head. "Don't even know his name. Mom thought it would be better that way, and I've never wanted to know. My mom was enough for me."

"Even though he was a musician, like you?"

Laughing, I tuck her hair behind her ear and shake my head. "My love of music has nothing to do with him, no matter what talent he might have had. It's all me, and I'm lucky my mom is emotionally resilient enough to separate me from the trauma he put her through."

Kasey's fingers find their way to my wrist and brush along my whale tattoo, sending a shiver through me. It's like she knows how different my life could have been without my mom being as amazing as she is. Or maybe I'm just responding to her soft touch and trying not to react and scare her off.

I really don't want to scare her off.

"Are you sad she lives so far away?" she asks.

I snort. "Santa Barbara is barely over an hour away in good traffic."

"Yeah, but you can't leave your house right now, so she's an hour too far if you ever want to see her."

I guess I hadn't thought about it, and suddenly I wonder when I last went to visit her. She came to one of my shows a few months ago, but I didn't get the chance to talk to her. It was just a wave from the stage and a smile in return. I used to be better about calling her, but lately…

There's always been something in the way. A recording session, an interview, meetings with my agent or Ethan. The longer I'm in this world, the busier I get. But what has been my excuse since getting trapped here? My entire life, I've always tried to live in a way that my mother would be proud of. Punching a guy in front of my fans? Not exactly pride-worthy. I'm hoping I can get through my hearing and make it through the other side of this whole mess before she finds out about it.

I clear my throat, suddenly uncomfortable. "I think we should move outside. Give Nelson the freedom to do whatever he wants for a bit without risking your pretty little head."

Kasey looks up, and Nelson flaps in response, making her wince. "You'll protect me?"

"Just stay right where you are and stand up with me."

We stand slowly, both of us watching Nelson to make sure he doesn't make any sudden moves. Seriously, I can't decide whether I should strangle the bird or reward him for tonight's display of aggression. I want Kasey to like him, but I also don't mind the way she wraps her arms around my torso and holds on tight.

It is taking everything in me not to catalog how it feels to wrap my fingers around her waist, the way she leans into me, how her hair smells like the drugstore shampoo I used to use until my agent snagged me an endorsement deal with a hair care brand that actually keeps my hair from getting out of control wild. I kind of miss the old stuff, and I am so tempted to bury my nose in Kasey's hair while we walk.

Because that's not creepy at all…

We make it to the back patio without incident—bird-related or creepy sniffing—and only when I've closed the door behind us does Kasey slip out of my arms and run her fingers through her hair to smooth it. Her hair is mostly straight, but there's a wave to it, and I wonder what my shampoo would do to it. Would it give it a little curl, like it does mine?

"Thanks," Kasey says, her cheeks red. "Honestly, I have no idea why birds scare me so much."

Right. I should probably focus on the actual problem of the moment, not on thinking about Kasey washing her hair in my shower. "I think he was excited to make a new friend, but he overdid it. I'm sorry."

Thankfully, she smiles at me and then settles on one of the pool chairs, relaxing even more now that we're out in the fresh air. Her eyes are molten gold in the sunlight, and I'm suddenly transfixed. "Outside of your name, I never would have guessed you were Irish."

"Yeah, well, it's hard to feel Irish when you grow up from Nebraska to Texas and everywhere in between. Oklahoma definitely isn't Ireland."

"Why did you move so much?"

As I settle beside her, I try to think of the answer that doesn't make my mom look bad. She did her best—above and beyond, when it comes to music—but from an outside perspective, I can see how other people might think she did me a disservice by living the way she did rather than giving me some stability. It's one of the big reasons I don't tell people about my past, and it's not something I want the world to know yet.

My popularity is still new and clearly unstable, given the reactions to my recent altercation with the guy at my show, and it wouldn't take much to send me back to living off of pennies and struggling to get my music heard.

I'm not as much a fan of the fame and fortune as I am of the connection I get with people when they hear my music. Playing sold-out shows is the most exhilarating thing I've ever done, and nothing else has ever come close to the feeling of singing my heart out on a stage and having a whole stadium of people singing back to me.

I don't want to give anyone a reason to think I don't deserve to be where I am because my life hasn't been sunshine and rainbows like everyone thinks. I've spent my whole life working hard to get here, and my mom has sacrificed so much to help me on my way. I'm not ashamed of my past, but the tabloids have a way of twisting the truth to get attention.

"I won't tell anyone," Kasey says, as if she can read my thoughts. My hesitation is probably all over my face because I still haven't mastered the art of hiding my expressions like Ethan keeps telling me I need to.

I sigh and stretch out, enjoying the warmth of the sun. It's almost as nice as the warmth from holding Kasey. "We lived wherever my mom's boyfriends lived. It was easier to live with whoever she was dating at the time, but most of her relationships didn't last long."

Well, I don't think I succeeded at softening the truth, so I throw a question back at her, wondering if she'll answer this time. She's pretty good at changing the subject. "What about your parents? Are they still in Kansas?"

She nods slowly. "Yeah. Dad's a retired English teacher, and my mom worked at the same school in the admin office."

I'm assuming that means they're still together, which is becoming more and more rare. "What brought you to California?"

"Hollywood."

I can't stop the thread of unease that always makes an appearance in my belly when the subject of Hollywood comes up. We've both been good at avoiding it for the most part. I know why I stay away from it, but I wonder why she does. She knows I'm good friends with two prominent actors, and Kasey wants to get into the movie business as a writer. These two things go so well together, and yet neither of us has made that connection out loud.

I do want to introduce her to Derek, or at least see if he has any contacts who could be helpful to her. But I want her to ask. I want to see the look in her eyes when she does so I can know if she plans to disappear as soon as she has her foot in the door. I'd rather have some time to prepare myself for my return to a life without Kasey in it.

The silence between us stretches longer than I'd like, so I clear my throat and look toward Ted's yard. "I hate that we haven't seen Ted or Martha yet."

Kasey lets out her breath, like she's sighing with relief. "Seriously, I almost wonder if something happened and they're both lying dead in their kitchen."

"Morbid, much?"

She lifts an eyebrow. "Okay, maybe they went on vacation."

"Boo. That's too boring." I could ask Johnny at the gate if Ted has been in or out lately, but that feels like cheating. "I wish I could go next door with some cookies or something so I can check on them."

"Do you bake?"

I laugh, shaking my head. "My kitchen may look nice, but the only thing I use it for is the microwave and blender. Nobody wants my hands making food."

"Now I understand why I keep bringing food with me." Kasey stands again and moves to the wall that separates my property from Ted's. The trees don't give us much access, which is why we've mostly been up on the balcony. "Hmm, I think I might see something, but I'm not tall enough."

I'm still buzzing from holding her inside, and I can't get used to that shift in our relationship. I reluctantly stand and move to her side, knowing I'll have to get close to know where she's looking. Outside of holding her hand that first night she came back, I've barely touched her. Until today.

I stand just behind her, putting my hand on her shoulder so she knows I'm there. It's like I can't help but have some sort of contact, and my fingers tingle with the warmth of her. "Where?"

She points, leaning into me as if that will help me see what she's looking at. It doesn't. "See it? Against the house there?"

"I don't see anything." And I really need to put some distance between us. No one has ever affected me like this, and I'm starting to think maybe there *is* something I'm afraid of after all.

If I fall for her any more than I already have, I think it might break me when she leaves.

"Stand here," she says, moving behind me and then tugging me to the left.

When my foot lands, pain shoots through it and up my leg. I hiss and stumble back, falling directly into Kasey, and we both tumble backward into the pool with a splash.

CHAPTER TEN

KASEY

How many times does a girl need to almost drown before she starts steering clear of pools? Apparently it's at least twice, though this time isn't nearly as traumatic as the first because Liam is right there, hands snaking around my waist and lifting me up high enough to get my face out of the water.

I know he'll save me, but instinct tells me to cling to him for dear life as I cough and gasp for air. He stumbles when I wrap around anything I can hold on to, submerging us both once more before he regains his footing and hops to get to the shallower end.

"You okay?" he gasps, coughing a few times as he keeps moving.

I can barely breathe, but I nod. I try to relax, but it's not easy with the water still swirling around us.

"Hey." Liam stills, adjusting his hold on me with slow and careful movements. "I've got you, Kase."

Kase. I like that. Mostly because it's coming from Liam's smooth-as-chocolate voice that is my new favorite thing. Over the last few days I've done my best to keep him talking or singing as much as possible because I could listen to him all day long.

"What happened?" I ask, both to hear his voice and because one minute I was looking at what I'm pretty sure is a shiny, brand-new shovel leaning against Ted's house and the next I was inhaling first Liam's tantalizing scent and then water. I didn't even have time to register what was happening before I was in the pool.

Liam turns a shade of red I've never seen on him before. "I, uh, fell."

I can't help but laugh. "I figured that part out. Why?"

"My foot." He grimaces and glances down at the offending limb. "I keep forgetting it's fractured."

Guilt pools in my belly. "And I made you step on it wrong."

"It's fine. I should be wearing the boot." He brushes his fingers through my hair, pushing it away from my face in such a gentle way that it's like he's trying to use the gesture to reaffirm what he said. "I'm glad we landed in the pool instead of on the stone, but I'm sorry for inadvertently pushing you in."

"Thanks for saving me again." My teeth start chattering as my panic subsides, and I pull closer to Liam's warm body. I almost wish he wasn't wearing a shirt right now; I'd bet his bare skin would be warmer than the wet cotton.

Liam moves us to the edge, pausing when I don't make any attempts to release him. "I'm happy to help you out," he says, though his comment is open-ended, like there's a 'but' in there.

I shake my head. "Give me a minute. I'm not sure I properly internalized this the last time, so I figure I should take a second to process." Is that my lame way of not wanting to leave the circle of his arms? Yes. I got my taste when his evil parakeet attacked inside, and now I'm addicted to the embrace of Liam Connolly.

His fans would kill to be in my position, and I'm not going to take this for granted.

"Well..." Liam bobs up and down a few times, and then he wraps me up tighter. It's probably because I'm shivering, but I'm telling myself it's because he likes holding me as much as I like being held by him. "Did you see anything at Ted's before I messed it all up?"

"Just a shovel." Okay, I'm shaking so much now that I'm barely comprehensible. I'm not sure I'm clever enough to come up with another reason for Liam to hold me like this, but I'm bound to get hypothermia.

Yeah, I know no one gets hypothermia when it's seventy-five degrees outside, but I have the worst circulation and should probably move to Florida or Texas or something. Phoenix? Southern California is on the list of warmest places to live in the US, but it's clearly not warm enough for me.

"Okay, we need to get you into dry clothes." Prying himself free, Liam wraps his fingers around my hips and lifts me up and onto the pool's edge like it's nothing, even though he's only standing on one foot right now. Then he pulls himself out, showing off his arms as his pale blue t-shirt clings to his body in the best way.

It's next to impossible not to admire this man when he has clearly put in the hard work to look this good.

Liam doesn't give me much of a chance to trace his shoulders with my eyes. As soon as he's on his feet, he wraps me up again, pulling me tight against his beautiful body. "Still with me, Kasey?"

"Barely," I admit, though it's not just because of the cold. "You know they have heated pools, right?"

"Says the girl who can't swim."

"Maybe not, but I can appreciate a good hot tub."

We both look over at the covered hot tub, and fire spreads through my limbs at the thought of sitting in the scalding water with Liam Freaking Connolly. It has been strange enough to hang out with him the last few days, not to mention *sing* with the man and pray no one listens to that demo. I don't need something as intimate as a hot tub blurring the friendship lines that already feel vague as it is.

"It would warm you up," Liam says, nodding toward the spa.

I shake my head. "How about I test out that waterfall showerhead in the guest bathroom after I raid your closet again?"

Have I brought back the shirt and sweats combo I borrowed the first time I was here? Intentionally no. I figured if our friendship doesn't last, I could sell them on eBay and use the profits for rent money. Besides, I don't know where this man buys his sweatpants, but they are insanely comfortable and might have been my pajamas for the last week. Val keeps making fun of me for the amount of laundry I've been doing.

Liam starts moving us toward the door, still with his arms around me. "You can have anything you want from my closet except the shirt from Indiana Brews."

I frown when we reach the glass doors. "What's Indiana Brews?"

"It's a coffee shop in San Francisco. I was playing there when my agent found me."

Oh, to be a fly on that wall. Or even to know Liam before he was famous. I can imagine sitting in that coffee shop and hearing the smoothest, calmest voice coming from the speaker. Maybe he didn't even use a speaker. Coffee shops generally aren't very large, so he might have been playing acoustically.

"How did a guy from Oklahoma end up in San Francisco?" I ask as we head inside. I flinch when Nelson chirps something, but he's in a different room. Hopefully indefinitely. "Why not come straight to Los Angeles?"

Liam chuckles, shifting so one arm is draped over my shoulders rather than both his arms tucked around me. He's limping, though he's doing his best not to make it obvious. "One of my favorite artists came out of San Fran," he says. "Jack Hawthorne."

I've never heard of him, but Liam gets a wistful look in his eyes as we start up the stairs.

"He's not a big name," he continues, "at least not compared to some, but his songs really influenced my style. He's the kind of guy who sings from the heart and really means every word, and I wanted to be that kind of musician."

"I'm pretty sure you became that," I tell him. "I don't even like music, and I already preordered your next album."

He laughs, filling the hall with light as we reach the top of the staircase. "I would have given you a free copy, Kase. After all, you're going to be on it."

I know he's teasing. At least, I'm mostly convinced he's teasing, but panic still sets in at the thought of my voice being on his album. "You had better not put me on the final recording, Liam Connolly. You might like being famous, but I don't need that in my life."

For some reason, that brings out a wide grin on his lips, which are far too close to mine right now for me to be even remotely calm right now. "You don't want fame and fortune?"

"Fortune, sure, but people don't need to know my name."

"I thought you wanted to make a career out of being a screenwriter."

He makes that sound so simple, like it's something I can actually do. Without a connection like Derek, there's no way I could write enough to make a comfortable life for myself.

That could have been you last year, a tiny voice in my head says. He-Who-Will-Not-Be-Named sold my script for almost fifty thousand dollars. *My story* was worth that much. But the only reason it sold was because he had the connections and I was stupid enough to let him take it. I even met the guy who bought it, some Hollywood producer who came to visit campus and talk to the film students, so I could have given him the screenplay myself if I hadn't been so trusting.

"Kase?"

"I'm freezing," I say, which is true both literally and emotionally. I desperately want to trust Liam and his friends, but I've been down that road before. I *loved* the man who stole everything from me, and that's not something a girl can easily recover from. Logically, I know not everyone will be out to screw me over, but there's a reason I haven't been able to write anything since my script was stolen. "I should really warm up before I shiver to death."

Liam's face drops with disappointment, but he's quick to slap on a smile and direct me to his closet so I can snatch a pink t-shirt with a flamingo on it and a pair of light gray sweatpants. While it's true what they say about how good guys look in suits, Liam's relaxed sense of style is fine by me.

"Thanks," I tell him before wandering down the hall to the glorious shower that awaits me.

CHAPTER ELEVEN

LIAM

"Wait, she's in your house right now?" Cole brings his face closer to the screen, as if that will help him see beyond my face. He's a smart guy, but he probably had practice today and looks a little worse for wear with several bruises on his face. I can't help but wonder if he got hit in the head one too many times.

I swear, rugby is way more dangerous than people realize, though Cole has always been casual about the fact that he is regularly tackled without any protective padding.

I roll my eyes and turn my laptop so the only view outside of my head is the bedroom wall behind me. Kasey is still in the shower, and I intend to keep this call quick and painless. I only joined in because I got a text from Freya that said she would fly all the way to the States to make sure I'm alive and well if I didn't show my face, and she is terrifying if she gets off schedule by anything unplanned.

"Will you guys calm down?" I say, my voice low. "I only have a minute before she's out of the shower."

"Why is there a woman showering at your house?" Bonnie asks. She, apparently, has been too preoccupied with Derek next to her to pay attention to anything we've said so far. Not that it's been much. Derek started the call by asking me if I'd seen the Diner Delivery girl again, and I utterly failed at hiding the heat in my face, which prompted Freya to gasp and guess that Kasey was here.

"We accidentally fell into the pool," I say as casually as I can.

Derek frowns as he wraps his arm around Bonnie's shoulders. "Again?"

"*Again?*" Freya repeats, eyes going wide. "Just how many times has this girl been in your shower, Liam? I thought you were not interested in dating."

"It's not like that." I glance at my open door. It was closed while I showered and changed, in case Kasey decided to waltz right in again, but she's taking a lot longer than I expected her to. Uncertainty weaves its way into my belly, and I'm tempted to go make sure she's still here and didn't sneak out while I was in the shower.

"What's that face for?" Cole asks, squinting at the screen. Seriously, he's looking a little dazed, though no one else seems worried.

I do my best to cover my worry—both for Cole and about Kasey—with a smile. "What face? I only have one face. I didn't make a face."

"Subtle," Derek says, rolling his eyes at the same time everyone chimes in with a chorus of, "Lies."

I sigh, doing another check to make sure the hallway is clear and Kasey won't overhear me. I shift my laptop again, too nervous to sit still. "I'm getting attached," I admit with a grimace.

All four of my friends glance around, probably checking each other's expressions to see how they're supposed to respond. It's Freya who speaks first, looking impressive in a gilded room and a high-backed chair behind her. She may not have taken the throne yet, but she's already taking on a lot of the responsibility from her parents, who are eager to retire. Every time I see her, she looks more like a princess.

"Liam Connolly," she says stiffly, "you are aware that you get attached more easily than anyone I know, yes?"

"That's not true," I argue, prompting another round of, "Lies," from my friends. I get where they're coming from, but they're wrong. I enjoy being around people, and I'll admit I've been on my fair share of dates. *First* dates. Rarely anything more. Those women have always felt like new friends rather than someone I might see as something more. "You know I don't do relationships."

"But you trust too easily," Cole says.

"That's not the same as getting attached."

Freya scoffs. "But you are—"

"I think he's right, Peach," Derek interrupts, a thoughtful look on his face. "I saw him almost a week after he met her, and he was all sorts of messed up."

"Thanks?" I say, though I'm not sure if that's what I'm supposed to say to his comment. "I'd barely known her for twenty minutes, so I'm not sure I could call myself messed—"

"How did you meet her?" Bonnie asks. Her eyes are alight with interest, probably because she's been in enough romantic movies now that she can't help but see romance everywhere.

"She was his delivery driver," Derek says before I can come up with a nicer way to say it. "I'm guessing she's the reason you've been so quiet this week?"

I shrug. As if Derek isn't unequivocally right. "She's been helping me with the album." *Barely.*

"Is she a musician too?" Bonnie asks.

"No."

"She delivers food," Cole throws in unhelpfully.

I roll my eyes. "She only does that to pay the bills. She's actually a…" I stop myself, wondering if I should tell them about Kasey's screenwriting goals. Derek and Bonnie could both help her, but that same fear that I'll lose her as soon as that happens keeps my words caught in my throat.

"A what?" Derek asks.

I bite my tongue.

"Liam?" Kasey's voice in the doorway pulls my eyes to her immediately. She looks pink-faced and adorable in my too-big clothes, her hair still wet as she folds her arms in a strange way. One hand is up by the opposite shoulder, the other gripping the other arm.

"Is that her?" Cole asks way too loudly.

I wince. "It's a video chat with my friends," I tell Kasey. "We do it a couple times a week, but I missed the last one so I thought I should hop on quick. Let me just—"

"We want to meet Kasey!" Bonnie shouts, making Derek flinch beside her.

I meet Kasey's gaze again. "Do you want to—"

"Of course she wants to!" Freya snaps, almost as loudly as Bonnie. "Give her the computer, Connolly."

It's as close to a royal edict as you can get, and I sigh. "What do you say, Kase?"

She turns a brighter pink and inches her way into the room. "Your friends?"

I nod, though I'm still tempted to shut my laptop and delay the inevitable a little longer. "I promise they're harmless. Mostly. Freya might make you feel inadequate, but she does that to everyone."

Freya gasps. "I do not!"

Kasey stops dead, halfway to the couch where I'm sitting. "Freya?" she whispers. "As in the princess of Candora?"

I grin despite the apprehension building in my gut. "See?" I say, at full volume rather than in a whisper. "You're already scared of her."

Freya glares at the camera. "What have you been telling her about me, Connolly? I am not frightening!"

"She's really not!" Bonnie throws in.

Kasey cocks her head, a question in her eyes.

"It's all of them," I tell her. "Her Royal Highness, Derek Riley, Bonnie Aiken, and Cole Evanson."

"She's not going to know who I am," Cole says.

"Actually." Kasey takes a step forward, still a bit wary but more interested than she was a moment ago. Probably because I mentioned Derek. But then she says, "I do know who Cole is. I love rugby."

Those three words send a rush of relief through me. It's not a guarantee that she'll stick around for me, but at least in this moment, she seems more interested in the rugby player than the connection she could get from Derek.

"You hear that, Cole?" I say as I scoot over so Kasey can sit beside me. "You're not completely unknown!"

"Very funny," Cole grumbles back. Though, he's less grumbly than normal, probably because someone recognized his name. "You keep forgetting I played in a Superbowl."

Honestly, I do keep forgetting about that because Cole never talks about it. It's weird that he even brought it up today. My response gets lost when Kasey settles directly beside me, our thighs touching. She looks nervous, but there's excitement in her eyes also.

I'm too focused on how close she chose to sit to remember I should be making introductions.

"Hi, Kasey!" Bonnie waves emphatically, and I'm glad she's the first person to interact. Few people in the world dislike Bonnie Aiken. "We've heard so little about you, but it's probably better to get to know you ourselves rather than trust Liam to do you justice. He can write some amazing songs, but he's not nearly as poetic in real life."

"Hey," I complain, but Derek starts talking.

"Thank you for keeping Liam from going stir crazy so far," he says with a smirk.

Kasey doesn't respond. I can't decide if it's because she's overwhelmed, confused, or terrified by all of this; her face is a mixture of all three.

Cole speaks next. "Who's your favorite rugby team, Kasey? And you don't have to say the Thunder. My ego can handle it."

Kasey glances at me, as if looking for confirmation, and I nod. It's about all I can do because she's sitting so close, and I worry that if I try to say anything my voice will crack and squeak. Why I fear that, I have no idea. That only happens when I overuse it.

"I don't really know the teams in the US league," she says slowly, "but I like the All Blacks."

Cole pulls his dark eyebrows together. "New Zealand? Everyone likes them. Who would you like if you weren't boring?"

"He's joking," I assure Kasey quickly, though I'm questioning myself because Derek frowns at the camera and then grabs his phone. Probably to text one of us, something he does often during these video chats. The guy likes to have multiple conversations at once.

"Liam!" Freya speaks so sharply and suddenly that most of us jump, Kasey included. "She's wearing your clothes?"

I raise an eyebrow. It's not like this is something scandalous, though maybe things are different in Candora? "She fell in the pool, remember? Her stuff is soaked."

"Well, then get the girl a sweater or something." She says it like I'm an idiot for not doing that sooner, though Kasey looks plenty warm.

"Oh, you're hopeless," Bonnie moans.

I frown. "What?"

"Her bra got wet, obviously."

"So?" I glance at Kasey right as her face turns beet-red at the same time she adjusts her arms to an even more awkward position, covering up her chest. Then it clicks. Her bra is wet, which means she's probably not wearing one right now, and she's got nothing on but my thin t-shirt. "Oh!"

Dumping the computer onto the cushion on my other side, I scramble to the closet and hunt for anything she can wear, though I rarely wear anything warmer than a t-shirt unless I'm in a suit, so my options are limited. I find a sweatshirt with a giant picture of Nelson printed on the front—a gag gift from Cole—and hurry back out to give it to Kasey.

She takes it without a word and quickly pulls it on while I resituate the laptop.

"You should have said something to him, Kasey," Bonnie says sweetly. "These boys aren't always the brightest bunch."

"I'm feeling fine!" Cole snaps, his eyes on his phone. Like I suspected, Derek must have texted him to check on him.

I groan as Derek starts typing something else. This is going to descend into madness quickly if we're not careful. "Guys, I should probably get going."

"You still have songs to write," Freya agrees.

I hadn't planned on writing anything tonight, at least not while Kasey is here, but Freya's words start a rhythm in my head, followed quickly by a melody that I try to ignore. I've spent enough time writing around Kasey, and I'd much rather give her my full attention.

"I'll send you the next song as soon as it's done," I promise. "They've been coming a lot more easily since Kasey—" I swear and then clench my jaw as all four of them start talking at once. Though I can't understand any of them, I can guess pretty easily that they're all coming to the same conclusion that I have been mostly ignoring for days: my block is gone because of Kasey.

I shut my laptop despite the continued conversation, throwing us into silence. I can't even look at Kasey, though I'm dying to know what she might be thinking. I didn't say anything specific. Maybe I was going to say I've been writing more since the day Kasey brought me ice cream.

Ice cream I've barely touched.

"So," Kasey says, wrapping her fingers around the ends of her sleeves. That sweatshirt is so big on her, but she looks impossibly comfortable and all around adorable. The sight of her tiny arms coming out of the sleeves makes me want to pull her up against me and snuggle in close, but I can't do that because I'm pretty sure I'm still only one mistake away from sending her running.

"So," I reply, waiting to see what she wants to do.

She waits until I look over at her, and then she smiles. "How do you know Cole Evanson?"

"Derek."

"And you never did tell me how you became friends with a princess."

I chuckle. "Derek."

"Okay, so how did you meet Derek? Does he know, like, every famous person to ever exist?"

Relaxing even more, I set my computer on the couch next to me and then stretch my legs out. My foot is still throbbing, and the adrenaline crash after rescuing Kasey again has left me exhausted.

"It feels like it sometimes, but no," I say with a chuckle. "Derek happens to be incredibly personable, which is how he managed to start dating Bonnie when half the world wants to be her boyfriend. And it's how he didn't get shot when he entered the grounds of the royal palace in Candora in an attempt to personally ask permission to film a movie in the capital city. Freya was so impressed with his gumption that he basically has diplomatic immunity in Candora. And it's how he found *me* when I performed at an awards show for the first time and puked my guts out backstage from nerves. He was the one announcing that I was going on, and he stalled for a good ten minutes so I could get my crap together. I thought the audience would be calling for my head, but no one cared because he's Derek Riley. Basically, he's annoyingly likable."

Kasey nudges my arm with her elbow. "You do know that you are also annoyingly likable, right?"

Oh, I like the sound of that a little too much, and the spark of excitement that spreads through me seems to take over my limbs. I watch in consternation as my hand slips over the top of hers, and my fingers slide in between hers so easily. It's not quite holding her hand, considering my palm is pressed against her knuckles, but the contact still sends a thrill through me.

I wasn't kidding when I told the gang I was getting attached, which is a problem. No matter how much I like her, it's not going to go anywhere. I don't do relationships. As much as it is a lack of good examples, I'm on the road way more than a partner should have to tolerate, and that's not going to change. Especially if this album does as well as I hope it will. And, assuming my luck with music continues, my fame will grow. Kasey has already told me how much she doesn't want fame, and she would be better off without me, assuming she is even interested in me to begin with. She may enjoy my company, but that doesn't mean she's attached like I am.

I wish she were. I wish I could know she would be here waiting for me when I come back from a tour, celebrating with me when I hit a streaming milestone or get an award. Inspiring songs simply by existing. What would a life with Kasey look like several years down the road?

It's time to change the subject before my mind goes too far down that path. "Tell me about your screenplay."

Kasey meets my gaze, a crease forming between her eyebrows. "What?"

"I want to know about the story you've written."

"I've written a bunch."

"Oh."

Sighing, she stretches out the fingers that are wedged between mine, though I don't think she's hinting that I should let go. It's almost like she's feeling things out, trying to decide if she fits. "None of them are good enough for Hollywood, so I need a new idea. Something compelling."

"Have you sent them to anyone?" Maybe she already has contacts and doesn't need me to get anywhere, and I can stop worrying for nothing.

But Kasey shakes her head, killing my hope in an instant. "But I will. When I have something good."

"What makes a good—"

An angry shout outside pulls both our attention to the balcony doors, which I opened as soon as I got out of the shower. We look at each other, confirming that the other person heard something, and then we both hop up and hurry outside. Kasey's faster—stupid foot—and heads straight for the best view of Ted's yard.

By the time I reach her side, Ted is stomping across his lawn with a murderous look on his face. He's dripping wet, but only on his front half, like something splashed him, and he shakes his arms out as he turns back to the house.

"I've just about had it with you, Martha!" he snarls. Then, much softer but still loud enough for us to hear, he adds, "Why won't you die already?"

Kasey squeaks and drops down below the balcony railing, out of sight, and then she tugs me down after her. "Did you just hear what I heard?"

"I'm hoping I heard wrong," I mutter. He wants Martha dead? I mean, sure, people get angry all the time. Just this afternoon I told Nelson that I wanted him to get eaten by a cat and the cat to get eaten by the devil. Not exactly kind words. But I didn't mean them.

Ted seems to mean them as he continues to grumble incomprehensible things in his backyard.

"I'm starting to worry about Martha's safety," Kasey mutters.

As much as I don't want to admit it, so am I. I want to admit even less that I'm glad for the distraction. Glad that, for now, I can pretend that my growing attraction for Kasey doesn't exist and that I'm not careening toward emotional disaster at a speed I'm not sure I can stop.

Like with most things in my life, none of this is going to end well.

CHAPTER TWELVE

KASEY

AFTER TED PACED AROUND his yard for a bit, he went back inside and we didn't hear or see him again. As we halfheartedly played a game of Monopoly on the balcony to give us an excuse to keep an eye on the house, Liam said more than once that Ted was overreacting and everything was fine, but I know he doesn't believe his own words.

He's been tense ever since, to the point where I don't want to leave him here by himself tonight even though I told myself that I need to make a few deliveries if I don't want to go completely broke.

Right now, he's downstairs trying to catch Nelson and get him back in his cage so I can leave in peace, which means I'm up on the balcony on my own as I look out over the neighborhood and debate my options.

It's a nice neighborhood, and I can see why Liam likes it here. When he told me all about his neighbors, he mostly only had good things to say about everyone, though that could partially be because he's such a nice guy that he probably thinks the best of everyone. Either way, with only six large houses lined up around the gated cul-de-sac, it's good that he doesn't hate everyone.

From my spot on the south side balcony, I can see every house but Ted's, as well as the little green park-like area in the center of the curved street. The park doesn't boast much, just a fountain and a few benches, but right now there's four people hanging out on the grass as the sun begins setting over the ocean to my right.

I'm guessing the man is Leonard Curry, given his silver hair. According to Liam, he's ex-military and was quite possibly a literal spy in his younger years, though Liam has never gotten him to confirm it. The women are harder to guess, though I'm pretty sure the one wearing too-short shorts and a sports bra is Gina Grady. Liam says she always flirts with him if he's ever outside, despite her being married to a tech CEO. Liam says he's often out of town on business trips, and Gina seems to enjoy the freedom his absence gives her.

As for the other two women who are gabbing away with Leonard, I have no clue.

"Oh, Mrs. Buford is out and about," Liam says behind me. "That's unusual."

I try to remember as he comes up to my side. "She's the one whose husband died last year, right?"

"Yep. She's on the far end there, next to Patty Carmichael." He chuckles when he looks at me. "Patty is the resident gossip."

"Ah, right. All good neighborhoods need one of those." I squint at the odd grouping. Over the several days I've been here, this is the first time I've seen any of Liam's neighbors interacting with each other. "So outside of you and Ted, that's one person from every house."

"I thought Patty and Gina couldn't stand each other." Liam frowns. "Granted, I don't pay that much attention to my neighbors when I'm here, but Patty has told me plenty about how she thinks Gina is a…" He stops, his face turning slightly red. "Not something I want to repeat in polite company."

I snort. "What, do you think I couldn't handle it?"

Grinning, he bumps his shoulder into mine. That smile is a sight for sore eyes, so I'm determined to keep this conversation going as long as I can. "No, I think Patty is petty, and Gina doesn't deserve me thinking poorly of her because someone else doesn't like her."

"You said Gina flirts with you even though she's married, right?" I don't like the way my stomach twists when I think about that. Not because of Gina being married (which isn't great) but because I don't like people flirting with Liam. Mostly because I don't like the thought of him flirting back. I tuck my arms around my middle to try to quell the uneasy feeling.

Liam laughs. "Yeah, but old ladies in grocery stores flirt with me too. Or, one time a woman with four kids and a husband in the car came up to me at the gas station to tell me she liked my hair."

I like his hair too. I still don't know if it's naturally blond, but it has this carefree wave to it that is so like Liam. Outside of the uncertainty with Ted today, he is always so calm and chill and unbothered, and I wish I could live like him.

Unable to stop myself, I run my fingers through Liam's hair. It's as soft as I expected it to be, and I don't want to stop. So I don't. Liam's eyes turn to me with an intense look I'm not sure I could describe if I tried. My stomach ties itself into a knot or two as he leans closer.

"I like when you do that," he says, his voice dropping low.

Good heavens, I like when he does *that*. If Liam sang country, I think women would keel over dead the minute he opened his mouth. His actual songs are bad enough, but I think country songs by Liam would break the world. I want to hear him sing one immediately in this deeper-than-normal register he's using.

"Do you have any more song ideas rolling around in this head of yours?" I ask, still running my fingers through his hair because there's no reason for me to stop now that I've started. I feel like if I hold still, something might happen. I'm not sure I can let something happen, even if I want it.

"Oh, I have plenty of ideas right now." Liam's eyes trail from my face down to my arms and then back up again. "But none of them have to do with music."

That's when his hand finds my waist, slowly making its way to my back. His fingers dig in slightly, drawing a shaky breath out of me, and then he pulls me toward him in a motion so smooth that I feel like I'm floating.

"Ideas?" I whisper, completely breathless. Where did this come from? I'm blaming the bird, who forced me into Liam's arms and gave me a taste of something I like a little too much. I press my hands against his chest, feeling the way his heart is pounding just like mine. I'm so glad he's wearing a shirt right now, though I'm getting some great flashbacks from that first day I met him and I got up close and personal with his muscles.

He's so warm, and it's taking everything in me not to curl up against him.

Liam nods slowly. "Ideas like this." He tucks my hair behind my ear. "Or maybe this." He presses a kiss to my forehead, leaving a burning spot behind while his thumb strokes my cheek.

I close my eyes, suddenly unable to hold them open anymore. "Anything else?"

His breath brushes across my mouth. "Maybe something like—"

"Liam?"

He swears and pulls away, looking down at the sidewalk in front of his house. Patty Carmichael is standing there, beady eyes staring up at us and her phone gripped in her hand in a way that makes me wonder if she just took a picture of us. She looks down long enough to type something, and then she gives us a gleeful smile.

"What's up, PC?" Liam calls down, his voice falsely calm. I know it's false because he's clenching his hands behind his back.

Patty's eyes linger on me for a moment before she returns her focus to Liam. "I haven't seen you out and about much the last couple of weeks," she says, her tone as much a question as it is a statement.

Liam shrugs. "I've been busy working on a new album."

Movement catches my eye, and I look up to see Mrs. Buford walking arm in arm with Leonard toward the smallest house on the block. On the other end of the neighborhood, Gina looks over at Patty before slipping through a side gate. I don't know which house belongs to whom, but that looked mighty suspicious.

Maybe I'm just projecting. Seeing things that aren't there.

"I always see you coming and going with all your lady friends," Patty says, pulling my attention back. "I'm surprised to see you've kept one around longer than a day or two."

A sickening combination of anger and hurt bursts to life in my belly, forcing me back a step. "Who says something like that?" I ask out loud, though my voice is small. My follow-up question is silent. *And is she telling the truth?*

Liam glances at me, his eyebrows pulling low before he turns back to Patty. "Hey, Patty, I've noticed Ted isn't as chipper as he usually is. Is he doing okay?"

I take another step back. I don't know what I expected him to say, but I guess I was hoping he would defend me. Tell Patty that I'm just his friend. His friend he almost kissed just now.

I can't help but think about how he almost kissed me on the day he met me too. He said he's not a friends-with-benefits kind of guy, and I believe him. But I also think Liam is far more casual with physical intimacy than I am, which means I have no idea where we stand. A kiss for him probably doesn't mean the same that it would for me.

"Ted?" Patty glances at the house next to Liam's. "Oh, he's been having some trouble with Martha, but things will work themselves out before long. I've been keeping my eye on other, uh, individuals lately. Nothing you need to worry your pretty little head over."

Her comments about Ted make me feel a little better, but Liam only seems to be tenser than before as he leans on the railing. "How are things with you?" he asks. "Paul doing okay?"

Paul, I think, is Patty's husband, though right now I don't really care. I'm still processing what she said about me. Me, and Liam's many lady friends. Am I simply the latest in a long string of flings? He said he didn't want to mix our friendship up with any kind of deeper intimacy, but that doesn't mean he's not fine with *casual* intimacy. Lots of people see kissing as meaningless.

He's clearly attracted to me. Maybe he's been building up to the kissing and beyond because he knows I wouldn't have jumped right into it without a little persuasion. And boy, is he persuasive. I don't know if anyone can say no to this guy.

My phone buzzes, and I dig it out of the massive pocket of these sweatpants I borrowed.

I smile and inch my way around the balcony to the chairs on the back, leaving Liam to his conversation with Patty. Milo and I only have each other's numbers because we got our orders mixed up one too many times. I wouldn't call us close—at nineteen, he's four years my junior—but I've missed running into him at various restaurants throughout the day.

Kasey:
I wish I was on to bigger and better. I got caught up in a project this week, but I'll be out there tonight.

I regret it as soon as I send it, though I'm not sure Liam has even noticed I left his side. I can hear him talking to Patty, but I can't make out what he's saying.

Milo:
Right on. I wondered why I kept getting access to the Malibu jobs all week, but I'm glad you'll be back.

I'm not sure he means that last part, given the insane tips people give out here, but it's nice to think he at least sort of likes me. We started as rivals, fighting for space in a competitive and exclusive market, but then we found our rhythm and sort of became friends.

Milo:
You missed the motherload though. (Because I got it lol.) Ever done a delivery to Brent Fallsteen?

My stomach drops. That's the name Liam uses.

Milo:
Apparently he's a crazy tipper and someone got almost a grand from him last week. I'm hoping he's feeling extra charitable tonight.

Kasey:
You're delivering to Brent?

Milo:

Almost there. Wish me luck! Gotta rizz him up.

I don't know why I'm freaking out, but I'm freaking out. It's not like Milo will see me, but having him in this space that has been a strange haven away from the rest of the world feels like the bubble is going to pop, and I'm not ready for that yet. Then again, nothing about this afternoon has felt right. Ever since Ted made his appearance, everything has been off balance, and I hate it.

Headlights pull onto the darkening street from the direction of the gate at the same time Liam comes around the corner, his phone pressed to his ear and his eyebrows pulled low.

"Hang on a sec, Ethan." He presses his phone to his chest and glances at the approaching car. "I ordered us dinner after getting Nelson put away, but I forgot to add a tip and my phone is about to die. Would you mind grabbing some cash from the office at the end of the hall and giving it to the driver?"

So much for not seeing Milo. I'm about to object, tell him that I should really be heading out to do my own deliveries, but then he shifts his expression to one that is closer to pleading.

"I have to take this call, Kase." But it's pretty clear that he doesn't want to.

"Okay," I squeak out.

"Give him as much as you want." Then he disappears into the house.

Though I follow soon after, Liam is nowhere to be found. I'm assuming he went downstairs somewhere, maybe to one of the rooms in the hall before the music room, and I feel weird wandering around on my own like this. Still, Liam is the kind of guy whose pout makes him impossible to disappoint, so I head to the end of the hall right as the doorbell rings.

The office isn't much more than a starkly empty desk and a couple of leather wingbacks, which probably means Liam rarely comes in here because none of it feels like him. The drawers are almost as empty as the top of the desk, but the biggest one has an unlocked safe inside. Inside that safe is an obscene amount of cash sitting there all innocently in its neat little wrapped stacks.

This safe has more money inside it than my entire bank account, and I actually tear up as I grab a few hundred bucks. Liam's life is so completely different from mine, and I think I've been fooling myself the last few days, thinking I could be a part of it.

Even when talking to Derek and Bonnie and *Princess Freaking Freya*, I still thought in my core that Liam and I weren't so dissimilar because of the way he grew up. Oh, how wrong I was.

Liam is wealthy and popular and has lots of lady friends, and I'm just a struggling graduate with nothing to show for my years in film school.

The doorbell rings again, and I hurry down the stairs with my handful of cash and a resolution to clear out and let Liam live his fancy life with his fancy posse and fancy lady friends. I need to get back to my life, where I can't afford the pathetically cheap rent my best friend is charging me because my student loans are drowning me more than Liam's pool.

I can't even write a new screenplay let alone sell one, and Liam has plunked out three amazing songs in the last few days alone.

We're not the same at all.

When I open the front door to a rousing rendition of the *Ghostbusters* theme song by Nelson the parakeet, I've almost forgotten that I know the guy on the other side. But as soon as we lock eyes, time seems to freeze for a second.

Milo blinks. Looks down at the bag of food in his hands. Back at me. Then he scrunches his face up and looks up, as if the house might explain why I'm standing in front of him.

"Uh, hey, Milo," I say, tripping on the words.

His eyebrows shoot high. "Dude, are you secretly rich?"

"What? No! If only."

He takes in my clothes next, fixating on the large, printed photo of Nelson on the sweatshirt I forgot I was wearing. It doesn't help that the bird is still singing his little heart out, filling the air with his screeching song and putting me on edge.

"So…" Milo shifts the brown paper bag from one hand to the other. "So what, you're some kind of bird babysitter?"

I frown. "Is that a real thing?" That's when the smell of the food hits me, and I look closer at the bag. "Wait, is that from Sadie's Diner?" *My favorite…*

"Hmm? Oh, yeah. Weird thing to deliver in a place like this." His gaze falls to my hand, and I practically see the dollar signs pop up in his eyes. "Kasey, are you going to tell me why you're at Brent Fallsteen's house?"

"I…" I don't know how to explain this without explaining the truth, but I don't want to out Liam like that. He uses a fake name for a reason. "I, uh, know him. Sort of. I've been helping him write—"

"Is he a screenwriter?" Milo rises to his toes to peer over my shoulder. "I hope your project this week was working on your script because I hear screenwriters can make bank."

They can if they manage to *sell* a script to one of the big studios, but that's not me. I don't even have another good one written. Still, I don't bother correcting Milo. It's one more layer of protection for Liam.

"Anyway, Brent's phone died, so you get your tip in cash."

Milo trades the food for the cash and then nearly screams when he counts the four bills. "What? Kasey, you can't be serious."

I would think it's too much if I didn't have firm memories of Liam paying me more than double that much with my first delivery. Shrugging, I try to play it off like it's nothing to hand over that much money. Milo deserves it, but that money could help pay my rent if I was the one earning that tip.

I really need to get out there. My paycheck this week is already going to be horrible.

"Like you said, Brent is a good tipper," I mutter.

"Am I?" Liam's voice right behind me makes me jump, and I spin around only to collide with him and drop the food at my feet.

He gives me a brief smile before draping his arm around my shoulders and looking at Milo. "How much did she give you?"

Milo looks like he'd rather not say, in case Liam decides to take it back. But I must have read his expression wrong because as soon as he manages a breath, he points at Liam and says, "You're not Brent. You're Liam Connolly." He looks at me, jaw gaping open. "Kasey, you know Liam Connolly?"

I can hear the question he's not asking. I don't blame him for wondering if I more than *know* Liam, given the familiar way he's holding me right now.

Thankfully, before I stumble through what is likely to be a terrible explanation, Liam speaks first. "Kasey and I have been friends for a while. How do you two know each other?"

"We work together?" Milo says, though it sounds like a question.

I sigh. "We run into each other all the time while on deliveries, so Milo and I have become friends."

"She gave me four hundred dollars, Mr. Connolly, sir," Milo squeaks, holding it out as if he intends to give it back.

Liam clucks his tongue. "Kasey, I'm ashamed of you."

I *knew* it was too much! "Sorry, Liam. I just thought—"

"I would have tipped at least six," Liam interrupts. Then, to Milo, "Once my phone charges, I'll add a few hundred to the app so you don't look bad."

"Ha!" Milo claps a hand over his mouth. "Oh, you're serious."

"Any friend of Kasey's is a friend of mine." Liam holds out his fist, which Milo bumps with obvious glee. I'm worried he's going to say something about never washing his hand again.

"Dude, you are the coolest rich person ever!"

Liam grins and looks at me. "You hear that? At least *someone* thinks I'm cool."

I look down at my bare feet. As much as I love him doing this for Milo, he's only making the differences between us more and more obvious. Wiggling free of his arm, I bend down and pick up the food.

"I'll take this to the kitchen before I head out. Milo, it was good to see you. Hopefully we start running into each other again once I'm back on my regular schedule."

"Wait," Liam says, but I'm already walking. And maybe holding back tears because I don't want to say goodbye to him even though I have to.

I set the bag on the kitchen counter and then head for the stairs. My clothes should be fairly dry by now, so I'll change quick so I don't steal another outfit.

"Kasey, wait!" Liam curses when I hit the stairs, probably because his foot is bothering him so he can't move as fast as I am. "Where are you going?"

I keep my gaze straight ahead as I hurry up the stairs. "I told you. I need to go make some deliveries tonight."

"But—" He swears again, this time in Irish, but he's faster than I expected and right behind me when I hit the guest room. "Kasey!" He grabs hold of my arm, his hold tight but not painful. "What's wrong? What did I do?"

Why does that question tug at my heart? It's enough to make my tears spill over, though I swipe them away as I keep my face turned away from Liam. "You didn't do anything."

"I clearly did. Can we talk about this?"

"There's nothing to talk about." I tug my arm free and go into the bathroom, where I hung my clothes to dry. But Liam is still standing there when I come back out, looking at me with the most heart-wrenching expression. I groan. "Liam."

"Kasey." He clenches his jaw.

Hoping he'll figure it out without me having to say it, I let the silence build between us until I can't stand it anymore. "You don't get it, Liam. And I don't think you'll ever get it."

"Try me. Why were you so weird with your friend?" His frown deepens, and he glances at the bedroom door behind him. "Unless he's more than a friend?"

"What? No. Ew. I mean, Milo is great, but he's not..." I shake my head, refusing to get off topic and draw this conversation out longer than it needs to be. "It's not about Milo."

"Is it about what Patty said? Because she was talking nonsense, and—"

"It's not about Patty." I toss my clothes onto the king-size bed and fold my arms. "Not entirely, anyway."

Liam groans, running a hand through his hair. It reminds me of how it felt to do that same thing a few minutes ago. Right before he almost kissed me a second time. "Just tell me, Kasey. You were giving me all sorts of signals a few minutes ago, so what is it about me that's suddenly so repulsive?"

"It's your money!" The words fall from my tongue so easily, but it feels like they take all of my energy with them.

He grows still, eyes so focused on me that I want to hide. "My money?"

How can he be surprised? "This has been a problem since the day we met," I remind him. "You were just so good at distracting me."

"Distracting you from what?"

"The fact that we're from two different worlds, Liam! People like you and people like me—we don't mix."

His eyebrows drop low, almost in anger. "Says who?"

"Says everyone!" And the fact that he can't understand this only highlights my point. "You are so disconnected from the real world that you can't even see how wrong this is." I gesture between us. "You have three cars in your garage, each of which is worth triple what mine would cost brand new, and I've had my car since I was sixteen and will drive it until it falls apart. You live in a mansion in Malibu with a security guard and a view of the ocean, and I can't even pay my friend a measly six hundred dollars to live in her two-bedroom house in East Hollywood because I'm in so much debt that I'm probably going to be paying things off for the rest of my life. You give a random delivery driver hundreds of dollars for a thirty-dollar meal and don't even realize how crazy that is!"

I'm still crying, but it feels like it's only adding to my argument. Only, Liam looks like I punched him in the gut, and my guilt keeps me talking even though I know I should stop because I've clearly made my point.

"I know it's not your fault," I say, "and you're such a nice guy that you have no idea how it feels to be on my end of things. To be a charity case who can't say no to a guy who is willing to pay someone to hang out with him even though it makes me feel insanely guilty. And I have loved these past few days with you, Liam. It's felt like a dream that I will remember for the rest of my life. But it's time for me to wake up now."

Gathering up my clothes again, I head for the door. But Liam is standing in the way. I expect him to step aside and let me disappear from his life before I have to find more excuses why it won't work, but he doesn't move. In fact, he puts his arm out and stops me, closing his eyes with a pained expression.

"Before you go," he says, "I need to tell you something, and you're not going to like it."

I already don't like it, and I have no idea what he could possibly tell me. "What?"

He winces. "It was my publicist who called me, and... Can I see your phone? Mine is charging downstairs."

I would so much rather leave before this gets harder, but curiosity gets the better of me. I hand my phone over, holding my breath as he taps a few times and then hands it back.

He opened up a tabloid article, the kind that Val and I like to make fun of because they always sound so ridiculous. My stomach drops as soon as I read the headline:

Liam's Staycation with His New Lover?

I read the article quickly, though by the end of it—and when I see the picture of us almost kissing on the balcony—my head is spinning too much for me to think straight.

"Kasey?" Liam says my name carefully, like he knows I'm about to snap.

Snap, no. Instead, I run straight for the bathroom and empty the contents of my stomach.

Hollywood Hot Scoop

Liam's Staycation with His New Lover?

I KNOW ALL YOU Scoopers have been patiently waiting for Liam Connolly news, and we here at *Hot Scoop* have finally hit gossip gold. Despite his recent altercation, Liam has been cozy at home in Malibu, and it looks like he's found himself a new lady love to help him pass the time.

While we're still working out who this mysterious beauty is, sources say she's been glued to Liam's side for weeks. (Talk about clingy!) We know this sounds like bad news for us single ladies, but not to worry, Scoopers. Liam Connolly is not one to commit to someone for long, especially someone unimportant like this most recent affair. She may have made herself right at home in his clothes, but we all know the drill. He'll be back on the market before we know it, ready to snatch up another longtime Liam fan and give her a whirlwind romance like he has the rest of them.

Until then, make sure you subscribe for more juicy photos of Liam's new fling as things start to steam up in Malibu. I have a feeling it's going to get good. XO

CHAPTER THIRTEEN

LIAM

I'VE NEVER HATED MY fame more than I do now. I'm stuck just sitting here, nothing I can do as Kasey paces the length of the lounge, clearly on the verge of a full nervous breakdown as she processes this development.

At first I was glad when Ethan called; he gave me an excuse to end that horrid conversation with Patty. But then he started talking, and every word he spoke brought me crashing down in a way I've never felt before. Up until now, my fame has only affected *me*. Now that someone else has been dragged into this world when she clearly doesn't want to be a part of it, I'm seeing red.

Patty is lucky I've got this ankle monitor preventing me from marching over to her house and giving her a piece of my mind. I don't know what I would do if I had a chance.

"Can we press charges or something?" Kasey asks, speaking for the first time in almost ten minutes.

I take a slow breath, trying not to imagine what it would be like to punch Patty. After my response to the harasser at my last show, I don't like the way this all makes me feel like a violent person. I'm not, but I'm not sure that will always be true. If I'm this protective of Kasey when we're not even dating...

Then again, Kasey made it pretty clear I'm not what she wants. Our situation isn't likely to change for the better, and I have to be okay with that.

"Charges against whom?" I ask, though I don't really need to.

Kasey scoffs. "Patty! Obviously."

"Do you have proof that it was her?"

"Who else would it have been?"

I shrug, rubbing the headache that is forming in my temples. "Even if we do press charges, the damage is done. *Hot Scoop* has a crazy wide reach, and that story went viral in minutes."

I have no idea how that stupid website got it up so fast or how Patty knew exactly who to send that photo to. Maybe her love of gossip is because she works for *Hot Scoop*. I wouldn't put it past her to be behind the whole site entirely.

"How are you so calm right now?" Kasey asks. There's a bite to her words that I really don't like, but I deserve it.

"I'm not calm," I reply calmly. "I'm angry."

"That's why we should go after Patty!"

"I'm angry with myself," I clarify, still just as even-toned. I'm too exhausted to put any real feeling into my words. "It's my fault you're in this mess. I'm the one who almost..." I can't bring myself to admit out loud that I almost kissed her. I was already on edge from the whole Ted and Martha thing, and the tumble into the pool, and Nelson being an idiot and attacking Kasey. Then she started running her fingers through my hair, and I couldn't resist her pull anymore.

Now look where we are.

I really need to work on not pushing boundaries, but it feels like I'm wired to toe the line, no matter what it is. That, plus my bad luck, and I should have stayed away from Kasey in the first place. I know better, but something about her messes with my head.

She makes me think I can have more in my life.

Kasey drops onto the couch next to me. "How long until it blows over?"

I am not about to answer that question.

She groans at my silence. "So what does this mean for me? They didn't say my name or anything."

It's the one positive from all of this. "Ethan thinks your identity will be safe for a little while, but he's not confident that you'll remain anonymous for long."

"But how would anyone figure it out? That picture barely shows my face."

"The paps have discovered identities with less." Sighing, I slump down in my seat and close my eyes, trying to think. The article wasn't exactly flattering toward Kasey, and if someone does figure out who she is, they won't leave her alone as they try to get all the dirty details about her relationship with me. This is exactly why my mom uses a fake name and doesn't often come visit me. It's safer for her if we stick to phone calls and video chats.

Man, I miss her. But if I call her now, she'll pick up on my stress, and I don't particularly want her to know about yet another mess I've gotten myself into.

"What does your publicist think I should do about this?" Kasey asks, and I can hear the strain in her voice. She's in over her head, and she knows it.

My phone died before I could have a good conversation with Ethan. I should probably call him back and get the rest of his game plan, but I can already guess what he's going to say.

"Are you really struggling to make ends meet?" I ask instead of answering her question. I look over at her, hating how defeated she looks.

She shrugs. "No more than other people."

"Kasey. I can handle the truth. How bad is it?"

"I went to USC," she says without looking at me. "The film school. And even after financial aid and scholarships, it wasn't cheap. Neither was my dorm. So I've got all sorts of student loans I'm trying to pay off, but I deliver food for a living. Not everyone tips as well as you do."

I chuckle, though I don't feel like laughing. "A moment ago you were angry with me for tipping as much as I do."

"No, I was angry that you think it's normal."

"I don't, for the record." Shifting, I turn to face her and lift my lips in a half smile. "I was twenty-three when I got picked up by Groupline Records. Before that, I was playing in bars whenever I could. Half the time I didn't get paid, and when I did it was next to nothing, so during the day I picked up any odd jobs I could find. Anything to keep my nights free so I could keep playing in front of people and hope something caught on. Meanwhile, my mom worked fifteen-hour days at the salon so we could pay our rent."

Derek is the only person who knows any details about my pre-fame life, and it feels good to let someone else in on the secret. It makes this friendship with Kasey feel more real, even more so than this afternoon. This is the hard stuff. The gritty, uncomfortable stuff that doesn't fit the shiny, carefree persona I let the rest of the world see.

This is me.

"When I was sixteen, my mom found me a music teacher," I continue. "A really good one. I thought he was teaching me out of the goodness of his heart, but it turned out my mom was working night shifts while I was asleep so she could pay for the lessons and afford rent. That teacher taught me so much, but paying tuition took a toll on my mom and nearly broke her before I found out how much she was working. I quit lessons so I could help with the bills, and she didn't complain, which told me just how tired she was. If I can make sure she's taken care of for the rest of her life, I'll die happy. And if I can help other people avoid that stress, I'm going to do it because I know how much it sucks to stress out about having enough money to put dinner on the table every day."

I close my eyes, hating the memories that surface from that time of my life. Those days are part of the reason I've struggled writing another album. The novelty of being famous wore off after my last release earlier this year, and I know how quickly all of this can go away if I don't put out good music. The pressure is enough to stifle anyone's creativity, but the underlying fear is just as bad. With my savings and some investments Cole suggested, I'll likely never slip back to poverty, but I don't really want to take the chance.

To my surprise, Kasey reaches out and takes my hand, tucking it between both of hers. "Liam, I had no idea."

"No one does." It's as much a justification for her ignorance as it is a warning to keep it to herself. I don't need pity driving my success. "I'm just saying I get it. And I'm sorry if I made you feel bad by unintentionally flaunting what I have. That was never my intent."

"I'm sorry for yelling at you." She swallows and looks down at our hands. "Liam, what do we do about this?"

My part is easy; I can't leave anyway, so I just need to lie low and not give Patty any other photos to share. But Kasey... I grimace. "I think you need to stay here for a bit."

She looks up, some fear entering her golden-brown eyes. "How long is a bit?"

"That depends on how long it takes for the internet to lose interest in you."

"A couple of days?" When I don't answer, she squirms and pulls her hands away from mine. "How long, Liam?"

Before I can tell her it's going to be at least a couple of weeks, probably longer, my phone starts ringing on the end table where it's been charging. I'm surprised it took this long, though I'm curious about who is on the other end. Could be Ethan, but I have a feeling it's not.

Kasey looks over, since she's closer. "It's Derek," she says, blushing slightly.

I don't like her reaction.

Tempted to ignore him, I stand and pick up the phone to answer it. "Hey, man."

"It looks like you've got a serious security breach in your neighborhood," Derek says.

"Tell me about it."

"And you're clearly attracted to your 'friend' no matter how many times you deny it."

I really haven't denied it, but I'm pretty sure Derek is trying to understand my level of involvement here. "I didn't mean for this to happen," I tell him, which is true. "And now Kasey has to deal with *Hot Scoop*."

"Is she still there? Can I talk to her?"

I frown. "Talk about what?"

"Give her the phone, Connolly."

I don't want to, but I hand the phone to Kasey, who looks at it for a second before taking it and muttering, "Hello? Yeah, I saw the article." A pause. "I appreciate that."

Derek is happily in a relationship, I remind myself as I start pacing. *He loves Bonnie and isn't making a move on the girl you're falling...* I pause before I finish that thought. I'm not falling. I won't let myself fall. Kasey doesn't want to be part of this life, and I don't know how to be in a relationship in the first place so I would mess things up.

My bad luck would mess things up.

I can't afford to fall, no matter how much money I have. Millions aren't worth much when it comes to happiness.

"Liam thinks I should stay here for a while," Kasey says after listening to Derek for a while. "What do you think?"

Oh good, she trusts a guy she's spoken to for half a second over the guy she's been hanging out with for a week. That makes me feel great. *This* is why I didn't want to introduce them to each other, knowing they would become fast friends. That's not the *whole* reason, but I'm going to tell myself that and hope it makes me feel better.

"How long?" she asks. Then her face falls. "What if I can't?"

"What's he saying?" I ask, unable to hold back my curiosity.

Kasey looks at me but doesn't say anything, listening intently to the man who is soon to be my former best friend. After a long moment, she pulls the phone away from her ear and hits the speaker button. "Okay, go ahead."

I'm instantly at her side.

"You might get lucky with this one," Derek says, "but you might not. It's hard to say where things will go, especially if any other pictures surface."

"That's easy to avoid," I say, though I can't help but remember how close I came to kissing Kasey and caused this whole problem in the first place. This would be easier to bear if I hadn't been interrupted because I feel like I'm paying for a crime I didn't commit. "I can't leave the house anyway, and we'll stay away from the balcony."

"I wouldn't be surprised if your neighbors start coming over," Derek continues. "Probably best to keep them out as much as you can, and don't let them know Kasey is around."

"I'll move her car into the garage tonight." We should have done that as soon as the article dropped, but then I would have had to leave Kasey's side, and I don't want her to feel like I'm not here for her.

Derek hums. "Kasey, I know you're freaking out about being stuck there, but you couldn't be stuck with a better person. Liam is one of the best guys I know."

I smile at the praise. "Thanks, man."

"I've got some table reads this week, but I'll stop by when I can. I know you're struggling, Liam, but Kasey will need someone in her corner with all of this."

As I meet Kasey's gaze, I wonder if she agrees that she needs me. Or anyone. She could probably head back to her friend's house and go about her deliveries and feel a lot more comfortable about things for a little while, but as soon as one of her customers recognizes her—and it *will* happen—she's done for.

I pull my eyebrows together. "You could go home," I tell her, even though I don't want to. "Lie low in a place that's familiar to you, and it would be just as effective as staying here."

"But believe us when we say this kind of attention isn't easy," Derek continues for me. "Even for those of us who have been dealing with it for a long time, it can be hard to bear."

I nod. "No matter how strong and independent you are, it takes a lot of practice and support to survive the attention that's waiting for you out there."

"Paparazzi will be watching the neighborhood soon," Derek says, "so once you decide what to do, you're pretty much stuck with that choice unless you want to make sure everyone gets a clear photo of your face."

Kasey's eyes are anxious and wary, but she seems to be looking at me as a source of hope, not as the reason she's in this mess. She should blame me—I'm definitely to blame—but I think she's smart enough to realize she can't do this on her own. She shouldn't *have* to do it on her own.

She swallows, speaking to the floor instead of to me. "I think it's better if I stay here. I don't know what to expect, and that's terrifying."

"You'll be okay, Kasey," Derek says. "We'll look after you."

"Come over if you have the time, Derek," I say. "We'll make it work here, but I'm going to have to give it my all to keep Kasey from going insane being stuck here with me." I grimace when she raises an eyebrow at me. "She could probably use more than just me with all this."

"I would send Cole over, but he got a concussion at practice today, so I don't want him driving anywhere."

"Oof." My head hurts just thinking about getting tackled hard enough to get a concussion. "Is he okay?"

"I'll make sure he is."

Kasey looks over at me once again, a clear question in her eyes.

I smile. "Derek is protective," I explain, not caring that he can hear me. "Once you're in his inner circle, he'll make sure you're taken care of."

"Like now," Derek confirms. "I'm sure Ethan will be doing as much as he can to quell the interest in Kasey, but if you need some more power behind you, let me know. I know a few people who can help."

I groan, but this conversation is making me feel better. "Sometimes I wonder if you're an actor or if you're actually a spy, Derek Riley."

He laughs. "I'm not a spy."

"That's what a spy would say."

"Just because I played a spy once, it doesn't mean I am one."

"Yeah, but—"

"Thank you, Derek," Kasey says, and I'm pretty sure she's trying to end this conversation. "We'll figure it out. And thanks for making me feel a bit better about all of this."

"You've got this," he replies. "You'll get an up close look at the way Liam and the rest of us live and can decide if you want to be a part of it."

My stomach drops. Why did he say that? Though I'm surprised she chose to stay here instead of hiding at home, I already know Kasey is likely to disappear as soon as she knows it's safe. Derek is practically telling her that she's better off without me, and I said something just as damning a moment ago.

I'm really bad at talking myself up, apparently.

Kasey meets my gaze one more time before handing me the phone and returning to her spot on the couch. She's so hard to read right now, but she certainly doesn't look happy.

"Got anyone who can shut *Hot Scoop* down?" I ask, switching the phone off of speaker and holding it up to my ear.

Derek barks out a laugh. "If I did, I'd have done it years ago. That website is the worst. I'm glad it hasn't hit Bonnie and me yet."

My eyebrows pull together as I consider those words, though it's not like he said anything strange. We talk about the gossip sites all the time and how nice it is that we can avoid them for the most part. Glancing at Kasey, I speak quieter. "Do they have any reason to come after you two?"

"What? No, of course not."

"Lies," I mutter, though I'm not quite loud enough for him to hear me. Derek never lies, which made this little fib starkly obvious. As far as I know, Bonnie is as unproblematic as Derek, outside of her many short-lived relationships, and I can't fault her for her dating life when I'm in the same boat.

"Hey, I should go," Derek says. "You sure you're okay? This will likely turn ugly."

"Mm hmm." But wait, he told Kasey there is just as much of a chance that it will blow over. "Derek, what are you thinking?"

"I'm thinking you should brace yourself. And maybe get that album finished so you can distract people. You're about to get a lot of attention—you already are—and people are starting to speculate about why you're not making any public appearances. Keeping Kasey out of the tabloids is as much for your benefit as it is for hers. You need your trial to go well, Liam."

"I know that." And up until now I wasn't worried. I send a prayer to the heavens, wishing I knew a few in Irish so I could cover all my bases.

"I'll be fine." Do I believe that? Probably not, but negativity isn't going to do me any favors. "Thanks for looking out for me. And for Kasey."

"Good luck."

I hang up the phone and stand in silence for a moment, playing through all the different scenarios in my head. Best case, people get bored before anyone figures out who Kasey is, and she can go back to her real life without any lingering effects from the story. Worst case... There are a lot of things that could go wrong, but I think the worst is Kasey becoming some sort of pariah, though that's a bit of a leap from my new girlfriend. That article wasn't kind to her, and I've seen *Hot Scoop* throw out some pretty slanderous stories that have hurt their targets even when the gossip isn't true.

My stomach clenches when I think about what could happen to *me* if they decide I'm a villain. Their last story about me still felt pretty positive, but they could change their tune in a heartbeat if it means more hits on their site. And if I get convicted for assault, I'll probably lose my contract. Lose my rapport with my fans. Lose one of the few things that have truly made me happy. I can always write songs for other artists, but playing live is half the reason I love what I do.

"Liam?" Kasey comes up to my side and puts her hand on my arm. For the first time since our run-in with Patty, she looks more concerned for me than for herself, and my heart beats harder. I love that she's trying to look out for me, but this is my mess. I need to fix it and look out for *her*. I owe her that much.

"Can I have your keys? I'll get your car inside, hopefully before Patty thinks to get your license plate number and hand that off."

I make it two steps out of the garage when the black box on my ankle beeps, and I freeze, backing up quickly and holding my breath as I wait for it to do something else. It looks normal. Hopefully that was only a warning that I was approaching the edge of my limit.

I let out a curse, tempted to kick one of my cars in frustration. How in the world am I supposed to protect this woman if I can't even step into my driveway? She'll have to move the car herself, hopefully without being seen.

I hate this. I hate all of this.

And yet, as I head back inside to return Kasey's keys, I can't help but be a little bit glad that she's now stuck here with me and I'm no longer on my own.

CHAPTER FOURTEEN

KASEY

ALL THINGS CONSIDERED, MY situation isn't all that bad. I have a massive guest room in a Malibu mansion all to myself, complete with a balcony view and the most luxurious bed I've ever slept in. I have a chef who comes in every other day to drop off pre-made meals that taste like heaven because Ethan decided Liam shouldn't have constant delivery drivers showing up every meal. I even have a sort of paycheck coming in, which Liam assured me was perfectly normal and coming out of his security fund to replace the money I might have made making deliveries if I wasn't stuck here. Ethan's reasoning is that my identity staying secret is helping Liam's image.

But I'm not sure I can do this.

It's only day two of my quarantine with Liam, and I'm already losing my mind a bit. It's like my feet are itching to run for the first time in my life, and a treadmill in Liam's home gym just doesn't feel the same. It almost makes the feeling of being trapped so much worse, like those dreams where no matter how far I run, I can't go anywhere.

Honestly, I don't know how Liam has made it more than two weeks through his house arrest without going completely mad, and I almost understand the parakeet's usefulness. Almost. I've been avoiding him as much as I've avoided Liam.

Val calls me while I'm sprawled out on my bed and staring at the ceiling, and I'm so glad for the distraction.

"How are you holding up, girly?"

I groan. Val is the only person I was allowed to tell once I agreed to hang out here until the tabloids give up on me, mostly because Ethan didn't want her filing a police report and blaming Liam when I didn't show up after a few days.

"I am so bored, Val! How am I supposed to go weeks with nothing to do? I feel like I'm in a strange version of that *Jury Duty* show and I'm the only one who doesn't know this is all fake."

"Oh, I loved that show. So funny!"

"Val, you're not helping."

She laughs, and I can picture her in her studio, performing some crazy feat of yoga with ease. She's tried to teach me some things, but I never had the patience for it. Maybe it's time I start watching more of her videos. What else am I going to do?

"Hon," she says, "you're looking at this all wrong. This isn't a punishment but an opportunity!"

I roll over onto my belly and turn my head so I can breathe, though my voice comes out slightly squished. "An opportunity for what?"

"One, to get yourself a kiss from that beautiful man."

I roll my eyes. "Liam doesn't want to kiss me." He's been avoiding me as much as I've avoided him.

"Girl, I saw that picture. That man has it bad for you and probably doesn't want to make it weird now that you can't leave."

That man is currently swimming laps in the pool, though I've refused to let myself go out to the balcony and watch. Look at me, with my great self-control!

"Val, I think it was just a weird moment because he's been stuck here for so long without any, uh, female company." I know he said he's not that kind of guy, but it's still hard to believe Liam hasn't had intimate relationships with his past girlfriends. I'm not sure any woman could resist him, and he's a guy. In my experience, they're all pretty much the same.

"I'll let you think what you want to think," Val says, her tone indicating how dumb she thinks I'm being. "The other opportunity is a chance to finish that script you've been working on for months!"

I let out a short laugh. "You mean the one I've been avoiding for months?"

"The one you haven't had time to work on because you've been so busy making deliveries to pay off your loans. Now you have time! Not to mention a new boy toy whose best friend is one of the biggest names in Hollywood right now and could get your script into the right hands. Don't think I have forgotten about that, Miss Graham."

I am so glad I haven't told her about the two conversations I've had with Derek, or she would be incredibly mad at me right now. In my defense, I don't actually have a completed script I could send to Derek, even if I wanted to. Not a good one, anyway.

Groaning, I pick myself up off the bed because I've been lying here for at least two hours and should probably move around a bit. I might even take up swimming if I'm here for too long, just to spice things up a bit. "I will think about working on my script," I tell Val, mostly because it's what she wants to hear. "But I will not be kissing Liam. Things got weird the other day, and I'm not about to make things more awkward than they already are."

"You're making a mistake, Kasey, and I think you know it. I would kill for a chance to make out with the likes of Liam Connolly."

"Better not let Vince hear you say that."

"He would probably encourage me! That's a once-in-a-lifetime opportunity that I wouldn't let go to waste if I were you."

It's a good thing she's not me; Val would probably drive Liam crazy.

The doorbell rings, and I immediately go on high alert. The chef won't be here again until tomorrow, and Derek said he wouldn't be able to stop by for a couple more days. That means it's probably one of Liam's neighbors, hoping to scope out the truth. I'm surprised it took them this long.

"Hey, I gotta go, Val."

"Kiss that man!"

With those parting words, I hang up and hurry down the stairs to let Liam know someone is at the door. We've agreed that I should make myself scarce, and he should pretend everything is normal whenever his neighbors come prying.

He's still in the pool when I get to the backyard, and I can't help but wonder how long he's been swimming back and forth. Maybe close to an hour? He's so focused on his strokes that he doesn't notice me as he reaches the near wall and does a fancy little flip in the water to head in the other direction.

The doorbell rings again.

Nerves building, I kneel down and stick my hand in the water so he'll for sure see me when he comes back this way. The cool water brings back memories of the two times I've been inside this pool, neither of them especially pleasant. But both of those mishaps got me closer to Liam.

It's weird to think that one food delivery led me to all of this.

"I'm not sure I like your sense of humor, universe," I grumble right as Liam comes up to me and lifts his head out of the water, pulling off his goggles.

"Hi," he says, out of breath. Seriously, how long has he been going at it? He looks miserable and exhausted and worried, which isn't how he's supposed to look.

I haven't seen him smile in days, and he's starting to look like a different person.

I smile, hoping he reciprocates. "There's someone at the door."

He swears and pulls himself out of the pool, heading straight for the cabinet of towels. You'd think at this point I would be used to seeing his beautiful body, but when it's all on display right in front of me, I can't stop the flush that rises up my face. It feels like I haven't seen him in days, even though we've eaten all our meals together, and apparently I've missed the sight.

Val's words pop into my head, telling me that I'm a dummy for avoiding Liam. She didn't say that exactly, but the implication was there.

Once he's somewhat dry, Liam tugs on his shirt and then hurries inside when the doorbell rings again. He grabs his crutches—two of them—and shoves his foot into the boot that he was wearing the first time I met him. Ethan thought it would be a good idea to play up the injury so people will think he's just recovering and not stuck here.

He's halfway to the door when I realize his ankle monitor is on full display. "Liam!" I point to his foot.

He swears again, looking around for some way to hide it. But it's already been a long wait for him to answer the door, and he apparently decides he'll have to try to hide it as he tucks his good foot behind the boot and opens the door.

I duck around a corner, close enough to hear but out of sight.

"Bonnie?" Liam's voice is as full of surprise as it is excitement.

Bonnie Aiken? As Nelson starts chirping excitedly, I peek around the corner. Yep, it's definitely her. She may not be quite as famous as Derek, but being his girlfriend has quickly helped her rise through the Hollywood ranks. Not that she needs his help. She's one of the better actors out there.

She takes in the crutches and the boot Liam's wearing, frowning in a way that doesn't give her any wrinkles. "What's with the getup? I thought your foot was doing better."

"I thought you might be one of the neighbors coming to sneak a peek."

Bonnie looks up and to her left, one eyebrow higher than the other. "Why didn't you just check the camera?" *That's* where the camera is? I kept looking for it in the wrong direction.

Liam drops his head with a sigh. "I'm obviously not thinking very clearly. Come on in."

Bonnie spots me quickly, and her eyes light up. "Kasey! It's so nice to meet you in person."

Is it, though? Because if I wasn't here, Liam wouldn't be in this mess. "Um. Nice to meet you too, Bonnie Aiken." Did I really just use her full name? Blegh, that is so cringey, even for an awkward duck like me.

"What're you doing here?" Liam asks as he tugs himself free of the boot.

"Making sure you two are still alive over here." She hands a large duffel bag over to him. "Derek's doing a chemistry read with Sylvia Rodriguez, or he would have come with me."

"Are you okay with that?" Liam asks. I don't blame him. Bonnie said it so nonchalantly even though her boyfriend is probably flirting with another actress.

Bonnie laughs. "Why wouldn't I be? It's all part of the job. Now." She comes forward and grabs my hands, catching me off guard with her sudden nearness. "I thought you and I could use a spa day."

A spa day? With the most beautiful woman on the big screen? She's got to be kidding. "But we can't go anywhere."

She leans in and gives me a conspiratorial smile. "That's why I brought the spa to you."

My goodness, she's gorgeous. But it's not an otherworldly kind of gorgeous. It's all natural beauty, girl-next-door vibes and effortless softness in her features. If she wasn't already dating Derek Riley, I would be worried about her catching Liam's attention and pulling him away from me.

Not that I would care. Because I don't.

I swallow, all too aware of Liam studying me from behind Bonnie. "I'm sure you have better things to do than—"

"Hush." Bonnie squeezes my hands. "You have spent the better part of a week in this house with a man who has no clue how to pamper a woman." She holds out my arms so she can study the t-shirt and linen pant combo I'm sporting right now, all of it far too big for me like everything else I've borrowed from Liam. "I brought you some clothes as well. Liam, darling, will you take those upstairs for us?"

I expect him to argue or roll his eyes, but he smiles for the first time in days and passes us without a word. I only get a glimpse of that smile, but it eases some of the tightness in my chest as I watch him make his way upstairs. At least I didn't break him entirely with this tabloid mess. He's still got some sunshine in there somewhere.

"Hmm," Bonnie says.

I frown, my face flushing with heat. "What?"

"Oh, nothing. You're younger than I expected you to be."

"Is that bad?" I'm pretty sure she's in her late twenties, which puts me several years younger than her and makes her even more intimidating. Liam and I are only a few years apart, but most of his friends are older than him. Standing next to Bonnie in the midst of all this tabloid stuff is making me feel like a kid, and I don't love that. I haven't felt young since the mess with my screenplay.

"No, it's not bad." Bonnie's smile is warm and comforting as she tucks her arm through mine and starts leading me up the staircase to follow Liam. "I'm just surprised how well you're taking all of this. I had my first real scandal at twenty-two, but I'd been in the thick of this world for more than three years at that point."

"Does it get easier?" I hope so. I don't think I could survive for long if I always felt this helpless.

"Hmm," Bonnie says again, her blue eyes taking me in with more interest than before. They're almost green, like the color of the ocean, and not as bright as I expected them to be after seeing her in movies. "It does get easier. And having a good support system helps. Especially someone you can hold close when you're going through particularly stormy seas."

"Does Derek make it easier for you?" I don't know why I ask that when it's pretty obvious that he would be that for her, but I'm really curious to see how someone as sweet as Bonnie portrays Derek Riley. Maybe I'll find the courage to finally trust him if I get a better sense of the kind of man he is.

Her smile brightens as she pauses in the hallway. I don't know where Liam is, but for now we're alone. "Derek is my best friend. We've gotten each other through a lot of things, both good and bad, and he has always been my biggest supporter. So yes, he does make it easier. He makes everything easier, for everyone he cares about."

My heart throbs as her words wash over me. Not just because my gut is telling me Derek is as good as Liam believes but also because it's so nice to know people in their world can have happy, healthy relationships. With all the gossip columns and tabloid articles, love in Hollywood seems more like a fantasy than reality.

And since I want to be in Hollywood, though not necessarily in the spotlight like they are, I think I've been holding a lot of fear about finding future happiness if I ever get my career started. It certainly doesn't help that my one and only attempt failed because of a relationship.

Bonnie pulls me tight against her side. "Is there a specific reason you're crying, Kasey, or is it general overwhelm?"

"I'm crying?" I brush a hand across my cheek and laugh when it comes back wet. "I'm guessing it's overwhelm, but also..." I don't know why I so easily trust this woman who is so out of my league, but I do. "I'm glad there's hope for celebrities to find love. People like you and Derek, I mean. And Liam. I'm glad the fame doesn't get in the way."

Chuckling, she guides me forward again, heading for the guest room I've been staying in. "Oh, it gets in the way, but at the end of the day it's nice to go home to someone who won't be watching your every move. Someone who knows you're still human, no matter how people see you. Isn't that right, Liam?"

He pops out from the walk-in closet, making me jump. I had no idea he was in there. "I wouldn't know," he says, still with a small smile playing on his lips. "I've never had a relationship like what you and Derek have."

"You haven't had a relationship, period," Bonnie counters.

My heart stutters when Liam doesn't deny it. He hasn't? But what about his reputation of dating around? And all the stories and articles online that I definitely haven't been slogging through for the last day and a half. (I have. It's awful.)

Liam's eyebrows twitch downward as he watches me, and I can't help but wonder what he's seeing. Whatever it is, it's confusing him. "Hey," he says, blinking and turning to Bonnie. "Did you know Kasey is a screenwriter?"

Bonnie's eyes go wide at the same time my heart does more than a stutter. Why did he just say that?

"Are you?" Bonnie claps her hands even though she's still linking arms with me. "That's amazing! Has anything you've written been made into a movie yet?"

The easy answer would be no, but there's something about Bonnie that brings a ball of guilt into my stomach as soon as I think about telling her anything other than the truth. How does she do that?

"Uh, yeah, actually," I say, though my words come out small because I wasn't ready to admit this to anyone outside of Val.

"Wait, really?" Liam says. "What movie?"

I'm already regretting this, but it's too late to turn back. "Um. *Figure Eight Dollhouse*." I send a silent prayer to the heavens that neither of them have seen it.

"I thought Mitchell Crane wrote that one," Bonnie says, furrowing her brow. "Or are there two different movies and I'm mixing them up?"

"No, it's that one." I sit on the bed and shut my eyes, refusing to look at them and see whether they believe me.

"I'm sensing there's a story here," Bonnie says gently.

I nod. "Mitchell was my TA in my final screenwriting class at USC. And..." I swallow. If I just let it all out, it will be like ripping off a Band-Aid. Maybe. Or maybe they'll think I'm full of it. "He was also my boyfriend for a few months. We both met a producer who came to campus and seemed interested in my script when I told him about it, and Mitchell told me he got a meeting with the guy during one of my finals and offered to take my script to him for me. Next thing I know, my professors are all celebrating because Mitchell made that successful leap into film when so few do."

Silence fills the air around me, broken only by incomprehensible words and phrases from Nelson downstairs. I feel sick, a little bit dizzy, but I also feel lighter than I've felt in a long time. I don't feel as alone as I've been for the last year. Whether or not they believe my claim, speaking the words out loud felt like setting down a backpack full of rocks that I've been carrying since last December.

The mattress sinks beside me, but it's not Bonnie who sits next to me. Liam's warm and solid body is almost familiar even though we've only been this close a couple of times.

"What did he tell you when you asked him about your script?" His voice is soft, but there's an edge to it that makes me shiver. He's angry, but he believes me. That's more than I could have hoped for.

I drop my head onto his shoulder, needing some of that support Bonnie was talking about. He tenses, but then his arm wraps behind me and holds me close.

"He didn't say anything because I never got a chance to ask," I say. "He blocked my number and started having one of his friends answer his phone for him, like he was suddenly some big shot. I guess he is a big shot now."

"That movie did really well," Bonnie says.

"Exactly."

"No, I mean..."

I look up at her, not sure how else I could interpret her comment.

She lifts one shoulder. "I mean that story was amazing. It may not have been an international record-breaker, but that's because it was low budget and had a short production time. Mitchell shouldn't have sold it to the first bidder like he did."

"He shouldn't have sold it in the first place," Liam snaps. "And that producer is as much to blame if he knows who actually wrote it."

"No, I know, I just—"

"He stole from Kasey!"

"It's okay." I take Liam's hand, not sure if I'm hoping to calm him down or because I'm trying to take strength from his indignation. "At this point, it's too late to do anything about it, and I doubt Mitchell has been able to sell any other scripts since then. He isn't a very good writer.

But now…" I take a deep breath. "I want to keep writing, but it's been hard. I've been stuck ever since I found out what he did."

"You're scared to go through that again," Bonnie guesses. "I don't blame you." Her eyes suddenly light up, and she glances between the two of us. "Maybe Liam can help you get over your block!"

"What?" we both say at the same time.

Bonnie nods wildly, like this is the best idea she's ever had. "Yeah, this could totally work. You helped him with his block, after all."

"That's ridic…" Liam purses his lips and then looks at me. "Okay, maybe you did."

"I don't understand," I admit, lifting my head.

Liam's smile has grown, though it's not out in full force like I want it to be. "I've been trying to write my album for months, but I've had nothing."

"But I watched you write a song," I argue. "Multiple songs."

"Yeah. *After* you showed up on my doorstep." He rubs his jaw and looks up at Bonnie, though I'm having a hard time processing the idea that I might have inspired any of those amazing songs he's written. "How am I going to help Kasey if I don't know exactly what she did to help me?"

Bonnie rolls her eyes and then grabs Liam's hand, pulling him to his feet and away from me. "That's what you need to figure out. We have a spa day to enjoy, so you need to clear out." She literally shoves him out into the hall, surprisingly effective considering he's so much bigger than her.

He turns around, eyebrows furrowed and jaw clenched. "What am I supposed to do?"

"Go hang out with your terrifying bird or something."

Okay, I knew I liked Bonnie, but that just sealed the deal. I have a new best friend.

Liam starts to argue, but Bonnie closes the door. The last thing I see is Liam's eyes on me, and his gaze sends a shock through me because it's far more intense than I would have expected.

And the burning sensation that pops up in my chest when I lose sight of him is just as intense. I feel as if something has come to life inside me, and I know it's entirely because of him and the way he lets me be real and raw. Liam is unlike anyone I've ever met, and I'm starting to think he's going to be hard to leave behind when all this is said and done.

That's assuming I'll even want to leave him behind.

Maybe Val isn't so crazy.

CHAPTER FIFTEEN

LIAM

"What happened to staying off of social media?" I stretch my legs out on the couch in my music room, wishing I hadn't answered the phone when Ethan called. "If you want me to act normal, getting on social media is going to be the opposite of that."

"People need to see you, Liam. I've been combing through all the comments and theories, and that's what you need right now. Most of the talk… It isn't good."

"Good buddy bird," Nelson replies as he hops along the back of the couch, enjoying his view out the west windows.

I figured if Bonnie was going to kick me out of time with Kasey, I might as well have some company, and he's been thrilled to be out of his cage again. I don't know how long Bonnie is going to claim Kasey, but it already feels like too long.

Staying away from her yesterday was the worst, but I could tell she needed time to process. But today? Today she told me why she's so jumpy whenever I bring up screenwriting, and I love her for it.

Not love. That's a big word. But I'm so glad to know she trusted me, even if it was because of Bonnie.

"What should I post?" I ask reluctantly. I'm only considering this so I can ask Ethan for a favor in return. And maybe because Ethan is echoing what Derek said the night the photo surfaced. I'd rather not have people figure out that I'm under house arrest, because they'll turn this situation into more than it is. "In case you forgot, I don't get on social media, so I don't know what people are doing nowadays."

Ethan breathes out an audible sigh of relief. He must have expected me to fight him on this. "I thought maybe you could do a live video and show people one of the songs you've been working on. Highlight your foot and that you're taking the time to heal and tell people that it's been really good for your songwriting muscles to have some downtime."

"That sounds easy enough." It really does. I might even bring Nelson into the video with me, since videos of him seem to do pretty well, according to my social media gal. He's got stardom potential when he's not going all murder-bird. "Hey, Ethan, while I'm figuring out this live thing, can you do something for me?"

"Do what?"

"I need you to look into someone." I pause for a second, wondering if I should give him all the info or keep it as vague as possible. He'd probably better know as much as I can give him if I want his searching to be productive. "Someone who hurt Kasey."

I explain the situation, and though Ethan tells me he isn't sure what he'll be able to dig up, he promises to try. I end the call by telling him he's almost as cool as Jordan, which makes him laugh.

And I relax a little. Kasey says there's not anything that can be done, and maybe she's right. But I want to make sure she's *really* right.

After I text my social media coordinator for my password—it's been too long since I actually logged in—I hold out my finger for Nelson to hop on. "What do you say, buddy? Want to help me with a video?"

"Good bird!"

"I'm assuming that means yes."

I get him situated on my shoulder and then grab my guitar. Hoping for the best, I hit the live button and throw on a smile.

"Hey everyone! Long time no see. I know there's a lot of talk going around right now, so I wanted to give you all an update on what I've been up to. Nelson and I have been hard at work on my new album—isn't that right, buddy?"

He nods his head with excitement, though I'm pretty sure it's because he sees himself on my phone screen. Most of the comments showing up are about Nelson, which is good. Hopefully he'll keep people's attention off of Kasey.

"Buddy bird!" Nelson says happily. "Chicken soup. I knew you were trouble."

I reach up and pat his head. "Anyway, I've been stuck at home for the last little bit after injuring my foot, but I'm happy to report things are healing nicely." I lift my foot up to show an awkward angle of the boot, and the comments start going crazy. "It's kind of the worst. You know me; I can't sit still, and I'm really hoping my foot heals up quickly so I can get back out there with you guys. I think Nelson has enjoyed having me around, though, haven't you, buddy?"

He starts whistling one of my new songs, and I can't help but grin. That's the perfect segue.

"Oh, I like the way you think, buddy. You guys want to hear one of my new songs?"

I watch the comments for a second, glad to see the growing excitement from my fans. Ethan was right, and this seems to be helping my image. If nothing else, I'm reminding people that the reason they care about me is because of my music, not because of a random picture of me and a girl.

"I don't know…" I scratch my chin and then run a hand through my hair, which prompts several emoji explosions. "I'm not sure you guys really want to hear it."

The comments keep coming, and my view count starts climbing. People must be telling their friends that I'm about to drop some new music, and my smile grows. I've missed this. Not the social media part but interacting with my fans. They always manage to fill me with light and life and make everything feel okay.

I knew this house arrest was wearing on me, but I didn't realize how bad it was getting. Suddenly I can breathe again.

When the viewers start getting impatient, I grin. "Fine, I'll play you a little something."

Resting my fingers on the first chord, I close my eyes and let the music fill me from my chest to the tips of my fingers. I've never fully understood where the music comes from, but it feels like a part of me. Something I can't ignore or pretend it's a figment of my mind. It's tangible and electric and alive.

When I pluck the first notes, a simplified version of the first song Kasey inspired, I know immediately that I picked the right song for how I'm feeling today. This one is about fate bringing two people together. At first, I'd thought it was about friendship, but this doesn't feel like friendship.

I wouldn't be angry with Bonnie being here if Kasey was just a friend. In fact, I'd be glad that others in the group are accepting her. But the only thing that has kept me downstairs is knowing Derek would thrash me if I was rude to Bonnie and kicked her out so I could reclaim Kasey's attention for myself.

Once I play through the intro, I start singing.

Middle of the night, with the moonlight smiling down,
I thought life was pretty perfect in my sleepy little town.
Then a star flew 'cross the sky and pulled my gaze down to the street,
And there I found you walking with no shoes upon your feet.

The chorus is all about the woman in the song telling me that I've been living in fear and I need to embrace life and live it to the fullest, and I can't stop my smile. I close my eyes as I move into the second verse, singing about a spark that has come to life from my encounter with this fearless girl and how it feels like something bigger than us brought us together when we meet again at the diner in town.

It's a flipped narrative from reality—Kasey seemed so afraid to live when I first met her—but I still feel this song deep in my chest as I think about the last three years. I've always been an open person, comfortable in my skin, but finding my friends changed me. When Derek brought me into his little fold, I realized I could decide whose opinions mattered to me. I could lose my fame overnight, and it wouldn't change who I am. I don't think I would have found that peace without fate putting me in Derek's path. All of us have helped each other in some way over the years, and I wouldn't trade any of them for anything.

The third and fourth verses are all about how there are no coincidences in life and how everything is determined by our choices, and my choice led me to this fearless girl who has shown me a better way to live. The final chorus shifts a bit, switching from living life in fear to living life with intention. Accepting that there are some things that are so important that our choices will always lead us to them. Those are the things we don't want to ignore or forget.

I sing the last line with a bit of a break in my voice because it's so tightly woven into my soul that it tugs at my heart.

Maybe fate was right all along.

The outro comes easily, ending on a hopeful note that settles deep in my chest. I really do think Kasey and I were meant to meet. Even if it only ends up being friendship on her end, she came into my life at a time when I would have drowned without her. Ha! Irony. But I was starting to forget what was most important to me, and I needed something to remind me why I worked so hard to get here.

Nelson starts whistling the tune of the song I just finished, tugging me back to reality and reminding me of the camera pointed at me.

I chuckle and hold my finger out to him so I can bring him closer to my phone. "And now for the real star. Show them what you've got, Nelson!"

I give him a few more seconds to sing and dance with himself on the camera, and then I pull him back and give my fans a wide smile. "Let me know what you guys think of the song! I'm hard at work getting more music out to you all, so keep a lookout for my next album. Maybe even some more surprise song drops!"

Though the comments keep coming, I end the live and save it to my profile so people can watch it even if they missed it today, and then I fall back onto the couch with a weary sigh. The high of performing is wearing off quickly, leaving me restless. Ethan was right to have me do that, but now I feel more trapped than ever knowing my only link to the outside world is that phone, and singing to a little screen isn't nearly as fulfilling as singing to a packed stadium. I'm only two and a half weeks into my house arrest, with another three and a half to go, and now I need to make sure Kasey is doing okay and not losing her mind alongside me.

Three more weeks before I can leave this house and show her what my world is really like. Why I love my life despite its pitfalls and struggles. I can't help but think that if she sees the side of it that I love, then maybe she'll understand why she doesn't have to be afraid of this world. She doesn't have to leave.

Fate brought us together, but in the end it's going to have to be her choice on whether she embraces it or lets a good thing pass her by.

Chapter Sixteen

Kasey

When Bonnie leaves, she does it with an enthusiastic hug and a promise to come have dinner with me as soon as she has a free night. I don't want her to leave, though I have no idea how she became such a dear friend in only a few hours. She's the kindest, sweetest, most unassuming person I've ever met, and that is the farthest thing I suspected from one of the biggest names in Hollywood.

Derek must be really great to be dating someone like her.

Bonnie also promised to tell Derek about my writing so he can ask around and see what studios are looking for. It's not a promise to get a script into someone's hands, but it's a way to give me a direction to go as I figure out what to write.

"Be patient with Liam," she tells me as she grabs the handle of the front door. There's a twinkle in her eyes that has been there all day, even though she hasn't brought up Liam like I expected her to. Though she's said his name a few times, it was mostly in relation to the others in their little friend group. Now, however, she seems to be insinuating something with her smile. "He is a really good guy, but when it comes to relationships, he's always been a bit lost. He never saw what a good relationship should look like."

"He told me something about his mom's many boyfriends," I reply. "But not much."

Bonnie nods. "I think his mom did her best. I know some of what that's like. Sometimes you have to experience something to learn it, but I think Liam is ready to take on the challenge." She winks. "If you are."

Am I ready? Liam has been a friend, and the last couple of days have been stressful and weird. But after a day of pampering with Bonnie, I'm feeling calm and relaxed and up for anything. Especially where Liam is concerned. I've weirdly missed him over the last few hours, like I've misplaced something important and can't remember where I put it.

"We'll see," I say, though I can't stop my smile from spreading across my lips.

Bonnie grins and glances behind me. "I think you two might be good for each other."

"Does this mean I'm allowed into the rest of my house again?" Liam's smooth voice fills the room with warmth. Even my cheeks blush hot, and I refuse to turn around and show him how much he affects me now that I don't want to avoid him anymore. I'm not ready for him to have that power, even if I don't know what he would do with it.

He would probably kiss me. Finally. And I would let him.

"I was bored out of my mind," he continues as he reaches me.

Bonnie snickers and shakes her head. "I saw that video you posted, Liam. You were perfectly fine. I like the new song, by the way."

Which song? I immediately want to grab my phone and search for whatever video Bonnie must have watched while I was in the shower, but I resist the urge and keep my hands tucked behind me.

It's a good thing too, because Liam's fingers brush against my shoulder as he passes me and pulls Bonnie into a hug. "Thanks for taking care of Kasey. You're the best."

I'm not jealous of the way he's holding her. I have no reason to be jealous. But that doesn't mean I like how he leans his whole body into that hug. I wouldn't mind a hug like that, and *okay fine I'm totally jealous!*

Wrapping my arms around myself, like that might curb my sudden need to be held by this handsome heartthrob, I focus on keeping my expression neutral and unbothered.

Bonnie looks over at me as soon as she's free. Though she's make-up-free and in casual clothing, she's still absolutely gorgeous as she smiles at me. "Kasey, you're strong enough to get through this. I promise."

"Thanks," I say, since that's better than telling her I don't believe her. It's only been two days, and I have an indeterminate amount of time ahead of me. I'm not sure if anyone is strong enough for something like this.

"I'll be back!" Bonnie says and heads out.

Liam waves, but two seconds later he stiffens and says something in Irish again before he slams the door shut.

My heart jumps into an uncomfortable rhythm as he stuffs his hand into his hair and looks back at me. "What was that?" I ask, though I can guess pretty easily that he was swearing again and something is wrong. "What happened?"

"Paps."

"Paparazzi? How did they get in the neighborhood?"

Liam moves to the window and peeks through the blinds, his expression tight. He already has his phone pressed to his ear. "Johnny? Why are there paps in front of my house?" He groans, pressing a hand to his face. "Of course they did. Can you... Yes, I would appreciate that. They accosted Bonnie on her way out. Thanks."

As soon as he hangs up, I leap forward and look outside with him. Only, Liam has those accordion blinds that are all one piece so I have to look in the same place he's looking on the side, which means I end up pressed against him. I'm as focused on the warmth of his body behind mine as I am on the three guys still trying to get photos of the house.

I duck down in case they notice us in the window. "What did they do to Bonnie? Is she okay? Do I need to go rescue her?" That would be quite the sight for the tabloids—me running at them with my arms in the air and complete terror in my expression. I act confident and unbothered, but I'm not that brave.

"No, she's fine." Liam crouches beside me, and his hand rests on my shoulder as he continues to gaze outside. If it could stay there forever, that would be great. It's not a hug, but it's contact. "She deals with paps all the time and knows how to handle herself. That's not the problem."

Can I be Bonnie when I grow up? "What's the problem?"

Liam growls. "I guarantee there will be a story in the next five minutes about how Bonnie is cheating on Derek with me." He huffs a humorous laugh. "On the plus side, that might get you off the hook if they decide that it was Bonnie up on the roof with me. You two do look fairly similar, and your face wasn't clear in the photo."

Is it bad that I'm feeling hopeful about that outcome? I don't want Bonnie's life to get difficult or Derek to think his friend is being a world-class jerk, but I wouldn't mind the chance to get back to my normal life.

"So..." I settle myself on the floor. "Are we just supposed to wait around for this story to show up?"

To my delight, Liam sits next to me, one of his knees pressed against mine. It's weird, sitting here on the floor by the window, but I'm not about to move. "Waiting is pretty much our only option. If we tried to head off the story, it would look like we're hiding something."

"Which we are," I point out.

"But we don't want them to know that. We want them to think I'm living my normal life, free of drama and mysterious, beautiful women."

I tilt my head to one side. "Did you say women plural? Am I not your only secret lover?" As soon as the word leaves my mouth, heat splashes across my face.

Liam traces the blush with his eyes, which only makes it worse. I didn't fully comprehend how close he is until I made eye contact with him. "What," he says, "you want to be my one and only secret lover?"

I shiver. "I hate that word. *Lover*. It sounds so..."

"Intimate?" Liam's lips twitch. "That's what makes it so fun, isn't it?" Then he catches me completely off guard when he reaches over and brushes his finger across my cheek. Apparently it wasn't enough to trace my blush with his gaze; he needed to touch it. "You look different," he says, and his voice has dropped half an octave.

Chuckling nervously, I look down at the tank top and leggings that I picked out from among the clothes Bonnie brought. She brought me a variety of things, but I've gotten used to lounging around in Liam's clothes. This felt like a good middle ground.

"I'm finally wearing something more my size," I say with a shaky laugh. "No more teenage hooligan vibes for me."

"No." Liam's finger moves to my other cheek, though I doubt it will feel any different from the first. Not for him, anyway. On my end, it feels like he's lighting my skin on fire. "No, *you* look different. I think having Bonnie here was good for you. She's better company than me."

"That's not true." I grab his hand, both to save myself from blushing even harder and because I want him to believe what I'm about to say. I don't know where my sudden boldness is coming from, but I'm willing to run with it while it lasts. "You're great company when I'm not too busy avoiding you."

"You were avoiding me?" Goodness, he looks miserable.

I wrinkle my nose. "You seriously didn't notice?" What does that say about me? For the last two days, I've been missing his presence but haven't been confident enough to be around him, thanks to this whole mess Patty started. If he didn't even notice I wasn't around him...

He laughs and laces his fingers between mine. "Oh, I noticed. I just didn't realize it was intentional. I hoped you were just overwhelmed."

"I was. But also..." I take a slow breath and then sigh. There's probably no value in keeping things to myself, given our forced proximity. Honesty is the only thing that will keep us sane. "I'm worried you're going to get sick of me."

For a moment, Liam seems completely stunned, like he couldn't have imagined that response. His eyebrows are pulled together, his mouth slightly open, and his hand squeezes tighter around mine. Then he laughs, and the sound fills me with relief. I've been missing that sound as much as I've missed his smile.

"Kasey," he says, inching closer. "You forget that I spent more money and time than I care to admit trying to get you back here after that first day we met, and I've found reasons every day since to keep you here. If anyone is going to get sick of someone, it's you."

I don't think anyone could get sick of Liam Connolly. His positivity and cheerfulness are infectious, and I've never met anyone who can be so talented but so down to earth. Plus, he has this habit of humming and singing under his breath pretty much any time he isn't talking, and I'm not sure he even knows he does it. It's the cutest thing.

I was brave when I told Liam and Bonnie about Mitchell and my script. Maybe I can be brave again and let this man know that I want to be here.

"What if we start over?" I say, pulling my hand free of his and then holding it out for a handshake. "Hi, I'm Kasey. I am a screenwriter who hopes to write something worth putting on the screen."

Liam studies my hand for a moment, and then he grins widely and takes it in a firm hold. "Hey. Liam Connolly. You've probably heard of me."

I think about it for a second. "Hmm. Don't think I have. Are you a friend of Val's?"

He laughs, and the sound fills me with life. I need to get that laugh out of him whenever humanly possible if I'm going to make it through this ordeal. "Okay, I'm sorry for being an egotistical idiot. I'm Liam, and I'm a musician. I write songs that make you see the world differently. At least, that's my goal."

"If your other songs are anything like the three you've written this week, you're definitely reaching your goal."

He gasps, putting his free hand to his chest. "Are you telling me you haven't listened to any of my other songs? Kasey, I thought I'd gotten through to you!"

I grin as the last of my nerves melt away. "We just met, remember?"

"Fine. In that case, you should listen to 'Tangle' because I think you'll really like it."

"You wrote a song called 'Tangle'? That sounds naughty."

There's that laugh again, and he swaps hands and holds mine in a more comfortable position, entwined together on his leg. "It's not how it sounds. It's about getting caught up in the busyness of life and forgetting what's important."

"I love that idea. Can we listen to it right now?"

Liam grabs his phone so quickly that I can't help but laugh at his excitement. But before he can pull up his music app, Ethan's name lights up his screen. He sighs, looks up at me with an expression that says *I told you so*, and then answers the call on speakerphone.

"Let me guess."

"Maybe clear it with me before you start bringing your friends into this," Ethan replies. "You're just making this messier, Liam."

"It wasn't his fault," I complain.

Ethan's quiet for a second. "Hi, Kasey."

"Bonnie came over on her own," Liam says. He's grinning at me like he doesn't have a care in the world. "I'm already forbidden from leaving my house; don't you dare tell me I can't see my friends either. I don't want to have a reason to fire you and bring Jordan back."

I raise an eyebrow. "Who's Jordan?"

"Only the best publicist in the world."

"Why aren't we working with him?"

"Because he went and got married, the loser."

"Why does that make him a loser?"

"Well, because he—"

"Liam!" Ethan lets out a deep sigh. I have a feeling he does that a lot when working with Liam. "In case you haven't seen it, there's a new picture of you on *Hot Scoop*. You and Bonnie."

"You mean me waving goodbye to Bonnie?"

"Wait," I say, suddenly realizing something. "How did they get in the neighborhood in the first place? The guard didn't let them in, did he?"

"He did," Liam says, "but it's because they were delivering food to one of the other houses. Someone must have noticed that I was getting a lot of deliveries and thought they could get in that way."

"That's a serious weakness in the neighborhood's security," Ethan says. "I'll fix that. And no, Liam, it is not a picture of you waving to Bonnie. It's a picture of you welcoming her *into* your house. Which, frankly, is worse. Why did she have a duffel bag?"

Liam frowns. "She brought clothes for Kasey. Why did it take this long for them to post something? Bonnie just left, but she got here hours ago."

"Maybe they were hoping for something juicier," Ethan says. "Regardless, *Hot Scoop* is trying to convince everyone that you and Bonnie are an item, so now I get to deal with Fran on top of everything you've already given me."

"It's not my fault," Liam says.

"Yeah, I know. It's never your fault."

I meet Liam's gaze, and though he's clearly frustrated, he's still smiling. It seems doing a re-meet was a good idea, and maybe I can keep him happy like this going forward. *Maybe.* That might depend on what happens now that this new story is out there.

"Who is Fran?" I ask so I can stay in the loop with everything.

"Derek's publicist," Liam says at the same time Ethan says, "Bonnie's publicist."

I raise my eyebrows. "They're dating *and* they have the same publicist?" I don't know why, but that sounds strange, like there's a weird conflict of interest in there somewhere.

Liam studies me for a moment before turning his attention back to the phone. "What do we need to do to fix this, Ethan? And what does it mean for Kasey?"

I love that he just asked that. Technically, Liam being in a romantic entanglement with Bonnie probably puts me in the clear, but I'm glad he's still worried about me. It makes me more convinced that he's not going to hate me by the end of this.

"Let me talk things over with Fran," Ethan says. "And please, for the love of all that is good and holy, stay away from windows and doors. If I see your face, chest, butt, *anything* on *Hot Scoop*, I really might quit. Got it?"

A laugh breaks out of me as soon as Liam hangs up the phone. "Butt? Please tell me your *butt* hasn't been on the internet."

Liam groans as he gets to his feet. "I can't do that."

"Liam!" I take the hand he offers, still laughing as he pulls me up. "Why—and when—was your butt on the internet?"

"It wasn't my fault!" Red in the face, he starts pulling me toward the kitchen, hopefully because he's as hungry as I am. I didn't realize it because Bonnie is so distracting, but I'm starving. We didn't eat lunch.

"I have a feeling you say those words a lot," I say.

Sure enough, we stop in the kitchen, and Liam starts rummaging through the meals the chef left in the fridge. "That's because it's usually true. Orange chicken or braised pork and asparagus?"

"Oh, those both sound good."

"Both it is." He pops the two meals into the oven and flips a switch to turn it on. I'm pretty sure it's not a normal oven; if I tried doing that at home, the food would burn to a crisp during the preheat stage. But so far all of our meals have turned out delicious. It's magical.

Liam hops onto the edge of the counter and smiles. "Really though, I have terrible luck. Always tend to be in the right place at the wrong time, no matter what I do."

"That sounds like an excuse, Liam Connolly." But I smile to let him know I'm joking. "Is that what happened at your concert? When you punched that guy?"

He nods. "I don't condone violence unless absolutely necessary, but there was no one else around to protect the girl. I couldn't not help."

I'd almost forgotten about the reason behind his house arrest. It's hard to believe I actually thought this guy was anything but purely good when he keeps giving me reasons to see the best in him.

"So... Why was your butt on the internet?" My face flames again as soon as I ask the question. I may have seen this man naked the first time I came over, but he was sitting down. I did not see his butt. And it's not like I *need* to see his butt, but curiosity has gotten the better of me.

Liam narrows his eyes. "I feel like you're going to look up the story as soon as I tell you."

I bite my lip. "It's either that or start searching for it blindly, and that feels dangerous." I would never do that, but he doesn't need to know that.

Wincing, he seems to debate with himself for a moment before he drops his head and says, "I was going for a run on the beach and there was a bee swarm that someone was relocating right as I ran past, and they needed help lifting the box they were using. I somehow managed to startle the bees, and several of them flew up my shorts." He shudders and shakes one leg, as if he can feel the insects again. "By some miracle I didn't get stung, but I did lose my shorts and everything else in the process. Dove into the sand to keep the rest of me hidden."

I'm trying so hard to hold it together. Laughter is building in my chest, but I press my hand over my mouth to keep it in because this isn't the sort of thing I should laugh at. But how can I not?

Liam rolls his eyes. "Go ahead. My friends had a good laugh about it too."

I crack, busting up so hard that I can't stand straight. "Poor Liam," I gasp. Somehow I've ended up closer to him, practically leaning on his knees as I fight to curb my amusement.

His fingers find my hair and run through it. That shuts me up immediately. "It's funny now, but it wasn't so funny in the moment. I was pretty new to the celebrity scene and had no idea what that kind of, uh, exposure would do to me."

I look up, and though his hand in my hair is incredibly distracting, I try to stay focused because this part of the conversation is important. "So you know how I feel right now?"

His smile turns soft as he continues to play with my hair, which is far silkier than it's ever been because Liam's shampoo is as magical as his oven. "I know exactly how you feel," he says. "And more. I've been through it all, Kasey, so no matter what Ethan and Fran decide we need to do, I know we can get through it. Do you trust me?"

My natural instinct is to say no, but the word catches in my throat. I don't know how he worked his way past my defenses so quickly, but he did. I nod. "You've given me no reason to believe otherwise."

He beams at that, his hand moving from my hair to my neck so his thumb can rub my cheek. "Thank you." He cocks his head to one side. "And thank you for telling me about Mitchell and what he did with your script. That sucks, but I'm glad you told me."

I duck my head. "It does suck. But I've gotten over it. Mostly."

"I would love to help you with a script, if that's what you want to do while you're stuck here."

There's something thrilling about the idea of Liam Connolly being a part of my writing process. I got used to getting critiques in school, but getting feedback from someone as important as Liam, even if he's in a different industry, feels like taking a step in the right direction. Plus, his friends are exactly the people I should know if I want to break into the film industry.

Looking back up at him, I smile and press my hand over the top of his. My hips are pressed against his knees now, and I'm genuinely surprised by how easy it is to get this close to the man. We're not a couple, despite what the tabloids thought the other day, but I can be comfortable with this man in a way I've never been before. I like that.

"Well," I say, "I did promise Bonnie that I would try to get a script finished by the end of the year."

Liam chuckles. "Is that the only thing she made you promise? She's good at convincing people to do things."

"If she wasn't so nice, I would be terrified."

"You know it's October, right?" Liam asks next. His other hand moves to my waist as he adjusts his knees and pulls me closer. "That doesn't leave you a lot of time."

This kitchen is entirely too warm now. I smile, though it's shaky. "Luckily, I seem to have all sorts of time on my hands now that I can't do any deliveries. Maybe you'll be able to inspire me to finally finish something." Oh, that felt a lot like flirting. Am I flirting? Liam seems to be, with the way he's still stroking my cheek with his thumb and holding me close enough that we're tangled up together.

"I'll happily inspire you," he says huskily.

I figured starting over would start us at the beginning of whatever this is, but Liam seems to be moving right along, just like he did the first time we met.

As thrilling as that is, it's also terrifying.

Swallowing, I put my hands on his arms because it feels like the most natural place. His muscles flex beneath my fingers, and his smile stretches wide.

"Liam?" I say, my voice coming out small.

"Kasey?" His eyes are roaming my face so tenderly that it almost hurts.

"What are we doing?" That question is too vague, so I ask another to clarify. "What's happening between us?"

It's the kind of question I was never brave enough to ask Mitchell, though I wish I would have. In my mind, we were long term. According to his friend, I was just a means to an end. I should have realized that Mitchell only paid me any attention after he read my script the first time. Should have noticed the way he gave my work such deep workshopping when he should have spent the same amount of time with it as he did all the others.

Liam tucks my hair behind my ear and then moves that hand to join the other at my back. "We are…using this opportunity to get to know each other better," he says slowly. "As for what's happening between us…" He leans forward and presses a kiss to my forehead. "It feels like something good. But…"

I meet his gaze, holding my breath. "But?"

"But I don't want to ruin whatever this is by making this a right person, wrong time situation. You're stuck here, and that may or may not change for the foreseeable future. I don't want to take advantage of that. Take advantage of you."

Oh, my heart. That is one of the swooniest things I've ever heard. "You'd better be careful, Liam Connolly, or the world is going to find out you're a big softy under all this muscle."

I poke his stomach as if I need to demonstrate what muscle I'm talking about, and he curls in on himself and straight up giggles.

I raise an eyebrow. "Are you ticklish?"

"That's not a question I'm going to answer honestly." He grins and takes hold of both my hands. "I have a proposal, Kasey Graham."

"Oh?" Whatever it is, I'm probably going to want to say yes.

Nodding slowly, he pulls our clasped hands together and holds them against his chest. "I propose that you and I get to know each other over the next few weeks, or however long I get to keep you. No strings, no pressure, just two people learning more about each other."

I put on a thinking face, even though I don't have to consider this at all. "Hmm, I think I can get behind that idea."

He snorts. "Oh, you think?"

"I'm still hoping this new development with Bonnie gets me off the hook." It's supposed to be a joke, but as soon as I say it, my heart sinks. I don't actually want that. I want an excuse to stay here, away from reality, for as long as I possibly can.

So when Liam wraps his legs around me to tug me closer, I can't help but match his grin. "Call me selfish," he says in a low voice, "but I hope you're wrong. I'm not ready to let you go just yet."

Would it be a terrible thing to kiss him after a line like that? I'm thinking not, and I even lean in. But my mouth has another idea first. "That sounds like a good song lyric," I murmur and then close my eyes.

Liam never comes the rest of the way. Though he's still holding on to my hands, he's suddenly tense, and his heart rate has picked up a notch against my fingers. When I look at him, he's gazing back at me but with a distant look in his eyes.

"Liam?"

"Hold that thought." He grabs his phone and starts singing into it. *"Maybe it's a lifetime, maybe it's a year, maybe we were never meant to be, but to be clear: I'm not ready to let you go just yet."* He hums a couple more lines of melody and then stops recording, his eyes bright and excited. "Well, I know what I'm doing tonight. Want to help?"

Uh, he's asking if I want to help him write a song? I felt weird enough singing harmony to the other one, and I'm no poet. I'd probably make it sound terrible compared to the magic that Liam just pulled out of thin air.

Laughing, Liam nudges me to the side so he can jump down and check on the food in the oven. "Whatever you're thinking, I'm sure you wouldn't be that bad at songwriting. But if you don't want to help, maybe you can work on a script while I get this song hammered out?"

"Oh, I like that idea. But I don't know what to write. My last project fizzled, and I don't see it really going anywhere."

"So you need something new?" Liam grabs a towel and uses it to pull the food out and onto the counter. It's steaming and looks absolutely delicious, though I still don't know which one sounds better.

He grabs two forks, handing one over to me, and then he starts eating, alternating bites from each. "What kind of stories do you like to tell? You said something about mystery the other day, and *Figure Eight Dollhouse* was pretty cerebral."

My eyebrows shoot high. "You watched it?"

"Derek told me it was good when it came out, and I trust his opinion when it comes to what movies to watch."

Suddenly I feel dizzy. It was weird enough to know Bonnie had seen the movie that came from my script, but Derek is a much bigger deal. "Derek...saw it?"

Liam nods, unconcerned as he keeps digging in. "You could write another one like that."

"I don't think so." Before he can eat all the orange chicken, I take a bite, groaning when the tangy sauce hits my tongue. "Oh, this is amazing! I might never leave if it means I can keep eating meals from this chef of yours."

Liam's face lights up. "I'll keep that in mind. Why don't you want to write another thriller?"

I shrug. "Because it'll make me think of Mitchell and his dumb face."

"I don't know what he looks like, but he must be dumb if he let you go. I won't make the same mistake." He winks, sending a wave of heat through me. "So you might write something different?"

"Maybe a comedy. Though, I'm not sure I'm funny enough to write comedy."

"I think you're plenty funny," Liam argues. "You could write about my neighbors. I'm sure they've got all sorts of good material they could give you, even if Ted and Martha might be more of the true crime type of story."

I take a bite of the pork, which is just as good as the chicken, and then sigh. "It's going to be a lot harder to check up on your neighbors if we can't go onto the balcony."

"I'm sure we'll find a way, and the back balcony should be safe." He perks up. "For the others, I could order a bunch of cameras and get them delivered in a couple of hours, and then we could install them in the dead of night so no one sees us."

I laugh and point my fork at him. "I know you're joking, but I like the way you think."

"I don't have to be joking." Liam grabs his phone again and pulls up a shopping site, searching for security cameras while he keeps humming the melody he recorded a minute ago. "I've never been all that curious about my neighbors, but after this murdery stuff with Ted, and Patty being her busybody self, I want to see what all the hype is about."

I glance at his phone and nearly let a curse slip out when I see the total cost in his cart as he finishes adding everything he wants. Oh, to be able to drop thousands of dollars without flinching.

"Someday I'll throw around money like you," I mumble.

Liam looks over at me. "You're not still mad at me about this, are you? Because I can pretend I don't have money. I got really good at living the frugal life for a while, and it's not a bad way to live."

Be still my heart. Reaching over, I hit the order button and give him a smile. "That feels like a waste. You do have money, after all, and you might as well do something with it."

I don't think Liam could be happier if he tried, and for a moment I can't look away. It's so easy to make this man's day, and I can only imagine what a lifetime with him would be like. In fact, I *want* to imagine that. Eating meals together, working on our projects, going for drives along the California coast... It may be hard to imagine Liam away from his house because I've only ever seen him here, but I'm loving this little fantasy I've fallen into.

I'm starting to really like the idea of keeping this man in my life.

"Kasey?" Liam moves close, so our shoulders are pressed together, and his smile falters a bit. "Do you think you can be happy here?" It's like he's in my head.

I drop my head onto his shoulder, like I did in the bedroom earlier. He liked it then, and he seems to like it now as he relaxes against me. "I think so, Liam."

"Good. Will you tell me if that ever changes?"

That feels like openness and vulnerability, which hasn't been my thing since Mitchell. Liam makes it look so easy to be genuine, and something in me wants to return the honesty he's given me. Somehow, he seems to have seen the frightened woman behind the shield I've carried all year, and it hasn't scared him off. Besides, if I can't trust *Liam* with all my softest parts, who can I trust? "I'll tell you."

"Promise?"

I take a deep breath and tell myself to keep being brave. I think it will be worth it. "I promise. But for now, I'm not ready to let you go either."

Hollywood Hot Scoop

Has Liam Found "The One"?

SORRY, LINNIE FANS, BONNIE's still happily in love with Derek despite strong signs that our favorite actress was making a move on her beau's best friend. While I'm as disappointed as all of you that we won't get to enjoy a thrilling affair full of drama, there are plenty more mysteries to unravel. We're all wondering what was inside that duffle bag Bonnie brought to Liam's house. Leave your theories in the comments!

Looks like Bonnie is still loyal to Derek, much to everyone's surprise. The dynamic big screen duo was seen keeping their romance alive all over Los Angeles this week, including on the roof of Liam Connolly's Malibu mansion, and I think we can all agree that Dennie is still one of the cutest couples we've ever seen. I for one am hoping for some dazzling news—AKA a shiny new ring on Bonnie's finger—in the near future!

As for Liam, he has yet to make an appearance in public since his last show, which has us here at *Hot Scoop* wondering if Liam has found his soulmate and wants to keep her all to himself. Our sources are certain the pair have been enjoying a staycation of epic proportions—could the duffel have been for Liam's lady love?—and we'll be sure to give you all an update as soon as we figure out who the mysterious beauty is. After all, the two of them can't stay in loveland forever! Regardless, Liam was looking mighty happy during his time with Bonnie and Derek, and only love can give a man that kind of smile.

This girl could be the one.

Stay tuned and be sure to subscribe for all your Liam's Lady news here on *Hollywood Hot Scoop*! XO

CHAPTER SEVENTEEN

LIAM

"WHAT'S ANOTHER WORD FOR being in love?" My brain feels fried, though that's probably because it's almost one in the morning.

Kasey looks over from her spot on the couch. She looks half asleep just like I am. I missed the point where she burritoed herself in blankets, but the little of her that I can see now is adorable. She's always adorable. "How many love songs are you writing, Connolly?"

I smile and stretch my back. I've spent too much time sitting on the piano bench lately, but Kasey has gotten comfortable in her spot on the couch, and I'm not about to mess with the status quo. It's been two weeks since Bonnie's visit, and they have been two of the best weeks of my life.

I've never had a sounding board when it comes to my music, at least not one who doesn't have skin in the game, and Kasey is surprisingly good at critiquing. For someone who claims to not like music, she has a lot of opinions on my songs and isn't afraid to tell me when something isn't working. She's almost always right.

Maybe it's just the fact that a lot of these songs are about her, but Kasey has helped make this album my best one yet.

"They're not all love songs," I say, though eight out of ten is a strong argument for this album being a love album. If Kasey has been my inspiration, these songs are probably trying to tell me something.

I've been ignoring them.

The album is the cherry on top of a friendship unlike anything I've ever had. Yeah, Derek is great, and so are the others, but Kasey is so down to earth and real that she makes me feel normal again. She's not afraid to make fun of me and tell me when my jokes are stupid, but she's also quick to laugh and build on inside jokes in the best ways. She's smarter than she lets on, and she's kind to my staff when they show up, and the longer she's been here the more comfortable she's gotten. Sometimes I even imagine her walls are down all the way and she's letting me see the whole woman she is beneath the fear and uncertainty.

What I wouldn't give to know for sure that she trusts me with everything. I feel like there's still so much I can learn about her that she won't let me see.

I know I'm falling and falling hard, but I'm so afraid of messing things up that I haven't let myself think about my growing feelings for Kasey. She has seemed happy to stick to friendship, so I keep telling myself to be happy along with her. It's better than letting my bad luck curse scare her off. Until I get some sort of sign from her that this could be something more, I'm keeping the ball in my court. Biding my time.

Failing to fight a yawn, Kasey sets my laptop on the floor and resituates herself into a tighter ball. "It's okay if they're all love songs. I like those. Smitten, enamored, charmed, captivated, mad."

I raise an eyebrow. "Mad?"

"You know, like when you're mad about someone? It feels more British, though." Her words come out mumbly and cute as she closes her eyes.

We should go to bed, but every night it gets harder. She sleeps just down the hall from me, but it feels too far away. I keep pushing things later and later each day, delaying the moment of goodnight. For some reason, it's even harder tonight to call it a day and head to bed. We've been in the music room for the last six hours, and it almost feels like she likes it in here as much as I do.

Aside from Nelson, she's the only other person I've allowed in my music room. Not even Derek comes in here.

Maybe she'll want to hang out for a bit longer without working?

"How's your script coming along?" I ask. I get up slowly, moving closer to her and wondering how she might react. "You've been pretty focused all day."

She smiles without opening her eyes. "Well, it helps that your neighbors are getting more interesting. They make for good inspiration."

Chuckling, I sit on the end of the couch by her feet, lifting them up and moving them to my lap. This isn't a new position for us, but usually she's more aware of me. That means tonight I have to keep my hands to myself. *Well, that makes me sound like a creep.* I clench my hands into fists to stop myself from doing anything like massaging her feet. I mean, who wouldn't want a foot massage? No one. But Kasey hasn't asked for one, so I can't give her one. I'll keep my hands away from her.

But I end up holding my hands awkwardly above her legs, which is dumb.

Why am I being so weird? This wasn't the plan when I came over here. I mean, I didn't have much of a plan to begin with, but it certainly wasn't to act like I'm afraid to touch her. Even if I am.

"Yeah," I say, trying to dispel the awkwardness that seems to be filling the room like floodwater. "I don't care what you say; I'm pretty sure Gina is having an affair with Patty's husband."

Kasey opens one eye, lifting an eyebrow to go with it. I fold my arms so she doesn't see the way I've been hovering them above her. "You're just hoping for drama, Liam Connolly."

"I hate drama!" I hold my hands up again, this time in a show of innocence. "But you can't tell me Gina going into the Carmichaels' backyard in the middle of the day while Paul works from home isn't totally suspicious." When I put my hands back down, they happen to land on top of Kasey's legs. Not intentionally, just naturally because it's the most comfortable spot.

Kasey doesn't react to my touch, though her lips twist up in a smile. "There could be all sorts of reasons she would go back there."

"Every day? And name one good reason to go into someone's back-yard without them knowing." My fingers twitch, wrapping around Kasey's ankle. Involuntarily, of course. I'm not even technically touching her because the blanket is between my hands and her legs.

Kasey rolls her eyes. She's waking up now that we've broached the subject of my questionable neighbors, which probably means my hands are going to move again so she doesn't think I'm trying anything. "Maybe she's checking to make sure Paul hasn't flipped a lid and buried Patty in the backyard like Ted did to Martha."

"We haven't seen Ted in over a week," I argue. "For all we know, Ted was in a whole murder-suicide situation."

"Why are we so dark and gloomy?" Kasey stretches, arms coming out of her blanket and a huge yawn making me yawn in return. Then she sits up, legs still over my lap, and drops her head onto my shoulder.

I stop breathing. She's basically cuddling with me, which *is* a new development, and I have no idea what to do with this situation. You would think, after spending all day with a person for more than two weeks, I would have figured things out with this woman, but each passing day makes me less and less certain about what our future holds.

I know her so much better now from all our time spent talking about our lives, speculating about the neighbors, and eating the amazing food my chef brings over, but I have no idea if she'll ever want more than friendship.

I've never wanted something like this, so I don't know how I'm supposed to get it. Asking her feels like a good way to scare her off.

"Do you think Derek and Bonnie will come over again?" she asks, yawning again. "They're still filming their movie, right?"

I nod. "But they're filming in LA for a couple more days, so they might have some free time before they head to Europe."

After Ethan talked to Derek's publicist, Fran, the two of them decided Derek and Bonnie should come over and have a barbecue on the balcony with me so we could all put on a show of being good friends with no drama. Derek and Bonnie amped up their relationship anytime one of my neighbors was outside. They spent plenty of time making out, which made me want to go inside to the office where Kasey had started working on a new script out of sight. But the plan seemed to work, and the internet stopped speculating about a relationship between Bonnie and me, switching back to wondering who my new lady friend is, even though there's been no new evidence of her.

I have no idea why everyone is still so interested or how they know Kasey is still here. One of my neighbors, probably Patty, must be keeping tabs.

That means Kasey is stuck, but she hasn't complained. Neither have I. I've never written so many songs all together like this, and Kasey says she is on a roll with the script she's working on, even if she won't tell me what it's about. Apparently I have to wait until it's finished before I can read it.

My phone buzzes in my pocket, and I have to reach around Kasey to get to it. That also means I end up wrapping my arms around her, but if the way she snuggles closer means anything, she doesn't mind.

I snort when I see the text and hold it out for Kasey to see.

Cole:

> Freya is coming into town tomorrow and has ordered that I join her in checking on you and Kasey for brunch tomorrow.

Kasey lifts her head to look up at me. "Does Cole not want to stop by? I thought you guys were friends."

That makes me chuckle. "We are. But Cole is grumpy on a good day, and he doesn't do well with people telling him what to do."

"Is that why he left the NFL? I guess it would make sense that he plays scrum-half so he can call a lot of the shots."

Laughing, I shake my head. "I still can't believe you're a rugby fan. That alone should have been enough to get him here." He's famous in his sphere, but not enough so that your average person knows who he is unless they're a football fan with a good memory. Everyone and their dog has heard of Derek, and I think that bugs Cole sometimes, but he's the one who gave up his promising career in a multi-billion-dollar industry to play on a team that only sees action a few months of the year.

Kasey takes a deep breath, leaning more heavily against me as she exhales. I take a leap and tighten my hold, elated when she smiles. "And do you promise Freya isn't as intimidating as she sounds?"

"Nope. She's every bit the princess you would imagine she is. But she's also incredibly kind, if a little pushy, and she'll only push in ways she thinks are good for you. She's usually right."

"As long as she doesn't expect a lot from me."

"She's going to love you." I love that she's trying to understand my friends. It makes this all feel like it could last. "But maybe I should let you get your beauty sleep, just in case."

"My room is so far away," she moans as she hides her face in my shoulder.

My phone buzzes again, this time with a text from Freya.

Freya:

Apologies for the late text, but I thought you should know that I am bringing Cole over in the morning before I attend a business meeting. You should ensure Kasey is prepared so I do not catch her off guard.

Liam:

I don't think it's possible to prepare anyone for your presence Peach.

Freya:

Then do your best. I do not wish to scare her off when she has clearly been good for you.

Liam:

Then why bring Cole with you?

Freya:

Because Cole has broken with his girlfriend and needs to be around other people.

"What?" My audible question makes Kasey jump and look up.

"What's wrong?" she asks, rubbing her eyes. Had she fallen asleep while I was texting?

Though I'm tempted to call Cole, I doubt he'll answer the phone. He and Sage have been together for *years*. A breakup is no small thing. "Apparently Cole and his girlfriend broke up."

I send a text to Derek instead, wondering if he's even awake. He tends to stick to a schedule when he's filming, and it's exceptionally late. To my surprise, he answers quickly.

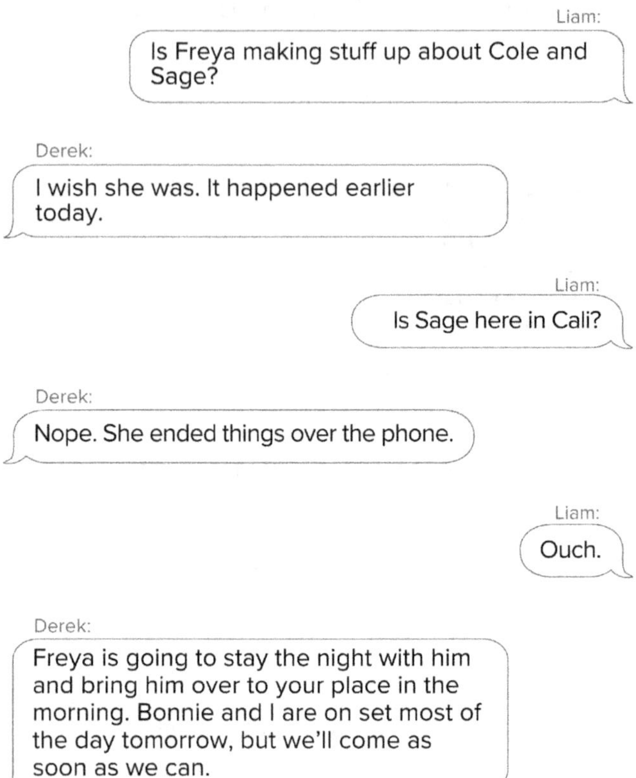

I frown. That sounds like Derek wants me to keep Cole here until he can come over. I mean, I love Cole, but I'm not sure I can handle the heartsick version of him for very long. Not when I'm just barely making some headway with Kasey. His grumpiness, which in this instance is warranted, might set the two of us back another couple of weeks, and I don't know if I have that kind of time.

I *know* I don't have that kind of patience. The line I set for myself with Kasey is begging to be crossed.

"Sounds like your whole group is coming over tomorrow," Kasey says, clearly still reading my texts. "We should have the chef bring more food when he comes in the morning."

"That's a good idea."

"We can eat outside by the pool. We haven't used the dining area in the backyard yet, and I've been wanting to use that fancy china you have for some reason."

Does she know how domestic this all sounds? She's talking about my house like it's *our* house, and I've never heard anything better than that. I'll give her everything I have if she stays. And I need to give her every reason to stick around.

"I know you didn't get much of a chance to talk to Derek when he was here before," I say. "And who knows when he'll be able to come over again, since he and Bonnie are heading to Europe to finish filming. What do you think about showing him your script tomorrow?"

She stiffens. Maybe I said the wrong thing. "I don't know," she says slowly. "It's probably not very good."

"I would disagree, but I haven't actually seen it."

"That's because I'm pretty sure it's awful, Liam."

"I highly doubt that."

She sits up and scowls at me, though right now it's just as adorable as her sleepy face and I can't really take her seriously. "Liam, you don't know anything about how I write."

"Obviously you write well enough to get something turned into a movie."

She huffs a frustrated sigh. "That was probably a fluke. It doesn't mean I can do it again."

I could argue, and I want to, but I know imposter syndrome when I see it. It wasn't until well into the success of my second album before I believed I could make it in the music industry, despite being a household name by that point. Eventually I figured out that life is a lot less miserable when I allow myself to feel proud of my accomplishments and talents. I won't always write Billboard hits, but I know I'm a good songwriter.

I'm just not sure how to help Kasey get to that point with her screen-writing.

"What if you let me read some of it?" I offer, though I already know what she's going to say.

Wincing, she looks down at my laptop. "I don't know, Liam. I feel like you're the kind of person who will tell me it's good even if it's terrible."

"Why would I do that?"

"Because you're unerringly nice. Like, the other day." She pulls her legs from my lap and tucks them underneath herself as if she's gearing up for an argument. "I *know* you wanted the last slice of cheesecake, but you gave it to me."

I lift an eyebrow. "That's your argument? Cheesecake? I hate to break it to you, but this lactose-hating belly doesn't do well when I eat too much ch—"

"You always do my dishes for me."

"That dishwasher is really hard to load," I say with as much sarcasm as I can. "Besides, I don't even put it away. Lucy does that when she comes to clean—"

"You sent your housekeeper home with a box full of food the last time she was here," Kasey interrupts, pointing at me. "And put in a grocery order to send to a homeless shelter."

"You saw that?" The back of my neck starts to feel hot, but I have a feeling she's not done.

Kasey rolls her eyes. "You get up an hour earlier than me every morning so you can let Nelson out of his cage for a bit without scaring me, and don't think I haven't noticed you distracting him every time I have to go near the front room."

I'm trying to make sure she's comfortable here while she waits out the tabloids' interest in her. "Kasey, that's not—"

"That's why I think you won't be able to give me honest feedback. It might kill you to tell me it's not any good."

I narrow my eyes. "Is that what you think?" I've given feedback before, when I've met other musicians or done workshops at high schools or music camps. I can usually work in some actual critique among the praise. But if Kasey doesn't think I would actually be helpful, I'll have to give her someone who would be.

Unlocking my phone, I type out a quick text and send it before Kasey can look over.

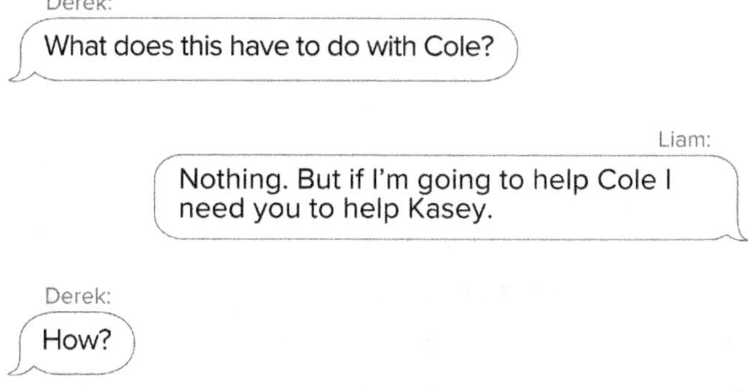

"Who are you texting?" Kasey asks, her eyes going wide.

I jump up before she tries to grab my phone and see, glad that my foot isn't giving me any problems tonight like it usually does when I've been sitting for a while.

"Liam?" Kasey stands too, though she has to untangle herself from the blankets, which buys me a little time. "Liam, you'd better not be doing what I think you're doing."

Derek:
What if she doesn't want me to read it?

Liam:
She wants to be in Hollywood. She can't do that if she doesn't put herself out there. She's dying for you to read it even if she doesn't know it.

"Liam!" Kasey lunges for my phone but ends up smashing into me instead. I lose my balance as well as my grip on my phone, and we tumble backward toward the piano. Thankfully, I hit the bench instead of the baby grand, landing flat on my back with Kasey on top of me.

My phone buzzes with a text, and we both turn our heads to look at the screen as it lights up on the floor. Most of the text is cut off, but we can see the first bit.

Freya:
Cole thinks he would rather be alone, but he

Kasey frowns at the phone. "I thought you were texting Derek."

Thank goodness he didn't respond yet, though he's bound to do so any minute. I need to distract Kasey before he does. I wrap my arms around her back, holding her against me even though this position is wildly uncomfortable. This is closer than we've been in weeks, and I feel like our snuggly moment on the couch a moment ago was like my first taste of authentic Mexican food, and now I'm addicted.

I don't know how much longer I can keep thinking of Kasey as a friend.

"You know," I say, "if you wanted to cuddle, we could have done that on the couch a lot easier."

Her cheeks blaze with a delightful pink. "As nice as that sounds, that isn't—" She cuts herself off when I grin. "Liam Connolly, you are trouble."

"So everyone says, but they tend to keep me around anyway. It's probably because I'm so nice."

Scoffing, she tries to push herself free, but I've got her locked in. "Liam."

"Kasey."

"I'm exhausted, but I'm not going to fall asleep on top of you like this."

"I wish you would." Ah, I probably shouldn't have said that. I'm as tired as she is and enjoying her nearness a little too much. Still, it's too late to take the words back, so I push forward even though she's blushing like crazy now. "I'll release you," I tell her, "but only because I want you to want to be in my arms. I already told you I don't want to let you go—wrote a whole song about it—and that hasn't changed. I'm..."

No, I can't tell her how much I like her. Not while she's still a prisoner.

I swallow and loosen my arms. "I'm nice to you because I want you to be happy here."

To my surprise, she doesn't get up, resting her head on my chest with a sigh. "I am happy here, Liam. More than I thought I would be."

Did she really just say that? She must hear the way my heart starts pounding like crazy, but she keeps talking as if she didn't say the words I've been aching to hear for weeks.

"I didn't realize how much I missed writing until I got this chance to do it again."

Oh. Okay, so her happiness has nothing to do with me. That's fine. Totally fine.

I sit up, pushing her with me until she's straddling my lap. This is the kind of place I've started imagining her being, but I highly doubt reality is going to follow my fantasy, where we end up making out in front of the piano.

Okay, yeah, I'm definitely getting creepy. We've been locked up in this house too long.

Making a mental note to check on the status of things with Ethan tomorrow, I smooth Kasey's hair and give her a soft smile. "You can't keep your writing to yourself forever, Kase. Someday, you're going to have to be brave and put it out there, or what's the point?"

She shrugs, her eyes on my collarbone rather than my face. "What if I'm not cut out to be a writer?"

Words of encouragement make it to the tip of my tongue before I hold them back. She thinks I'm too nice to be helpful, but those two things aren't mutually exclusive. Maybe I can show some tough lo...like. Tough *like*. That's a thing.

"If not a writer, then what?" I ask.

Kasey's eyes jump up to meet mine. She's tired and needs to get to sleep soon, but not yet. Not until she gains some confidence. "What do you mean?"

I shrug. "If you don't want to write screenplays, what do you want to do with your life? Deliver meals to people who probably have plenty of time to cook their own food but choose laziness and convenience, like me?" There's nothing wrong with the way I live, but I'm trying to paint a certain kind of picture to help my argument. "Keep driving a car that looks like it's one pot hole shy of falling apart? What's Plan B?"

She blinks. "I don't...I don't have a Plan B."

Letting my smile grow, I lean forward and kiss her forehead, stroking her hair while I do. I've done that a couple of times since meeting her, so I hope she takes it as a gesture of comfort. "Then maybe don't freak out about Plan A not working out until you've given it a real shot? If it's not meant to be, you'll figure out what is."

"Easy for you to say," she grumbles, looking around the music room. "You're a literal rags to riches story come to life, Liam Connolly. You have everything you could ever want."

Not everything. And I had to work for all of this. I know she knows that, but I can't blame her for seeing the end result of all my hours spent playing to indifferent crowds. I've talked about my past struggles multiple times over the last couple of weeks, but while we're surrounded by the opulence of my impulsive home purchase, I can see how it would be hard for her to imagine my life before all of this.

Before my agent walked into the right coffee shop at the right time in one of the rare moments things worked in my favor.

When fate decided to give me something good.

It's the same thing that brought Kasey to me, and I know better than to let her slip through my fingers. When life hands you lemons after a lifetime of rotten fruit...

"We should go to bed," I say and gently lift her to her feet. "You're going to meet royalty tomorrow, remember?"

As she nods and follows me upstairs, fear fills her expression and leaves her a bit green, and I hope she can get some decent sleep tonight even with that prospect before her.

"Freya will love you," I remind her when we reach her bedroom.

We both pause, a silence settling between us that makes me antsy. Even having Kasey here hasn't completely cured me of my aversion to the stillness of an empty house. I think it's because she's only temporary. As soon as it's safe for her to leave, she's going to go, and I'll still be stuck here.

At least until my trial, which is still almost a week and a half away.

Ten days is an eternity when it comes to my house arrest, but it's not nearly enough time when it comes to having Kasey nearby.

"Thanks for trying to make me feel better, Liam," she says, the first to break the silence. She's always the one who ends up calling it a night. If it were up to me, we would never leave each other's sides. "I'll think about what you said when it comes to my script, but I'll mostly be focused on the whole princess encounter I'll be having."

Rolling my eyes, I ignore the buzz of my phone in my pocket and take a step closer to Kasey. "She's going to love you," I say once more. "Just like I..." I choke on my words and swallow them back down.

"Goodnight!" Kasey squeaks that word and disappears into her room, shutting the door behind her with *oomph*.

"Nice going, Connolly," I grumble on my way to my own room. I check my phone before tossing it onto the couch with a sigh.

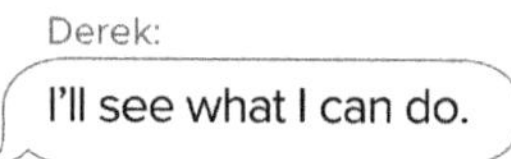

Derek can do a lot of things, but I'm not sure even he can make things happen with Kasey when she's so hesitant to trust people. I hope she'll show him her screenplay, but if she doesn't...

I may have to accept that our friendship has a time limit, and one of the best friends I've ever had is going to go back to her own world as soon as she gets the chance to leave mine.

Chapter Eighteen

Kasey

There are no internet searches to prepare you for meeting a princess. (Trust me, I looked.) Instead of sleeping, like I should have been doing, I spent much of the night studying up on etiquette and customs, how to bow and words to avoid. But when Princess Freya Alverra of Candora steps through Liam's front door, all of that research suddenly feels like gibberish.

My confusion starts when Liam runs straight for the gorgeous blonde, head down low like he's going in for a tackle. It almost looks like an extreme bow but in motion, and Freya's eyes go wide as he approaches. The dark-suited man behind her—the one with every outward indication of being a royal bodyguard—flinches but otherwise allows Liam to wrap Freya up in a bear hug and lift her off her feet.

And Freya *laughs*. It's not a prim and proper laugh but a honking sort of giggle that is instantly endearing.

"Will you put me down, you big oaf?" she says as Liam spins her around a couple of times. Her accent, a mix between posh English and gentle Scandinavian with a dash of something unique, is stronger than it was when I heard her on the several video calls Liam has been on with his gang of famous friends. Her beauty is stronger too. Like Bonnie, she has that natural sort of porcelain beauty that is either real or the product of thousands of dollars of treatments and skin care regimens but no one will ever know for sure. Her blonde hair is thick and glossy and perfectly styled, her blue eyes bright and intelligent. Outside of being far smaller, she and Liam almost look like siblings with their similarities, which is exactly how I'm going to think of them so I don't get overwhelmed with wild jealousy.

"Where's Cole?" Liam asks as he steps back from her.

We all follow Freya's eyes toward the open door, where the rugby scrum-half is leaning against the door frame with his hands in his sweat-pants pockets and a surly glower in his eyes.

"I figured I'd let you get all the excitement out of your system," he grumbles to Liam before stepping inside. He *looks* annoyed, but he opens his arms anyway and accepts the enthusiastic hug Liam gives him.

I guess they really are friends, like Liam said last night.

I swipe my fingers under my eyes while everyone is distracted by the tender man-embrace happening, hoping I covered my exhaustion well. Even before my deep dive into royal etiquette, I was up later than I should have been. I barely remember my conversation with Liam outside of complaining to him that he's too nice, which probably means everything else I said was equally nonsensical.

I do remember Liam looking at me differently and feeling a tug in my gut as he did, though that tug has been regularly making an appearance for the last two weeks, so it's nothing new. It has been incredibly hard not to imagine my life staying like this, and it's going to feel like the rug being pulled out from under me when it all calms down and I have to go back to real life.

Liam has quickly become my best friend, a position Val was eager to concede even though I've been pretty tight-lipped about my growing affection for the man. It's so easy to be comfortable and open with him that sometimes I forget how terrified I am to fully let him in. I even find myself imagining far into the future, picturing us both old and gray as we keep creating our respective art, laughing at little jokes we share and giving each other a safe space to be vulnerable. It's such a warm and happy future that it's becoming a nightly sort of dream as I lie in bed and wonder if he'll let me stay after everything shifts back to reality.

I'm not ready to lose him. I don't know if I ever will be.

"You must be Kasey."

I realize too late that Freya is coming my way and I should have come forward instead of hiding by the stairs and daydreaming. I tense up, forgetting everything about bowing and what to call her and how I should avoid eye contact.

She only makes it a few steps before her bodyguard steps in front of her and narrows his eyes at me. "State your name and your business," he says in a commanding tone. His accent is far thicker than Freya's, sounding more Dutch, almost German, and his gruff voice makes him instantly terrifying. It doesn't help that he's somewhere in his fifties and built like a bear.

Before I can even open my mouth—not that I would be able to say anything anyway—Freya puts her hand on his arm and gracefully twists around him, bringing herself far closer to me than I would have expected. "Don't mind Gregor," she says, rolling her eyes in a way that suddenly makes her look less like royalty and more like a friend. "He doesn't trust as easily as I do, despite posting men at the entrance to the neighborhood *and* along the property lines." She looks up at him with frustration in her eyes. "When are you retiring, Gregor?"

"As soon as I have found you a viable replacement," he grunts back.

Freya sighs. "Kasey is not a threat to me. Are you?" she adds, turning back to me.

I shake my head, which probably isn't very convincing.

"There, you see? Go play with Liam's cameras. I hear he has added several more since the last time we were here."

Something like glee enters Gregor's eyes, catching me off guard, and when he heads down the hall to the little office that Liam set up as his security room—where we've been watching his neighbors—everyone else seems to relax. Even Freya.

"Wow," Liam says, his eyes on the hallway where the bodyguard disappeared. "That was easier than I expected. The first time Gregor met me, he threatened to pull out his lie detector."

Freya scoffs. "Yes, well, Gregor has since learned to do his background checks *before* meeting people. My sincerest apologies, Kasey," she says to me, her smile growing as she looks at me freely now. "He is getting extra protective in his old age, and as he has been my protector my entire life, you cannot blame him for struggling to find the motivation to leave my safety to someone else. May I hug you?"

My eyes go wide. "What?" I choke out, my tongue dry.

"Do you not like hugs? That is no problem." She holds out a delicate hand, which I take with shaking fingers. "Oh, you are even more darling than Liam has described you!"

"Hey!" Liam complains. He's still standing in the foyer with an arm around Cole's shoulders, even though Cole is far broader than him. Cole doesn't seem to love the affection, but that scowl could easily be his default. "That makes me sound like I haven't been singing her praises."

"You did her an injustice, Liam. She is far more beautiful than you painted her."

"I said she was gorgeous!"

Did he? Heat splashes across my face as the two of them continue.

"Perhaps," Freya concedes, "but you didn't say she looked so shrewd."

"I said she was—" Liam grunts when Cole elbows him in the ribs.

I wasn't nervous to meet Cole, but as he turns his gaze to me, suddenly I feel exposed. If anyone in this group is shrewd, I'd put my money on him. Plus, he somehow manages to make Liam look small, which I didn't think was possible. "I suggest you stop talking about Kasey like she isn't standing right here," he growls. "Kasey, it's nice to officially meet you."

"Oh!" Freya spins around, taking both of my hands. "Yes, it is lovely to finally meet the woman who has turned Liam Connolly's head. I was beginning to think she wouldn't exist."

I honestly have no idea what to do with that, though my blush decides to grow. I don't think there's any makeup in the world that can hide the color rising in my cheeks, but I can't turn my face away because a princess is holding my hands. *A literal princess.* There were no forums on the internet that told me what to do in this situation, and I'm pretty sure my palms are starting to sweat.

"Freya," Cole says, more gently this time, "you're scaring her."

"No!" Finally my tongue unsticks from the roof of my mouth, and I shake my head wildly. "No, I'm just...surprised, I guess?"

"Liam!" Freya scolds. "You said you would prepare her."

He grins. "I also said there's no preparing for someone like you, Peach."

"Psh." Pulling me toward her, Freya smiles warmly as she squeezes my hands. "Yes, I am the heir to my throne, but I have learned to be more..." She cocks her head to one side and looks at the men. "What is the phrase you like?"

"Down to earth," Cole says at the same time Liam says, "Peasant-like."

She rolls her eyes as she turns back to me. "Down to earth. I have learned that from my American friends."

I blink, and while I know I shouldn't say it, I can't help myself. "I hate to break it to you, Your Highness, but I'm not sure celebrities are your best bet for learning something like that."

Liam busts up laughing, and Cole cracks a small smile, which feels like a win because he got dumped and probably isn't in a smiling mood.

Freya shrugs. "Perhaps. But anything is better than the life I know in the palace."

"It's more of a castle," Liam argues, which makes Cole's smile grow.

Something tells me this group knew what they were doing by bringing Cole here, of all places. Not only might it help Liam feel less trapped, but also I don't think even a heartbroken man could be miserable around Liam Connolly. I know I can't, even with all signs pointing to my life never going back to normal. Liam's publicist wasn't thrilled about the latest *Hot Scoop* article—no one is losing interest in figuring out who I am, like, *at all*—but my worries about it all have been shoved to the side thanks to Liam and his friends. Today, I've been too focused on making sure everything is perfect for Freya's visit.

Liam kept telling me all morning that she really is pretty chill, all things considered, but that hasn't made me any less nervous. It's not just Freya. It's Cole too, and Derek and Bonnie will be here later, and it feels like the bubble I'm in is once again getting close to bursting from growing too large.

"Well," Freya says, lifting her head high in a straight posture I don't think my shoulders are even capable of. I feel like I'm standing like the Hunchback of Notre Dame next to her. "Something smells absolutely delicious! Did you cook for us, Kasey?"

I snort a laugh. "Definitely not."

"We know Liam didn't," Cole says and makes his way toward the kitchen, following Freya.

Liam pauses by my side, his eyes bright and his smile easy. "Are you totally traumatized?" he asks.

I wrap an arm around my stomach, running my finger along the silk fabric of the blouse I haven't worn before today. Though Bonnie brought me a whole bunch of stuff, I've mostly stuck with Liam's clothes because they're far more comfortable. But I thought I should wear something nicer to meet Freya. "I think I'll survive, but I feel totally lame and unimportant."

"You get used to it."

I elbow him in the side, making him laugh. "*You* get used to it, but I'm on a whole different playing field here. How am I supposed to relate to a *princess*?"

Tucking his arm over my shoulders, Liam starts directing me toward the voices that have made their way out to the patio and the brunch spread I laid out after the chef dropped it off. "You don't have to relate to her, Kasey. Just be you. She'll appreciate that a lot more than you fawning over her or treating her like she's royalty."

"But she *is* royalty."

"I know. But trust me. One of the reasons Freya comes to the States as often as she does is because she can be herself around us. Living the life we do, we all need to feel normal sometimes."

We haven't talked much about our different worlds over the last couple of weeks. At least on my end, talking about our differences only makes them more pronounced, and it's nice to pretend we have things in common. No matter how much he struggled in the past, he doesn't live like that anymore and probably never will. Especially not with his new album being as amazing as it is. His new songs are going to make him more famous than he already is.

"Is that why you call her Peach?" I ask, forcing my thoughts away from our different lifestyles.

Liam chuckles. "She looks like the character from the Mario games, and I accidentally called her that the first time I met her because I was pretty starstruck. She had no idea what I was referencing at the time, but she liked it so much that it stuck."

Cole and Freya are already sitting at the outdoor dining set when we get outside, both of them at ease in Liam's house in a way that makes it clear they've been here many times before. Obviously Freya lives in Europe—Candora is a small island between England and Denmark—but Cole has his own house somewhere in the valley, just like Derek and Bonnie. I wonder if they have a sort of rotation on where they go when they hang out or if they're the type of friends who show up at random times because they know they'll be welcome.

Aside from Val—and maybe Milo—I don't have friends. I left everyone behind when I moved to California, and I was so focused on school that I didn't bother making friends in any of my classes. Except Mitchell, of course, and that clearly didn't work out for me. I wonder what it would feel like to have a whole close group like this. People who know each other well enough to tease and joke but still look after each other when things are hard.

Liam doesn't move his arm from my shoulders until we're practically sitting, and I don't miss the way he sits in the seat directly next to mine and scoots his chair closer. I may not remember much about last night, but I remember him holding me close. I remember him saying he wishes I would fall asleep on him. Did he mean it? His nearness feels slightly possessive, and I wish I could know what's going through his head. He's not humming anything right now, so it's hard to guess.

Most of the time, I can figure out exactly what he's thinking about by looking up the lyrics of the song currently stuck in his head, though I usually have to ask what it is first. He was easy to read to begin with and doesn't hide much, but his constant humming gives me a way to dive even deeper into Liam's soul. I love it more than I can say, and I wish I was brave enough to be as open with him as he is with me.

Once I'm settled in my seat, I feel Cole's gaze on me. I look up and meet his eyes and, unlike Liam's, his expression is pretty much impossible to pin down. He seems to be studying me, his brown eyes jumping to Liam before he turns his focus back to Freya as she tells him about some dignitary she was dealing with before her flight yesterday. I'm not sure what he sees, and I definitely don't know what he thinks.

I'm pretty sure Cole won't be singing anything while he's here, so I'm flying in the dark with this guy. I don't like it.

"Relax," Liam whispers, his hand resting on my shoulder blades. "They're even less likely to eat you than Nelson is. Especially when you managed to convince the chef to bring all of this on such short notice."

While I was technically the one who messaged Liam's chef early this morning, I doubt he acquiesced because of me. I'm pretty sure everyone who works for Liam is more than happy to do whatever he asks, not only because he pays well but because he's always quick to show his gratitude.

"I need to get me a chef during the off-season," Cole says when Freya finishes her story. He has piled his plate high with a little bit of everything, which makes sense given his size. Liam has a lot of muscle, but he's nothing compared to the all-star rugby player who looks like he could fight a bear and come out the victor. I figured Cole would be fit, but he's beyond athletic. He probably eats a million calories a day.

If these guys ever bring another man into their friend group, he's going to be hard-pressed to stay in shape. Derek is just as cut as Liam, something I know more from watching his movies than from the limited time I saw him when he came over last week. I barely spoke to him, using some lame excuse to stay out of the way while they did their little display for Patty and the other neighbors.

"I have a chef," Freya says as she nibbles on a pastry, "but he has a fondness for traditional Candoran cuisine which, in my opinion, is lacking in..."

"Flavor?" Liam suggests, popping a grape into his mouth. "Face it, Peach, Candoran food is blander than an English breakfast. And that says nothing about all the eels..."

Freya sighs. "That is exactly what I was saying, yes. I have half a mind to hire a new, young chef so my family can enjoy some variety. And maybe cut back on the eel."

"As long as you also hire a new, young bodyguard," Cole replies with what I'm assuming is a chuckle, though it's more of a grunt. "Gregor should have retired years ago."

"You are telling me things I already know, boys. But I have no say in Gregor's replacement, as he is head of Alverra security. I only hope he finds someone soon, before I have to force him to step down."

"You mean before you have your mother force him to step down," Liam argues. "You forget you're not on the throne until next year."

I must look entirely lost because Freya reaches over and takes my hand. "The Candoran monarchy is passed from eldest child to eldest child, though we also hold elections in case the people feel the next in line is unsuitable for the throne. My mother has ruled for the last fifteen years and is beloved by the people, but she is ready to live a quieter life with my father. If all goes well next autumn, I will take my mother's place and begin my reign, as I was born to do."

I can't imagine having my life planned out for me from birth. "Have you always wanted to be a queen?" I changed my mind on a prospective major three times before I ever got to college, and even now I'm still questioning my choice to go into film.

Liam laughs at my question, Cole smiles, and Freya gets a far-off look in her eyes, as if she's imagining something. "Oh, yes, I have always dreamed of helping my country thrive, and there is no better way to do that than by being queen. Though, if I am not elected, I will simply run for office in Parliament and do my part there."

"But you'll be intolerable if you lose," Cole mutters before taking a massive bite of frittata.

"You've got that right," Liam agrees, offering his hand for a fist bump.

Cole simply looks at it before returning his focus to his food.

"And what of you, Kasey?" Freya asks, ignoring the men. "Liam tells us you are writing a movie. You are in the right place for that."

"I guess so." I don't like all the attention that is suddenly on me, though I don't know what I expected. I'm the odd man out and probably the most interesting person to them. Or, I will be until they realize how little there is to learn. "I haven't decided if that's the direction I want to go."

"You are young," Freya replies with a smile. "You have plenty of time to find your path. My only suggestion is that you do anything but hold still. History is only made by those who keep moving forward, and many have lost their souls by refusing to take a step."

Cole shifts in his seat, like he's suddenly uncomfortable.

"Take Liam, for example," Freya continues, pointing to Liam as he slouches in his chair next to me. I'm pretty sure his feet are up on the chair across from him, which weirdly helps me relax. If he's totally okay sitting like that in front of a princess, maybe I can stop straining my shoulders by trying to sit up straight.

Liam smirks at Freya and gives her a salute. "What about me, Peach?"

She sighs, as if his lack of decorum is simply one of many grievances she has against him. I mean, she clearly likes him, but despite their physical similarities, they are total opposites. "Despite his success," she says, "he continues to improve himself and write more music, though we have you to thank for his recent victory over writer's block. For the most part, Liam is a paragon of never standing still."

"That's because he's literally incapable of sitting still," Cole says with a roll of his eyes. "I'm amazed you're not moving right now."

Something tells me Liam's current calm has a lot to do with the hand he still has pressed to my back. I've noticed it a few times over the last few weeks, the way he seems to be anchored when he's with me. I can't say I've ever seen him when he's *not* around me, but I've learned enough about him through his many stories about his life to know that he's a fairly restless soul. I like to think I've helped with that.

Glancing at Liam, since we talked about this last night (I think), I put on my best smile and say, "I'll figure out what I'm doing, whether it's writing for the movie industry or something else. But I don't like sitting still any more than Liam does."

"That's unfortunate," Cole says. He raises an eyebrow when we all look at him. "Because you're as stuck here as Liam is," he explains. "Unless you want the world to suddenly learn who you are, of course."

If Cole is right, and I'm pretty sure he is, my chances of things going back to normal are pretty slim. "Do you really think someone would recognize me so easily?" I ask, wrapping my arms around my stomach. It's growling, but I'm not sure I can eat anything right now.

"Never underestimate someone's drive to learn every detail they can about someone they will never meet," Freya says. "You would think Candora would be too small for me to be recognized among the crowds here in the States, but I can't go anywhere without someone alerting the press. It is why Gregor and his team must come with me even when visiting dear friends."

"Even I've still got a few fans who always seem to know where I am," Cole says with a shrug. "Drives me crazy, and it makes it really hard to go on a date..." His sentence falls off on the last few words, his expression falling. I wonder if he forgot, just for a moment, that his girlfriend dumped him yesterday. Poor guy.

Liam clears his throat and sits up. "There has to be something we can do to help Kasey, right? I hate that she's stuck in hiding just because I..." He drops off too, a bit of a blush rising up his neck as he glances at me.

That's another thing we haven't talked about. He almost kissed me two weeks ago, but he hasn't come anywhere close since then, keeping things platonic—exactly as he said he would. I talk a big game every time I tell Val I'm not going to kiss Liam, but it's becoming harder and harder to keep the thought out of my mind. I don't know if I'm falling for him because he's the only guy around or if it's real interest fueling the fire in my belly whenever we're together, but outside of last night, I haven't seen many signs of attraction on his side lately.

I'd bet Freya would just ask Liam if he's interested, were she in my position. She seems confident like that. But I'm not the princess of Candora, and I would die of mortification if Liam actually answered that question, assuming I ever found the courage to ask it. Even if he said yes, I'm way too confused about my own feelings for my response to be anything but fear and discomfort.

So I don't plan on talking about that almost kiss. *Any* of our almost kisses. If Liam wants this to be something more than friendship, he's genuine and confident and charming enough to make it happen.

Cole clears his throat, breaking up the building silence that has fallen around the table. "Unless you have a way to rid the internet of that picture, I don't think you have any hope outside of time."

"Or," Freya says, her perfectly sculpted eyebrows rising high.

When she doesn't say anything else, Liam frowns. "Or what?"

She looks at me when she continues. "Or you embrace it, Kasey. Accept that you are a part of this world now and learn to live in it. It isn't so bad once you get accustomed to being watched, and it is far easier when you have friends who understand your struggles."

I jump when Liam takes my hand, and though he immediately tries to pull back, I grip him tightly. I need some sort of anchor as I consider Freya's words. "I'm no one special," I argue. "I'm a delivery driver."

"A screenwriter who wrote a pretty spectacular script," Liam argues.

"You haven't even read—"

"I'm talking about *Figure Eight Dollhouse*. It might not be your name on it, but you wrote it. And it was really good."

"I saw that one," Cole says, his eyebrows pulling low. "Why isn't your name on it?"

I would have thought Liam would have told all of his friends about Mitchell, so it surprises me when Cole and Freya both look shocked and confused. Swallowing, I keep my eyes on my hand locked with Liam's. "My boyfriend—ex-boyfriend—sold it to the studio and took credit for it."

Cole swears under his breath.

"It's fine," I continue. "I don't have a way to prove that I wrote it, and Mitchell's a terrible writer so it's not like he's going to get any other contracts even if he tries."

"Nothing about that is fine, Kasey," Liam says, leaning close enough for his shoulder to press against mine.

"I just..." I look over at Freya and shrug. "I just want to move forward, you know?" I would especially love to move forward from this conversation.

Thankfully, the princess smiles and nods. "Sometimes, that is all you can do. And who knows? Maybe you'll write something a hundred times better, and you won't even care about what came before."

I think I'll always care about what Mitchell did. He was the first person I really trusted with something that took so much heart out of me. But I hope she's right. I hope I can get over this fear and eventually make something of myself. It probably won't be with this script I've been working on—it's more for me than anything—but someday. Someday I'll write something I can be proud to put my name on.

"Your Highness." Gregor appears in the doorway, though his eyes are on Ted's house instead of Freya. Did he see something? "You should be on your way."

Freya sighs and nods. "Yes, yes, I know. Candora never sleeps, so they say."

"I don't think they say that," Liam says with a grin. "Thanks for stopping by, Peach. You'll come by later?"

"If I can. I have a meeting in Portugal tomorrow afternoon, but I can always sleep on the plane. It all depends on how long-winded my counterparts will be." She bends and kisses his cheek, triggering a stupid bout of jealousy in my belly.

I want that level of familiarity with someone. With Liam. I was proud of myself for getting close to him last night, a feeble and sleepy attempt to see what he would do with it, but it's clear Liam is simply comfortable with all his friends. Him holding my hand is nothing more than a gesture of support. A gesture I will cling to as long as I can.

Freya blows a kiss to Cole, who nods once in return, and then she follows Gregor into the house and leaves the three of us in silence.

Liam doesn't let the silence last for long. "So, Cole, what are your plans during your off-season?"

Cole's expression immediately darkens. "Well, I was *planning* on spending some time in Oregon."

Liam winces. "Oh. Sorry."

I'm assuming Cole's ex-girlfriend is in Oregon, and my heart goes out to the guy. "How much time off do you have?" I ask, hoping that won't make his mood worse.

He shrugs. "A while. Practice will start up again soon."

"Maybe you could take a vacation?"

His face twitches, like he's trying so hard not to glower at me like he did Liam. I appreciate Cole's attempts at civility, given we just met, but I hope someday he'll be comfortable enough with me to let his emotions be at the forefront. "I don't have anywhere to go," he mutters, dropping his gaze.

"You can always hang out here with us!" Liam suggests, though I can't tell if he's serious. He's smiling, but it looks forced.

Cole shakes his head. "Thanks. But that would be a bad idea, and you know it."

Liam leans against me again and gives me a smirk. "Last time Cole and I spent any significant time together without Derek around, we nearly destroyed our esophagi while eating ghost peppers because we were bored."

Cole actually chuckles at that. "Like I said. Bad idea. Though, I ate more than you did." Then he frowns again, looking over his shoulder toward the front of the house. "Freya was my ride," he mutters, his words coming out growled, and then he swears under his breath. "Let me borrow one of your cars, Connolly."

"Absolutely not," Liam says with a grin. "You're the worst driver in the world."

"Well, I can't call a ride because your neighborhood is on lockdown."

"Sorry," I squeak. According to Liam, no one new can get into the neighborhood until things die down, which has frustrated his neighbors but prevented more paparazzi from getting inside. All deliveries are left at the gate with the guard. Honestly, I'm surprised it hasn't been that way since the beginning, though I'm glad it hasn't. I never would have met Liam that way.

"Just stay here, man," Liam says, though I can see Cole ready to argue.

Maybe Freya's right. Maybe I need to embrace my ridiculous celebrity status and hope I'm strong enough to endure my newfound fame. With any luck, people will figure out I'm a nobody and decide I wasn't worth their time in the first place. It would free everyone except Liam, who still has more than a week before his hearing.

I don't want him to feel completely alone, and if I reveal myself, I won't be able to justify the paycheck I'm getting to stay here. My guilt would drive me back out to do deliveries, and Liam would be on his own when I know that isn't good for him. When Cole is the only one with a free schedule right now, and apparently the Cole/Liam combo being dangerous, that doesn't leave him a lot of options for company.

"There's no way to win," I mumble without meaning to. I've gotten fairly good at holding back my under-the-breath comments, but apparently I don't have the skill today.

Both men look at me, and I sigh. "This whole thing… It's not good for any of us. And there's really no way to make anything better." I grab a muffin and stuff it into my mouth before I say any other depressing things.

While I chew, the two of them look around as if searching for a new topic. Cole is the first one to find one.

"How's the album coming?" he asks Liam.

They break into a discussion of the new songs and how Liam thinks they'll do with his audience, and I sit quietly in my chair, far too aware of the fact that Liam is still holding my hand but doesn't seem to notice.

CHAPTER NINETEEN

LIAM

She let me hold her hand. For almost an hour. I'm glad Cole wanted to talk about music because it is possibly the only topic that could have kept my attention on anything but the way Kasey kept her fingers laced with mine all through brunch. I've tried to come up with some sort of explanation for it, like she didn't realize she was still holding on to me, but she ate her entire meal with her left hand despite the fact that she is very much right-handed.

She held my hand *on purpose*.

The only reason I let go is because Derek and Bonnie show up, and it is physically impossible for me to greet Derek without leaping onto him.

"Whoa!" he says when I tackle him, nearly knocking him into the pool. "Cool your jets, Connolly."

"No one says that, you old man." He's only a few years older than me, but I never let him forget that he's over thirty.

"One of these days you're going to break me," he complains and shoves me off of him.

I poke him in the gut. "You're made of steel, and if they ever do another Superman remake, which is likely, you'll be perfect for the role."

"Shut up." He stuffs his hands into his pockets and looks over at the table, where Bonnie has joined Kasey and Cole. "How is he?"

It's not late enough in the day for Cole to have had any time to wallow, though I'm pretty sure he brought up music because he wanted the distraction as much as I did. "Okay for now, but you can't leave him here without some sort of supervision. The trouble we could get into..."

Derek winces. "Good point. We don't have long before we have to get back to set, though, so we have to think of something. I don't love the idea of him being on his own. What about Kasey?"

I flinch, an unsettling feeling of jealousy pooling in my belly. "What about Kasey?"

Derek rolls his eyes. "Would you relax? I just mean she can keep the two of you from being idiots."

That had better be all he meant, because right now Kasey and Cole are talking, and Cole is almost smiling. I'm all for him moving on and finding someone who won't drop him out of the blue over a phone call, but I won't let him make Kasey a rebound. Not that I think Kasey would go for that in the first place. Then again, she *is* a rugby fan, and Cole's a good-looking guy, and I'm pretty sure rugby players take the cake when it comes to athleticism.

"Dude." Derek shoves my head and then heads over to the table, taking Freya's vacated seat at the head of the table.

I don't know why that strikes me as odd that he would choose to sit between Kasey and Cole rather than next to Bonnie, who sat on

Kasey's right. Derek doesn't have to constantly be next to his girl-friend, obviously, but this is the first time he *hasn't* chosen to be beside her.

Thoughts roll through my head as if *Hollywood Hot Scoop* has taken over my mind. *Could there be trouble in paradise for the starlet and her leading man? Maybe Bonnie was just putting on a show, and her real love has been the mediocre musician, Liam Connolly, all along.*

I shake my head. I've clearly spent too much time in the tabloids lately, trying to find a way to get Kasey out of her predicament.

Since there aren't any open seats next to Kasey now, I reluctantly take the seat opposite Derek and try to tune in to the current conversation. Something about a new role Bonnie is taking on in the spring.

"And I *love* his books, so you can imagine how I nearly died when I got the call!" Bonnie says, waving her hands around with excitement.

"Whose books?" I ask.

"Henry McAllister!"

I can't claim to be much of a reader—too much time sitting still involved in reading—so I have no idea who that is.

"He's a fairly new mystery writer," Kasey explains, almost with the same level of excitement as Bonnie. "But he's brilliant! I'm dying to read his next book, but no one knows when it's coming out."

Bonnie groans. "Seriously. This slow burn has been killing me!"

"Bonnie got the lead," Derek says with a smile, probably because he can tell I'm still lost. "It's a pretty big deal."

"It's a much more serious role," Bonnie agrees. "I'm a little bit terrified but also super excited, and I hope I get to meet McAllister!"

Kasey lets out a wistful sigh and sits back in her chair, her hand on the table. It's practically begging to be held, but I'm too far away unless I want to reach across Bonnie to grab it, like a weirdo. "Man, if I had the chance to adapt a book like that, I would have so much fun writing that script!"

"How's your project coming, anyway?" Bonnie asks. I don't know if she's genuinely asking or if it's because Derek filled her in on my request, but it doesn't matter. Kasey immediately closes off.

"Oh, it's coming okay, I guess."

Her hand slips from the table to her waist, and it takes everything in me not to jump over there and start telling her (again) how amazing she is and how she doesn't need to be afraid of putting her work out there. I know it won't help, but I still want to try. I'll tell her again and again until she believes me.

"It's been nice having all this time to write, at least," she finishes, and she obviously wants this conversation to be over because she starts picking at the crumbs on her plate.

I make eye contact with Derek and silently tell him to work his magic.

Though he rolls his eyes at me, clearly telling me he probably won't be able to help, he shifts in his seat and makes himself look casual and unconcerned. "Sometimes I get these scripts from my agent that are the worst," he says lightly. "It makes me wish I'd taken some writing classes at some point so I could know how to make them better, you know?"

"Oh, me too!" Bonnie agrees with her usual enthusiasm. "Actually, this Gabrielle Frost script is a little iffy, but I'm hoping once we start filming it all of the kinks work themselves out. If not, you might be getting several phone calls from me while I'm on set, Kasey."

Kasey flashes an uncomfortable smile.

I'm halfway out of my seat, ready to pull her aside and say whatever I can to make her feel better about things, when Derek starts talking again. "I don't know what it is about some of the big screenwriters that are out there right now, but it's like they've run out of ideas. Like this movie we're doing right now."

"Oh, it's awful!" Bonnie says. "Cole, remember that movie you and I saw like two years ago about that man walking across the country?"

Cole's expression contains nothing but boredom as he lounges in his chair. "You mean the one where he met a prostitute and convinced her to walk across the country with him?"

"Yeah, that one. Remember how boring it was?"

"Because the characters were entirely flat."

"Nothing about them felt real," Bonnie agrees. "The movie we're filming right now is just like that, and I'm glad I'm working next to Derek because otherwise I would be dying of tedium. We need more stories about real people. Or at least stories written by people who haven't already written dozens of movies."

Okay, *this*. This is what I was hoping for. A natural conversation that isn't centered around Kasey but will hopefully help her get out of her own way. Since I don't have anything to add to the conversation, I keep my eyes on Kasey, curious to see how she takes it all. At the moment, she's still staring at her plate like it holds the answers to the universe.

"Honestly," Derek says, "I'm tempted to start doing more indie films and stay away from the big studios. They always seem to have the better stories because their writers and directors aren't held to any certain expectations."

"I'd guess the money isn't as good," Cole says. Either he has no idea what Derek is trying to do, or this is part of the plan, though I don't know how this is going to help.

Derek shrugs. "Maybe not, but it's not like I need it."

"Can you imagine how well an indie film would do if you were in it?" Bonnie says, stars in her eyes as she looks at Derek.

That, at least, calms my weird thoughts that something is up between the two of them. Especially when Derek sends a warm smile right back at her. They're fine. They wanted to make Kasey feel welcome by putting her in between them.

"I don't know if I'll ever be able to stop making movies entirely," Derek continues, "but I'm getting tired of making the same movies over and over."

He's either really leaning into this thing with Kasey, or this is all real. In the three years I've known him, Derek has loved playing the action heroes and confident leading men, and it's hard to imagine him wanting to do anything different. He's too good of an actor for me to tell if he really means what he's saying.

That's never bugged me before. Probably because he's never *acted* around me before.

"That's why I'm so excited about this Frost movie!" Bonnie says. "It's something totally different from what I've been doing."

Derek smirks. "You're just excited because you're secretly the president of the author's fan club."

Bonnie laughs. "If I get a chance to meet him, I'll be sure to try to get you there too, Kasey."

She finally looks up and smiles, the expression more believable than the last time. "I would love that. I'm not brave enough to ever try writing a novel, but I'm sure there's a lot I could learn from a guy like him. He knows how to write real characters."

"Absolutely," Bonnie agrees. "Just like Liam knows how to write real emotion."

I snap to attention, pulling my gaze away from Kasey before she realizes I've been watching her. "Oh, we're talking about me now? And here I was thinking you guys came over to keep me from going stir crazy."

Cole barks out a laugh. "You would have gone crazy weeks ago if not for Kasey. She might be the best thing to ever happen to you, Liam."

She is. I know she is, and there's nothing I can do about it until I find a way to free her from this prison that is my house. I know she picked being here over going back home in the beginning, but until she has a choice in whether she stays, I can't ask her to love me. I think that's what

Freya was trying to do by suggesting she lean into the possible fame. Still, I can't picture Kasey willingly stepping into the limelight.

That's not going to make a relationship very possible, given my regular life, and my spirits start to sink. I've been falling for this girl since the day I met her, but I don't know if she'll want everything that comes with me. I can't force that on her.

Kasey's back to staring at her plate, her face bright red, so I sit up and change the subject. "I think I only have one more song before the album feels finished, and then I need to get into the studio as soon as I possibly can and get it all recorded. I have a good feeling about this one."

"It's because of the emotion," Bonnie says again. "You always write songs that make me feel like you're singing stuff straight out of my soul."

I've never disliked Bonnie—that's impossible—but she might be my third favorite person now, following Kasey and my mom. Take that, Derek.

Grinning, I shrug my shoulders like it's no big deal. Inwardly, my chest is blazing from the praise. "I write from the heart, you know?"

"Creativity without heart is never as good," Derek says. Then he pulls out his phone and frowns at it. "Give me a second, guys."

As he wanders to the far side of the patio to take the call, I take advantage of his empty chair and move closer to Kasey. She peeks over at me, red creeping up her face again, and I try not to get too hopeful that there might be some kind of deeper feelings on her end.

While I was failing to fall asleep last night, I came to the renewed conclusion that no matter what she may or may not be feeling, Stockholm syndrome isn't something I can take advantage of. Of course, setting that rule for myself only makes me want to break it, so it was probably a bad idea to make it an actual rule instead of just a guideline we agreed upon at the start of all of this. But after last night, when I came so close to crossing some lines, that wall needs to be built up higher if I want to stay on this side of it.

"Cole, what are you going to do with all your time off before the next season starts up?" Bonnie asks.

With those two now occupied, I reach over and take Kasey's hand. Her shoulders relax, and she looks up at me with a small smile.

"I'm fine," she says before I can ask. "I'm just thinking about a lot. I thought you were going to stick with ten songs on this album."

If my album is the reason she's got a crease between her eyebrows, we've got bigger problems than tabloids and paparazzi. I never want to be the reason she is worried or stressed. It's not much better if it's her own creativity that's bothering her, but at least that's something I can help with. Or try to.

"I thought it could use a slower song in between 'Maybe it's You' and 'Say More'," I say, trying to keep my words casual and unconcerned. "If nothing comes to mind before I can get out to the studio, I won't worry about it."

Kasey looks over at Derek, and I can practically see the wheels turning in her head as she purses her lips. "Does Derek read a lot of scripts?"

I almost laugh. "Are you kidding? He's such a big name now that he can be extremely particular about which projects he takes on, but everyone wants him to be in their movie. I'm pretty sure he gets several scripts a week, if not more, and that's after his agent filters through the ones that aren't worth his time."

Honestly, Derek's life sounds exhausting. Maybe that's why he's changing his tune and thinking about going the independent direction. I'm not sure what his ultimate goal in life is outside of continuing to tell stories on film; maybe he's starting to feel restless. Looking for something new, outside of his career. I know he wants a family eventually. Maybe he's thinking it's time.

I glance at Bonnie, who also happens to be looking at Derek. She's been good for him, but is she the settle-down type? I've never thought so. I watch Derek pace on the phone and wonder where his head is at with his relationship with Bonnie. They've been together longer than he's been with anyone before, and it will either end or progress to something new.

"Is there a reason we're all staring at Derek?" Cole asks, making me jump.

I shake my head and slap on a smile. "Can you blame us? He's Hollywood's hottest man alive. Look at him!"

Cole grunts, glances at Bonnie, and then narrows his eyes at me. I'm not sure what he's trying to say, but I have a feeling we'll be having a conversation later.

"I'll be right back," Kasey says. She pulls her hand free before I can ask where she's going and disappears inside, leaving me with the overwhelming urge to rush after her and make sure she's okay.

She's been gone all of ten seconds, and already I ache for her.

"Um, wow," Bonnie says.

I shift my gaze to her. "What?"

"You're in love with her, aren't you?"

I keep my mouth shut. I don't need Cole and Bonnie to call out my lies, but I'm not willing to admit anything out loud.

"You've only known her for a few weeks," Cole points out.

"But they've spent literally every minute together," Bonnie argues. "Plus, Kasey is adorable, so it makes sense that he would fall for her."

Cole grumbles something under his breath, and then he says, "He might be infatuated because of their proximity, but I doubt he knows her enough to—"

"Of course he knows her!"

"I don't." I frown, slumping in my seat. "I don't know her. After everything that happened with her screenplay getting stolen, I think she's too afraid to open up to anyone again, and it's killing me that she still doesn't trust me."

There. It may not be an admission of my growing affection, but it's nice to say my fears out loud. I've learned so much about Kasey since the day I met her, but I know there's so much more to discover. So much underneath the surface that she's not willing to show me. I was fascinated from the start, and I've only grown more interested as time has gone on. There are times when she's open, but sometimes she feels as closed off as she did in the beginning.

Bonnie grabs my hand, squeezing it and giving me her signature smile, the one that can make anyone feel better. "As someone who absolutely hates sharing personal things, I can understand where Kasey is coming from. She needs to know she has someone in her corner, you know? Before I met Derek, I kept everything bottled up inside, and no one should live like that. People need someone to know their fears and dreams and everything in between."

There's a lot to unpack in that, including my sudden realization that I don't actually know Bonnie all that well despite the fact that she's been dating my best friend for the last year and has been part of the group even longer than that. It's probably not the right time to point that out, so I keep my focus on the current problem. "But how can I know all of those things if she won't tell me?"

"She probably doesn't know you're willing to listen," Cole suggests, his eyes on the ocean. "Probably has no idea that you've been waiting for her to tell you everything she's struggling with."

I swear under my breath, both because he's right and because he's probably speaking from experience. I don't know if he's the one who wasn't willing to share or if that was Sage, but I'm going to guess their relationship came to an end because the communication wasn't where it should be. I can't imagine long distance was easy for them.

"And what if I tell her I'm here, and she runs away?" I ask, shaking my head. "I can't chase her. Literally or emotionally." It's hard enough thinking about a serious relationship when I have no idea what that's supposed to look like; if Kasey is resistant the whole time, I'm going to run out of fuel before it ever becomes something good. Besides, I don't want to push her into something she doesn't want. And yet... There have been enough moments for me to think I have a chance. Not knowing is maddening.

I think I'm starting to understand what people mean when they say they're mad about someone they love.

Bonnie squeezes my hand again. "I'm the worst person to give you advice, considering I haven't..." She pauses, purses her lips, and then shakes her head. "But maybe don't go jumping to conclusions without taking that first step. Cole's right, and you need to let her know that you're here to help her. That she *can* trust you."

"It's not like I've given her any reasons *not* to trust me," I complain.

My phone buzzes, and I glance at it out of reflex, ready to ignore Ethan or my agent or whoever is getting in the middle of my much-needed therapy session with my friends. But my heart kicks up a notch when I see that it's Kasey.

Kasey:

> Hey, I'm up in the office, and I could use your help with something.

I'm on my feet in an instant, ignoring Bonnie's and Cole's questions as I dart inside and up the stairs. "Kasey?"

She's sitting at the desk, the ocean glittering behind her and making her look ethereal. Ethereal, but also seasick.

"What's wrong?" I ask. I'm out of breath from my mad dash up the stairs, but I hurry to her side anyway. "What happened?" Then my eyes lock on the document on the screen of my laptop, with a bold title that says *The Song of Icarus* and her name right beneath it. "What's..."

"I want to give a copy to Derek," she says, her voice tight and her hands trembling. "Do you have a flash drive or something?"

People don't use those anymore, I want to say to her, but I keep that thought to myself. If she's wanting to take this step, I'm not about to convince her not to by telling her to use the cloud. "I'm sure I've got one somewhere," I say and start digging around in the drawers.

Kasey's arms wrap around her middle, nearly halting my search so I can hug her and try to give her a boost of confidence. Not sure how a hug can do that, but I want to hold her regardless. She takes a shaky breath. "Maybe I shouldn't..."

"Found one!" My fingers wrap around the little thumb drive like it's the only thing that can save my life. I have no idea what's on this thing, but it's going to Derek so it's not like it matters. "Here."

It takes her four tries to get the drive into the USB port, which makes me laugh, though I bite it back as best I can. I'm here to support, not chuckle at the universal conundrum that is USB positioning. "I hate those things," I say, which feels innocuous enough.

"I guess I could have emailed it," Kasey replies, though she continues with saving the screenplay to the drive. "But this feels more...real? I guess." When she pulls the thumb drive out, she holds it on her palm like it might explode. Her eyes are wide, her lips in a thin line, and she's clearly terrified.

"Derek's not going to steal it from you." I hate that I even have to say that. If she'd had a chance to really get to know him, she would know that Derek Riley is almost incapable of doing anything to hurt someone else. He's got an ego sometimes, but it's one he deserves, and he doesn't need someone else's talent to make himself feel more important.

Kasey sighs. "I know that. I really do. Your friends are all amazing." Her fingers curl around the drive as she closes her eyes. "You're really lucky to have them, Liam."

She's preaching to the choir, but I can't figure out why she's still so scared if she's not worried about Derek. "You can talk to me, Kase," I tell her, crouching down beside her. I want to take her hand, the one not holding the drive, but I don't know if that will do any good. "Why are you afraid to put yourself out there?"

Opening her eyes, she looks at me with an expression I haven't seen from her before. It's vulnerable and open, but she's still so hesitant. It's like she wants to let me know her but doesn't know how. "What if I'm not good enough?" she whispers.

As a man who knows the importance of using the right words, I don't miss the subject of her question. *What if I'm not good enough?* She's not talking about her screenplay.

I grab hold of her hand, pressing it between both of mine and holding it close to my chest. "Kasey, I've only known you for a few weeks, but I happen to be an excellent judge of character."

That brings a smile to her lips, exactly as I'd hoped.

"You walked into a stranger's house with your head held high and demanded what was promised to you. You have told me over and over when something in a song isn't working despite knowing nothing about music because you're unafraid of letting people know your opinions. You have been faced with a situation that would make lesser women either fall apart or find a way to manipulate things for their own benefit, and you have kept your cool and shown a level of patience I can only dream of."

Where was I going with this? I got caught up singing her praises.

I clear my throat and stand, pulling her up with me. It's both because I think she'll feel more confident if she's on her feet and because my own foot is screaming from holding my weight in a crouch. The pain quickly fades as soon as I realize she's gazing so intently into my eyes that it's like she's desperate to hear what I have to say.

"I have no idea what's in that screenplay besides a killer title," I continue less confidently, "and I can't promise Derek will like it or that it will end up on the big screen. But I know you, Kasey Graham, and I know you're meant for more than driving food around the valley. You're for sure meant for more than babysitting me."

She laughs, and this time her smile stays in place.

It's killing me standing here with just her hand, so I tug her closer and wrap my hand around her back. It's as much to steady myself as it is to steady her. "You'll never know if this story is going to go anywhere if you don't give it a shot," I tell her. "And giving it to Derek is like jumping in a pool instead of taking the stairs into the water. Scary, but it gets you somewhere a whole lot faster."

"You forget that I can't swim," she whispers. Did she just lean closer? I'm pretty sure she leaned closer. She definitely tilted her head back. And she let her eyes slip down my face to my mouth. And rest there.

I also may have forgotten how to breathe just now. "That's what you've got me for," I whisper back and lean in.

"Hey Liam, Bonnie and I need to..." Derek's words drop off, but it's too late. Kasey is already pulling away and shoving the flash drive into my chest. "Sorry," he mouths at me.

I sort of want to punch him, but I also know it's a good thing we were interrupted. Our situation hasn't changed, and I shouldn't be taking advantage of a high-emotion moment. I shake my head right as Kasey mutters, "I'll go say goodbye to Bonnie," and slips out of the room.

Derek lifts an eyebrow. "That was new."

"That was a bad idea," I argue, running a hand through my hair. And it was hardly new. I've gotten close to kissing this woman too many times, and I might go crazy if I get that close again without actually kissing her.

"Why?"

I've told myself this so many times that it's starting to feel like beating a dead horse. "Because she's stuck here, and I don't want her to think I'm into her because she's the only woman within reach."

"Wow. That's really good of you."

Scowling, I step toward him and hold out the flash drive. "I don't like your tone of surprise, Riley. Here."

"What's this?"

"It's a flash drive, you dummy."

Derek's expression flashes with irritation, but he rolls his eyes and it's gone. "I can see that. What's on it?"

"Kasey's screenplay."

"Oh!" To my relief, his face lights up with interest. "I didn't think I'd managed to convince her."

"Neither did I, but I guess we were wrong." Granted, I had to do some convincing even after she'd made the decision, but we got here in the end. "Will you read it?"

"I said I would." Derek puts it into his pocket, and suddenly a flash drive doesn't seem secure enough. What if it falls out? Someone could find it, and anyone with half a brain would recognize a good screenplay when they saw it and probably do exactly what Mitchell did. My overthinking must be on my face because Derek rolls his eyes again and pats his pocket. "I'll take care of it, Liam. I promise. You should be worrying about you."

"What about me?"

"Are you sure you're ready for a relationship with this girl?"

That was not the question I expected him to ask, especially after what I just told him. "I'm not planning on—"

"Say Ethan comes up with some way to get her out of the public eye and back to normal life," Derek says in a warning tone that turns my blood to ice. "Say Kasey gets to go home tonight but tells you that she wants to keep coming around because she's into you, which she obviously is."

"She is?" My stomach does a flop. If Derek sees the same interest that I saw...

"What will you do then?" Derek puts his hand on my shoulder, his grip firm. "For as long as I've known you, you've not only avoided relationships but actively been against them. Why has that changed with Kasey?"

I can't help but think back on my conversation with Jordan weeks ago. My old publicist was entirely focused on his job when I knew him, which worked out great for me but clearly not for his wife at the time. Now he's married again, and he seems happy. Different. But it was only a month ago that I was making fun of him for tying himself to a relationship.

"I didn't think love was real," I say with a half-hearted shrug. "It's not like I've ever seen it. Except with you and Bonnie, of course."

Derek frowns, his jaw tightening. Seriously, what is up with him today? "Love is...complicated," he says, almost growling the words. "And you can't use my relationship with Bonnie to... Are you in love with Kasey?"

"Derek, is there something—"

"Answer the question, Connolly. I have to head back to set, so I need to know you're going to be okay. You're not acting like yourself."

"Maybe that's a good thing." I've never been in love before, no matter what I sing in my songs. But I've also never felt the way I feel with Kasey. Whatever this is, I don't want to let it go because it feels like there's more to my life than myself. "Yes, I'm in love with her," I say. The words are terrifying and exhilarating all at the same time. "But like I said, I can't do anything about it."

"You *shouldn't* do something about it," Derek says. "But that doesn't mean you can't. Maybe..." He grimaces and shakes his head. "Maybe tell her how you feel. The circumstances aren't ideal, but if you really love her like I think you do, it won't matter. She'll know you mean it because you can't hide what you're feeling any more than you can play a show without taking off your shirt."

He starts heading for the door but pauses when he reaches the hallway. "Why do you do that, anyway?"

I'm surprised he's never thought to ask before now. I smile despite the way my heart is pounding in my chest with fear and excitement at the idea of telling Kasey how I feel. "Because it gets hot on stage," I say with a shrug. "And because I spent my summers half naked when I was a kid and would do it as an adult if it wasn't frowned upon. Way more comfortable that way."

He chuckles. "You are one of a kind, Liam Connolly. Tell her, okay? It'll make you feel better."

He's probably right, but it will open me up to the risk of rejection. I've been rejected plenty of times by people who decide my music isn't for them, but no matter how much my songs come from the heart and are important to me, this feels bigger. With my music, I can always play it somewhere else. Find another label who will produce it or even go indie. I don't need validation or acceptance to find joy in writing and performing my songs.

But with Kasey? If she decides I'm not what she wants, that's it. I don't think I'll ever find someone quite like her. Someone who inspires music in a way nothing ever has.

If Kasey rejects me, I'm not sure I'll ever recover.

chapter Twenty

KASEY

Liam spends the rest of the day watching game shows with Cole, who keeps threatening to walk out of the neighborhood and call a car to take him home but hasn't looked at his phone even once since getting here. I'm pretty sure he's secretly glad to have a friend around to keep him distracted from his breakup. He's a quiet guy, but I've quickly figured out that he is the type of person who feels a lot and feels it deeply, despite his fairly stoic exterior.

After three straight hours of *Family Feud* and *The Price is Right*, I ask them why they don't find something else to watch, and they both laugh at me.

"Everything else is too problematic," Liam explains. "Movies and TV series? Derek and Bonnie would be so much better than the main actors, and they tend to complain about the mediocre storylines."

"Sports are just as dangerous," Cole grunts. "None of them are as good as rugby, and we all have different teams anyway."

"Reality TV hits too close to home," Liam says.

"Never get into anything with music with Liam," Cole adds. "He'll spend the whole hour telling you why that singer should open their vowels or why the percussion was the wrong choice."

"And I'll be right," Liam argues.

I leave it alone after that and use their diverted attention to go sit on my bed and tell Val that I finally bit the bullet and gave Derek my script. Well, I gave Liam my script so he could give it to Derek because I was way too much of a chicken to do it myself.

As expected, Val screams and takes all the credit, telling me that I am going to be famous before the end of the year, which definitely isn't true. Even if Derek says the script is the best thing he's ever read, which absolutely won't happen, I know it still needs a lot of work before it's ready to be shopped around. I haven't even written the ending yet because I don't know how it's supposed to end.

"Look," I say when she's done gushing over her genius plan to get me famous. (I'm not sure how Patty's photo became her plan, but I'm too tired to argue with her on that.) "It's probably not going to go anywhere, and that's not the real reason I called you."

Val gasped. "You kissed Liam?"

"What? No! Why would you…" I shake my head. "No, but I *almost* kissed Liam."

"Oh." She sounds way more disappointed than she should about that.

I curl my legs up against my chest, knowing I'm going to regret this whole conversation. "Oh? Why is that your reaction?"

"Because you have been in that man's house for more than two weeks, girly, and an *almost* kiss is basically nothing. Have you always been a nun?"

Yep. All the regrets right now. "Val, this whole thing with Liam is too complicated for me to just go around and kiss him all the time."

"Why? It doesn't mean anything."

Maybe it doesn't mean anything for her, but I've only kissed three men in my twenty-three years of life. The first was Chandler Gray in the fifth grade when we played Spin the Bottle, a game no ten-year-olds should be playing. The second was a boy in high school whose name I can't even remember because he was from the next town over and doubled with Val and her boyfriend at the time. He needed a date, and somehow Val convinced me to hold off watching the movie I'd rented and go out with them. The kiss was wet and sloppy and made me wonder what the big deal was with kissing anyway.

The third was Mitchell Crane. Mitchell, who rented a study room in the library and brought snacks and was so charming and sweet that *I* kissed *him* when he walked me back to my dorm. Mitchell, who basically taught me how to kiss but made my naivety sound exciting, like I had the rare opportunity to learn perfect chemistry without previous experience getting in the way. Mitchell, who told me our relationship had to stay secret and only kissed me in dark corners and late at night when we were alone.

Val has always been more open with relationships, to the point where I'm surprised she settled with Vince so easily, and she forgets that we're not the same in that regard. Or any regard, really. I love her, but she doesn't often get me like I wish she would.

Not in the way Liam's friends seem to get me after so little interaction with me. I've never been as comfortable around people as I am around them. Even Freya, though she's still intimidating.

I hug my knees and take a deep breath. "Val, I really like Liam, and I don't want to mess things up. Especially because we're both stuck here." She doesn't know about Liam's ankle monitor, believing he's avoiding the paparazzi like I am, but a part of me wishes I could tell her the truth.

Maybe then she would understand that I'm worried Liam is only taking an interest in me because he doesn't have any other options. I know he said he didn't want to take advantage of me being stuck here, but it's been *weeks* since then. "What if I make a move and he—"

"Don't you dare finish that sentence," Val snaps. "I saw that photo just like everyone else. I'm tired of telling you that that boy is madly into you, so you just need to start believing me and let yourself live again. Or, you know, start living for the first time."

What if she's right? My life in Kansas was quiet. My town was too small to know a lot of people, and I spent all my free time watching movies. Writing stories. Then I went to college and kept my eyes on the prize. I'm twenty-three, and my relationship with Mitchell was the only time I focused on anything beyond my future as a screenwriter.

And yeah, that didn't exactly turn out well for me, but I'm smart enough to know a single instance isn't going to be the ultimate rule.

"If anything is going to happen with Liam," I say slowly, "it's going to be the real thing, Val. Not just a fling while I'm trapped here."

"Even better!"

"No, because dating Liam Connolly isn't something simple. He's world-famous. A millionaire. He goes on late-night TV shows and will probably play a Superbowl halftime show at some point and can't even exist in his own home without someone watching his every move." I take a deep breath, holding it in my lungs. "That would be my life, Val." Not to mention Liam isn't the kind of guy who gets into relationships to begin with, but that's a whole different point I'm too tired to make right now.

To her credit, Val doesn't argue. She knows me well enough to know that I'm not a spotlight kind of person. Yes, I was in the drama club, but I was on the stage crew during the school plays. Background. Effectively invisible.

"Here's my take," Val says, her tone gentle. "Someday, you are going to be a famous screenwriter with Oscar-winning movies. And no, people won't recognize your face, but they'll know your name. You were meant to shine, Kasey Graham, and it would just look a little different if you got with Liam. That's not necessarily a bad thing, is it?"

I don't get a chance to answer because movement catches my eye, and I look up as Liam fills up the door frame with a warm smile. Dang, he looks so good. It's his messy hair and bright eyes and all around happiness and light. That's a sight I don't think I'll ever get tired of.

"I've got to go," I tell Val and hang up before she can shout any last words of wisdom. Like *get some* or something equally embarrassing.

"Sorry," Liam says immediately. "I didn't mean to interrupt."

"I'm glad for the interruption. Val was getting too philosophical for my taste."

His smile growing, he leans one shoulder against the frame and stuffs his hands into his pockets. He's pulling off the casually sexy look a little too well. "Someday I want to meet your roommate."

"Technically you're my roommate," I argue. "And you don't want to meet Val. She's one of your rabid fans and would probably try to ditch her fiancé and go after you."

"Would you keep me safe?"

A blush heats my face, but I don't try to hide it. I may not end up being brave enough to tell Liam that I'm falling for him, but I'm going to try. Maybe. Probably not. Yes?

"Anyway," Liam says, "the sunset is looking promising, so I wondered if you would sit on the balcony with me to watch it."

This gorgeous man wants me to watch the sunset with him? There is no circumstance in which I would say no to that. Hopping up, I grab a sweatshirt from the closet—one of Liam's—and follow him to the outer door by the office. "Where's Cole?"

"Sound asleep. I don't think he slept at all last night."

I haven't been on this side of the balcony—Patty shared that photo before I got a chance to explore the whole thing—and the view from this west side is absolutely incredible. Since we're up higher than the lounge, there aren't any trees or bushes to obscure the view. We can even see the beach from here, though it's far enough down that I can't make out any faces on the few people wandering the sand.

I tug the sweatshirt over my head and then join Liam on the railing. "I feel like this is technically breaking Ethan's rules."

Liam shrugs. "If anyone is looking at us instead of this sky, they've got issues."

He's not wrong. The clouds are a soft orange as the sun sinks lower, and it's looking like the colors are only going to get more vivid. There are hints of pink building on the edges, bathing everything in a golden glow while the ocean glitters almost magically.

This might be the most romantic place I've ever been.

For some reason, I feel the overwhelming urge to fill the silence before it lasts very long. "Thank you, by the way. For today."

Liam glances over at me. "Which part?"

"Ha! Well, all of it. For sharing your friends, and for helping me not freak out about meeting a princess. And..." I tug on the cuffs of the sweatshirt, pulling them over my hands and then fisting the fabric. "For helping me be brave."

He's still watching me, even though the sunset is quickly deepening. "You didn't need me to help you be brave. You made the choice."

"And you gave Derek the flash drive." I glance at him. "You did give it to him, right?"

I feel a strange sense of accomplishment when he laughs, even though it's so easy to make him laugh that there's no reason for me to take any pride in the fact. Maybe I just like knowing that he can be happy around me, even when my life is a mess.

"Yes, I gave it to him." Still grinning, Liam turns his focus back to the setting sun. "He seemed excited to read it."

"Really?"

Instead of answering, Liam reaches over and places his fingers over my hidden hand, chuckling as soon as he does. He pulls his hand back again and purses his lips. "I saw that going differently."

I quickly free my hand and grab hold of him, willing myself to take strength from his touch and tell him I don't want to be just friends. "More like that?"

"What's your screenplay about?"

Huh? I wasn't expecting that question, and it came out of nowhere. Though Liam threads our fingers together, he drops his head as if disappointed. Frustrated?

I'm not entirely sure where this conversation is going, but I do know I don't really want to answer his question. It was hard enough to give the script to Derek, but Liam... If Derek actually reads it, I know he's going to talk to Liam about it, but I'd like to stay behind this shield of Liam's ignorance for a little longer.

"Um. It's about a guy." I grimace as soon as those words leave my mouth. *About a guy?* That's the best I could come up with? I clear my throat. "Sorry, it's hard to think straight with a sunset this gorgeous." And by sunset I mean man, and by gorgeous I mean...well, gorgeous, but also confusing.

I was gearing up to be open with him and tell him how much I like him when I took his hand, and he basically shot me down by changing the subject.

Maybe he has decided that things went too far in the office earlier and he's finding the right way to turn me down. Keep things in the friendzone. Then again, *he's* the one who took my hand. Unless that was supposed to be a friendly gesture and I turned it into something more?

Ugh, why can't I read this man tonight? I need him to sing his feelings to me so I know what to do, but he's completely silent right now.

I swallow, wishing I could pull my hand away from his but not finding the motivation. "If Derek likes the script, I'll let you read it." Liam is probably never going to see that script because Derek is never going to like it. He might tell me it's okay, but he'll be lying to be nice because that seems like the kind of guy he is.

Plus, as soon as Liam learns what it's about, things are going to get awkward.

I turn my eyes back to the sunset, taking it all in. "This is so beautiful."

"Yep."

I feel his eyes on me, but I can't bring myself to look at him. He's probably wondering why I'm acting weird, even though he's being just as weird. We're just two weirdos enjoying the best sunset I've ever seen in my life.

Liam shifts until our arms press together, and then his thumb rubs along mine in a soft touch. "Kasey."

That's all he says, which is enough to get me to look at him even though I'm afraid of what he's going to say next.

His lips twitch up, but he looks more nervous than anything. "I know things have been kind of crazy since we met."

That's one way to put it. And yet I've enjoyed every minute of my time here with Liam. Anyone else, and I probably would have gone completely nuts. I would have been desperate to get out of this house and return to normal life. But something about Liam messes with my natural inclinations. I don't act like myself around him, but I don't know if it's a bad thing.

He makes me calm. Relaxed. He convinces me to take life at a slower pace instead of sticking to the grind like I've always done. He makes me feel confident again, which is something I wasn't sure I would ever experience. He's my best friend and would be my biggest supporter if I let him.

Liam swallows, his Adam's apple bobbing as he leans closer. "But I want you to know that I've been so glad to have you here. Maybe it's not the way you expected to spend the last couple of weeks, but hopefully it hasn't been too bad."

I still don't know where this conversation is going, but I like this a whole lot better than talking about my script. "Honestly, it's been better than not too bad." I swallow too because it feels like my words are sticking in my throat. "Liam, I really like being here."

His eyebrows pull low. "But?"

Be brave, Kasey. I shake my head. "There's no but."

The smile that breaks across his face is so much better than the sunset, which is bathing us in a deep orange glow. Everything about his expression is warm and bright and feels like home in a way nothing has in a long time. I don't want to ruin this friendship we've been building, but I'm not sure I can hold my feelings back anymore.

His fingers trail along my jawline as he moves in close enough that his breath brushes my lips. "I promised I wouldn't do this until you were free," he murmurs. Then he waits because that's the kind of guy he is. He won't do anything unless he's sure I want him to.

I want you to.

My own breath catches in my throat. "Please," I beg, closing my eyes.

His mouth presses to mine so softly that I almost don't feel it. It's just a touch, a whisper so full of hesitation that my immediate thought is he doesn't want to do this and is simply humoring me. *Why won't you kiss me?* my thoughts beg.

Only, I'm pretty sure I said those words out loud because suddenly Liam claims my mouth with the enthusiasm of someone whose resolve has disappeared. There's no way this kiss is an obligation because Liam's hands move to my waist and pull me close at the same time he teases my lips open and deepens the kiss. I match him eagerly, gripping his biceps until he nudges my arms up and around his shoulders so he can move his fingers into my hair without losing his hold on me. I run my own fingers into his mess of blond and across his scalp, loving the way he smiles into his kisses in a way only he can do effectively. The sunset has nothing on this kiss as he works to make me forget anything exists in the world but him.

Liam kisses as passionately as he writes his music, and I'm done for. There's no going back from this.

When he finally breaks away, we both struggle to breathe. I'm on the verge of collapsing as my knees threaten to give out, and Liam is now gripping the railing so tightly that his knuckles are going white.

"Wow," he says and presses his forehead to mine.

I let out a shaky laugh. "You stole my line."

"I've wanted to do that since the day I met you."

A zing of excitement shoots through me, even though that's not exactly news to me. "I haven't."

He laughs and kisses me again, threatening to render me completely melty in his arms. "I know. I blame Nelson."

Honestly, his parakeet hasn't bothered me in over a week. It's probably because he hasn't been out of his cage around me since the time he attacked me, but his songs and chirps have become a familiar part of the background noise, to the point where I almost don't notice him.

I run my fingers along Liam's smooth cheek, suddenly wondering if he's ever tried to grow a beard. It's a weird thing to wonder in this moment, but it makes me smile. "You are more than your murder bird, Liam Connolly."

As he opens his eyes, which are still bright despite the darkening sky overhead, he studies my face with an intensity that sparks a fire in my belly. "I don't..." He swallows, looks down, then looks up again with vulnerability in his eyes. "I don't want you to think that I only kissed you because you're stuck here and I don't have any other options."

I love that he's still thinking about that. I run my hand through his hair again, prompting another smile. "I know."

"And I didn't kiss you because I want something from you."

"I know that too." Mostly because I have nothing I could give him.

But Liam's expression falters. "Kasey, what Mitchell Crane did to you was horrible, and I never want you to think that I might—"

"Hey." I take his cheeks in my palms so he has to focus on me. "Remember that time I said you are too nice? I meant it. As soon as I really got to know you, I knew you could never be the sort of person who uses someone else for his own gain."

The problem is me. I want to think I agreed to hang out with Liam because of him, but there's a ball of unease building in my stomach that reminds me how connected this man is. His best friend is a movie star with genuine influence in the industry I want to be a part of. He has been paying me to sit around and write instead of busting my butt making food deliveries and never having a spare moment to put words to paper. His life—at least right now—lets me feel like I'm living in a fairytale.

I know I like Liam, but this whole thing is still so complicated. I can't keep taking advantage of his good heart without the guilt eating away at me. He's already given me so much, and what have I given him in return? Nothing. He deserves so much better.

"Liam," I say, my heart sinking. This isn't going to work. We're from too different worlds, and someday he's going to realize that I'm just riding on his coattails and using his celebrity status to benefit my own life because there's nothing I can give him in return.

As if he's reading my mind, his whole expression drops. "Don't," he begs.

A gruff, agonizing yell splits the air around us, and my blood turns cold.

That came from the direction of Ted's house.

CHAPTER TWENTY-ONE

LIAM

Kasey and I run to the other side of the house, though we both duck down as soon as we reach the northeast corner. Ted's right outside his back door, pacing across a few feet of space with his hands in his hair and muttering to himself. He's not loud enough for us to hear him, but that scream definitely came from him.

"What's going on?" Kasey whispers, her voice trembling along with her body.

The urge to wrap an arm around her is so strong that it physically hurts to hold myself back, but I do it anyway. Despite giving me the best kiss of my life, she was about to tell me that she doesn't want to be a part of my world, so she's not mine to hold.

I get it. My life is crazy, and what she's seen of it has been pretty crappy. But it's not always like this. When I'm free of my house, I get to travel all over the world and see places I could only dream about when I was a kid. I get to meet all sorts of amazing people, and I have the chance to see the way people light up when they share my music with me. It's amazing.

But the fame is…hard. I know that. I just thought I was worth enduring that.

Apparently not.

Ted growls low in his throat and then stalks to the side of the house, the part Kasey was trying to see a couple of weeks ago. We don't have a good view from here, and I'm tempted to head down to the patio and lift her onto my shoulders so we can get a good sense of what Ted is doing.

It doesn't matter. He comes back a moment later, a shovel in hand, and moves to the corner of his property that is closest to mine. He's just out of sight again, but we can hear him as he starts digging, still mumbling to himself.

"Is he digging a hole? In the dark?" Kasey slowly rises to her feet but ducks back down a second later. "I can only see the top of his head, and I don't want him to see me."

It's dark, but not so dark that he wouldn't notice us if he looked up and we were standing there.

"Maybe he's doing some late-night gardening," I suggest.

Kasey looks back at me with narrowed eyes. "You don't believe that."

"I don't believe that," I agree. "But I don't like the alternative that I'm thinking of."

"Me neither."

"Good riddance," Ted spits, making me tense up. He can't hear us, can he? "She was useless anyway."

Kasey shifts so she's sitting with her back to the railing, her wide eyes on me. "Martha?" she guesses. "What if he…"

I would so much rather go back to making out with Kasey in the sunset than be crouching in the dark, wondering if my neighbor just murdered his wife.

My foot starts aching, so I sit as well, keeping enough distance between us that I won't accidentally touch Kasey, but close enough that I can protect her if something happens. What that something would be up on my balcony at the back of the house, I don't know, but I want to be prepared. I'm in love with this woman, and I won't let anything happen to her.

Even if she doesn't love me back.

"Ted has always been a nice guy," I mutter, shaking my head as I press my hand over my aching heart, as if that might hold it together. I force my voice to stay even and calm. "I have a hard time believing he would do anything to hurt Martha. Not after the way he talked about her."

"But he's been acting weird for weeks," Kasey argues. "Any time he's been on the cameras, he's always tense and shifty. And he's been ignoring everyone else whenever they go to his house, even when he's home."

Those cameras were a bad idea. It was a fun way to convince Kasey to stay here with me, but they made it so easy to forget that my neighbors are real people. Not characters on some strange TV show.

I shake my head. "We don't know anything, Kasey. And we shouldn't—"

"Something is going on in this neighborhood, Liam, whether you like it or not. Gina sneaking into the Carmichaels' backyard, the little get-togethers in the square, Ted digging a *giant hole in his backyard in the middle of the night.*"

It's barely seven o'clock. Not exactly the middle of the night. I groan, wishing I had tried harder to keep Cole awake so I would have had an excuse to not find Kasey and make the monumental mistake of kissing her.

I'm never going to come back from that. She kissed like a woman who had a song in her heart begging to come out, and I'm never going to sleep until I figure out what that song is. She may have ruined me for anyone else, which is probably fine because it's not like I was big on relation-ships to begin with.

They only ever end in heartache. For all I know, Derek and Bonnie aren't even really dating and it's all just some scam for publicity's sake.

The ache settles heavier in my chest, more uncomfortable than painful. At least I know where Kasey stands now so I can stop won-dering. Stop wishing.

Stop caring.

With the full moon giving us more light as it rises, we sit in silence for a long time, listening to the steady *shunk* of the shovel sliding into the dirt. Ted keeps muttering to himself, usually too quiet for me to catch any words but sometimes loud enough to know he's talking about Martha and how he can sleep easily now that she's gone.

I keep waiting to hear some kind of proof that Ted is doing some-thing nefarious—and hoping for proof that he isn't—but it's hard to imagine anything but the fact that Ted is currently digging Martha's unofficial grave to cover his tracks.

Feels oddly fitting, given the way the evening has gone.

After maybe half an hour, the shovel stops, and Kasey and I both stiffen and look up in time to watch Ted lumber back inside his house.

"He must be tired," Kasey says, frowning at Ted's yard. "There's no way he dug a hole big enough." There's not a lot of emotion in her voice, which doesn't surprise me. She's not a heartless person, and I doubt she enjoyed turning me down. Even if she clearly enjoyed that kiss.

My lips tingle as memories of that kiss rise to the surface. My head's a little full of panicked imaginings of what is inside Ted's house, and yet the feel of Kasey in my arms still lingers in the back of my mind, waiting to be revisited on repeat when I'm not thinking about murder.

"Maybe we should see if the camera picked up anything," I say.

"Do you think we should call the police?"

"And tell them what?" I huff out a humorless laugh, trying to calm my racing heart. I'm letting my imagination run wild, and that's a bad idea. "That we saw my neighbor digging in his yard for an hour? We don't have any proof that something happened, and I don't need the police giving me any more attention than they already have. Not until after my hearing and I'm cleared of charges."

Kasey stands and stretches without looking at me. "I didn't think about that. Sorry."

I haven't really been worried about my hearing, but right now I'm not feeling especially optimistic. About anything. Plus, I have no doubt that there are still paps crawling around outside the neighborhood, and they would *love* to turn my secret love affair into a scandal if the police came blazing in. They could say anything they wanted, and people would believe them, and I'm not sure my reputation could handle that kind of backlash even with proof that nothing bad has gone down.

That would *definitely* make Ethan quit.

"Let's—" My words catch when Ted appears at his back door again, his back to us as he drags something outside. I swear and grab Kasey, pulling her back down so we're more hidden.

"Is that Martha's body?" Kasey squeaks in alarm.

It's a black garbage sack, so we can't actually see what's inside, but it's big and bulky and clearly heavy. Ted is grunting and groaning as he drags it across his yard. It's not long enough to be a human, but it's lumpy enough that it looks like...

"He must have cut her up into pieces." Kasey sounds too intrigued for my liking.

I grimace, slightly queasy as Ted dumps his sack into the hole. "We shouldn't be out here," I say, my words hoarse.

"Ted?" A female voice makes us both jump. "Ted, sweetie, are you okay?"

"Wait, is that Martha?" Kasey asks, craning her neck to try to see over toward the street.

I shake my head, and my voice comes out raw. "Pretty sure that's Patty." It sounds like she's at Ted's front door, but she's shouting loud enough that we can hear her from here, as if she knows Ted is in the backyard.

I swear again. "Is she an accomplice?"

Kasey slips out of my grip and darts around to the front of the house. There's a light in the square, so she'll be a lot more visible over there, and I let out a string of expletives as I hurry after her. I don't want to be seen, but I'm not about to leave her to fend for herself.

Sure enough, Patty is in front of Ted's house, though she's making her way toward the side gate with a determined look in her eyes. "Ted, I know you're back there!"

She looks up, and I dive onto my stomach in a feeble attempt at hiding. What is even happening right now? I wait until Patty disappears into Ted's yard, and then I scurry forward until I reach Kasey where she's crouched in the corner.

"We need to get inside," I growl at her.

"We need to figure out what is happening with your neighbors," she argues.

"I'm calling the police."

Before I can even unlock my phone, Kasey swipes it from my hand. It slips from her fingers, though, and tumbles over the side of the house until it crashes on the pavement below, shattering.

"Oops." Kasey winces at me. "Sorry. I'll buy you a new..." She stops when she catches the angry look on my face, which is as much for the idea of her paying for a phone she can't afford as it is due to our current situation. "Like you said, calling the police is a bad idea," she says after a moment. "Not just for your own sake, but we need to know more about what's going on before we jump to any conclusions."

"Says the woman who is convinced Ted chopped his wife into little bits before burying her in the backyard." My stomach heaves, and I take a few deep breaths so I don't throw up. I don't do well with blood and gore, and everything feels too hot. I'm tempted to take off my shirt so I don't overheat and pass out as I try to sort through what's happening right now. "Kasey, we need—"

I cut myself off again as Ted and Patty come around to the front of the house, Patty's arm around Ted's shoulders as they walk slowly down the sidewalk toward my house. I scramble backward and out of sight, silently begging Kasey to do the same.

She doesn't move, keeping her eyes fixed on the pair below.

"I know it feels like you did something wrong," Patty says, her words sickeningly soothing. "But she was making you miserable."

"I don't know how to go on without her," Ted replies. "She was the only family I've got."

Patty hums in sympathy. "Martha lived a good, long life, but it's time for you to move on. Get yourself something younger. More...lively. You've still got some spring in your step, and you need someone who can keep up with you."

"I should have saved her," Ted moans. "But I just sat there while she choked to death!"

Kasey turns to me, her eyes wide.

I know exactly what she's thinking. Does it technically count as murder if he didn't step in to help when Martha was choking?

"There's nothing you could have done," Patty says. "Come along. Gina will help you feel better, and then I'll help you with Martha's body."

Their voices fade until we're left in a heavy silence that feels suffocating.

"Oh. My. Gosh." Kasey says, crawling over to where I'm practically gasping for air. "This is crazy, Liam! I don't even know if we can call the police for something like this."

I run a hand through my hair, sorting through the things I know out loud because it's the only way to keep my thoughts straight. "Martha is dead. She choked, and Ted didn't do anything to save her. Patty knows Martha is dead and is encouraging Ted to go find some comfort in the arms of Gina, who is probably sleeping with everyone in the neighborhood except me. Not that I want her to, but..."

Kasey almost smiles, even though this is hardly a laughing matter. "Well, she *does* flirt with you."

"Not the point." I groan, wishing I had my phone so I could call Derek and get his opinion. He may be just an actor, but I'm sure he'd know exactly what to do in this situation.

"Why would he bury her in the backyard instead of calling 9-1-1?" Kasey asks as she settles against the side of the house next to me. "That's the part that doesn't make sense. He didn't kill her, he just...let her die."

"Not sure if that's better." I close my eyes, still fighting the urge to throw up.

Kasey groans and stands up. "What if the whole neighborhood is made of serial killers?"

Grimaces, I look up at her. "Seriously?"

"Liam, you could be living in a hotbed of murderers, and all we would need is a little proof."

I don't realize what she's doing until she heads for the door, but even then my mind is slogging through too much input. She can look at the cameras all she wants, but I doubt she's going to learn anything new. The cameras only show what's outside my house, and Patty and Ted have disappeared on the other side of the circle. I don't know if they went to Gina's or Patty's, but at this point I don't care.

Though it started off great, today has sucked.

A door closes somewhere below, and I frown, forcing myself forward so I can see who is—

"Kasey?" My heart leaps into my throat. She's on the sidewalk, stalking toward Patty's house. "Kasey, what are you doing?"

She glances up, her face full of determination. "I'm going to get some answers."

Movement catches my eyes in the moonlight, and I look across the square to Gina's house. She's heading toward Patty's as well and will probably reach it at the same time as Kasey. Not only is Patty probably going to recognize Kasey from when she took our picture, but I have no idea how Kasey is going to get any proof without revealing what we saw tonight.

Panic sets in, pushing me to my feet even though I feel too dizzy to stand. She's going to get herself killed!

Everything is a blur as I hurry down the stairs and to the front door. A vague sense of warning pops up in the back of my head as I race toward the other side of the circle, but all I can think about is keeping Kasey safe. I don't know if my neighbors are capable of hurting her—I haven't talked to them enough for that—but I do know I won't let anything happen to her.

Right as I reach the Carmichaels' house, a shriek pulls me to a dead stop. That had to have been Kasey inside. Am I too late? Did they already kill her? I can't breathe, can't move, and I stand frozen as my mind runs through all the horrible things they could be doing to her in there while I'm out here, useless. It's like my limbs have been trapped in cement, and no matter how many times I silently scream at myself to go in and save her, I can't do it.

Honestly, I don't know how long I stand there in the middle of the sidewalk, my heart racing and my mind spinning and my stomach forcing its contents out into the bushes in front of Patty's house. *Minutes.* I haven't heard a thing since that scream, and now I'm too much of a coward to keep moving forward and see Kasey's dead and mangled body for myself.

What kind of a man does that make me? The woman I love is being slaughtered and all I can do is stand here.

Someone inside Patty's house laughs, and the sound settles into my body like lead. The panic subsides into complete numbness, and I find myself taking a heavy step forward. Then another. It's too late for me to save her, but I can't let myself abandon her forever. If nothing else, I have to find out what happened inside that house so I can tell her story. That's assuming my murderous neighbors let me live in the first place.

At this point, does it even matter if I survive?

I ring the doorbell with a trembling hand, exhausted and sweaty and wholly unprepared for Gina's smiling face.

Her smile falters when she takes me in. "Liam! I haven't seen you around in a while. Are you okay? You look..."

I swallow as my stomach threatens another upheaval. "Where is she?"

Her expression falling, Gina pretends to be confused for a moment. "Do you mean Kasey?"

"Where. Is. She?"

"Liam, are you—"

I push past her and make my way into the house, which isn't as snobby as I expected from someone like Patty Carmichael. It's actually quite homey, but that doesn't matter because it's a murder house. I can hear voices near the back, so I make my way in that direction, aware of Gina right behind me but hardly caring. I need to see her. Find out what happened to her. Once I know that, then it doesn't matter what...

My steps still as soon as I reach a sort of mud room leading from the garage. Kasey's there, but she's very much alive. She's *laughing*.

Because she's surrounded by half a dozen husky puppies who are climbing all over her.

Something snaps in my brain. All thoughts gone.

Ted is also sitting on the floor like Kasey, and though he has tears in his eyes, he's snuggling a puppy close and kissing the top of its head with a tenderness that a murderer couldn't have.

"Oh, Liam!" Patty says, coming from another room with a bag of dog treats and a fully grown husky on her heels. "What are you doing here?"

"Liam?" Kasey's head snaps up, her eyes going wide. She stares at me for a long time, even with the puppies crawling all over her, and then her eyes drop to my feet.

Where my ankle monitor is beeping as a red light flashes angrily.

Crap.

CHAPTER TWENTY-TWO

KASEY

As MUCH AS I would love to spend the night cuddling Patty's dog's puppies, I hop up and grab hold of Liam's hand. "You need to get back home," I tell him, though he looks pretty shell-shocked and barely acknowledges me.

Why is he even here? I texted him to tell him... Oh. His phone shattered on the sidewalk when I dropped it. Right. Which means he did not get my quick text telling him that it was Ted's geriatric *dog* Martha who died after being sick for months.

"Thanks for letting me play with the puppies!" I tell Patty and then start dragging Liam toward the door. I know his neighbors noticed the monitor and are probably fully aware that Liam is outside his designated area, but they're kind enough not to say anything. At least not while we're still here. *Hollywood Hot Scoop* is probably going to have the story blasting out to their followers in the next five minutes, but that's a problem I'll deal with *after* I get Liam back into his house.

Once we're outside, Liam is even harder to move, like he's completely shut down. His grip is so tight on my hand that it's starting to hurt.

"Liam, you need to keep walking!" I tug, but I barely manage to force him to take a single step. "Liam!"

"I thought you were dead," he says hoarsely. His eyes meet mine, full of terror and pain. His anguish settles deep in my chest. "I thought something had happened to you, and I couldn't... Kasey, I don't know what I would have done."

I lift my free hand and press it to his cheek, alarmed when he closes his eyes and starts crying. He's always worn his heart on his sleeve, but this is... I think I've underestimated his feelings for me. "Liam, I'm fine. I promise. Everyone's fine."

Based on the way his monitor won't stop beeping, Liam is probably not fine, but unless I can get him to snap out of whatever this is, I won't be able to help him.

He shakes his head. "Kase...I..."

A siren blares to life in the distance, making me jump. Is that for him?

"Liam, you need to—"

"It's too late," he says. Then he sighs, and it's like all of his strength leaves his body with his breath. He looks so worn down, just like he has since he kissed me, and I can't stop the guilt that builds up in my gut. I did this to him. I pulled him from his house, and I broke his spirit, and I messed everything up the minute I showed up at his door and pretended I could be a part of his world.

Tears prick my eyes. "Liam, I'm so sorry."

A cop car zooms into the neighborhood, lights flashing, but the officer turns off the siren as soon as his headlights hit us. The lights are blinding, so I keep my focus on Liam.

He smiles a little as the car approaches and his neighbors come piling out of the house in curiosity. "I'll be fine," he says, clearly not believing it.

"Liam Connolly, I'm going to need you to come with me." The cop approaches warily, but he doesn't need to worry.

Liam holds his hands up and doesn't fight when the officer puts him in handcuffs and stuffs him into the car. He meets my gaze, his smile sad, and I watch in misery as he's carted off. That seems excessive for a guy who was only a couple houses down from his own, but what do I know? For all I know, Liam could have completely lied about the fight that got him put under house arrest in the first place.

No. I refuse to believe that Liam would ever lie to me.

"Kasey!" Cole hurries over to me, though his sleep-filled eyes are on the retreating police car. "Was that Liam?"

I nod. "He broke his house arrest."

"Why?"

"Because he thought I was in danger." It doesn't sound real, even though Liam told me himself.

Cole swears under his breath and has his phone out in the next second, probably to call Derek and let him know what just happened.

I look behind me and glare at the phone in Patty's hand. "Don't tell me you've already sent a picture."

She blinks. "What?"

"Can't you let him live his life in peace?"

"I didn't—"

"Oh, shut up," Gina says and rolls her eyes. "We all know you sold that last photo of Liam and..." She looks at me and cocks her head to one side. "Was that you?"

Before I can say anything, Cole takes my hand and starts pulling me back toward Liam's house. He's on the phone, listening intently to whoever's on the other end of the line, but his scowl is enough to keep me silent. Probably smart not to confirm anything, though it's pretty obvious who I am when I walk into Liam's house like I own the place.

"I hate Liam's neighbors," Cole growls as soon as we're inside. Nelson greets us with an excited rendition of a song that I'm pretty sure is by Taylor Swift, but we both ignore him. "That's what he gets for interacting with them. Curiosity. No, they arrested him." He says that last part into the phone.

While I can't say I like Gina, we were wrong about her. She's apparently a vet and has been helping with the puppies. And Ted has never been married, but Liam never met Martha the dog because she was too old to go on walks. Patty is...still the worst.

"Yeah, she's right here." Cole hands the phone over to me.

Hopefully Derek has some words of wisdom like he always does. "Hello?"

"Kasey, you need to tell me everything you can."

"Ethan?" I don't know why I'm so shocked that it's him, but I am.

"This is going to get out fast, so I need details. What happened?"

Though I'm not sure he needs to know about our murder conspiracy, I tell him anyway, ignoring the skeptical looks Cole gives me as I lay it all out for Liam's publicist. "He was trying to make sure I was safe," I finish, hating the guilt pooling in my belly. That's not going to go away any time soon, and I have a feeling it's going to keep getting worse. "Ethan, I swear I didn't mean for this to—"

"Liam Connolly has a habit of being in the wrong places for the right reasons," Ethan interrupts. He sounds tired. "He would have gotten into a mess like this with or without you because that's what he does."

I don't like the way he makes Liam sound impulsive and thoughtless. "Liam is one of the best guys I know."

"I agree, but luck is never on his side. We're used to it."

I don't like that either. "So what now?"

"Now you and Cole should get out of there while you still can. Paps are going to be swarming the place, and short of calling in the National Guard, there's not much we can do about that. Your anonymity is probably toast, I'm afraid to say, but you'll at least be able to avoid questions for a while if they don't know where to find you."

I meet Cole's eyes, and though his expression is calm, his whole body is tense. "He thinks we should leave," I tell him.

He nods once. "I agree."

"But I don't want to abandon Liam."

"Liam will be fine," Ethan says. "I'll take care of him. But he'll most definitely fire me if I don't take care of you first, Kasey, so please take my advice and go home for now."

"Okay."

"I'll be in touch with updates."

He hangs up, and I stand there in the middle of the entryway, unsure what to do. I'm still gripping Cole's phone; it feels like my only tie to sanity. Go home? I haven't been back in weeks, and Val's house almost doesn't feel like home anymore.

Not like Liam's.

Cole watches me for a moment, his dark eyes unreadable in the dim room. I don't know for sure how he knew to come outside, but I'm glad he did. I'm glad I'm not alone in this now that Liam is...somewhere. "You okay?" he asks eventually.

"I don't know how to answer that question."

He smiles and stuffs his hands into the pockets of his sweatpants. He looks so much softer when he smiles, like he's got this big, scary mask on most of the time and only drops it when he smiles. "Welcome to our world. Don't let it scare you. Liam is worth it."

"That's not what I'm worried about." It is, but even knowing Patty probably got a clear shot of my face and has my first name to go with it, I don't feel as anxious as I should. Handing Cole's phone to him, I hug my middle and sigh. "Why would Liam want to be with someone like me? I'm not famous—at least, I wasn't—and my life is so much smaller than his. There's nothing I could ever give him."

Nelson starts whistling a melody I've never heard before. I like it, but it sounds sad. It fits the mood.

With his hands still in his pockets, Cole shrugs and drops his eyes to the floor. "I probably can't speak for Liam, and I'm nowhere near as well-known as him nowadays. But one of the reasons I loved Sage was because she was outside of the fame. She kept me grounded in a way not even my friends can. Liam has only been a part of this world for a few years, and I know he's terrified of losing his roots. Maybe..." He shrugs again. "Maybe you feel like home."

Warmth spreads through me, loosening my tense muscles and making it easier to breathe. I *really* hope he's right. Especially because that's exactly how Liam feels to me.

"I'm sorry about your girlfriend," I whisper, wondering if that's a good idea after the way he reacted last time someone brought up his breakup.

He glances up, and I get the slightest glimpse of sadness before his face is a blank slate again. "Thanks. She has her reasons, and I won't fight them."

I wonder if she *wants* him to fight them.

"Anyway." He coughs and looks around the house, which is far too dark without Liam here. And I don't just mean because most of the lights are off. "We should probably go. If *Hot Scoop* doesn't know everything already, they will soon, and the paparazzi will be coming in droves."

I don't want to leave, but I understand that it might be the best option unless I want to be under siege here by myself. Holding down the fort with an overexcited parakeet doesn't sound all that appealing.

"Do you need a ride?" I ask, suddenly wondering where in the world my keys ended up. I haven't needed them for weeks. I don't even know if my car will start.

Cole shakes his head. "I'll borrow one of Liam's cars. He can't tell me no."

We lock all the doors, Cole throws some extra food and water into Nelson's cage, and then we part ways in the garage, me to my beat-up Honda and Cole to the charcoal-gray Jaguar that sounds like it's purring rather than chugging gasoline.

I drive away first, since Cole has the remote for the garage, and it's all smooth sailing until I get outside the gate and am suddenly faced with a dozen flashing camera lights that leave me nearly blinded as I make my way to the highway. Ethan wasn't kidding, and I imagine every oncoming car is holding several more paparazzi hoping to get an inside look into the drama of Liam Connolly's life.

I hate this. I hate that I'm leaving, that Liam is in trouble because of me, that even if they let him go back home I won't be there waiting for him. I hate that he can't live his life in peace just because he writes incredible music and that I might never understand how it feels to be famous the way he is.

I hate that there's nothing I can do to help.

I'm sobbing by the time I pull up to the curb outside Val's house, and the only reason I didn't pull over somewhere to have a good cry was because I was terrified someone would see me and realize who I am. How does anyone live like this and still find ways to smile and be happy? How is Liam so impossibly perfect despite everything he deals with?

When I walk through the front door, everything about the house looks wrong. I've lived here for almost a year, but none of it feels right anymore, like this is someone else's life that I'm trying to step into. I don't know how a few weeks with Liam can completely change my comfort zone, but they have, and I'm already desperate to go back.

"Kasey?" Val appears from her bedroom, her eyes wide as she takes me in. "Girl, what are you doing here? Are you—"

I rush forward and collapse into her arms as my crying turns critical. "I don't know what to do," I wail, holding on to her like she's the only thing that can hold me together.

She's not Liam, but she's the next best thing.

"Oh, honey, tell me everything."

Hollywood Hot Scoop

From Deity to Delinquent: Liam Connolly's Downward Descent

IN A SHOCKING TWIST, Liam Connolly was arrested tonight in his own neighborhood after breaking a court-mandated house arrest. Yeah, I'm as heartbroken as you are, Scoopers. While we know Liam lost it at his last concert, we didn't think he would go the way of many of our heroes and spiral. While there's no news on if he was intoxicated or under the influence, here's the one thing we do know:

Liam's mystery woman is Kasey Graham, a delivery driver for a popular food delivery service here in Los Angeles. While I was hoping for someone more interesting, Kasey's nobody status does make me wonder if there really is hope for the average Jill finding herself in the arms of one of our favorite famous men.

What does Liam see in her? We may never know. This Scooper has a theory that in his desperation Liam was holding her against her will, as Kasey was seen fleeing Liam's house immediately upon his arrest. That, or she is actually his dealer and didn't want to take the heat for dosing up our beloved singer-songwriter.

Liam will be at trial in a few days, and we'll be there to give you all the insider info as this story unfolds! In the meantime, we'll be taking a closer look at Kasey Graham and figure out how she turned Liam's head. Maybe we can learn a thing or two from her and snag ourselves a rich and handsome celebrity as well!

Be sure to hit that subscribe button so you don't miss your chance at a famous boyfriend. XO

CHAPTER TWENTY-THREE

LIAM

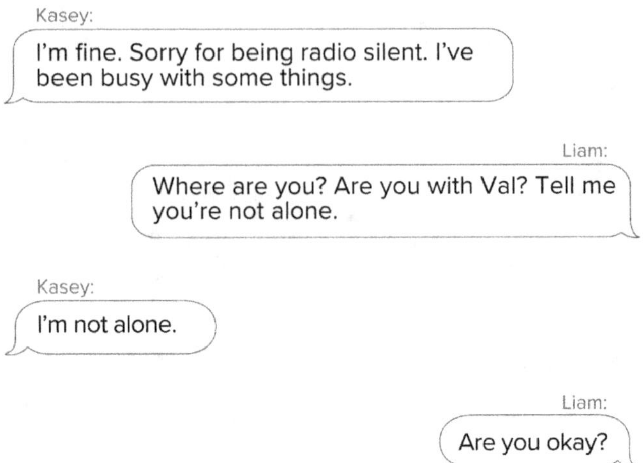

"Liam?"

I blink, still staring at the text that has been on read for almost two days. I thought the night of the "murder" sucked, but this is so much worse. At least that night Kasey was still within reach, and now it feels like I've lost her entirely. I can't even blame my new phone because she *has* responded. Just not in the way I wish she would.

"Liam," Derek says again, and based on the sound of his voice, he's said it more than twice. "You've got to talk to me, man."

I swap my phone back to the call so I stop staring at Kasey's lack of response. "And say what?" I snap. "There's nothing to say."

He doesn't deserve my anger. In the six days since my arrest, Derek has been doing everything he can to keep my spirits up, spending all of his free time on the phone with me even though he and Bonnie have flown to Europe to finish filming their movie. I don't even know what time it is there outside of being late. Very late.

I don't know what time it is here either. My eyes flick to the clock at the top of my screen. Five. At night. I shift on the couch in my music room, though I should probably get up and walk around at some point. I've spent too much time in here over the last few days, and even my guitars are starting to judge me.

With nothing else to do, I've been recording and mixing all of my songs myself until they're perfect. Who needs a studio and sound mixer when I've got misery fueling my obsession? All of these songs remind me of Kasey, and they're all I've got left.

My producer doesn't like it, but I'm not letting anyone touch these songs but me.

"Liam, you need to snap out of it. Your hearing is in a few days, and—"

"They'll decide whatever they decide," I grumble back. With the way the media is currently painting me as a felon and a druggie and a danger to myself and others, I'm not sure things are going to go well for me. "I'll understand if you no longer want to associate with me once my fame is gone."

"Liam, I'm not friends with you because you're famous. Please tell me you know that."

All of Derek's friends are famous. There's no other reason for him to keep me around.

"Liam," he growls, and it's like he's reading my mind. "You were barely on anyone's radar when I met you. Bonnie was a C-list background actress who was only cast to be a pretty face. Freya was—okay, well, she's been famous since before she was born. The point is I've never cared about how famous any of you are, and that's never why I've wanted to be around you. So get your head out of your butt."

I snort. It's like a reflex, even if I don't feel like laughing. "You said butt."

"Are you twelve?"

"If I was, do you think Kasey would actually talk to me instead of ignoring me?"

Derek groans. "I know you've been reading all the articles about her. Will you cut her some slack? She's new to all this."

"I just want to know if she's okay."

"She texted you, didn't she?"

"Barely."

Derek's quiet for a minute, during which I decide to restring my favorite guitar because I need something to keep me occupied. I've thought about hanging up and rerecording a section of "Lull," one of the first songs of my new album, but at this point I don't even know if anyone is going to want to listen to any of my songs.

Most of the world seems to hate me at the moment.

The doorbell rings, and since Derek is still silent, I pull up the camera feed to see who decided to bother me this time. A couple of my neighbors have stopped by, but I've ignored them. This time it's Patty, and though she's high on my very short list of people I don't like, I'm extremely curious to know what she might want to say to me. Plus, she's holding the only thing that might bring me a spot of happiness right now.

"Hang on a sec, Derek," I say, struggling up to my feet and shoving my phone in my pocket. I don't bother muting it, mostly because I know I'm more likely to be civil if I know Derek is listening to the conversation.

When I open the front door, Patty's eyes go wide, like she wasn't expecting me to answer. "Liam."

I pluck the puppy out of her arms without a word, hugging it to my chest and keeping my eyes on the dog's icy blue eyes as it tries to lick my chin.

"Um." Patty lets out a sigh. "I thought maybe you might want a dog to keep you company, with you here, uh, by yourself."

I scoff. "You're the reason I'm by myself." Though, I can't really blame her for Kasey's lack of conversation. There's nothing stopping Kasey from coming back except her own choice to stay away.

Patty is quiet for long enough that I look up, and she winces as soon as my gaze meets hers. "I'm sorry, Liam. About the photo."

I grit my teeth. "Which one?"

"I only gave them one. I don't know how they figured out Kasey's name, but I'm sorry for that too. I never should have..." She drops her eyes to the cement beneath her feet. "I know a puppy doesn't make up for what I did, but you can have him. If you want him. He's purebred and—"

"I can't keep a dog." It's tempting, especially as the little ball of gray and white fluff curls up against me with a yawn. Though there's the chance my life will change after the hearing, I'm hoping it all goes back to normal. I'd be traveling too often to take care of a dog, and I already feel bad enough as it is leaving Nelson in the care of my housekeeper when I'm on tour. "I'm not home often enough to look after him. I mean...usually."

Patty's eyes flick to the monitor on my ankle, and she folds her arms, looking wildly uncomfortable. "Did I make it all worse?" she whispers. "I swear, I just thought it would be a bit of fun when I sent in that picture, and I've never seen you with anyone like that so I figured it was a relationship people would want to know about."

I honestly don't know what to say to that. "You know I'm a regular person, right?" My words come out sharper than I mean them to, but I'm so tired of people thinking that just because they know who I am, they have instant access to my private life. "And whether or not I'm dating someone isn't anyone else's business. I'm entitled to my secrets as much as you are."

A flash of guilt pools in my belly as I think about all the time Kasey and I spent watching my neighbors on the cameras, and I clench my jaw before holding the dog out for her to take him back. I don't deserve puppy snuggles. And I have some cameras to take down.

"We don't have to be friends," I say quietly. "But we're neighbors. That means we should be looking out for each other."

Red-faced and frowning, Patty nods. "You're right."

"I don't have any sugar, but if you ever need to borrow..." I search for something I do have, though I'm not coming up with much. Just a whole lot of ice cream, more than I can ever eat myself. I sigh. "If you ever need someone to sing at your niece's birthday party, give me a call."

She lets out a disbelieving laugh. "You remember my niece? You met her once. More than a year ago."

I shrug. "I appreciate your apology, Patty. Can I get back to my wallowing?"

That makes her expression fall again, and she seems to struggle for something to say. She settles with a nod, tells me I'm welcome to request a visit from the puppy anytime (until someone buys him), and then I'm on my own again, with nothing but Nelson's forlorn whistles to fill the air. I should probably get another parakeet so he doesn't end up miserable like me.

"You're a good man, Liam," Derek says when I flop onto the couch in the lounge and pick up the phone conversation again.

I scoff. "Basic human decency isn't—"

"Do you trust me?"

I glance at my phone, wondering where this change in topic is coming from. "That's a stupid question."

"That's not an answer."

I know it's not, and I trust Derek. I trust him more than I trust anyone. But right now I want to brood, and that's very hard to do when the sexiest man alive is about to give me a pep talk. (That's the internet's assessment of Derek, not mine. Even if it's true.)

"I trust you," I grumble anyway.

"Good. Then don't hate me for what I'm about to say."

I sit back up, my curiosity piqued. "Okay?"

"I talked to Kasey a few hours ago."

If he wasn't in Germany right now, I would punch him. "What? Why? And why won't she—"

"She has her reasons, and they're good ones. And that's all I can tell you. But you need to stop moping around. Give her some time, and she'll come back."

"Will she? Because she won't even send me a text."

My phone buzzes, and I already know what I'm going to see when I pick it up again.

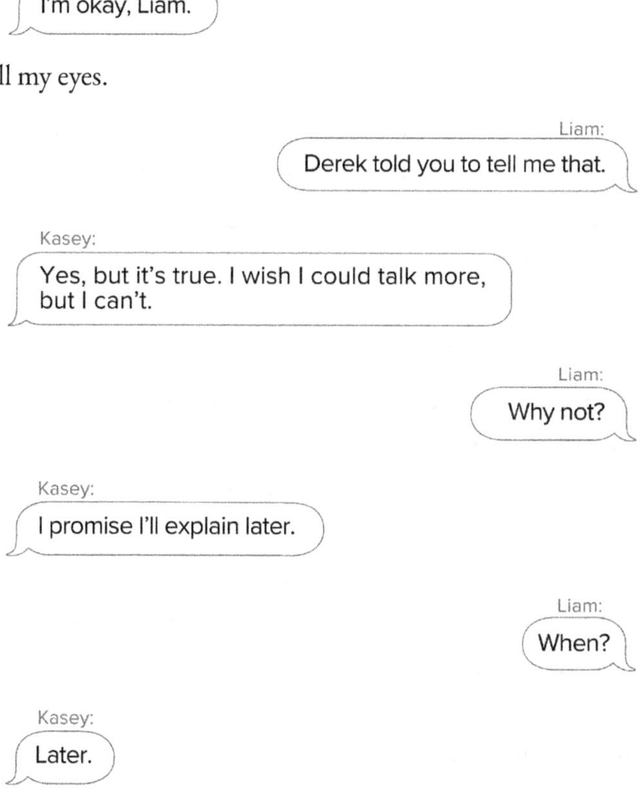

I roll my eyes.

I groan and toss my phone into the plush pillow next to me.

"Relax, Liam," Derek says, his voice muffled by the pillow. "It's not as bad as it seems."

"The woman I'm in love with will barely talk to me because I kissed her and she doesn't know how to turn me down. How is any of that good?"

"You kissed her?"

Yeah, and I can't stop dreaming about it.

"Did you tell her how you feel about her?"

"I didn't get that far," I grumble. "I messed everything up, Derek. I scared her off, and then I went and got myself arrested because I chased after her."

"The police just wanted to make sure you stayed within the bounds of your house arrest," Derek argues. "Especially with all this *Hot Scoop* stuff floating around."

"I hate that website. I hate it so much."

"We all do." There's an undercurrent of something in his voice, but I'm too tired and restless to interpret it. "Will you promise me you'll stop being so gloomy? You're not acting like yourself, and not in a good way."

"Love turns all men into idiots," I mutter, though I smile a little as a melody pops into my head to go with it. Actually, it's a melody that Nelson has been singing ever since I got back from my night out with the cops, though I have no idea where it came from. It's a somewhat jarring collection of notes, but it aligns with my current mood quite nicely.

Even when she's not here, Kasey is inspiring songs.

"I'll try not to be such a buzzkill," I tell Derek, though I won't try very hard. I've been optimistic enough for a lifetime, and I deserve some time to brood. "You should get some sleep, Derek." In other words, I want him to hang up so I don't feel rude, and then I can write this angsty song that's building in my head.

"I should go," he agrees, "but I have one more question."

I already know I'm not going to like this question, whatever it is. "What?"

"Have you read her script?"

I roll my eyes, glad he can't see me as I stand and make my way back to the music room. I would like nothing more than to say yes to that question, but I can't. Kasey didn't trust me enough. "No. Is it any good?"

"Liam..." He seems to be searching for the right words to say.

I grip my phone, suddenly nervous. "Oh, is it terrible?"

"I mean, it's not perfect, but it's a first draft written by someone barely out of school, so of course it's not perfect. But honestly, it's one of the best scripts I've seen in a long time."

"Oh. That's...that's good, right? That sounds like a good thing." So why does Derek sound weird?

"Liam, the story is about you."

"It's...what?" I'm pretty sure I heard him wrong, but Derek is nothing if not an enunciator. "What do you mean, it's about me? Like, some kind of exposé or—"

"I mean it's the story of a musical genius kid from the Midwest who makes his way across the country playing in bars and dives until he meets a record label exec who gives him a shot, and then he makes it big."

I sink onto the piano bench, unsure how to feel about what Derek just told me. "She wrote my story?"

"It's a different name, and there's a romantic subplot, but yeah."

My heart latches on to the last part, and I am way too hopeful for my own good, given how rough the last few days have been. "What kind of romantic subplot?" When Derek's quiet on the other end, I raise my voice. "Derek, what happens in the subplot?"

He sighs. "She's a waitress. He meets her in one of the bars he plays, and she follows him to California after they hit it off. She has dreams of being a musician as well and works alongside him, taking advantage of his fame to boost her own. But she goes too far and gets credit for some of the songs they've written together."

I don't like the sound of that. "But she clears the air, right? Sets people straight?" I need that nameless waitress to do the right thing and not leave me behind as soon as she gets her connections.

"It's just a story," Derek says instead of answering my question.

Groaning, I get up and start pacing because sitting still feels like letting the story come true. "You're telling me the waitress uses the musician's fame for her own gain and then carries on her merry way?"

"I don't know."

"*Derek.*"

"She hasn't finished it, Liam. The story's not done yet."

The story's not done yet. I was supposed to help Kasey write this screenplay, to inspire her to do something she loves, and clearly I did that without knowing it. But maybe I can also help her write the ending. Show her that there's a happy ending for her characters.

For us.

I can't do that if I don't know where she is or if she's really okay.

"Derek, I need you to send me that script." I need to see if there's anything in there that can help me.

"If she didn't give it to you, I don't think—"

"She told me that if you like it, I can read it. Send it to me. Please."

He must hear the desperation in my voice because he sighs and says, "Fine. But you need to tell her that you have it so I don't end up looking like a bad guy."

I laugh despite the way my heart has started to race at the thought of finally reading the thing Kasey has been spending all her time on. "Derek, I'm pretty sure it's impossible for anyone to think of you as a bad guy. You can't even get cast as a villain because you're too good at being good."

Kasey wrote my story. And yeah, she wrote it before I kissed her, but one kiss can't be enough to make her completely lose interest in me, can it? It's not like I told her I loved her (though I came close) so there's no way I scared her off.

What if she was as scared of her own feelings as I've been by mine?

I'm probably grasping at straws, but I've got nothing else to hold on to. If there's even a chance she'll come back, I'll hold on to that chance for the rest of my life.

"Derek, do you promise everything will be okay?"

"I can't promise that, Liam."

"Please."

"Be patient. It will be worth it."

"Okay." If that's all he'll give me, I'll take it. "Give me that script."

I hang up because I still have a song to get out of my head. Then I have to find a way to convince Kasey to finish the story with a happy ending. I'm not sure how, but I'll figure it out.

I have to.

Chapter Twenty-Four

KASEY

I can't believe I'm doing this. Yeah, I've spent the last year knocking on strangers' doors and hoping I don't get murdered during a delivery, but this feels way more dangerous.

For one, people have started recognizing me on the street, though no one has been brave enough to make contact. It's just a lot of pointing and whispering and a couple of guys camped out in front of Val's house, only to be disappointed by the same shabby outfit I've been washing and wearing every day. (That was Bonnie's recommendation; she figured all of the pictures would look the same so no one would pay for new ones.)

I actually sent Vince out to get me tampons at one point because I didn't want the world to start talking about my lady time, and Val was busy doing a live yoga session. Thankfully, her fiancé is a gem and didn't bat an eye at my request, allowing me to avoid public notice for a full morning before I had to go out for a meeting.

Another reason I shouldn't be doing this right now? I have no idea if it's going to work. It might even blow up in my face.

It's been a week and a half since I left Liam's house, and it has been the strangest ten days of my life. More than strangers knowing my name, I have talked to more people than I could have dreamed I ever would. People who have influence, people who couldn't care less about my drama, people who know way more than they should but for some reason keep it to themselves.

"Oh, honey, you look like you're going to a funeral." Val clicks her tongue as she comes into my room, eyeing my outfit with what I can only describe as disgust.

It doesn't help that I literally wore this dress to my grandma's funeral.

I glance at the pile of clothes I've already rejected. I wish I had grabbed some of the clothes Bonnie gave me, but I wasn't exactly thinking straight the night I left Liam's house. "What am I supposed to wear to an interview that might be the end of my life as I know it?"

She snickers. "Girly, there's no *might*. As soon as you set foot in that restaurant, your life is kaput. Bye bye, anonymity! What little is left of it, anyway."

I know she's right, but it's not as terrifying as it was a month ago. No matter what happens today, I'll be fine. "I need this to go well for Liam."

Wrapping her hands around my upper arms, Val rests her chin on my shoulder and smiles. "I think it will work. You've done your research, and unless this Brian guy decides to twist all your words and edit you into oblivion, which would not go well for him, this will work."

Her smile turns more mischievous. "If nothing else, it's going to get you another toe-curling kiss from Liam. Maybe even more."

I smack her. "I never should have told you about that kiss."

It came gushing out along with everything else when I got back, and of course she's of the opinion that I'm doing the wrong thing by keeping my distance from Liam.

Sometimes, I think she's right. It's been killing me being away from him, and every time he sends a text—which is painfully less frequently every day—it takes everything in me not to cave and tell him the whole plan. But I can't do that. I've spent the last week and a half digging into Liam's life as much as I possibly can to try to save his reputation and career, and it would kill me if I got his hopes up and it all came to naught.

I've made sure to text him every day and beg him to be patient with me, but I'm starting to worry that hasn't been enough.

No, I *know* it hasn't been enough, but I don't know what else I can say to him without breaking my resolve and spilling everything.

"I have an idea," Val says and disappears to her own room. When she comes back, she has a pair of wide-legged black slacks and a bright red sleeveless blouse. "I think you need to go bold today. Prove that you're confident."

I laugh. "I'm not confident."

"This will help."

She's right, and as soon as I put on her clothes, I stand taller. This outfit isn't me, but it's what I need.

I've been ignoring my phone all morning, but as I step out into the crisp morning air, I check quickly to make sure this Brian guy is still planning to meet me. I have to sort through a million social media notifications—I should really turn those off—but I find a message from Brian, telling me he will be at the restaurant at the agreed-upon time. Honestly, I don't know if he's actually from *Hollywood Hot Scoop*, but when I contacted the website and told them I was willing to speak to them about Liam, he was the one who responded.

Thank goodness he agreed to meet in a public place, or I would never be brave enough to do this.

I wave to the cameraman chilling in his car outside, though he's clearly sound asleep, and can't help but smile as I climb into my own car. Interest in me is already waning, but what I'm about to do is going to put me front and center in the gossip mill. If it helps Liam, I'm okay with that.

As I head to Santa Monica Boulevard to go deeper into Hollywood, I flip on the radio and start taking slow, deep breaths to keep myself calm. Someday I'll be a world-renowned screenwriter and have to do interviews all the time, so this is just the first of many. I can't let myself panic. Especially not for Liam's sake. If I come across as nervous and twitchy, Brian will probably think I'm making it all up, even with my video and audio testimonials I have ready to go on a flash drive. Confidence is the only thing that will sell this story.

Despite the early time—the sun isn't even out yet—Sunset Boulevard is full of people, but I planned for the traffic. I figured the time could be good for me to review what I plan to say. Normally I would listen to movie soundtracks, but I figured I should act more like Liam this morning and see what is trending. The song that's playing right now is unfamiliar to me, but it's good. Not as good as Liam, but good.

"That was 'As It Was' by the one and only Harry Styles," the radio host says when the song finishes. "Now, hold on to your butts because up next is a brand-new song. It secretly released about an hour ago, so you're going to be one of the first to hear this masterpiece. If you're not sitting down, you might want to. Here's 'If I'd Known'."

A melody I swear I've heard before pops up on a lone violin, slow and heart-wrenching even though it's absolutely beautiful. A layer of piano joins in, just as simple and haunting as the string line, and I feel like something is reaching into my chest and grabbing hold of my heart, like that evil dude in *Indiana Jones and the Temple of Doom*.

And then a voice I know better than my own starts to sing.

If I'd known love would break me
I'd have hidden my heart away
But you would have taken it
Cuz I never had a say

"Liam!" I choke out right as the car behind me honks to tell me traffic is moving.

The rest of my drive is a blur, and I'm genuinely surprised that I make it to the restaurant in one piece. The song is one I haven't heard, all about how love makes fools of men but is somehow worth the pain. I know he's singing to me. He's hurting, and I don't blame him, and if I didn't have to hurry and fix my now tear-streaked makeup before rushing into the restaurant to talk to Brian, I would call Liam and tell him that everything's going to be okay even if I can't actually promise that.

There's just enough hope in the lyrics of this new song that I have to believe it's not too late for us.

But now that I've heard it, I'm feeling all sorts of feelings that are going to make it difficult to do this interview without falling apart. I take a deep breath, give myself a mini pep talk, tell myself that I have to do this for Liam, and then I hurry inside before I can chicken out.

Given the early hour, the restaurant is mostly empty, so it's easy to spot middle-aged Brian sitting in the corner, facing the door. His eyes lock on to me, taking me in, before he stands and gestures to the seat across from him.

"Miss Graham?" he guesses.

I shake his hand and then sit, pulling out the flash drive while he readies his camera. He must do this often because none of the restaurant staff are paying him any attention. He looks so...normal. Just some guy in a plaid button-up and glasses, his beard scruffy and a gold wedding band on finger.

I relax a little, hoping he won't be out to get me.

Once he's fiddled with a few settings, he hands me a microphone to attach to my collar.

As soon as I'm ready to go, he jumps right in, his expression hard. "First and foremost, I am not the proprietor of *Hollywood Hot Scoop*, nor am I employed by the website beyond contract work that fits within the legal bounds of free journalism."

I frown. I was really hoping for someone who was actually from the website that has been working hard to ruin Liam's life, but this is probably as close as I'll ever get. "Okay."

"It is also to be understood that nothing from this conversation is legally binding as fact. Agreed?"

I get it. He's protecting himself from lawsuits. But I don't like it. "Fine. But you promised you would get this story to *Hot Scoop*, and I expect you to hold to that agreement."

"I promised I would get it to them, not that they would publish anything said in this interview."

That's probably as good as I'll get. I take a deep breath, gripping the flash drive tightly. "In that case, I'd like to make it clear that I have recorded my own version of this interview, including all of the testimonials I'm planning to give you this morning, and it's ready to be published immediately in case *Hot Scoop* tries to twist my words into something they're not."

I have to be very careful about what I say today and make sure it doesn't differ from what Val and I recorded.

Brian smiles, which catches me off guard. "Great," he says, and I'm pretty sure he means it. I wonder how many times he's accidentally ruined someone's life by selling a story to *Hot Scoop*. "So you're here to talk about Liam Connolly."

"I am here because I just spent several weeks with Liam in his house in Malibu and don't like the way he's being portrayed by the media."

He lifts an eyebrow. "You're admitting you are the mystery woman he's kept locked up this month."

"I am admitting I was fortunate enough to enjoy his hospitality and friendship while we both have been keeping out of the public eye." I'm going to do my best not to talk about his house arrest, though that's common knowledge now.

"And why would *you* need to lie low?" Brian asks.

"I'm not here to talk about me."

"But you seem to be a large part of this story."

"You can say whatever you want when it comes to my part. I'm here for Liam and Liam alone. He is a good man who has done nothing wrong."

Brian smirks. "I think his recent house arrest says otherwise."

"Liam's house arrest was for his own protection, and he never argued against it." I think back on how Ethan told me I should word things. When he heard what I wanted to do, he was wary, but after talking through my plan with me, he agreed this might be the only thing that will help him. "After his altercation with an intoxicated attendee who was harassing another attendee at his last show, Liam thought it was best to keep a low profile and focus on his music."

"He punched a man in the face," Brian says with a scoff.

"He also saved me from drowning," I reply. "Twice. He paid for his driver's chemotherapy last year. He donates food and money to homeless shelters all around the country, in every city he visits. He gives out extremely generous tips to every service worker he interacts with." *He writes entire albums for a girl who doesn't deserve his tender looks and sweet smiles.* I don't say that last part out loud, but I want to. "When I met Liam Connolly, I was barely getting by, and he took me in without question, giving me a place to stay and helping me chase my dream because that's the kind of guy he is."

Brian folds his arms, sitting back in his seat with skepticism in his eyes. "And why should I believe you?"

"You shouldn't." I set the flash drive on the table in front of me. "But will you believe Derek Riley? Princess Freya Alverra of Candora? Maybe his longtime housekeeper or people who knew him when he was a kid?"

"A few testimonials hardly—"

"How about twenty-seven testimonials?" I ask, pushing the drive forward. "And that's just the ones I got on audio and video. There's also several written statements. You don't have to believe me, but I hope you believe some of the world's most influential musicians who were happy to praise Liam even though you'd expect them to consider him a competitor."

I did try to get Taylor Swift in on it, knowing how much Liam loves her, but she was annoyingly difficult to get a hold of because she's so busy being successful. I'm still hoping she posts something or says something at some point, but I'm perfectly happy with the artists who did respond when Derek reached out.

I wouldn't have been able to do any of this without Derek, and I really hope Liam knows how good of a friend he has.

Furrowing his brow, Brian picks up the flash drive and studies it for a moment. "Why would you go to all this trouble for a man whose net worth is higher than anything you could dream of? Is he paying you?"

Ethan thought he would ask something like this, so I have a ready answer. In case anyone looks into Liam's financials, I need to be honest.

"When that first photo of us surfaced, Liam covered my paycheck for a few weeks so I could avoid going out in public and face attention that I wasn't accustomed to. Beyond that, he's given me nothing but a place to stay and some really nice tips when I delivered his food when we first met."

"So you're doing this out of the goodness of your heart?"

"I'm doing this because I'm in love with him."

Oh. That's not what I meant to say. My face blooms with heat, my heart picking up an erratic rhythm, but it's not like I can take it back.

Those words are out there now for everyone to hear unless *Hot Scoop* decides not to publish them, which wouldn't make any sense at all. A random nobody food delivery driver proclaiming her love for one of the greatest musicians of the modern era? That's comedy gold right there.

I swallow, clasping my hands together in my lap. "Liam always seems to be in the wrong place at the wrong time, but that's just because he's such a good person that he's always trying to help, even when it damages his reputation. The night he broke his house arrest, he thought I was in trouble and came to help. He didn't care about himself; he just cared about me. You can't fault him for that."

I look at the camera instead of Brian when I say this next part. "If you listen to Liam's lyrics and watch interviews he's done, you'll know he's never spoken poorly about anyone. His whole life is about making the world a better place for the people in it, and his music reflects that. I've never met a more selfless person in my life, and anyone who thinks poorly of him has either gotten caught up in lies or doesn't understand what makes a good person."

I look at Brian. "He doesn't deserve all this hate, and I think you know that. Thank you for your time."

Before he can say anything else, I tug the mic free and then stand and leave the restaurant without looking back. He has the flash drive, and hopefully *Hot Scoop* tells the right story. If they don't, I'll tell it myself, and I'll have the backing of some of the most influential people I've ever known to help me get it out to as many people as possible. This plan will work.

It has to work.

When I get back to the safety of my car, I drive away before anyone tries to approach me. I was in the restaurant long enough for someone to recognize me, and I'm not sure I can emotionally handle anyone asking more questions. Brian was hard enough, and he barely asked me anything.

I don't know where I'm going, but I don't stop until I feel like I've driven through a good chunk of Los Angeles and ended up on the beach near Santa Monica Pier. I guess I'm hoping to blend in with the crowds, but mostly I don't know where else to go. Val will be at home, waiting to hear how things went, and Liam is...

Glancing at the time on my phone, I wince when I realize Liam is probably starting his hearing right now. Derek said it was today, which is why I did my best to get the story out as quickly as I could. It's not like my little interview would change a judge's decision, but I wanted to make sure there was something good for Liam, no matter what the judge tells him.

"Please let him go," I beg the judge anyway. Wherever the hearing is happening, I hope he hears my quiet prayer. I send a prayer to *Hot Scoop* too. "Do the right thing."

With my shoes in hand, I walk along the sand and take in the sunshine, which feels like a good omen, and then I find a place to sit away from anyone else. Once settled, I pull up the music app Liam forced me to download weeks ago and type his name in the search bar.

His new album, *Kismet*, is the first thing that pops up, and I'm genuinely shocked at the number of listens some of the songs already have despite the album launching this morning. I knew he was popular, but this is unreal. It's only been a few hours since it dropped, and yet hundreds of thousands of people have been listening.

I hit play on the first one, smiling when I recognize the song I first saw him recording. It's so much better than the version I heard. Either he got special permission to go into the studio, or he somehow managed to record this in his house, which is incredible. It sounds polished. Perfect. With all of the heart he puts into everything.

Exactly how Liam would want it.

The next song is more of the same, another familiar tune but so much better. I can't stop grinning as I hold my phone to my ear and let the music meld with the sound of the waves and people enjoying the sunny California morning. The breeze off the water is cool, but the sun is warm and comforting.

For a girl who grew up in the flat, waterless lands of Kansas and is afraid of deep water, this place feels so much like home. I'm not sure I'll ever be able to live anywhere else.

Halfway through the album, I suddenly hear my own voice crack and squeak through the harmony of a song. I drop my phone in alarm but pick it back up immediately, brushing off the sand and turning the volume higher. He kept it? I was supposed to be a placeholder until he recorded the actual harmony with a real singer, and I sound like a hoarse seagull trying to mimic a human voice. Granted, the rest of the song isn't as polished as the others I've listened to, so it all mixes together really well, but I'm not a vocalist.

"Why in the world would you keep this?" I ask my phone, as if Liam can hear me through it.

Before I can listen to the rest of the album, I have to know what people are saying about this song, "Say More." Maybe it's a sign that I've descended into madness with all this new attention, but I *need* to know.

And what I find is...confusing.

Generally, people like the song. They talk about how, unlike the others, this one has a rough and raw quality that feels intentional, like Liam is trying to say something with its quality. It's not like there are any actual mistakes in the instrumentation or Liam's singing, but everyone is talking about the imperfections of the song as a whole. Particularly the female vocalist's deliberate strain and breathiness.

Nothing about that was deliberate, and yet so many comments are talking about how human I sound. How Liam is telling the world with this song that you don't have to be professionally trained to sing your heart out.

No one has said I sound good, but no one has said they hate my singing either.

I don't know what to do with that.

A few people are convinced that it's me on the track, citing the date of my first appearance and the speculation that I've been with Liam ever since that point, while others think there's no way Liam could have written that song in the last few weeks. Clearly the latter group don't know him at all, and I wonder if anyone has ever seen his writing process the way I did.

He should show that to people. Be like that one guy—Charlie Puth, I think his name is—and compose a song on camera to showcase his brilliance. I know Liam doesn't like social media, but I think people want to know more about him. They already love his music; they should be able to fall in love with him just like I did.

Not *exactly* like I did, of course. I don't want anyone else loving him the way I do because I want to keep him for myself.

"Oh my gosh, I love Liam Connolly." Suddenly that hits me like I just got smacked in the face by a rogue wave. Apparently this fact didn't fully sink it when I said it in the interview. I mean, it shouldn't really come as a shock, given how amazing that man is, but I can't actually imagine what life would be like if I couldn't have him in my life from here on out. I suspected how I felt about him back when I was at his house, but there's really no way I can doubt it now.

Plus, I said it on camera.

I run a hand through my hair and hit play on the next song, hoping his music will keep me from panicking.

How long does a hearing like this last, anyway? Because I need Liam to be free so I can tell him to his face how much he means to me.

CHAPTER TWENTY-FIVE

LIAM

"OH, BABY, I'M SO proud of you!" My mom wraps me in a hug that is so tight I can barely breathe.

I don't even care. She's the only reason I made it through that hearing in one piece, and I'm so glad Ethan convinced her to come down even though there are cameras everywhere. I've missed her more than I can put into words, and I'm not sure I can keep pretending I'm fine keeping my distance. She paid for my music lessons; she's going to have to deal with the fame that came as a result.

Biting back tears, I hold her until she wiggles free and smacks my arm.

"Let a woman breathe, why don't you?" She mutters something in Irish that I don't understand and then shakes her head at me. "Why didn't you tell me you were in all this trouble?"

Her voice is the most familiar thing in the world to me, like a song I've known my entire life with the way it lilts and bounces. She may be reprimanding me, but I can't stop smiling. "Because I knew you'd be worried," I tell her, and then I hold her at arm's length to get a good look at her. Seriously, how could I have gone *months* without seeing my mom? She looks just as I remember, her auburn hair full of lively waves and soft wrinkles lining her sea-green eyes.

She shakes her head. "Liam Dónal Connolly, I'll be worryin' about you whether or not you're causin' trouble. At least you've gotten yourself out of this one."

I look across the courtroom, where the girl from the concert is talking to my lawyer. If not for Shaylee and her testimony, as well as those of her friends who were at the concert with her, I'm not sure I would have gotten off so easily. "I had help," I say, though at this point Mom knows pretty much everything. She heard the whole hearing and probably had a good long talk with Ethan at some point.

But there's one thing she probably *doesn't* know about.

I take a deep breath, making sure I've still got a bit of privacy despite the million reporters patiently waiting to talk to me. Lowering my voice, I lean in and say, "Mom, I met someone."

She smacks my shoulder again. "I know that. I can read, you know."

"But you never pay attention to the tabloids!"

Rolling her eyes, she pulls out her phone and shows me a picture I've never seen before. It's of Kasey and me the night of the sunset, locked together in a kiss that still haunts me a week and a half later. While I'm not mad about the reminder of something I dream about most nights, my stomach drops as I think about how this picture exists.

"Where did you get this?" I ask. *And why isn't it all over the internet?*

Mom clicks her tongue and takes her phone back, even though I wouldn't mind staring at that photo for the rest of the day. As much as I've missed my mom, I miss Kasey so much more.

"Ethan sent it to me," Mom says. "Thought I should know my son is in love for the first time."

"Love?" The word comes out in a squeak, and I grit my teeth when she raises her eyebrows at me. "Fine. I love her. But how did *Ethan* get this picture, and why isn't it—"

"Someone tried to sell it to *Hot Scoop*," Ethan says, coming up behind me. He gives my mom a warm smile and then turns to me. "But I figured you wouldn't want that one surfacing, so I pulled some strings."

"Why don't you always pull strings?"

He laughs, shaking his head. "I'm good at my job, but I'm not that good. This wasn't easy, so I hope you appreciate the hard work I put in. Congrats on getting the charges dropped."

Though he heads for the door, I grab his arm. "Thanks," I tell him as sincerely as I can. "I'm really glad you're my publicist, Ethan."

A flash of emotion crosses his face, though he hides it quickly. "Even if I'm not Jordan?"

"I don't think Jordan could have done what you've done for me. Thanks for looking after me all this time. And looking after Kasey too."

"It's my job, Liam. You pay me for a reason."

I shake my head, wishing I knew how to put into words how much I would have floundered without him. "I've been taking you for granted, and I'm sorry. You're the best."

He smiles, nods, and then leaves the courtroom.

Mom grabs my hand. "I think it's time you tell me about Kasey. And buy me lunch."

I laugh, glance at the reporters who perk up as soon as I look their way, and then kiss my mom's cheek. "Yes, ma'am, though we'd better hurry before they start hunting us down."

We meet my bodyguard outside the courtroom and hurry for the car that's waiting for me, ignoring shouted questions as we go. None of this is new for me, but it still feels strange to be back in the spotlight after spending so much time in the quiet stillness of my house. My ankle is free and clear, and I can literally go anywhere I want again, and yet I'm still drawn back home even though I should be sick of those four walls.

Home is full of memories of Kasey.

Lunch is nice. It's been so long since I really got to talk to my mom, and the restaurant she picks gives us a private room so we don't have to deal with people pressing their noses against the glass like I'm part of some zoo exhibit. *Here we see a Liam outside of his natural habitat. You can see by his fake smile that he would love to be somewhere else, with* someone *else.*

I love my mom, and I'm so glad I can tell her about what's been going on, but talking about Kasey is only making me miss her more.

"Why don't you go get her?" Mom asks while we wait for our dessert.

I slump in my seat, laughing without humor. "Because she doesn't want me to." I have treasured every text she's sent me, no matter how vague, but a few words on a screen don't compare to seeing the look in her eyes when I say something dumb. It's not the same as eating dinner with her and imagining what it would be like to see her backstage at all of my shows. To kiss her whenever she lets me. To know she'll always be there when my feet hit the ground after flying toward the sun.

"She told me to be patient," I say, folding my arms. "But you know how I am."

Chuckling, she nods and puts her hand on my arm. "Aye, but you know what they say. *Ní dheachaigh fear meata chun bantiarna.*"

I sigh, wishing I knew more Irish. "What does that mean?"

"Faint heart never won fair lady. It means you must be brave, Liam. I only know what you've told me about Kasey, but I have a feelin' she is afraid to take the next step because she doesn't know if she'll have a sure footin'. You need to tell her what she means to you."

I did that. I wrote a whole album and sent it out into the world this morning, though I have no idea how people are receiving it. I've kept my phone on silent since the moment I woke up. For all I know, Kasey might have sent me another vague text telling me to wait. Does she even know the album is out there? That I couldn't bring myself to record over her voice because that would feel like losing her?

I didn't put her name on it because I know she didn't want me to use her vocals, but that song is one of my favorites from the whole album because she's a part of it. She'll get royalties from it, which should help with her financial situation, but I want to do so much more for her.

I pull my phone out in case she has said anything, hating myself for how addicted I am to her at this point when she made it pretty clear after our kiss that a relationship with me is not what she wants.

"I know what's goin' through your head, and you need to stop," Mom says.

My eyes filter over the million and a half notifications. There's nothing from Kasey, but Ethan texted me about ten minutes ago. I open his message in case it's important and groan when I see the link to a *Hot Scoop* article.

"This should be good," I mutter, barely glancing at my name in the headline before I hit play on the video. They don't usually do videos, so I'm curious what—is that Kasey?

"I'm in love with him."

I drop my phone, which keeps playing underneath the table. Swearing, I duck down and fumble for it. Where did it go?

"That's right, Scoopers, we've got the ultimate scoop for you today!" an unfamiliar female voice says. "We've all been curious about what's really going on between Liam Connolly and his mysterious lady friend, Kasey, and it turns out this is a bona fide romance that has been brewing for weeks."

Finally locating my phone, I snatch it up and set it on the table so both Mom and I can watch.

Kasey's back on the screen, though the sound is muted as she talks to someone off-screen. The same unfamiliar voice continues over top of the video.

"Kasey Graham, recent USC graduate, met with one of our sources this morning to give us the real story, and I'm going to be honest with you—you might want to grab some tissues. But first, we reached out to some of your favorites to find out who Liam really is."

Suddenly Derek is on the screen, and he's not wearing his actor mask like he normally would when put in front of a camera. Maybe it's because this footage clearly came from a cell phone and he's in his hotel in Europe, but he's being entirely genuine as he talks. "I met Liam before he became a household name, and he's one of the best men I know. Always lights up a room, always makes sure everyone is comfortable and happy. His whole goal in life is to look after the people around him."

Raya Guerrera, a fellow musician with my record label, is up next, once again talking into a cell phone that she's clearly holding herself. For some reason, it makes the video feel more real. "Oh man, I don't even know where to start with Liam. He's like that guy who instantly makes you feel like you're a part of something, you know? We got signed around the same time, and you'd think that would make us rivals, but I can't count the number of times I've been in the studio and heard him cheering from the booth after a great take. He's even helped me with some of my songs because the man's a musical genius."

I don't know what's happening right now. And why can't we go back to what Kasey was saying? I'm pretty sure she said she's in love with me. Well, she said she's in love with *someone*, and it had better be me she's talking about.

Several more people pop up with nice things to say about me, including Bonnie, Cole, and Freya, as well as some people I've literally never spoken to despite being one of their biggest fans, Jack Hawthorne among them. He may have been my inspiration in the beginning, but I didn't think the guy knew who I was.

I was already feeling pretty good after the hearing and spending the last hour with my mom, but this is...

How am I supposed to feel right now?

The video shifts back to Kasey, who looks incredible in her red shirt and more makeup than I've seen on her before. Incredible, but not quite like her. "When I met Liam Connolly, I was barely getting by, and he took me in without question, giving me a place to stay and helping me chase my dream because that's the kind of guy he is."

But what about the *love*? I'm literally sitting on the edge of my seat here. I didn't imagine that word at the start of this. Did I?

The faceless narrator jumps into talking about articles posted about me by other media outlets even though *Hot Scoop* has by far been the most antagonist toward me over the last week. Heaven forbid they admit they were wrong.

"It seems Liam is just as golden-hearted as we've wanted to believe all along," she says, almost like she's wrapping up.

"That can't be it," I whisper to my phone.

The video pauses on a freeze frame of Kasey, whose cheeks are blushed with pink to match a look of surprise in her eyes. Surprise and something that tugs at my heart because it's the kind of look I've dreamed of getting from her for a long time. But is that look about me?

"While it may sound like Kasey is simply a pawn in a game to make Liam look good, we've done our homework, Scoopers, and this is the real deal. She's a woman in love, and I think we can all agree that Liam is lucky to have someone like this on his side. But we'll all be ready in case it doesn't last."

"It'll last," I whisper, though I bite my lip when the video starts playing Kasey again.

"I'm doing this because I'm in love with him," she says again, and then she makes that face it just showed a moment ago, the one that gives me renewed hope that things aren't over. "He doesn't deserve all this hate."

"There you have it, Scoopers," the narrator says. "We'll get you all the updates on this starstruck romance as it unfolds, so make sure you subscribe! XO"

The video ends, leaving me breathless and with no idea what to do now. My hands are literally shaking because this is the opposite of what I expected to get out of today. Not only am I cleared of any charges and ankle monitor-free, but also Kasey... Why would she do something like this? She put herself in the middle of all the gossip, guaranteeing herself a place in the spotlight. For me?

A text comes in, and I tap on it as soon as the notification pops up.

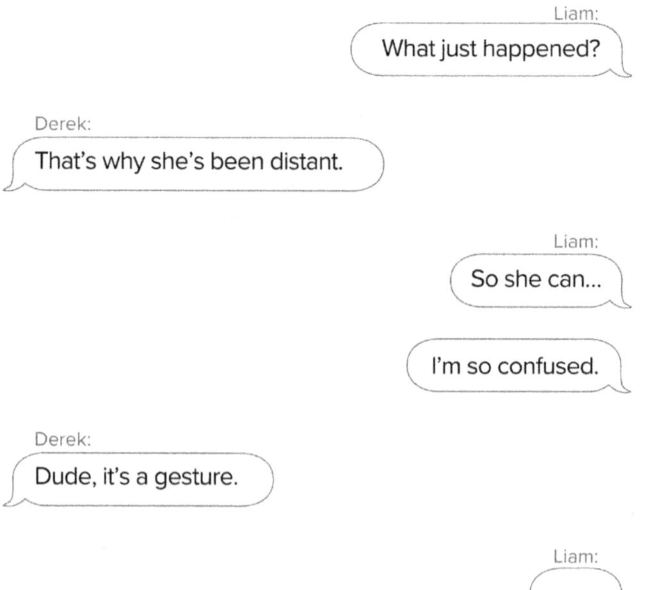

I can barely get my thumb to function as I type out a reply.

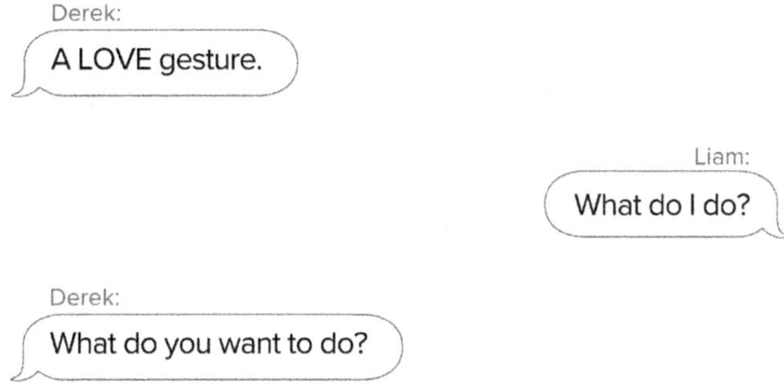

What a question. Though I can feel Mom's eyes on me, I keep my focus on Derek while I process the last ten minutes. What do I want to do? I want to find Kasey and tell her everything I couldn't put into words the last time we were together. A song is one thing, but telling her outright that I love her is another.

It's terrifying, but if that woman can do it in front of the world, surely I can say three little words to her face.

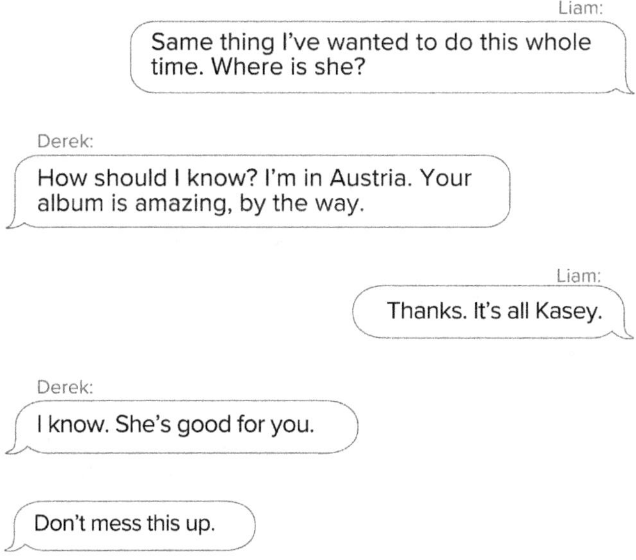

I exit out of the text thread, gloss over the texts my other friends have sent me even though I'm curious if they're commenting on the album or the video *Hot Scoop* just posted, and then pull up my texts with Kasey.

They're just as vague and distant as they've always been, but now I'm seeing them in a different light. I'm seeing her hesitation and fear leaking through as she takes a risk. I'm seeing the high likelihood that the video would have a different flavor and make things worse for both of us, so she probably didn't want to make me believe it would do what she hoped.

I'm seeing a woman who just did the most amazing thing for me and deserves everything in return.

I have never experienced such a strong sense of relief as the one that washes over me when Kasey texts me back immediately.

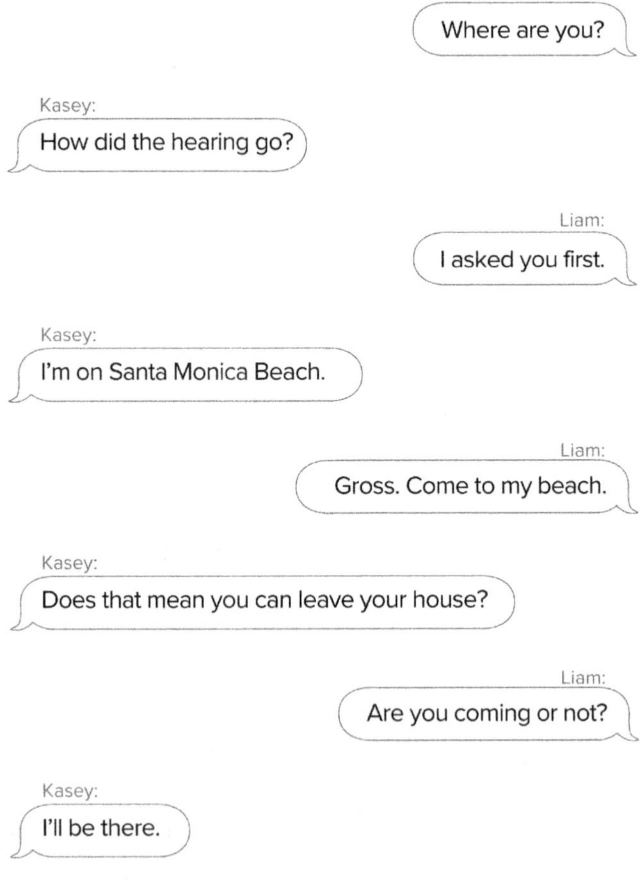

With that settled, I lock my phone and look at my mom.

She laughs, shaking her head at me. "I've never seen you like this, Liam."

"I've never felt like this."

She pats my cheek, her smile warm and familiar but not the one I want to be looking at right now. "Then you'd best go get her, *mo leanbh*." She hasn't called me her child in a long time, and the term of endearment feels like a boost to my already overfilled heart.

"Sean will take you home," I tell her, kissing her cheek and then passing the message on to my driver on the way out. I'll take an Uber and make someone's day because apparently I am a *great guy*.

Honestly, I may never stop smiling.

CHAPTER TWENTY-SIX

KASEY

WHEN I GET TO Liam's house, I can barely breathe. I'm assuming he saw the *Hot Scoop* video, which showed up way faster than I expected it to—must be a slow news day—and that's why he's so eager. He's been good about respecting my boundaries until today, so it's the only thing that would make sense.

But even with his enthusiasm, I'm not sure what to expect from this little reunion. Ethan confirmed that Liam was let off the hook and is now free to go anywhere, and I can't figure out why he wanted me to come back to his house where he's been trapped for so long. Or why he wants me to come in the first place. Is it just because he wants to celebrate with his friends?

I can be his friend.

Ha! No I can't. This week and a half away from him has been awful, and I never want to go through that again. But if I messed everything up after our kiss, or if Liam doesn't feel the same way I do, I won't be able to hang around as just his friend without my heart breaking the whole time.

Either today's meeting is the start to a real, hopefully lasting relationship, or this is goodbye.

Man, I don't like that second option.

He doesn't answer the door when I ring the bell, though I expect that. He said to meet him at the beach, after all. What I don't expect is the sound of the lock turning and a robotic voice that says, "Welcome, Kasey."

"That's new," I mutter as I step inside. And probably not as secure as it should be. What if someone printed out a picture of my face and wore it as a mask? I got approached by enough people on the beach to know my newfound fame isn't going away anytime soon, and interest in Liam Connolly is off the charts. His album alone lit a flame, and then I went and dumped a bucket of lighter fluid on top by basically telling the world that if they're not in love with him, they're idiots.

I need to know how Liam will respond to my interview—like, a bone-deep, never-going-to-sleep-until-I-know kind of need—so I push open the door and tell myself I can't be cowardly anymore. From here on out, bravery and honesty are the only way I can live if I want Liam to be a part of my life.

Nelson greets me with his customary excited shrieking, making me jump. I want to run to the back patio and the staircase that will take me down to the beach, but I force myself to stay put. Liam loves this bird, and Nelson spent more time than normal in his cage while I was here. I can't believe I'm saying this, but I feel bad for the little guy, and maybe I've misjudged him.

I tiptoe closer to the cage, gritting my teeth as I watch the bird bob up and down while he sings one of Liam's songs.

One about me.

"Here's the deal," I say, hating how much my voice wavers. This is a two-ounce ball of feathers who can't and won't hurt me, if Liam is right about him. I have no reason to be so terrified. "I'm going to open this door." I start unwinding the wire that Liam uses to keep Nelson from breaking out. The fact that he keeps using the wire even though he has had no indication that I'll ever return warms my heart.

"Good buddy bird!" Nelson says, bobbing his head wildly. I don't know if he's saying that as reassurance or because it's a thing he says all the time, but I'm taking it as a sign.

I nod. "I'm trusting Liam right now, so you'd better not make him look bad."

As I pinch the latch of the door, Nelson freezes, head turned to one side so he can stare at me with his beady little eye. Maybe I shouldn't do this. Not without Liam here. But I'm halfway there, and I want this bird to trust me as much as Liam trusts me, so I can't go back on my word.

I flick the door open, and Nelson zooms out with the fury of a caged animal intent on committing murder. I scream and duck, waiting for the sting of his beak and his little claws gouging my eyes out.

But it doesn't come.

I peek my eyes open, looking up at the murder bird.

He's whistling a cheery tune as he flies in circles over my head, and I can't describe his sounds as anything but pure happiness. I slowly stand up, and as soon as I drop my hands away from my head, the lemon-lime parakeet lands on my hair and hops around a couple of times, still singing his little song. Wait, I know that melody! It's the line of harmony that I sang with Liam!

I take a slow breath, tense but no longer panicking. "Maybe you're not so bad," I admit.

"Nothing but love," he says back, which is a line from one of my favorite Liam songs.

"I really hope you're right."

I spend a couple more minutes with Nelson, letting him explore my shoulders and even sit on my finger for a few seconds, and then I usher him back into the cage and close the door. I leave off the wire; if Nelson wants to get out, that's fine with me now that we've come to understand each other. Once he's settled on his perch, I head for the back door and the long, winding staircase that will take me to Liam.

Only a few people are down on the sand—boy, would I love to have access to a private beach like this—and Liam is easy to find. He's standing at the edge of the surf in shorts and a t-shirt even though there's a crisp breeze and what looks like a storm blowing in. I'm pretty sure he would dress like this even in the middle of a Wyoming winter and still complain that it's too hot.

Though I'm wishing I'd snuck upstairs and stolen one of his sweatshirts, I can't turn back now that I've seen him. He's the most beautiful man I've ever known, inside and out, and I already feel safe and warm despite the twenty feet between us. I won't survive saying goodbye if that's what he wants to do.

I could stand here for hours, admiring him against the dark waves and delaying everything, but that's not why I came here.

"You kept me on the song," I say when I get closer.

He spins around, and his instant smile when he recognizes me hits me with the full force of the sun, which has vanished behind a layer of clouds. Who needs sunshine when they've got Liam Connolly to brighten up the world? "You wrote a movie about me," he replies.

Oh crap. Derek told me Liam had the screenplay, but I was still holding out hope that he hadn't read it. I tilt my head to one side, doing my best to remain aloof. For some reason... "Who said it's about you?"

He chuckles and takes a step closer, so the water only licks at his heels rather than submerging his feet. Not close enough to touch, but close enough for me to see the way a fire lights in his blue eyes as he takes me in. "Please. The gorgeously handsome musician from the Midwest who falls for a woman who's way too good for him because he has a heart of gold and sees the best in people? You have me pegged."

With another small step, he reaches out and grabs a fistful of my blouse, using it to tug me closer to him.

My mouth is suddenly dry, my heart pounding, and none of my limbs seem to be working even though water now plays at my toes. Still, I smile and lean into the teasing because there is nowhere I'd rather be. "If that's the case, that would make me the antagonist who uses you for her own gain."

Liam shrugs. "You haven't written the ending yet."

That's because I don't know the ending, but I have a feeling it will be easy to write after today. With the way Liam's looking at me, his eyes growing dark with desire as his other hand joins the first and pulls me close enough that I have to press my hands to his chest, there's only one way this story can go from this point.

The antagonist realizes no career is better than the love of a good man. This man.

"There's an ending where we both can win here," Liam says huskily and traces my face with his eyes, landing on my mouth and staying there. Cold breeze who? I'm overheating.

"What is it?" I whisper, closing my eyes.

"It's not taking advantage of me if I'm giving it all to you willingly, and I would love to see you shine brighter than me. In any industry." He moves his hands to my hips and then presses his lips to the soft skin below my ear, dropping his voice to a whisper. "I'd give all of this up if it would help you achieve your dreams."

Oh. my. goodness. How is a girl supposed to breathe with a man trailing kisses along her jaw and saying the most romantic things? "But what about your dreams?" I manage to get out, though heaven knows how.

Liam chuckles, and the sound reverberates in his chest against my fingers. "I just want to make music. I don't care what happens with it once I do. But I'd give even that up for you in a heartbeat."

"Why?"

"Because I'm in love with you, Kasey Graham, and nothing makes sense anymore except making you happy."

I don't know how I'm still standing in one piece, and I'm so tempted to curl up into his arms and never leave. But I have to see his face, so I pull my eyes open and nearly melt at the expression on his face. His words were enough, but his face is saying so much more. He's always been easy to read, but this is Flynn Rider looking at Rapunzel in *Tangled*. Nick looking at Rachel during the wedding in *Crazy Rich Asians*. Mr. Darcy looking at Elizabeth in any version of that story.

I feel like I'm about to cry, which is ridiculous, so I let out a little laugh instead. "You love me?"

He nods. "I didn't think I would ever say that to anyone. What have you done to me?"

"Are you saying all of this is my fault?"

"Yes." His arms snake around my back, pulling me flush against him. To my surprise, he's not smiling, like he's entirely serious about what he's saying. "From the minute you crashed into my glass door and pretended it didn't happen, I have been captivated. Changed. Completely..." He frowns, as if searching for the right word. "Moonstruck."

I grin. "That sounds like the title of a song."

Scoffing, he shakes his head and then presses his forehead to mine. "Everything about you is the title of a song, Kase. I'm going to kiss you now." And then, after waiting a moment to see if I'll object, he presses his lips to mine so slowly and softly that all of my lingering worries fade away to nothing. This isn't a man hoping to score or enjoying a fling until the next thing comes along.

Liam loves me.

And I've been waiting ten days to kiss him again. Grabbing hold of his t-shirt, I tug myself closer and deepen the kiss. Maybe a bit too eagerly. My movement knocks Liam off balance, making him stumble back into the water. Though he catches himself easily, he swears as soon as his foot lands and falls backward, taking me with him because we're tangled up together.

And that's how I end up swimming in the Pacific Ocean for the first time in my life.

I thought pools were scary, and I went in a lake once as a kid and was terrified out of my mind. But the ocean? Which is not only freezing but *moves* you around and has things swimming in it that are bigger than I can even conceptualize? I scream as soon as I hit the waves, swallowing a mouthful of salty water as I scramble to find my footing even though it feels like there's nothing but water all around me.

Something grabs me and tugs, and that had better be Liam because I refuse to die in a shark attack. My foot finds something semi-solid, giving me enough leverage to push up. It slides in the sand under me, but at least I get my head above water.

"Kasey!" The word is drowned out by a wave that crashes over me, knocking me under again.

I'm going to drown in two feet of water. This is ridiculous.

By the time Liam manages to drag me to shore, I'm not sure if I'm crying or laughing in between my painful coughs as I try to dispel the seawater from my lungs. Liam is swearing up a storm, half in English and half in Irish as he runs his hands over my face, pushing my hair back and looking like he's considering mouth-to-mouth as I try to breathe again beneath him.

As nice as that sounds, I'm worried I'll choke water into his mouth if he does.

"Kasey, I'm so sorry. It was my stupid fracture, and then it dropped off right where... I didn't mean—"

"Is the ocean always that cold?" I gasp as a shiver runs the length of my body.

He relaxes only slightly now that he knows I haven't drowned. "Yeah," he says breathlessly.

My fingers find his arm and tug so he collapses on top of me in a blessedly solid blanket of warmth. "That's better," I say, my words hardly comprehensible through my chattering.

Dropping his face into my shoulder, Liam takes a deep breath and lets it out slowly. "Am I going to have to worry about you drowning for the rest of my life?"

The rest of his life. I like the sound of that.

I wrap my arms around him in case he gets the terrible idea to move. He's ridiculously heavy, but I'm pretty sure I'll freeze if he gets off of me. "Maybe you should teach me how to swim."

"I'm not much of a teacher."

"Then it will take a long time, and you might have to rescue me and give me mouth-to-mouth from time to time."

He slowly lifts his head, his eyes sparkling as they meet mine. "That doesn't sound so bad."

I grin. It still hurts like crazy to breathe, but I'm alive thanks to him, and I'm pretty sure he'll never let anything bad happen to me. Physically, mentally, emotionally. He'll take care of it all. "I know I said it to *Hot Scoop* this morning, but I love you, Liam."

And oh, how I love that smile of his.

After his eyes jump up in the direction of his house, he gives me a quick kiss and then starts pushing himself up.

"No!" I complain.

But he is too strong for me to hold and makes it to his feet. When he grabs my hands and tugs me up to join him, he immediately wraps his arms around me and pulls me close again. "I have an idea."

"Tell me." I'm chattering again, tempted to drop back into the wet sand and bring him down with me.

"How about we go up those stairs and get you some dry clothes."

"I like this idea."

"Order in some food from Sadie's Diner."

"Now you're talking."

"Make out on the couch for a while?"

I laugh, and the only reason I don't start kissing him now is because that would require movement from this spot, which will lead to cold. He's *so warm*. "What, exactly, is your definition of 'a while'?"

He chuckles. "I'm not sure I ever intend to stop kissing you, Kasey Graham."

"Good."

"I love you."

I can't help it. I tilt my head back despite the breeze that is currently turning me to ice, and I take in the sight of his familiar smile and warm blue eyes. "How did this happen?" I whisper, reaching up to touch his jaw, like I'm not sure I can believe he's real.

He closes his eyes at my touch. "I don't know, but I am the luckiest man in the world."

I'm the lucky one, but I don't bother arguing, instead rising up on my toes to kiss Liam the way I want to, *without* knocking us into the water.

EPILOGUE

LIAM

Sometimes, my life doesn't feel real. I mean, for the bulk of it I'm at home writing music or on tour *playing* my music, and that's always been something I love. It's the other stuff, like going on talk shows or seeing my picture on an online quiz titled "Which Alternative Rock Star Would Be Your Sugar Daddy" that make me feel like I'm living someone else's life.

It's the same feeling I have now, while I'm sitting in my chair in a tux that costs more money than I could have dreamed of as a kid and waiting for Raya Guerrera to announce who won "Album of the Year" at this year's Grammys. I was nominated for a few other categories—big ones, too—but I honestly don't care that I didn't win. It's this one that I want. That I'm almost desperate for.

While on the red carpet outside the Crypto.com Arena, so many of the reporters asked me which awards I wanted to take home tonight. It's the classic question, and I gave the standard answer. "I'd be happy to take home any of them, but there are a lot of deserving artists here tonight." I didn't mean it.

I mean, I did. Taylor Swift and Beyoncé are always going to deserve recognition alongside so many talented artists.

But tonight, *Kismet* is in the lineup for best album. It's Kasey's album, the one she inspired, the one that changed my life in the best way. I've been gripping her hand for the last several minutes while they've been announcing the nominees, telling myself that it will be fine if *Kismet* doesn't win. I don't believe myself in the slightest. This album—*our* album—is proof that Kasey and I are meant to be.

"And the Grammy goes to…" Raya opens the envelope and then squeaks in surprise. "*Kismet*! Liam Connolly!"

For half a second, it feels like the world stops, and then it catches up to itself in a rush of sound and color as so many different emotions flood through me. Hands are patting my back, people are cheering, and I can't do anything but bring Kasey's mouth to mine. But then she pushes me out of my seat, laughing, and I genuinely don't know how I make it onto the stage.

My hands wrap around the gold gramophone that Raya hands me, and I accept her hug and congratulations, still in a daze. Then suddenly I'm in front of a microphone, staring down the crowd of musicians and engineers and producers who make up the world I've been thrown into.

"Wow," I say, hearing my voice fill the arena. My hands are shaking, which is ridiculous because I won one of these last year for "Best Alternative Music Performance" so it's not like I haven't been in this exact spot. I even performed earlier tonight, singing "Let You Go" from my new album on live TV.

But this is different.

My eyes search the crowd, which is so hard to see because of the spotlights, but the moment I lock eyes with Kasey, everything stills. I grow calm. We've only been together for a little over three months, but everything is always better when I know she's there.

"Thank you," I say into the microphone, but really I'm saying it to her. "Writing this album was one of the craziest experiences of my life, and sometimes I wonder if it was all a dream. I don't think any of us ever *expect* to get on this stage and hold one of these, certainly not while we're hunched over a piano trying to figure out why that A minor seventh isn't the right fit." The crowd laughs, and my smile grows. "But it is truly an honor to stand up here, and I want to thank all the people who got me here. Everyone at Groupline Records. My incredible friends who refused to let me sit idly through writer's block." I blow a kiss to Freya, who's probably not watching. "And of course my wonderful mother, who has given me everything."

I grip the award tighter and lock eyes with Kasey. "Mostly, I owe this achievement to the love of my life. Kasey, you inspired each and every one of the songs on this album, and every day you're in my life is another day full of music that I want to sing to the heavens. You're my harmony, my soundtrack, my everything."

She's crying, and I know she's going to get mad at me for it, but I don't even care. I mean every word.

"This is amazing," I continue and hold up the award. "Thank you!"

When I get back to my seat, Kasey grabs my jacket and pulls me in for a kiss that is so much better than the one I gave her before going up to the stage. "I hate you," she says against my mouth.

I laugh. "I love you."

The rest of the night is a blur. Through interviews and photos and an after-party with my record label, I have eyes only for Kasey, who has taken to her newfound fame with ease. When she's not writing, she spends most of her time at home with me or hanging out with Bonnie or Val, but when she does go out and is recognized by fans—she even has her own fans now—she's always so kind and patient with everyone that *Hollywood Hot Scoop* and the other tabloids can't help but love her.

By the time we are finally set free late into the night, I want nothing more than to head home and hold this woman in my arms for the rest of the night. But I can't do that yet, and I tell Sean to drive to Derek's so we can celebrate with my friends.

Derek's bodyguard, Bruce, lets us into his house with a nod and a muttered congratulations, and I can't help but clap him on the shoulder because my win is starting to settle in and feel more real.

"Thanks, big guy!"

Kasey rolls her eyes, leading the way in and kicking off her shoes like she's right at home. I love that she has become comfortable with my friends so quickly and no longer overthinks everything when she's around them. "We're here!" she shouts into the house. "Finally," she adds in a grumble.

I fully plan to keep writing music, and hopefully that will lead to more awards. Plus, Kasey is likely to earn her own high-level of fame with one of her screenplays, so she'd better get used to nights like tonight. They're not going away anytime soon.

When we reach the massive lounge at the back of Derek's house—and when I say massive, I mean it, because Derek's house is at least twice the size of mine—everyone jumps up to give me a hug and tell me they were sure I would win and were glad that it actually happened. (Those two things don't fit together, but I don't complain.) Even Cole has a smile tonight despite his fairly constant moodiness since his breakup with Sage in October.

Bonnie gets Freya on a video chat, and the princess promptly takes half the credit for this album, giving the other half to Kasey, and then Derek breaks out the champagne.

It takes a while for us to settle down, but I'm more than happy to cuddle up with Kasey on the couch after we sneak off to change into sweats (and maybe make out a little while we're alone). I'm exhausted and happy and overwhelmed, and everything about this night is the best.

Someday, we'll be in this spot celebrating everyone else. Derek's up for an Oscar next month, and Cole's team is likely to take home the MLR Shield this year, and Freya inches closer and closer to her throne. Bonnie's rising as well with her upcoming detective movie, and Kasey... I've tried to get her credit for *Figure Eight Dollhouse*, to no avail, but someday she'll get to see her name in the credits of a movie. Hopefully someday soon.

And we'll be here to cheer her on.

"I have an announcement," Bonnie says right as I'm falling asleep with my cheek on Kasey's head.

I reluctantly open my eyes, checking her left hand in case I was somehow kept out of the loop of something. Her fingers are bare, so I don't have to fight Derek for keeping secrets from me.

Except, Derek's jaw is tight, and he's looking at Bonnie with a warning in his eyes. "You don't have to do this," he tells her.

Kasey and I both sit up straight. "Do what?" I ask, looking at Cole to see if he knows what's going on.

He looks as confused as I am.

Bonnie bites her lip, her cheeks turning a deep red as she glances among the three of us and ignores Derek entirely. "Um, so, please don't hate me, okay? And especially don't hate Derek because it's not his fault."

"Bonnie," Derek says, but he looks more resigned than angry.

She takes a deep breath. "Derek and I aren't really dating. It's fake."

I grab Kasey's hand, hoping the contact will give me some sort of way to process this. "Wait, are you serious?" I look at Derek, who drops his head and nods.

"Our publicist thought it was a good idea," he says, "and it's really done us a lot of good with this movie we've been working on."

"You're not actually dating?" Even saying the words feels wrong. "Since when?"

Derek sighs. "Since the beginning."

"But you two…" Okay, now my head is starting to hurt. "I know you're good actors, but that's…this is crazy, Derek."

Shrugging, Derek gets to his feet. He looks tired. More tired than he should be. "It's how it is, Liam. Bonnie and I have been friends since the day we met, and that has never changed."

Yeah, maybe, but I can't help but wonder if he wishes it was otherwise. Though I hate to leave Kasey, I untangle myself from her arms and follow Derek as he heads out to his back patio. The view from my place may be great, but it's nothing compared to his. Pretty much everything I have pales in comparison to Derek's version. Except Kasey, of course.

"Talk to me," I tell him, glancing back to make sure the door closed behind me and everyone else stayed inside. He won't bare his soul if he's got the whole group listening.

Derek grips the stone wall at the edge of the balcony, shaking his head. "Liam, I know you think there's something deeper here, but there isn't. Public relationships happen all the time, and it's just been part of the job."

"Why wouldn't you make it a real relationship?" I ask, folding my arms. "I know you love her."

He glances back, meeting Bonnie's eyes through the window as she talks to Kasey and Cole. There's a wistfulness in his eyes, but it's not longing. "Of course I love her," he says. "She's one of my best friends, and you know as well as I do that Bonnie is amazing. But she's not in a state of mind to be in a real relationship. You know what she's been through in the past."

I clench my jaw. Bonnie's relationships have all been rocky in different ways. Cheaters, womanizers, even one of her directors. *Blegh.* "I kind of hoped she'd figured it out when she started dating you," I admit. "I mean, it doesn't really get better than Derek Riley."

He chuckles. "I hate that you hold me up on this pedestal."

"You put yourself there, man."

He's quiet for a long time, eyes fixed on the black ocean reflecting back the moon. He sighs. "I want her to be happy, you know? Like you are. Like Cole *was*. It's all I've ever wanted for all of you, but our lives don't make love easy."

That's for sure. "What about you? I know you want to settle down."

"Someday," he agrees. "But it's not going to happen with Bonnie. Public opinion of our relationship is dropping, so we're probably going to have to stage a breakup sometime soon. Though, Fran would argue we need to do the opposite. This has been the easiest eighteen months of her life."

"Minus that little blip where Fran had to help fix my relationship," I point out. I've never liked Derek's publicist, but he's been with her since the beginning of his career, and she clearly does her job well. "So..." I swing my arms a few times.

Derek glances back and lifts an eyebrow. "What?"

"Well, I'm getting the sense that you need a change of subject, but I've got nothing." I could tell him about the diamond ring that I bought back in November and *almost* gave to Kasey over Christmas when we went to visit her parents in Kansas. At my mom's insistence, I decided to wait before I make that move. As Mom needlessly reminded me, I tend to rush into things and get into sticky situations, and this is one thing I really don't want to mess up.

I need to be patient, something I have learned well from Kasey.

But if I'm being honest, that patience isn't going to last long.

Though he narrows his eyes, like he knows what's going through my head, Derek pulls his phone out of his pocket instead and starts flipping through it. "Actually, I've got a subject change you'll like. I was going to come over tomorrow, but we're already in a celebrating mood. Or, we were."

One glance inside tells me everyone is on the somber side after Bonnie's admission. "What is it?"

He hands me the phone. "Some good news."

As soon as I read the email—honestly, I only have to get through the first few lines—I gasp and dart back inside, Derek right behind me. "Kasey!"

"What?" She flinches, staring at me like she's expecting me to dunk her in a pool or something.

"You're a genius!"

Wincing, she glances at Derek before looking back at me. "I know that, but why do you know that?"

Man, I am not doing this right, and I'm starting to think I should have let Derek break this news. But how could I wait? "Kasey, they want your script."

Her jaw slowly slips open. "*Who* wants my script?"

I start laughing because that's really the only way to express this kind of feeling. "*Everyone!*"

"As soon as you sent the finished *Icarus* script, I sent it to one of my favorite directors," Derek says, far more calmly than what I'm capable of right now. "Turns out he loved it and wants to make it into a movie."

Kasey's jaw drops the rest of the way. "Are you serious?"

"Yeah. But I also sent it to a couple other people, and—"

"And they also want it!" I finish. Derek is talking way too slowly. "Kasey, it's basically in a bidding war now. Your screenplay is going to be made into a movie."

Finally it sinks in, and her eyes go wide at the same time color floods her face. "It's what?"

I nod. "You did it."

"And they want more," Derek says, but he goes unnoticed as Kasey launches herself at me.

I'm ready for her, my feet planted and my arms out, and I hold her tight as we both start laughing and crying while she starts spewing incoherent sentences and exclamations. I knew she could do it. Her first draft was already amazing, and it kept getting better as she worked out the ending and let Bonnie read it too. The two of them perfected the script until it was ready to be sent around, and then Derek...

I look at him over Kasey's shoulder, tears in my eyes and my heart ready to burst. Best friend ever. "Thanks," I mouth.

He smiles but says nothing. He doesn't have to. He may be worried about the rest of us finding our happy endings, but he deserves one too. Whoever he ends up with, she's going to get an incredible man on her team.

"Liam," Kasey says, finally pulling away. Her makeup is a mess, her hair all over the place, but she's more beautiful than anything. "Can we go home? I need to scream into a pillow or something and then fall asleep because today has been..."

"A lot," I agree and take hold of her hand. "We're going to have a lot of these days, especially now that you're on your way to the big time. Can you handle that?"

She grins and leans up to give me a kiss. "With you next to me? Bring it on."

Also by Dana LeCheminant

Starstruck Love Stories
Moonstruck
Lovestruck
Dumbstruck
Thunderstruck
Awestruck
Wonderstruck

Love in Sun City
Kiss Me if You Can
She Likes It, Hey Micah
The Chad Next Door
Crossing the Brooklyn Briggs
Houston, We Have a Problem

Standalone Romances
For Butter or For Worse
The Fear of Falling

The Wonder Boys
Love on Camera
Love in Writing
Love on Display
Love in Disguise

Simple Love Stories (Sweet Love Stories)
Simplicity
Growing Young
Bittersweet Brews
In Front of Me
As Long as You Love Me
Dear Dalia
Let Go

Terms of Inheritance (Sweet Romance)
Forever You and Me
Holding On to Everything
A World without You
Love, Strictly Speaking

Historical Romances
The Thief and the Noble
A Twist of Christmas (part of The Holly and the Ivy anthology)
What Dreams May Come
This above All
Never Doubt I Love

About the Author

Dana LeCheminant writes sweet romantic comedies, heartwarming contemporary love stories, and swoony historical romances—with a twist. Known for putting a fresh spin on beloved tropes, she lets her characters lead the way, believing they always know their stories best. Her books are full of banter, emotion, and connection—all of the swoon without any spice. When she's not dreaming up her next twisty trope or emotional arc, she's hiking the remote Utah backcountry or cruising down rivers in search of new inspiration. Dana has been telling stories since before she could spell and has no plans to stop anytime soon.

Dana loves connecting with her readers!
You can find her on social media (**@authordanalecheminant**) and on her website, **lecheminantbooks.com**.

www.ingramcontent.com/pod-product-compliance
Lightning Source LLC
Chambersburg PA
CBHW060852210726

48293CB00006B/1760